# Happy Camp
## Discipline, Godliness, Fun!
### Ely North

Red Handed Print

# The DCI Finnegan Series

\*Note: All books are available from Amazon in ebook, paperback, and in **Kindle Unlimited** (excluding Aquaphobia). Paperbacks can be ordered from all good bookshops. **Boxset print editions are one book compiled from three books. They do not come in a box. \*\*\*** Pre-orders only apply to ebooks.

# 1

# 1985 – Good Friday – North Yorkshire Moors

Axles creak and groan like an old sailing ship battling a storm, as tyres bump along the undulating track. Optimistic, verdant tufts of grass snaking down the centre of the laneway contrast against the flaky, bleached gravel to the side. The singing from inside the battered old Ford Transit minibus is enthusiastic, boisterous, and for good reason. The song, Ten Green Bottles, may have originally been penned to teach children how to count backwards, but today it unwittingly conveys a prophecy... a prophecy the boys are blissfully ignorant of, as the invigorating scent of cut grass, drying in the fields, wafts into the vehicle.

From an emerald maze of paddocks, a flock of ewes watch on in curiosity as newborn lambs bleat dolefully under a balmy spring sun. Brakes squeal as the ratchet sound of the handbrake is applied.

'Young Tom, you can do the honours!' Doctor Henry Blenheim yells above the din. Eagerly, the lad leaps from the van and wrestles with the stubborn wooden farm gate. Blenheim turns his head to the passengers sitting alongside. 'Cyclone, make that gate the first job on your list. It's not fit for purpose. I'm sure the farmer will thank us.'

'No problem, Doc. An hour's work at the most to knock it back into shape,' he replies with a toothy grin.

Blenheim stares disapprovingly as Tom struggles with the gate. 'What is that damn lad playing at?' he grumbles, tapping at the steering wheel impatiently. The horn blares twice, making Tom jump. Blenheim sticks his head out of the window. 'Damn fool! Lift the blasted thing up, don't drag it!'

'Y... yes, sir.'

He shakes his head in obvious disgust. 'He's as thick as two short planks.'

With the gate fully open, the minibus creeps forward, pulling a large trailer behind it, as Tom hurries back to the vehicle.

The reverend, sitting next to Cyclone, now yells at the boy. 'Get back to the gate, lad! You need to close it once the delivery truck has come through after us, otherwise the sheep will escape.'

Tom, blushing at his callow ways, replies, 'S... s... sorry, reverend,' and scampers back to the gate as a flat-bed truck, laden with building materials, trundles through behind the minibus.

With the gate successfully closed, Tom hastily climbs aboard, joining the other children who bombard the four adults with a flurry of questions. Most go unanswered. As the vehicle nears the derelict stone barn, Doctor Blenheim glances in the rearview mirror.

'Everyone out of the van and line up in front of the barn. And listen to my instructions. I don't want to repeat myself. Understood?'

The unison is almost perfect. 'Yes, Doctor Blenheim.'

The eight boys scramble from the vehicle, laughing, fighting, pushing, making faces at each other, their excitement apparent. For most, it's the first holiday they've ever had.

'I said line up in an orderly fashion!' The harsh voice of Blenheim ricochets off ancient walls, and skedaddles across the idyllic countryside, bouncing across the languid river, eventually dissipating, absorbed by the open moors and rising fells. The sound is unnatural to the scene; unwanted... and unwarranted. The boys fall silent apart from a few sniggers as they array in an orderly fashion.

Rosco raises a hand. 'Doctor Blenheim?' The query is inquisitive, yet tentative.

'What is it, Rosco?' he replies with a sharp, disdainful sneer.

'Are we sleeping in the barn tonight, sir?'

His head shakes in consternation and disgust as he snaps back. 'No, of course not, you stupid boy. It's not yet fit for habitation. That's why we brought tents. Once the reverend has said a few words, we'll split into two groups. Red Group will help the truck driver unload the building supplies. Blue Group will unload the trailer and erect tents. Understood?'

Confused and apprehensive, Rosco averts his gaze, gathering the courage to ask the next question. 'Sorry, sir, but what group am I in; red or blue?'

Blenheim shakes his head in disbelief as Selwyn Morgan strides forward and jabs the boy in the chest.

'You ridiculous article! What colour is your T-shirt, lad?'

Rosco drops his head and checks. 'It's blue, sir,' he murmurs, the fun of his adventure already disappearing over the distant hills and waving a forlorn goodbye.

'Well then, what team are you in?'

'The blue team?'

'My God! At last, the penny drops.' He grabs him by the upper arm and yanks the boy forward. 'And it's sir, or Mr Morgan, to you, and don't forget it, my lad.'

Despite the stern authority of Blenheim and Morgan, it has not diminished the other boys' youthful exuberance. The reverend strides silently along the line, hands behind his back, exuding an air of esteem and gravitas. He performs the routine twice as the truck driver chunters in the background, unhitching ropes, then pulling at a tarpaulin.

'Supposed to be a bloody public holiday. I'm not even getting double-time,' he grizzles to himself.

The reverend finally addresses the gathering. 'Boys, I hope you are all aware of how privileged you are to be here. You were handpicked for the inaugural year in this brand-new charitable venture. Not only do I hope you all appreciate it, but I also want you to grasp this opportunity with both hands. I know some of you have not had the best start to life. Among you, there are those who have lost parents, others who have been abandoned, and some who have suffered neglect and maltreatment. But today, all that changes. You will learn new skills; we will build your confidence; we will turn you into young men full of fortitude and courage, ready to make the world a better place.' He turns and holds one arm out, moving it slowly across the horizon. 'This is God's own country. Open fields, wild moorland, rivers, becks, wildlife, and sweet pure air. Do not take it for granted.'

Ted Fairchild raises his hand in the air. 'Sir?'

A slap to the back of the head from Doctor Blenheim shuts him up. 'Don't interrupt the reverend while he's talking, Fairchild,' he hisses.

The reverend continues. 'Ahem, in many years from now, when you are all fine, upstanding young men, you will look back upon today as the end of one chapter in your life, and the beginning of a new one. Today... you are reborn.'

The adults initiate the enthusiastic applause, followed by the boys.

The reverend glances at Doctor Blenheim. 'I think it's time for the unveiling, Henry.'

'Indeed. Cyclone, have you the camera at the ready?'

Cyclone unzips his bomber jacket to reveal an Olympus dangling from a strap slung around his neck.

'At the ready, Doc.'

Blenheim grins. 'Actually, let's get a photo with all of us in it. For posterity. Ask the wagon driver to do the honours.' He glances at the children. 'No slouching. Heads up, shoulders back, arms by your side.'

As Cyclone explains how to operate the camera to the disgruntled driver, the boys adjust their posture. The three older men stand behind the row of boys, the reverend, closest to a wooden sign covered with a sheet.

The doctor is impatient. 'Come along, Cyclone! You kneel at the front. Everyone smile as the reverend unveils the plaque and name of our new venture.'

The driver stoops in front of them and squints into the viewfinder. 'Everyone say cheese,' he grunts in a broad Dales accent devoid of even a spark of enthusiasm.

'CHEEEEEESE!'

The reverend pulls the cloth from the sign as the camera clicks. Staring at the spectacle in bemusement, the wagon driver shakes his head as the boys split away and gather around the reverend and doctor for another photo. The reverend points at the words exquisitely carved into the oak plinth mounted on two wooden poles and reads them aloud.

'Happy Camp. Discipline, Godliness, Fun.'

# 2

# Modern Day - Sunday 23rd April – Pickering, North Yorkshire

Selwyn Morgan swallows hard as he peers out of the window into the fading twilight of a benign April night. After a day's labour in his cherished garden, he feels a satisfying weariness, the kind of tiredness that visits from a day spent doing what one loves.

Staring across the gravelled driveway at the Victorian rectory opposite his cottage, he tilts his head to one side and listens again.

The music has stopped.

'Hmm... about bloody time. Good,' he grumbles, glancing at the grandfather clock as it strikes the hour of ten.

The final chime fades, its cadence diminishing swiftly into silence, the sound absorbed by the weathered, floral-patterned settee and armchairs, and threadbare carpet. The familiar tone conjures reflection in the lonely, old bachelor.

He appreciates what he has. As a relentless servant of the Church of England for over fifty years, he was officially entitled to nothing apart from a modest pension once he retired. He'd served a dual role as sexton and verger for several small parishes over the years, ending his time at the rectory on the outskirts of Pickering, North Yorkshire.

A hundred years ago, the Anglican Church was front and centre of everyday life. A potent force with great influence and power. Today? An irrelevancy to all but the ardent few. Selwyn Morgan is one of the remaining few.

A developer bought the deteriorating rectory over a decade ago. It was gutted, then converted into ten luxury flats for retirees. The small housekeeper's cottage at the rear was retained by the church, renovated by the same developer.

In an act of Christian beneficence, the church allowed Selwyn the privilege of remaining on as a tenant at the cottage for as long as he wished or lived... whichever came first.

With his state pension, plus a modest monthly stipend from the church, and free accommodation, Selwyn lives a comfortable, if modest, life.

In his otherwise rather parsimonious existence, the sole annoyance is one of the residents from the rectory, opposite. Specifically, the intermittent disturbance of loud music late at night.

There's a strict ten o'clock curfew for music, but on some occasions, one particular individual flouts the rule. Selwyn has crossed swords with the transgressor on many occasions over the years. It's the only fly in his pastoral ointment.

He pulls at the cord on the curtains. As they lazily swish across the window, a fleeting silhouette melts into the shadows.

'Who the hell's that?' he murmurs. Yanking open the front door, he squints into the dusk. 'Hello? Who's there?' His brittle voice disappears into the void.

The sweet lingering scent of cherry blossom waltzes with the heady aroma of sweet pea, as a blackbird, way past its bedtime, warbles a heavenly requiem. Selwyn, usually attuned to such free delights, is oblivious.

'I know someone's there. I saw you. I demand you show yourself!' he commands, his tremulous voice undermining his authority.

The intruder emerges from behind the cherry tree and stalks forward.

The weak coach light from the cottage does little to illuminate the figure.

'Who the hell are you and what are you doing in my garden at this hour?'

The powerful beam of a flashlight hits him in the eyes.

He raises his hand to shield himself from the fierce glare. The light instantly disappears as Selwyn comes face to face with the stranger.

His trepidation eases somewhat.

'Tell me what you're playing at, otherwise, I'll call the police?'

'Don't you recognise me, Mr Morgan?'

Scrunching his eyes, he peers at the stranger's face. 'No. Should I? You're certainly not a resident of the rectory. Are you a guest?'

'No. I'm not a guest.'

'Then I demand to know who you are and what you want?'

'I'm your worst nightmare, Mr Morgan. I'm your past.'

He involuntarily shivers. 'My past?'

'Yes.'

Unnerved, he turns to head back inside. 'You're speaking utter nonsense. This is preposterous. Complete folly! I'm calling the police.' A hand clamps down on his shoulder and forcibly spins him around. 'What do you want with me?' he cries, trembling uncontrollably.

The emotionless voice is calm, measured, quietly confident. 'It's payback time!' The voice rises with a musical, humorous pitch.

'Pay... payback for w... what?' his voice fractures into a stammer, the words dissolving into the serene night air.

The smile of the stranger morphs into a disturbing grimace. 'Happy Camp,' the voice whispers, holding a finger to their lips. 'Shush. We must keep this a secret.'

In one heart-stopping moment, recognition dawns for Selwyn Morgan. 'My God... it's you.' His eyes bulge in terror. Laboured breath catches in his throat as he stares, transfixed, into the face of a memory he believed was forever buried.

Neither memories nor shadows can kill... but flesh and blood can!

# 3

## Monday 24th April

Prisha pounds down Church Street, her trainers thumping against the damp pavement, a metrical symphony in sync with her steady pace. She breezes past Arguments Yard, the historic alley, then darts through the old town square, inhaling a medley of aromas wafting from nearby bakeries and tea shops.

Crossing the swing bridge onto the west side of Whitby, the stringent seaweed tang accosts her nostrils, mingling with the sharp scent of freshly caught fish from the bustling market. As she approaches the cafe opposite, the rich fragrance of brewed coffee tempts her taste buds.

Balancing the warm cup of cappuccino in her hands, she saunters towards the end of the promenade, her eyes embracing the picturesque harbour. The call of seagulls cawing overhead mingles with the rhythmic lapping of the waves against the harbour walls, providing a soothing melody. Finding solace in her usual spot at the bandstand near Battery Parade, her heartbeat slows, and she surrenders to the harmony of sights, sounds, and smells that surround her. The vibrant hues of the fishing boats moored up create a vivid scene against the backdrop of the aqua sky, and the weathered church of St Mary's, with its ancient stone walls and stoic presence, standing defiantly atop the rugged east cliff. A silent sea breeze strokes her skin as she takes a sip of coffee, velvety foam coating her lips in a bittersweet embrace.

The serenity is rudely interrupted as the mobile vibrates in her bum-bag. She unzips it and pulls out the phone.

'Hi, Zac. What's up?'

'Body out at Pickering,' his soft Scottish brogue announces.

'Suspicious?'

'Very. Where are you?'

'Near the bandstand. Just finished my run.'

'I'll pick you up from your flat in twenty. We'll grab breakfast on the way. Bye.'

---

The tyres scrunch over pebbles laid thick on the driveway as Prisha and Zac feast their eyes on the magnificent old rectory, now better known as Peasholm Manor.

'Hell's bells, imagine living here?' Zac comments as he takes in the extensive and well-manicured gardens.

'Do you ever wonder where some people get their money from?' Prisha replies, mildly annoyed at her perceived injustices of life.

'Yeah, all the time. I mean, we could be considered to be on decent money, but I know for a fact those flats sell for upwards of eight-hundred grand a pop.'

'How do you know that?'

'I did a quick internet search on my phone.'

Driving to the rear of the rectory, they park up next to a low wall, the boundary to a beautiful, old stone cottage.

'This must be a bad one,' Zac notes. 'Four SOCO vans, plus Raspberry's Jag.'

'Oh, gawd!' Prisha groans. 'Doctor Bennett Whipple. He's such a sanctimonious, pompous prig.'

They both step from the vehicle and don their protective gear. 'Aye, you're not wrong. But he is a damned good pathologist. And it's always a source of free entertainment to watch him struggle to get in and out of his E-Type Jag. A man of his freakish proportions would be better off driving a bus, or a tractor.'

As Prisha zips up and slips into shoe coverings, she spots Charlene Marsden sauntering down the garden path, stopping occasionally to smell some of the abundant flowers in bloom. She pulls open the little picket gate and peels off her protective hair cap.

'Zac, Prisha, I trust you're both well?'

'Better than the poor bugger in there,' Zac says, nodding towards the cottage. 'Bad one?'

Charlene raises her eyebrows. 'Haven't seen one as gruesome as this in years. Selwyn Morgan. Eighty-one-year-old former church verger and sexton. Lived rent free in the cottage, courtesy of the church. He's not inside, actually. He's around the back, on the lawn. I hope you haven't eaten recently?'

'We stopped for a bacon and egg butty on the way down,' Zac replies. He pats his stomach and grins. 'But I have an iron-clad constitution.'

'Good. You'll need it. Come on, I'll show you the crime scene,' Charlene states as if she were an estate agent and not lead forensic examiner. 'My team is going to be here a while, so I probably won't have anything for you until tomorrow.'

The trio bypass the front door and make their way down a narrow brick path to the rear of the house, where a small lawn plays host to the white suits of eight Scene of Crime Officers. A small tent covers the victim.

'How long has Whipple been here?' Prisha questions.

Charlene slips her hair covering back on. 'About twenty minutes.'

'Good. He shouldn't be much longer, then.'

Charlene chortles. 'I've noticed something odd about the good doctor over the last two years of working with him.'

'Haven't we all.'

Charlene emits a throaty laugh. 'The grislier the crime scene, the more vested he is in his examination. Get a bog-standard dead body with no obvious sign of injury and he's almost bored. Something gory and he struggles to hide his glee. Right, here we are,' she says, pulling the flap of the tent back.

It's hard to make out the body in its entirety as the enormous frame of Doctor Whipple is crouched at the side of it, clearly fascinated with the cadaver. His gargantuan head turns slowly to spy the intruders.

'Ah! Inspector Kumar and Sergeant Stoker. We have a rare feast in store for you,' he states.

One couldn't describe his demeanour as joyous because Whipple has never shown joy in anything, but his deportment does belie a certain relish, a macabre fascination. He rises, not to his full, towering height but to a stooped stance akin to a colossal teddy bear kitted out in surgical attire. His head brushes the top of the marquee roof.

Prisha and Zac gawp at the dead body. Both swallow hard and curse.

'Christ!' Prisha gasps, baring her teeth as her cheeks rise.

'Slap my arse,' Zac murmurs, a dart of queasiness attacking him.

Much to everyone's everlasting astonishment, Doctor Whipple emits a deep baritone chuckle.

'Ha, ha, ha, ha. Indeed, behold the profound convergence of a corporeal enigma. A confoundment which could have only been spawned in the bowels of hell by Beelzebub himself,' he says, holding his hand out as if introducing someone at a dinner party.

The naked body of an elderly man, laid on his back, is pinned to the earth, a rag stuffed in his mouth. His arms are outstretched, crucifix fashion. Through either palm is what appears to be a tent peg. A burn mark is engraved on his brow, above which, another tent peg driven through his forehead. All his genitalia have been removed, leaving nothing but a bloodied gash.

Zac flinches. 'Talking of bowels, what the hell is that stuck up his backside?'

Whipple nods sagely. 'That, Sergeant Stoker, is a universal sentinel of waxen luminosity.'

'It looks like a candle. A very large candle,' Prisha notes.

'Indeed, inspector, indeed. A church or cathedral candle is my preliminary adjudication.'

'And what's happened to his ankles?' Prisha asks as she stares at the contorted mess and violent swelling.

'Ah, yes. The articulus talocruralis - to wit, the ankles. They have been broken, snapped in two. To achieve such a satisfactory outcome, I believe a solid object must have been placed in-situ between the medial malleolus, followed by a blunt force transmuted, with some energy to the tibia and fibula.'

Prisha and Zac glance at Charlene for clarification.

'I think Doctor Whipple means the inner ankles were placed against a length of timber, then a hammer was used to cause a break just above the ankle joint.'

'Your interpretation is rudimentary, Lead Forensic Officer Marsden,' Whipple says as he lumbers from the tent.

'It may be rudimentary, Doctor Whipple, but on the money,' she shouts after him. Turning to Zac and Prisha, she nods towards the tent entrance. 'We found a lump hammer and a piece of four-by-four outside. We'll check them back at the lab for prints.'

Prisha takes a tentative step forward and stares at the skull. 'Any significance to the burn mark?'

'Yes, it's more of a branding, actually. Hard to discern what it is because of the blood and swelling.'

Prisha drops to her haunches and inspects the mark. 'Looks like a motif; a head with one eye. Satanic, or Voodoo, possibly?'

Charlene shrugs. 'Not my area of expertise.'

Prisha notices a forensic cloth to the side of the head laid neatly out on the grass. 'I take it this is…' She gently lifts the covering to reveal the discarded scrotum, testicles, and penis.

'Excuse me,' Zac gasps, his face resembling the colour of a pistachio nut. He darts from the tent.

'Well away from the crime scene, Zac!' Charlene bellows.

A moment later, the unmistakable sound of retching can be heard some distance away.

'There goes his breakfast,' Prisha notes, without much sympathy, as she places the cloth down and rises. 'What's the wetness on his face and chest?'

Charlene scowls, bemused. 'Not sure, yet. It could be dew, or possibly sweat.'

'Then why is it only on his face and chest and not on the rest of his body?'

Frowns. 'Yes, it is odd. I'll take swabs and have it analysed.' Becoming distracted, she kneels at the side of the body and pulls out a small plastic sample bag containing a pair of tweezers.

'What is it?' Prisha asks.

Removing the tweezers, she carefully leans over and lifts something from the chin of the corpse, deposits it in the bag, then scrutinises it.

'If I'm not very much mistaken, it's a pubic hair with the root follicle attached. That should provide an excellent DNA sample.'

'Strange place to find a pubic hair,' Prisha muses, before blushing slightly. 'Considering the circumstances, I mean.'

Charlene chuckles. 'Yes, but those damn pubes seem to have their own migratory instinct. Anyway, it probably belongs to the deceased. Possibly fell from the genitalia as they were placed at the side of the head.'

Prisha shifts her attention back onto the body. 'The gag in his mouth tells me he was conscious when these atrocities took place.'

'We may never know, but if he was unconscious, or already dead, there would have been no need for a gag.'

'I'm assuming the fatal blow would have been the tent peg through the forehead?'

'It appears that way. It's possible a man of his age may have suffered a heart attack at any point during the ordeal. I'm sure Whipple will furnish you with the facts once he's conducted the post-mortem.'

Prisha shakes her head. 'Sweet mercy... imagine the pain. The ankles, the candle, the pegs.'

'I hope for his sake the ankles were broken first,' Charlene adds thoughtfully.

'Why?'

'After the initial excruciating pain, the body would have released a tsunami of endorphins producing an analgesic effect.'

'A numbing sensation?'

'Exactly. The body has its own built in safety mechanisms to prevent the mind from experiencing too much pain.'

'Did Whipple give an approximation of the time of death?'

Charlene rolls her eyes. 'You know what he's like. He's loathe to estimate the time of death. But he did indicate that some hours had passed since the cessation of life, as he put it. Rigor mortis has not yet set in.'

'So, possibly early this morning or late last night?'

'From past experience, I'd say you were in the ballpark.'

Prisha takes a deep breath. 'I hate the weird ones. Whoever did this went to great lengths to make a point.'

'Agreed.'

'Right, I'll leave you to it. Oh, who found the body?'

'According to the first uniform on the scene, it was one of the residents from the rectory.'

As she turns to leave, Prisha takes one last glance at the body. 'The poor old bugger has been crucified. And the candle up the bum... what's all that about?'

'Symbolic, perhaps.'

'Hmm... I think you're right. The whole thing reeks of symbolism. I pray to God this isn't the start of some occultist nutjob on a killing spree.'

'If it is... praying won't help you.'

# 4

On the outskirts of Whitby, a modern, architecturally pleasing, two-storey office block sits gleaming in the spring sunshine. A small contingent of assorted news media are setting up their microphones and cameras in the car park as dazzling light is reflected from the immaculate glass frontage.

Sebastian Thorne gazes down from his office window above and smiles.

'Well done, Dora. Our audience is expectant,' he states triumphantly, turning to his personal assistant. 'I take it we have some of the big boys awaiting my announcement?'

'Of course, Mr Thorne. BBC TV and radio. ITV, Sky News, and reporters from the Guardian, Independent, the Yorkshire Post, and a few from rival tabloids whose stories are typically syndicated to sister newspapers. And we also have our own crew filming so we can release it to all social media sites immediately afterwards.'

'Excellent.' He slides into his jacket and picks fluff from the collar. 'How do I look?'

She nods like a proud mother even though she's ten years his junior. 'Like a million dollars, as always, Mr Thorne.'

He grimaces. 'Hmm... tie or no tie?'

Studying him for a moment, she replies, 'No tie. Top button undone. You look smart, a man of the times, but not unapproachable. We must show the common touch.'

He chuckles. 'What would I do without you? Has the Opposition Leader arrived yet?'

'Yes, sir. Evan Tudor is freshening up downstairs.'

'And what about security? I don't want that rabid, communist lesbian, Amanda Chan, derailing the whole shooting match like she did last time.'

'Security is in the wings. And so far, she hasn't made an appearance.'

'Splendid! Let's do this, Dora. Upwards and onwards!'

———

Sebastian Thorne exudes an aura of refined success. His suits, tailored to within an inch of their life, whisper of wealth. The subtle, sophisticated scent of his aftershave—a fusion of citrus and cedarwood—leaves a tantalising trail in every room he glides through, a sensory signature of his presence.

To his supporters, of which there are legion, Sebastian's charm is effortless. His laughter, genuine. A sharpness in his eyes... like a falcon. Ever attuned to the subtle dance of commerce, they discern golden prospects where others see dung-heaps. Despite his current lofty stature, Sebastian's roots were humble. His rise to the top marked by a relentless drive and an innate understanding of the world.

A known philanthropist, he is often hailed as a saviour for his generous contributions to social causes. His support of the Labour Party in the UK underscores his commitment to social justice and economic reform. This blend of business savvy and compassion has made him a beloved figure of the British media, as approachable as he is respected. His story is one of transformation—from austere beginnings in the back streets of Leeds, to the peak of corporate influence, all the while maintaining a deep-seated desire to enact positive change. His bespoke calfskin leather shoes have graced the hallowed floors of Balmoral, Chequers, and the Palace of Westminster. To many, he's regarded as a national treasure, despite his relatively young age for such an accolade. His few, but

vociferous, detractors sing a different song. To them...
Sebastian Thorne stinks!

As he emerges into the light, accompanied by the
Opposition Leader, he beckons for the media scrum to
move in closer.

'Okay, guys, everyone ready?' he shouts to the gathered
pack. 'Good.' He throws a quick glance behind him at his
PA and receives a warm smile and the thumbs up. 'You
good to go, Evan?' he whispers.

He replies in his trademark lilting Welsh accent.
'Absolutely, Sebastian.'

Sebastian leans in towards the microphone. 'Thank
you for all attending Thorne HQ. It gives me great
pleasure today to announce another exciting new initiative
between Thorne Holdings and Thorne Construction,' he
declares. There's a ripple of applause from a small crowd
of supporters and a few ring-ins to swell the numbers. 'As
you all know, over the last decade, Thorne Construction
has converted many dilapidated buildings into secure
accommodation for the homeless and those who dwell
on the fringes of society. From Glasgow to Manchester,
Liverpool to Leeds, Newcastle to Blackpool, and today
I can announce our next project will be right here in
Whitby, my adopted hometown.'

The statement is not quite true. Sebastian Thorne lives on a luxury farm twenty miles away in an idyllic valley in the North Yorkshire Moors. One of many abodes throughout the land, and the world, but let's not split hairs.

'Now, a few words from the Right Honourable Leader of the Opposition, Evan Tudor!' Much to his chagrin, Evan receives less applause than Sebastian, but he hides it well.

'Thank you, Sebastian,' he begins as both men shake hands.

As he steps forward, Sebastian leans in and whispers, 'Short and sweet Evan, short and sweet.'

Evan readjusts the microphone and pauses a moment for dramatic effect as cameras whirr and click.

'This is yet another super initiative by Sebastian Thorne, and I wholly commend him on his philanthropic actions and unyielding commitment to giving the less fortunate in the community a leg-up, and more importantly, safe and secure accommodation. A right that most of us take for granted.' His generous smile melts away, a sure-fire sign he's about to kick the current government hard in the plums with a hob-nailed, steel-toe-capped boot. 'However, it saddens and angers me to think that after more than a decade of Tory rule, our nation has been reduced to relying on generous benefactors like Sebastian Thorne. It is not the role of private enterprise to solve the nation's housing crisis, it's the role of government. A role the current government is clearly unable, or unwilling, to do.' Gripping the edges of the lectern, he stares into the crowd with an angry, disappointed glare that has been rehearsed a thousand times before with his performance coach. 'I can assure you that should I ever be privileged enough to lead this great country of ours, then that state of affairs will change. I guarantee that under my first term in government, we will commit two billion pounds to the construction of homeless accommodation.' He again pauses to the let the claps and cheers naturally die away. 'We are one of the wealthiest countries in the world, and yet, we have thousands of people sleeping rough on the street every night, at risk of abuse and violence.' He feels a slight tap on his elbow from Sebastian. 'This must stop! This *will* stop! Thank you.'

He takes a step back as applause resounds throughout the car park. Sebastian shakes his hand and pats him on the shoulder, sporting a solemn frown, then faces the crowd.

'Any questions?' Sebastian declares.

A slew of queries rains forth, and he answers each one with grace and aplomb.

'Where exactly is this new development?'

'On North parade. The site is currently home to two rather old, dilapidated hotels. They will be demolished, and a new, modern, hi-tech, environmentally friendly row of three-storey flats will be built, providing accommodation for thirty tenants.'

'How much will the rent be?'

'There will be a six-month grace period before any rent is paid.'

'But how much after the grace period?'

'That hasn't been finalised yet. But I can assure you it will be a peppercorn rent. The whole point of the exercise is to help those unfortunate individuals who have fallen through the cracks and become trapped in a vicious cycle. Without somewhere to live, it is very difficult to hold down a job, and without a job, it is impossible to find accommodation.'

'When do you expect the flats to be ready to move into, Mr Thorne?'

'All planning permissions and permits were issued last week, so we begin work immediately. The first tenant will be moving in within eighteen months.'

'How much is this all costing you?'

He chuckles. 'I'm not at liberty to say, but it's not cheap, as I'm sure you can imagine. But I have made my wealth through hard work and endeavour. My family and I have more than enough. I know what it's like to struggle. I wasn't born with a silver spoon in my mouth, and that's why I feel duty-bound to redistribute my wealth for the common good. But I'm not here to talk about me.'

He has honed the ability to come across as humble, whilst miraculously blowing his own trumpet. A feat that few can pull off with any conviction, but Sebastian Thorne has mastered it.

The crackle from a megaphone has everyone spinning around.

'And what about your developments in Sunderland, Sheffield, and Nottingham, Mr Thorne?' a strident female voice booms out. 'They no longer have tenants. They were sold off to the highest bidder and are now owned by extremely wealthy individuals. This man is a liar, a cheat, and a charlatan. Do not be fooled!'

A slug of adrenaline shoots through Sebastian's body as he groans. 'Oh, no. Not that meddling bitch again,' he murmurs under his breath. He turns and nods at his PA, who reciprocates with a slight twitch of her head. Two burly security guards are already bearing down on the small slender woman with the megaphone, but not before she issues one more statement.

'My name is Amanda Chan. Please watch my YouTube channel to find out about the real Sebastian Thorne!'

As she's urgently frog marched away, screaming profanities, the media pack smells a story far more sensational than helping the homeless.

'Is that true, Mr Thorne? Have the flats in Sunderland, Sheffield, and Nottingham been sold to wealthy individuals?'

Sebastian waves his hands up and down and pulls his most gracious and reassuring smile. 'It's true there were some issues with those particular projects, but we have learnt from our mistakes. Let's call them teething problems. I was naïve when I first started this initiative and it's been a learning curve. But I can assure you that all the money made from the sale of those initial developments has been poured into new projects. Thank you for your time, ladies and gentlemen.'

With Evan Tudor at his side, they turn and head back inside the sanctuary of Thorne Holdings headquarters.

For once, Sebastian Thorne is slightly flustered.

Evan pulls him aside. 'Is it true what that woman said, Sebastian?' he hisses, his genial brogue replaced by rasping vowels and consonants.

'As I said, there were some issues with those particular projects.'

'What sort of issues?'

'Drugs. Our vetting process wasn't rigorous enough. Unbeknownst to my team, a lot of the early tenants had addiction issues, which then led to dealers entering the area and from there it escalated into a lot of anti-social behaviour. We received a lot of pressure from the local council and nearby residents to take action.'

Evan flicks his hand through his sleek silver locks. 'Damn it, Seb, I can't be associated with you if it's going to blow up in my face,' he spits in a forced whisper. 'It could cost me points in the opinion polls. As you know, as it stands, I'm on the cusp of winning the next election.'

'Calm down, Evan. It's all been taken care of. We now have a most robust screening process to ensure we get the right people in the flats. Clean, intelligent individuals who just need a helping hand for a few months before they stand on their own two feet again. All the other projects are working wonderfully well.'

His reassuring words appear to calm Evan. 'Very well,' he says, glancing at his watch. 'I'd hate our partnership to come to an unedifying and premature end.'

The veiled threat is as transparent as gossamer.

Sebastian raises one eyebrow and smiles. 'And I'd *hate* to stop my extremely generous donations to the party, Evan.'

*Touché*!

Both eyeball each other in silence, aware there is no friendship, merely a marriage of convenience between two men lusting for power.

Sebastian and his PA watch on as the Opposition Leader accompanied by his small entourage and security team head across the car park.

'Amanda Chan is becoming a problem, Dora, a big problem,' he reflects, eyes still fixated on Evan Tudor as he climbs into the back of a Jaguar.

'Indeed she is, Mr Thorne.'

'The woman is a tumour. And what is the remedy for tumours, Dora?'

'We cut them out, sir.'

'Yes... we cut them out,' he drawls slowly.

# 5

Gary Underwood places the tray down on the table in front of Zac and Prisha.

'Here we go,' he says, handing the cups out. 'Tea, black, no sugar for you, inspector. And a strong black coffee for you, sergeant.'

'Thanks,' Zac says, taking a sip of the brew as he scans the interior of the modern, refurbished, homely flat. 'Nice little setup you have here, Mr Underwood.'

'Call me Gary. Yes, it caters to all my needs.'

'I see you've a large record collection, Gary,' he notes, staring at a shelf packed with LPs and an eighties era hi-fi system. 'Old school as well...vinyl. What are you into?'

'All sorts really, but mainly modern jazz. Miles Davis, Herbie Hancock, John Coltrane. What about you, sergeant?'

'I like all the old sixties and seventies stuff. The Beatles, Stones, Kinks, The Who. Motown. They knew how to craft a good tune in those days. Although, my brother was into death metal for a while. It drove me mad.'

Prisha picks up a chocolate hob-nob and takes a nibble. 'How long have you lived here, Gary?'

'Oh, since the old rectory was renovated into flats about ten years ago.'

She runs her eye over him. *Late forties, early fifties. Lives alone. Slightly dishevelled. Old jeans, grubby top. Well-worn boots. Not how I envisaged a typical tenant of Peasholm Manor.*

'It must have cost you a pretty penny?'

Gary chuckles, then coughs, a hacking smoker's cough. 'Way out of my league, I'm afraid. I don't own it. It comes with the job,' he explains.

'Job?'

'Yes. I'm the facility manager. I'm employed by the management company.'

Zac leans in. 'You mean you're the caretaker?'

'Aye.'

With her doubts quelled, Prisha focuses on the job at hand. 'What time did you discover Mr Morgan?'

Gary grimaces as he recalls the grisly scene. 'About seven-thirty this morning. I'd just started the ride-on mower to give the grounds a good haircut. The grass grows like buggery at this time of year. I started at the stretch which runs along the side of the cottage. I saw summat on the back lawn. At first, I thought it was a scarecrow. I was thinking to myself, why the hell has Selwyn got a bloody scarecrow laid out on his back lawn? Anyway, as I drew level with it, I realised it wasn't a scarecrow. I turned the engine off and climbed over the wall, and...' He drifts away, staring at the carpet, slowly shaking his head.

'Take your time, Gary,' Zac offers quietly.

'Who'd have done such a thing? I mean, I know murders go on, you hear about them every day, but that... well, that's just bloody barbaric. Sick, twisted bastards.'

Prisha's intrigued. 'You used the plural.'

His eyes snap away from the floor. 'Sorry?'

'You said bastards, meaning more than one.'

Blinks, momentarily confused. 'Did I?'

Prisha throws Zac a glance. 'We think Mr Morgan may have been killed late last night or early this morning. Did you notice anything suspicious, hear anything, or see any strangers around?'

Gary shakes his head. 'No. Nothing. Just the same old, same old. There are ten flats, but only five are permanently occupied. The others are second homes, you know, weekend retreats. I know all the residents extremely well, and to be honest with you, they're all lovely people. Older folk, you know, sixties to eighties.'

'Were there any disputes between Selwyn and the residents?'

Gary shakes his head. 'Nah, not that I was aware of.'

Zac takes another slurp of coffee. 'When was the last time you saw Selwyn?'

'Yesterday afternoon. He was in his garden tending to his plants. Keen gardener, he was. I was out with the strimmer. I like to do all the edges first, makes it easier for the ride-on. I stopped and had a quick natter with him.'

'You got on well with him?'

'Aye. Agreeable chap. We weren't best buddies or anything. He kept to himself.'

'And how did he seem yesterday when you spoke to him?'

'Same old Selwyn.'

'Didn't appear distracted, or edgy?'

'No.'

'I take it he lives alone?'

'Aye.'

'Does he have many visitors? Anyone ever stay over?'

'There's one fellow that visits a couple of times a year and occasionally stayed for a night or two.'

'Can you remember his name?' Prisha asks, detailing every question and answer in her notepad.

Gary grimaces, then scrunches his eyes up. 'Now let me think. It's on the tip of me tongue. Another God botherer. Used to be a vicar or summat. Wilkes, aye, that's it! John Wilkes.'

'And do you know where Mr Wilkes may live?'

'If I'm not much mistaken, I think he may have hailed from Dalehouse near Staithes. But don't quote me on that.'

'And you think he used to be a vicar?'

'Aye, a vicar, or reverend. Summat to do with the church. I assume that's how he and Selwyn became friends as he was a verger for years.'

'And how long had Selwyn lived in the cottage?'

'He was here before I arrived. The church sold the old rectory over a decade ago to a big developer. They got it for a song by all accounts. Mind you, I heard it was in a bit of a state, derelict. Anyway, part of the deal was the old cottage and the land it's on remained the property of the church. That's how Selwyn ended up there. Rent free. I suppose after all those years of dedicated service, he deserved it.'

Prisha rises. 'If you could give us a full list of all the residents and their contact details, it would be appreciated, Gary.'

'Not a problem, love. I'll print one off for you right now.'

'Oh, one last question,' Prisha quizzes.

'Fire away, lass,' Gary replies as he lifts the lid on his laptop.

'The developer who bought the old rectory; can you remember their name?'

Gary snorts. 'Aye, it was that shiny-shit who thinks the sun shines out of his backside. Always in the news. Slimy prick. I can't stand the man.'

'Who?'

'Sebastian Thorne.'

# 6

Frank Finnegan strides purposefully across the incident room, a man on a mission. In his hand swings a plastic carrier bag.

'Prisha, Zac,' he barks. 'My office, now. You can give me an update on the murder out at Pickering. Whole bloody station is yakking about it. Makes me look like a right Charlie, when I'm in the dark.'

Zac and Prisha grin at each other and dutifully follow Frank into his office and take seats. Frank drops the carrier bag onto his desk, slips out of his overcoat and hangs it on the hatstand, then takes a chair.

Prisha extracts her notebook and takes him through the morning's proceedings. Her eyes flit between her notes, and Frank, as he lifts a can of dandelion and burdock from the bag, peels back the ring-pull and takes a thirsty slurp.

'Oh, yes. Grand,' he states with satisfaction.

Prisha reads from her notes, paraphrasing. 'Retired church verger, Selwyn Morgan, aged eighty-one. Lived alone at the back of the old rectory, now known as Peasholm Manor Retirement Apartments, on the outskirts of Pickering, five miles from the town centre. Quiet country road. Nearest building is a farm two miles south.'

As Prisha continues, Frank shuffles in the plastic bag and extracts a large bread roll, or as they're referred to in Yorkshire—a teacake. He lifts the top off the sliced teacake to reveal a generous slathering of butter.

'... tent peg through either palm. Crucifix position. And another tent peg...'

He now retrieves a packet of smoky bacon Seabrook crisps, yanks the pack apart and carefully shakes half the contents onto the teacake.

'... through the forehead. A burn mark, or branding on his brow which is, as yet, indistinguishable.'

Frank slams the top back on the teacake and squashes it flat to the sound of crunching crisps.

'And a church candle...'

He leans back in his chair and takes a giant bite of his sandwich, chews slowly, and closes his eyes.

Prisha falls silent as Zac smirks, accustomed to the unusual behaviour. Frank swallows, his barrel chest rises, his eyes flicker open.

'You just had an orgasm, Frank?' Zac enquires.

He takes another sup of his drink. 'Way better than an orgasm, lad,' he says with a grin.

Prisha rests the notepad on her lap. 'I've seen it all now. A bloody crisp sandwich, *and* for lunch.'

'You mean dinner,' Frank corrects. 'You're not down south now, Prisha. It's breakfast, dinner, and tea round these parts. You've been here long enough to know that.'

'I come from Birmingham, Frank. That's not down south.'

Frank winks at Zac. 'Anything south of Sheffield is down south. They think differently down there. Queer folk.'

'Queer?'

'Aye. Queer peculiar, before you go getting all politically correct on me. Carry on. A church candle?' he prompts, taking another bite of his sandwich.

'Ahem... a church candle inserted deep inside the anal cavity, and his genitalia removed and placed at the side of his head.'

'Sweet mother of Jesus! Can't you see I'm bloody eating?' he yells, throwing his sandwich onto the desk in disgust.

———◦———

Frank pulls a double teapot, hands on hips as he stands next to the window that offers him magnificent views of the harbour and the River Esk.

'It's a bloody rum 'un,' he states, deep in thought.

'Rumun,' Prisha repeats, turning to Zac for guidance.

'Rum one; odd, strange, queer... as in peculiar.'

'Don't you start,' she replies.

'Any previous convictions or misdemeanours on Selwyn Morgan?' Frank asks.

'No. A big fat zero.'

'As you'd expect from a church verger. What about the residents at Peasholm Manor?'

'The five permanent residents say they neither saw, nor heard anything unusual. They all have partners who vouched for each other's whereabouts last night. I'd say the youngest couple we spoke to would have been early sixties. It's like a little retirement village. As for the casual residents, we're still chasing them up.'

'CCTV?'

'It captures the areas directly around the rectory but doesn't pick up the cottage. And no, before you ask, the cottage doesn't have security cameras.'

'Not a lot to go on. What about forensics?'

'Charlene won't have anything for us until tomorrow at the earliest. There is one guy I'll chase up this afternoon or tomorrow. John Wilkes, possibly from Dalehouse, a retired vicar or something to do with the clergy. Apparently, he visited Selwyn a couple of times a year.'

'John Wilkes?' Frank says, worry lines splashed across his face. 'Why does that name ring a bell? Hmm... Next of kin?'

'One sister, Myfanwy Morgan. Lives in Southampton. Local boys have informed her. I'll give her twenty-four hours to come to terms with the shock, then call her and get some background on Selwyn.'

'Sounds like neither of them have been married. And possibly of Welsh descent. Anything else?'

'That's about it, boss.'

'What about the caretaker who found the body?'

Zac leans forward and picks up an errant crisp from Frank's desk and pops it in his mouth. 'Seemed straight enough. He's worked there for ten years since it opened. Keeps the place tidy. Does odd jobs. Gets along with all the tenants and was on friendly terms with Selwyn.'

'A retired church verger.' Frank mumbles to himself, deep in thought. 'The ugly question raises its head; is this the work of a random psychopath who has a grudge against the church in general, or was Selwyn specifically targeted?'

Zac stretches and yawns. 'I guess we won't know unless there's another murder.'

'What do you mean?' Frank queries, resuming his seat.

'If he kills again and there's a link between the latest victim and Selwyn Morgan, then they were probably targeted specifically. Then it's a case of finding out why. But if there is no link, then we've got an unpredictable nutter on the loose who has a beef against the church, or God, or fucking hymn books, candles, or whatever.'

Frank nods. 'Unpredictable nutters are notoriously hard to catch. And if they don't kill again?'

Prisha folds shut her notebook. 'To me, that would tell us the attack on Selwyn wasn't random. If this is someone with a grudge against the church or Christianity, then they picked a very soft target to exact their vengeance. Wouldn't they have gone for a high-profile member of the church? The Archbishop of Canterbury or York, or the Bishop of London? That would have sparked some serious headlines.'

Frank ruminates. 'Okay, let's dig into Selwyn's past. Speak with his friends, old colleagues, and relations. Maybe they can shed some light on the matter. And what about this burn mark on his head?'

'It appeared to be a small oval shape, but due to the blood and swelling, it was impossible to discern exactly what it was. Once the body has been cleaned up, it will be clearer.'

'Okay, keep me up to date on proceedings.'

'Will do, Frank,' they both reply in unison as they rise and troop from his office.

'Oh, Prisha, come back. I need a quick word. Close the door.'

She gives Zac a—not sure what this is about—shrug.

'Yes, Frank.'

'I'm making you the Senior Investigating Officer on this one.'

'SIO? Why?'

'Because you deserve it. Time to cut the apron strings.'

A scowl instantly appears. 'Don't tell me you're thinking of retirement?'

His laugh is genuine. 'Retirement... me? No, of course not. Still a few years left in this old dog.' He leans over his desk, hands clasped. 'When, or if, you have children, their first bike will have stabiliser wheels. They're the extra set of wheels attached...'

Prisha rolls her eyes. 'Yes, I know what stabilisers are, Frank. And I understand your analogy.' She turns to the door. 'Okay. Thanks. I'll try not to let you down.'

'Hang on. Not so fast. I still want to be kept in the loop. Think of me as a benevolent overseer; a father figure, if you would. Any brick walls you come up against, or heads that need banging together, then you let me know, and I'll sort it. Time to spread those wings, inspector.'

She smiles appreciatively. 'Got it.'

He glances at his wristwatch and emits a yelp. 'Hell's bloody bells!' he cries, leaping from his seat.

'What's wrong?'

'I'm late. Got an appointment with the quack,' he says, reaching for his coat.

'The doctor?'

'Aye.'

'Nothing serious, I hope?'

He grins. 'Nah. Stuff and nonsense. Usual mandatory, annual check-up.' He hurries past her. 'Now think on. And good luck. I believe in you.'

# 7

Frank slips into his shirt and fastens the buttons. 'What's the prognosis, Doc? Firing on all cylinders?' he says in a cheery, ebullient tone.

The doctor lifts his eyes from the computer screen and peers over his spectacles at Frank. 'Yes, I am. Thanks for asking.'

Frank chuckles. 'Most amusing.'

'You, however, are a different matter. Your blood pressure readings are still way too high, indicative of hypertension. Your BMI is above the optimal range by around ten kilos, and you have an irregular heartbeat.'

Unconcerned, Frank tucks his shirt into his trousers and fastens his belt. 'To be expected at my age, though, isn't it?'

'You're sixty, Frank. Not eighty. And if you want to make it to eighty, then you need to start looking after yourself. What's your exercise regime?'

He winces. 'Pretty rigorous. I walk the dog each night after tea. My office is on the second floor so I'm and up down those bloody stairs all day long. Oh, and I spend a lot of time at my allotment. Always something to do there.'

The doctor sits in his chair and frowns. 'That's hardly a regime, is it? That's normal everyday activity. When was the last time you had a holiday?'

Frank considers the question carefully. 'Now, let me think. Aye, that's right. Me and the missus had a long weekend in Cleethorpes not so long ago. Although, if you've ever visited Cleethorpes, it's more of an endurance test than a holiday.'

The doctor shakes his head. 'I'm not happy about it.'

'Oh, so you're familiar with Cleethorpes?'

The doctor glowers back at him. 'I'm being serious, Frank. Take a seat.'

Frank reluctantly sits down in front of the doctor and drops the false bravado. 'Come on, let's hear the usual mantra; cut down on red meat and saturated fats, eat more vegetables, more exercise, cut out processed food, alcohol in moderation, keep off the cakes and biscuits.'

'See? You know what to do, so why don't you do it? If you follow the advice, you may have another twenty years or more left in you.'

Frank's glum expression paints a revealing picture. 'Not sure I'd want another twenty years living like that. Basically, you want me to remove all the joy from life.

What's the point in living if you can't have moments of pleasure?'

The doctor slumps back in his seat and sighs. 'Can you not learn to love a salad?' he asks, exasperated at his incorrigible patient.

Frank's face creases in confusion as he stares at him as if he's barking mad. 'Love a salad. Have you had a bump to the head?'

'Have you tried the Mediterranean diet?'

'Does scampi and chips count?'

The doctor rubs at his eyes with forefinger and thumb. 'No, no, it doesn't. Have you given any further consideration to retirement?'

Frank folds his arms. 'You ask me that question every damn year. You just told me I need more exercise. What the hell would I do if I retired? Then I'd have no bloody exercise.'

'You have a very old-fashioned view of retirement. It's not the nineteen-seventies. These days people don't retire and vegetate in an armchair. They do things. They experience life. You can visit all the places you've dreamt of. Take up new hobbies like pottery, or painting. You could join a walking club, or a swimming group, or both. The world is your oyster.'

The very thought of organised group activity brings Frank out in a cold sweat. 'You have had a bang to the head.'

The doctor loses patience. 'I give up. I really do. Fine, you do what you want. But I'm warning you, if you don't make some drastic lifestyle changes soon, then you won't make it to eighty, you'll be lucky to make it to sixty-five.' He hammers at the keyboard, and with a flourish, hits the return key. The printer immediately whirrs into life. 'I'm sending you for an electrocardiogram and an echocardiogram. We need to get to the bottom of your irregular heartbeat. It could mean you require a stent or possibly a pacemaker... or both. Ultimately, the decision to undergo these tests and adhere to the medical advice proffered is entirely up to you. But I, for one, won't be coming to your funeral!'

The doctor hands the referrals to Frank, who, suitably chastised, rises and grabs his coat. As he makes his way to the door, the doctor calls out.

'Your wife, Meera, how old is she?'

Frank stops and turns, puzzled. 'She's fifty-eight. Why?'

'With the recent changes to the retirement age, she has another eight years to work before she's eligible for the state pension.'

'So?'

'You'll most likely be dead by then. Stop thinking about yourself and think of her. She's a lot healthier than you. That's a long time she's going to be alone. Think on that.'

Frank walks outside into the fresh air and rests on a nearby bench. 'That was fun. Bloody quacks,' he murmurs to himself as he gazes out at the grey North Sea and contemplates his future.

# 8

# Tuesday 25th April

With a solid run under her belt, a cold shower, and a healthy breakfast, Prisha enters the incident room still an hour early. She's surprised to see DC Clem Dinkel at his desk.

'Morning, Dinkel.'

'Good morning, ma'am.'

'Did you enjoy your day off yesterday?'

'It wasn't a day off, ma'am. It was a training day.'

'Ah, right, I recall now. What was the topic?'

'It was about the use of artificial intelligence in criminal investigations and the latest surveillance developments. Truly captivating stuff. Did you know that spy cameras are now so small and powerful they can be inserted into everyday objects most people wouldn't bat an eyelid at?'

'Such as?'

'Picture frames, books, toys, tissue boxes, artificial plants, lightbulbs, key fobs. And AI is now being leveraged to recover data from damaged devices, assist in examining crime scenes, and can analyse both fingerprints and handwriting. It's also used in comparing photographs. The algorithms in AI can detect subtle details that can escape the human eye. Some forces are now using AI for photo-fits.'

Prisha laughs and nods at Zac as he enters the room. 'You better lift your game, Dinkel, otherwise I can see the day when you're replaced by a robot.'

Zac takes a seat. 'Let's hope the robotic Dinkel comes with a personality.'

'Ha, ha,' Dinkel replies.

Prisha heads to the interactive whiteboard. 'I'm glad you're both in early. It shows you're keen. Now, Dinkel, are you up to speed with the murder out at Pickering?'

'Yes, ma'am. I'd just finished reading the report.'

She rapidly makes a list on the board.

## OPERATION GORSE BUSH

Selwyn Morgan - Murder

Friends / Family / Past / Peasholm Manor Casual
Residents - Zac

Rectory Cottage - Search - Dinkel

Forensics Lab - Prisha / Zac

John Wilkes Question – Prisha

Zac groans. 'Fuck me blue... Operation Gorse Bush. Is that one of yours?'

Prisha grins. 'Yes. Don't you like it?'

'Sounds like a makeover gardening show, not a murder investigation.'

'Yesterday, at Peasholm Manor, the scent of flowering gorse was delightful. Hence the name.'

'I like it, ma'am,' Dinkel concurs.

'Thank you.'

Zac sneers. 'No one likes a brown-noser, Dinkel.'

Prisha claps her hands together. 'Right, now we've agreed on the name, we need to dig into Selwyn Morgan's past. Zac, you tackle friends and colleagues and chase up the casual residents from Peasholm Manor. Let's see if Morgan had any skeletons in the cupboard. Once you've done that, we'll take a ride to see Charlene Marsden at the lab. Dinkel, get yourself over to Morgan's cottage and go through everything. Forensics have finished with it, but still wear gloves when handling anything.'

'What am I looking for?'

Prisha and Zac exchange glances. 'You're searching for clues. Anything that could tell us, or even lead us to, Selwyn Morgan's killer.'

His non-plussed expression exasperates Zac. 'For God's sake, man! Old photographs, diaries, scribbled notes on paper, the killer's name written in blood on the bathroom ceiling, anything that makes the hairs on the back of your neck stand to attention.'

Prisha tries a softer approach. 'Dinkel, you have a remarkable talent for extracting crucial information from what appears to be the most mundane details. Got it?'

'Right, got it.'

———◦———

The office is calm, the way Prisha likes it. Whoever thought open-plan offices were a good thing was, quite frankly, a dolt, and had obviously never worked in one. Data analysis and critical thinking require serenity, not the constant hum of chatter, printers, banging doors, and the occasional bout of laughter or angry shouting. Her eyes fixate on the boats on the river, which sway gracefully to the rhythm of the tide. A wisp of steam rises from her coffee cup, teasing her nostrils with a delightful aroma. She stares at the report in front of her, pleased with the first breakthrough in the case, albeit a tiny one. Once you have a starting point, things tend to gather pace at an exponential rate.

The peace is broken as Zac re-enters the office carrying a small paper bag. He sits down next to her and removes the contents.

'Here, I got us both a custard tart for elevenses.' He wastes no time in taking a large bite.

'Thanks,' Prisha replies.

'Has Frank been in?' Zac asks, scanning the office.

'He came in for about ten minutes, then left again. He was heading to the hospital for some routine tests. I assume it's something to do with the medical he had yesterday.'

Zac scowls. 'I don't like the sound of that. Did he say why?'

'No. He wasn't in the best of moods, so I didn't push it. Anything on Morgan?'

'Yes and no. The part-time residents from the manor didn't hold any surprises. Said Morgan was quiet, reserved. They also all had partners who vouched for their whereabouts on the night of his murder. Are all couples over sixty joined at the hip?'

Prisha pulls a face. 'Don't know. I'll get back to you in thirty years. What else?'

'I spoke with the vicar at St Mary's. He knew of Morgan, but as he's only been in the parish for three years, he couldn't tell me much we don't already know. However, it just so happened the cleaning lady was at the church. A nice old mare. Despite her senior years, she's as sharp as a tack. Memory like an elephant. She said Morgan had been with the Church of England for as long as she could remember. Worked a number of parishes around the area: St Mary's at Whitby, All Saints at Hawsker, St Hilda's at Hinderwell, and St Hilda's at Sneaton before eventually finishing up at the rectory in Pickering.'

Prisha takes a mouthful of custard tart. 'Who's this St Hilda when she's at home?' she mumbles.

'St. Hilda? Oh, she was a big deal in seventh-century Whitby. Ran the local monastery, which was the go-to place for learning and religion back then. She oversaw this important meeting, the Synod of Whitby, which shaped early Christianity in England. She's a bit of a legend around these parts. There are loads of churches and streets named after her.'

'I didn't realise you were such an expert in early Christianity.'

Zac grins and takes a sip of coffee. 'There are a lot of things you don't know about me. My mind is like blotting paper—soaks up everything.'

'The cleaning lady told you, didn't she?'

He nods sheepishly. 'Aye. Anyway, Morgan never married. Was quiet, respectful, good at his job. A confirmed bachelor. Worked way more hours than required, a real servant to the church. Well-respected by all. She hadn't heard about his death, so I told her we were still investigating and weren't sure what the cause of death was. No point starting the rumour mill.'

Prisha ponders. 'Never married, and a confirmed bachelor. Celibacy, perhaps?'

Zac snorts. 'Speaking as a man, and excluding any medical condition, celibacy is a myth. There's not a snowball's chance in hell that a man can live for eighty years and not have a sexual outlet.'

She rises and paces back and forth. 'Maybe he was gay and hid it. He's of that generation where it would have been deeply frowned upon, especially within the church.'

'Possibly.'

'The question is, why would a seemingly sweet old gentleman, a model citizen, a true believer, without an apparent enemy in the world, be so brutally murdered?'

'People only see what they want you to see. Behind closed doors, and all that.'

'Exactly. Was Selwyn wearing a mask, hiding a dark secret? Or, as we discussed yesterday, was his killing random?'

'That's a lot of effort and symbolism for a random killing.'

'I agree. Anyway, while you were away, I had a minor breakthrough, of sorts. I ran another query through the PNC. Yesterday, when we checked, we were looking for any convictions or cautions against Morgan. Today, I expanded the search to see if he'd ever been on the receiving end of a crime; you know, assault or burglary.'

'And?'

Prisha picks up the report and hands it to Zac. 'Four years ago, he was assaulted outside the Duke of York on Church Street. He received a minor cut to the back of his head but wouldn't press charges. As the perpetrator had a clean record, he was let off with a caution.'

Zac studies the report. 'And the offender's name is Marco Rossellini, from Whitby. Arresting officer, PC Jackson.'

'Do you remember it?'

'Nah. Uniforms jurisdiction. I know the officer, though, Grant Jackson. Good sort. He transferred a few years ago to the Roads Policing Unit. I can get onto control if you like and see if he's in the area? Get him to drop by for a chat.'

'That would be great.'

———— ◦ ————

'Thanks for coming in, Grant,' Zac says as PC Jackson takes a seat. 'Have you met DI Prisha Kumar?'

'No. I've seen her around the traps but never been formally introduced. Please to meet you, ma'am.'

'Likewise,' Prisha replies with a warm smile. 'I hope we didn't drag you from miles away?'

PC Jackson laughs. 'No. I was about five miles up the road. Just about to pull into a lay-by to eat my pack-up when the call came through. You don't mind if I...' he waggles a Tupperware box in front of her.

'Feel free.'

He peels back the lid and pulls out a mini pork pie. 'So, how can I help?'

Zac hands him the report. 'Four years ago, you arrested a guy called Marco Rossellini on Church Street. He'd assaulted an elderly man named Selwyn Morgan.'

Grant briefly studies the sheet whilst munching on his food. 'Oh, aye. I remember. Much ado about nothing, really. I was on the beat when I witnessed a fracas outside The Duke of York. Marco Rossellini had shirt-fronted an older guy. Had him pinned up against a wall. Rossellini had been drinking with his mates, but he wasn't hammered or anything. Anyway, I brought him back to the station and asked him to explain himself. He said he'd recognised the old man—Selwyn Morgan. According to Rossellini, when he was a kid, he and some other lads were playing hide and seek in a cemetery somewhere. Mr Morgan had collared him and given him a good hiding. Morgan was something to do with the church.

Well, Rossellini obviously has a long memory and holds a grudge, and with the help of a bit of Dutch courage inside him, he thought he'd square the ledger. The old guy had a cut to the back of his head. Well, more of a graze, really. He wasn't interested in pressing charges and as Rossellini had no previous, the desk sergeant let him go with a caution. Like I said, storm in a teacup.'

'When you say Rossellini copped a good hiding, how good?' Prisha asks.

'According to him, he said it was a right belting. But when I questioned Mr Morgan, he refuted that claim. He said he'd given the lad a quick clip around the ear and sent him on his way. I wasn't willing to get into a back and forth between whose version was correct over an incident that happened thirty-odd years ago.'

'Do you remember what Rossellini did for a living?'

'Aye. He's a mechanic. He owns the garage on the way out of Whitby. It's called Mike and the Mechanics, for reasons I never quite fathomed.'

# 9

Prisha and Zac gawp at the photograph in puzzlement.

'I don't get it?' Zac says, blinking as he turns to Charlene Marsden, the harsh lighting of the forensics lab almost searing his retinas.

She offers an enigmatic smile. 'No. It is a bit of a mystery.'

Prisha spins the photo every which way. There's no doubt it's an enlarged image of Selwyn Morgan's forehead. Above the small, round entry wound, created by the tent peg, is a definite motif. A small oval shape, no larger than the pad of a pinky finger. On top of the oval is what appears to be a clutch of short, tightly thatched, curly hair. Protruding from the hair is a single line, no more than a sliver, curling away at an oblique angle. In the centre of the oval is an eye, or at least, an eye shaped symbol.

Prisha places the photograph back on the bench. 'Putting aside what it actually is, or represents, what do you think caused the burn?'

Charlene raises her eyebrows. 'I'd say a signet ring, or possibly a small medallion or pendant designed with high-relief—alto relievo.'

'You just made that last bit up, didn't you?' Zac queries with a wicked grin.

Charlene laughs. 'Think of it as embossing, but with a PhD. It's typically seen in architecture where a figure or symbol is raised from the stone or marble instead of being flat. You see it on churches and ancient Egyptian, Greek, and Roman structures and artefacts. But it's also commonly used on jewellery and coins.'

Prisha nods, thoughtfully. 'The killer would have needed to heat it up somehow to create a burn mark.'

'Yes. The only thing I can think of that would be practical in such a time sensitive situation as a murder would be a small blowtorch and a pair of tongs or pliers to hold the piece of jewellery with, if indeed, it was jewellery that was used.'

'A final signature after the deed was done, perhaps?'

'Possibly, or maybe *before* the deed was committed. An initiation ceremony.'

Zac taps at the image. 'What about the motif itself? Does it signify some ancient cult? Is it the head of a one-eyed god?'

Charlene slips her spectacles back on and takes another look at the photo. 'If it is, then I've not come across it before, but then again I'm no iconologist, although...'

'Go on,' Prisha prompts.

'I have an old friend who was a professor of semiotics at Durham University; Marcus Eldridge.'

'Semiotics?'

'The study of signs and symbols. He retired some years ago, but lives in Runswick Bay. He's an expert in ancient religious and cult iconology from around the world. I can give you his telephone number and address if you'd like. It may be worth paying him a visit. I can text ahead to let him know you'll be calling.'

'Yes, thanks. That may be useful. If we can unlock the meaning behind the symbol, then it could be a game-changer.'

Zac strokes his beard. 'What about digital forensics? Anything of note on his phone or computer?'

'We're still analysing his laptop, but we've finished with his phone... and it wasn't a smart phone. An old Nokia, at least twenty years old. I'll give you a printout of all the calls and texts he's made in the last eighteen months, but it's a very short list. The last call was two months ago to his dentist.'

Prisha's ears prick up. 'Did you come across the name John Wilkes?'

'Yes, we did. Apart from another number in Southampton and an occasional call to a medical practitioner, that's about it.'

'Sounds like he didn't have many friends or acquaintances.'

'No. Which makes it even more baffling. The body is now at the mortuary, and I believe Doctor Whipple intends to carry out the post-mortem tomorrow.'

'What about fibres, hair, blood, DNA, fingerprints?' Prisha asks.

'Nothing so far apart from one shoe print from the crime scene that doesn't belong to the victim. Size eleven, and Selwyn is a size eight. I also checked the caretaker's shoe size, and he's a size ten.'

'Just one footprint?' Prisha quizzes, eyebrows arched.

She hands Prisha the shoe photo. 'Yes. It doesn't mean there weren't more. But there was only one that was discernible.'

'Do we know the manufacturer or the type of shoe?'

'Not yet.'

'What about the tent pegs?'

'Standard issue, heavy duty, ribbed steel pegs you can buy from any camping supply store. Twelve inches long.'

'And the candle?'

'Preliminary investigations suggest it's a Paschal candle used in liturgies within Western Christianity during Easter. The name Paschal is derived from the Hebrew, Pesach, meaning Passover. The diameter of this particular candle is three inches.'

'You mean the width?' Prisha questions.

'Yes. We have not ascertained the length yet as it's still inside the victim, but they can be twelve to eighteen inches in length, or longer.'

Zac gasps in disbelief. 'Shit the bed. I've heard of a bit of bum-fun, but a three-inch diameter is pushing the envelope to breaking point.'

Charlene cannot resist a chuckle. 'That's what I like about you, Zac; your gallows humour. Believe me, we need it. The depravity humans inflict upon other living creatures has no boundaries. I thought I'd seen it all, but I can still be surprised, even after all these years.'

'Anything else?' Prisha inquires.

'Still working on it. As you know, we are...'

'Understaffed, underfunded, and underpaid. I understand.'

'Very quick, Prisha, very quick.'

'Well, if anything interesting develops, please let me know immediately.'

———◆———

Zac parks the car on a piece of spare land at the side of the garage and turns to Prisha.

'Marco Rossellini— how do you want to play him?'

She purses her lips for a moment. 'Cool and easy. Simply routine. Let's see how he reacts. Deep down, I don't think for one moment he could have done that to Morgan over a so-called clip around the ear. And why wait nearly forty years? But we can't rule him out and at the moment, it's all we have.'

After locking the car, they amble towards the old brick workshop as music blares from inside. Prisha stares disdainfully at the sign affixed above the roller door.

Mike & The Mechanic's

Being an avid reader and a grammarian, she is affronted at the signage. The music from inside is a Neil Diamond classic, Sweet Caroline, a catchy little tune... usually. Unfortunately, for anyone with ears and a sense of pitch, the song is being mangled by the accompaniment of a voice which would be more suited to the role of town crier.

Prisha and Zac grin at each other as they enter the workshop and survey the scene. A Ford Mondeo is on a car lift as a man in blue overalls works beneath it singing, or shouting, his heart out. The workshop appears neat and tidy, with everything in its place. A small makeshift office is in a far corner next to a tiny corridor which looks like it may lead to toilets and a kitchen.

As the song reaches the unmistakable trumpet riff, the man spins around and joins in playing air-trumpet, although it could be air-trombone the way his right arm moves back and forth. Hitting the final note, he spots the strangers watching him from the entrance. He offers them a sheepish smile and immediately makes his way to a bench and turns off the music. They amble over as Prisha flashes her warrant card.

'I'm DI Kumar and this is my colleague, DS Stoker. Are you Marco Rossellini?'

'Yes, I am. How can I help you?' he says, wiping his hands on a grimy rag.

Zac takes the lead. 'It's about a murder we're investigating, and I'm not talking about the song you just slaughtered. That was a crime against humanity, not to mention Neil Diamond, and should be left to the International Criminal Court to tackle.'

His face noticeably darkens. 'Murder. Who?'

'A man named Selwyn Morgan.'

Both officers carefully study his reaction, which is a mixture of confusion, then remembrance.

He affects a cocky stance. 'Oh, I see. Is this about the little spat I had with him a few years ago?'

Prisha offers him a warm smile to put him at ease. 'Yes, it is. Can you tell me where you were last Sunday between the hours of 7 pm and 4 am Monday morning?'

'I was with my friend. We went out for the night. I arrived home about ten-thirty. Watched a bit of TV then went to bed. Got up next morning around six and opened up the garage around seven.'

'Where did you and your friend go?' Zac asks.

'We had a few drinks at The Fleece. My mate went home, and I went for a sit-down meal at The Jackdaw restaurant; fish and chips.'

'The staff at The Jackdaw should be able to verify that?'

'Aye. They know me in there. I go at least once a month, barring the holidays when it's overrun with bloody tourists. You say he was murdered. How?'

Prisha purses her lips. 'We can't divulge that information.'

He shrugs. 'Ah well, I can't say I'll shed a tear over his passing. Nasty piece of work.'

'I meant to ask you about that. According to the statement you gave to PC Jackson, you said when you were a kid, Mr Morgan caught you playing in the cemetery and gave you a hiding.'

'That's right. He knocked seven shades of shit out of me. Bloody psycho.'

'To the head, the body?'

'Head, body, face. Slapped me halfway across the bloody graveyard. As I ran away, I sprained my ankle. It was agony. I was on crutches for a week.'

'Did you tell your parents?'

He looks away. 'My dad was dead by then, and mum… well, she was having her own problems. I didn't want to burden her. Anyway, you've got to remember the times. It was the mid-eighties and knocking the shit out of kids wasn't as frowned upon as it is today. Now it's gone too far the other way.'

Zac and Prisha exchange looks.

'Okay, well, thanks for your time, Mr Rossellini,' Zac says.

'No problem.'

'By the way, I have the number of a vocal coach if you're ever considering applying for Britain's Got Talent.'

'Ha, ha. Piss off.'

As they head towards the entrance, Prisha half stops and turns. 'Oh, Mr Rossellini, when you were a kid, you said you were playing in the graveyard; which graveyard?'

'The cemetery out at Hinderwell. St Hilda's.'

'Thanks. And one last thing, the signage out front; there's no need for an apostrophe in the word mechanics. And if you follow normal title conventions, the word—the—should be lowercase.'

'Thanks for that. I'll get onto my signwriter right away—not.'

As they saunter outside, Zac asks, 'What do you think?'

'Seems legit. Wasn't fazed. But check out his alibi with the staff at The Jackdaw.'

# 10

Frank places the drinks on the table. One gin and tonic, a pint of Whitby Whaler, and a half-pint of Smugglers Gold. He pulls a packet of peanuts from his pocket and tosses them to Prisha.

'Cheers, Frank,' Zac and Prisha reply in unison.

Zac wastes no time in taking a hearty slug of his beer as he eyes Frank suspiciously. He smacks his lips together and wipes the suds from his top lip on the back of his jacket sleeve.

'This is a first,' he states wryly.

Frank takes a dainty sup of his beer. 'What's a first?'

'You, with a half-pint. It looks out of place. It's like seeing Mahatma Gandhi at the rifle range.'

'Very funny. You know me, everything in moderation.'

Zac snorts beer down his nose, coughing violently. 'Christ, I've heard it all now. You'll be drinking lager and lime next.'

Prisha offers Zac a tissue, then spills open the packet of peanuts onto the table. 'Frank, how'd you go at the hospital?' she says, taking a sip of her drink then popping a few peanuts into her mouth.

Frank groans. 'Bloody nightmare. Three hours sitting in the waiting room, then a heart test. Another hour waiting, then another ruddy test. And of course they don't tell you anything. It's like a closed shop. They send the report back to my doctor, who then, depending on the results, may or may not send me to a specialist.'

Zac and Prisha exchange worried glances. 'What's the issue?' Zac asks.

'Irregular heartbeat. Anyway, enough about me. Get me up to speed with the Pickering murder.'

Prisha pulls her notebook out and flicks through the pages. 'It's now called Operation Gorse Bush, if you don't mind.'

Frank pulls the face of a bulldog licking warm piss off a nettle. 'Operation Gorse Bush?'

Zac lifts his pint and says, 'Aye, I ken. Pure shite, eh?'

Prisha responds with scolding eyes... which is enough to silence both men.

'Shut-up. It's fine. Ahem, we're starting to make progress, but it's slow. Zac spoke with the cleaning lady at St Mary's and got some good intel on Selwyn

Morgan. Quiet man. Hard worker. Bit of a loner. Kept himself to himself. I spoke on the phone to his sister in Southampton, Myfanwy Morgan. She painted a similar picture. Selwyn was involved in a minor incident a few years back with a Marco Rossellini. He runs a mechanics workshop on the edge of town. He reckons Selwyn gave him a beating back in the eighties when he was a kid, and Marco pulled him up about it a few years back. We went to see him, but he has an alibi for Sunday night that Zac checked out. He said he was home by ten-thirty and didn't leave the house until the next morning. We think Selwyn died between ten on Sunday night and two or three the next morning. It's only a thirty-minute drive between Whitby and Pickering, so technically, it's still possible he was involved.'

'How did he react when you told him about the murder?'

'A bit surprised. But he didn't display any signs of stress or anxiety.'

'Forensics?'

'Not much so far. We've got some photos of the burn mark on Selwyn's head. It's a motif of some sort, but we can't figure out what it represents. Charlene gave me the number of an old friend of hers. A retired semiotics professor. I called him earlier and we're due to meet up on

Thursday to see if he can shed any light on it. Oh, and one foreign footprint. Shoe size, eleven.'

'And what about the occasional visitor to Selwyn's cottage, John Wilkes?'

'I obtained his phone number today from the report that digital forensics ran on Selwyn's phone. I called and arranged to meet him tomorrow at his home in Dalehouse.'

'And what's his story?'

'Don't know yet. He was hurrying to catch a train, and the line kept breaking up, so I only had a chance to tell him who I was, get his address, and arrange a time to visit.'

'At least it's a start. And what's Dinkel been up to?'

Prisha slaps her hand to her forehead. 'Hell! I forgot all about Dinkel. I sent him out to Selwyn's cottage to dig around.' She checks her watch. 'I bet he's still there.'

Zac chuckles. 'Aye, well, don't disturb the little ferret-worrier. We can leave him there for another day or two. Maybe a week.' He finishes his pint and glares at the other two. 'Come on, get them down. My shout.'

Frank holds his hand up and finishes the dregs of beer. 'Not for me. I've got some groceries in the car. My turn to make tea for me and the missus.'

Prisha knocks back her G and T and pushes the glass towards Zac. 'What's on the menu, Frank?' she asks, sporting an impish grin.

'Haddock fillets, seasoned and lightly dusted in flour, cooked in extra virgin olive oil with a Greek salad accompaniment. I'm going Mediterranean.'

'You're going doolally,' Zac says, experiencing a dizzy rush to the head as he collects the empty glasses.

— ◦ —

Frank is a dab-hand at cooking fish. Throwing together a Greek salad is a different matter. He has a Jamie Oliver cookbook open on the kitchen counter as Foxtrot stares up at him, either desperate for his own evening meal, or more likely perplexed why his master is attempting to make a salad. Frank adjusts his spectacles and reads out the list of ingredients, which seems like a hell of a lot for a simple salad.

'Roma tomatoes, cucumber peeled, red onion, green or red pepper, Kalamata olives - green or black, capers, feta cheese, fresh basil, fresh oregano, olive oil, salt and pepper to taste.' He rubs thoughtfully at his chin. 'Damn and blast. I don't have all the ingredients.' He stares down at his dog. 'Time for a little improvisation, Foxtrot.'

He pours himself a very generous glass of red wine to aid the extemporisation process.

———◦———

Meera is pleasantly surprised as she enters the house to the sound of relaxing, cool-jazz, and the usual banter Frank is engaged in with Foxtrot. She puts her bags down, disrobes from her overcoat, and enters the kitchen.

'You've already got tea on the go?' she says, exchanging a hug and kiss with Frank.

'Aye. You put your feet up, love. It's all in hand.'

'What are you making: steak and chips; egg and chips; bangers and mash; roast beef sandwiches; pork pie with Branston pickle; or is it your speciality, mince and tatties?'

Frank pours her a small glass of red and hands it to her. 'It's called Frank's Surprise.'

Meera is well known for not liking surprises. She eyeballs him, then the red wine, and performs a quick three-sixty of the kitchen, taking in every detail. Naturally, she's suspicious.

'Since when did you drink red wine?'

'I like an occasional glass.'

'There are five bottles in the normally empty wine rack.'

'A change is as good as a rest.'

'Hmm... are you in the mood? Because if you are, I'm warning you, it'll take a lot to fire my engine tonight. I'm dead on my feet and want to flake out in front of the telly and vegetate.'

Frank pulls an exaggerated, hurt expression. 'Never crossed my mind. Can't a loving, caring, considerate husband make his beloved wife a nice evening meal without there being an ulterior motive?'

'No.'

Frank shoots Foxtrot a sharp stare. 'Did you hear that, Foxtrot? You stay single, lad. You can't do right for doing bloody wrong when you're wed.'

Meera turns to leave. 'How long before Frank's Surprise?'

'Fifteen.'

'Okay. I'll take a quick shower and slip into my jim-jams for the night.'

As she leaves, Frank shakes his head at the dog. 'Jim-jams, also known as passion killers.'

---

Frank slides the food onto the dining room table as Meera watches on in mild amazement, or possibly mild trepidation.

Frank puffs his chest out as he takes a seat. 'Haddock fillets, lightly braised in extra virgin olive oil, accompanied by an authentic Greek salad,' he declares, as if he's solved the mystery of Lord Lucan.

Meera is impressed with the fish. The Greek salad... less so. To be fair, it is a salad—of sorts. Authentic Greek is pushing the boundaries of credulity somewhat.

'Frank, it looks divine. Is that chopped up cheese slices on the salad?'

'Aye. All out of feta.'

'Any olives or capers?'

'No. Out of them as well.'

'Herbs?'

'Of course. The herbs are mixed in with the cucumber, tomatoes, and white onion. Ahem, caraway seeds, a sprinkle of turmeric, and a dash of parsley—dried. I had to make do with what we had in the cupboard. They were all out of date by four years, but I don't think it matters with dried herbs—does it? But it is drizzled with extra virgin olive oil.'

'I'm sure it will be lovely,' Meera responds as she shovels a meagre portion of the *salad with no name* onto her plate, aside her fish fillet.

In her mind, she christens it—The Frank Salad. Once eaten, never forgotten.

———— •◇• ————

Frank collects the plates and cutlery from the table, feeling on top of the world.

'What do you reckon, love?'

Meera clasps her hand together. 'The fish was divine.'

'And the Greek salad?'

'Erm, yes... it was very... well, salady, sort of. Very... nice, edible... in a roundabout sort of way. Very exotic flavours.'

'Excellent. I'll make it again next week,' he replies, pleased as punch, heading into the kitchen.

Meera drops her head into her hands. 'Please Lord, help me out here,' she whispers, stroking her face in an agitated manner.

As they finish cleaning the kitchen together, Frank breaks the news.

'Meera, I've decided it's time for some serious lifestyle changes.'

'Go on,' she says, hanging the tea-towel up.

'A healthier diet, more exercise and lessen the workload. Take a bit more time off.'

She's been married long enough to spot the signs. 'It was your annual medical check-up yesterday, wasn't it?'

Frank averts his gaze as he tops up his wine glass. 'Aye. Nothing gets past you.'

'Is this what it's all about? The salad, red wine, and fish without batter?'

'No, of course not.'

She spins her husband around and fixes him with a withering glare. 'Don't lie to me. What's the matter with you?'

He sighs heavily. 'It's my heart.'

Meera clasps her hand over her mouth. 'Oh, sweet Lord. I've been dreading this day.'

Frank rests a hand on her shoulder. 'Calm down. It's nothing serious. An irregular heartbeat. I had tests today at the hospital. The doctor reckons it could mean I need a pacemaker or possibly a stent. These days, they're minor procedures.'

She slaps him on the arm. 'I've been telling you for years to look after yourself. You can't undo a lifetime of abuse by suddenly eating a few Greek salads and drinking red wine.'

'You want me to carry on with my old lifestyle, then?'

'No. Of course not.'

He drops his head. 'I need your help here, Meera. I can't do this alone. How about it? Healthy food, more exercise, less stress?'

She wipes a spot of wetness from her cheek. 'Yes. I'm sorry. We'll do this together.'

He leans in and pecks her on the lips. 'Good-o. And I think it's about time we had a holiday. What do you think?'

She turns to head out of the room. 'I'm not going to bloody Cleethorpes again.'

'I was thinking of somewhere overseas.'

'Really?' she replies in astonishment.

'Aye. Really. Push the boat out, pardon the expression.'

'Where do you have in mind?'

'Maybe the Isle of Wight or possibly even as far as Jersey.'

Spinning on her heels, she glowers at him. 'Jersey and the Isle of Wight are not overseas!'

He takes a cautious step back. 'Well, technically...'

'Frank!'

'Okay, okay. I tell you what, tomorrow during your dinner break, why don't you pop along to the travel agents and get some ideas? Bring some brochures home.'

'Which travel agent?'

'The one near the swing bridge.'

She shakes her head in disbelief. 'Frank, that travel agent closed down about a decade ago.'

He scratches his head. 'Did it?'

'Yes. Nearly everyone I know books their holiday online.'

'Is that safe?'

Her steely eyes bore into him. 'For God's sake. You're a man trapped in the 1980s. The world has changed, Frank, and it's left you behind.'

He raises his hands in a pacifying motion. 'Fine. I'll leave it all up to you. Wherever you decide to go, I'll be happy.'

'You mean that?'

'Yes.'

'Even Australia or South America?'

His face drops. 'Ooh, now hang on a moment. That's a hell of a long...'

'See, you can't do it, can you?'

'Do what?'

'Go out of your comfort zone. I tell you what, give me a couple of days and I'll present you with three destinations, then you can choose. Agreed?'

He unfurls the white flag. Arguing with Meera is like trying to drink a pint of beer underwater—futile. 'Aye. Agreed.'

Her stern expression evaporates. 'Good. That's settled then. Did the doctor say anything else apart from changing your diet and more exercise?'

Frank scratches his chin and decides to give it a whirl. 'Actually, yes he did.'

'What?'

'He recommended we have more sex. Apparently, it lowers blood pressure.'

The kitchen door has already closed behind Meera. 'I hope you and the doctor enjoy it. But do wear a condom,' she calls back.

Frank gazes down at the dog. 'That didn't go as planned, did it, Foxtrot?'

# 11

# Wednesday 26th April

Prisha glances at the rectory opposite, before focusing on the huge pile of diaries stacked high on the desk, as Dinkel laboriously trawls through them.

'Have you gone through this year's diary?' she asks.

'Yes, ma'am. I'm working my way backwards.'

'Anything illuminating?'

'Mundane stuff, I'm afraid. The time he woke up, his daily meals, and the plants he cared for. Certainly nothing to indicate anything untoward was happening in his life.'

'And he made an entry every day?'

'Unfortunately, he did. I'm going bog eyed. It's sad really.'

'Sad?'

Dinkel leans back in the chair and reflects wistfully. 'Yes. The scribbling of a lonely old man who had few family or friends, wiling away his last remaining years absorbed with the monotonous minutia of mundanity.'

Prisha raises an eyebrow. 'The monotonous minutia of mundanity? That's quite poetic, Dinkel. You continue to surprise me,' she says, flicking through a large stack of photographs.

'Thank you, ma'am.'

'It appears there is no mask, then.' She mutters the thought.

'Sorry?'

'From what we've ascertained so far, Selwyn Morgan was a quiet, reserved man with absolutely no distinguishing traits or habits. No skeletons in the cupboard. His diaries only confirm that impression. This man should have passed away peacefully in his sleep, followed by a dignified funeral, then been quickly forgotten about, as if he'd never existed. And yet... he didn't. Do you see the anomaly between his life and death?'

'Yes, I do.'

'And what do you deduce from that?'

Dinkel winces and scratches his head. 'Erm... I'm not sure.'

'The manner of his death tells us more about the killer than it does Selwyn.'

'How?'

'To cut someone's testicles and penis off, shove a large candle up the backside, crucify him, then drive a tent peg through the head and leave a burn mark... that's a lot of anger. They wanted to defile the body. It's an act of vengeance. The question we must fathom is, was it an act of vengeance against the church as a whole, or definitively against Selwyn Morgan?'

'Or both,' Dinkel adds, as he wearily picks up another diary.

'Hmm... good point.'

Prisha continues flicking through the multitude of snapshots. Most of the photos are of church architecture, graveyards, a few of Whitby Harbour, some of the North Yorkshire Moors. There is nothing artistic or striking about any of them. The composition is as dull as the man's diaries. She stops and holds one aloft. It's of Selwyn when he was a young man, early twenties perhaps. It's outside a church and his arm is entwined through the arm of a woman who bears an uncanny resemblance to himself. She flicks the photo over and reads the words.

Selwyn and Myfanwy.

St Hilda's, Hinderwell 1959

Neither he nor his sister appear particularly happy. She studies a few more images, finding only one where Selwyn has a smile on his face. He's bare chested, with a hammer in one hand and a nail between his lips. It's a hot, sunny day. In the background is a rundown old barn with a Land Rover parked next to it. In a distant field, children chase after a football. She flicks the photo over and studies the writing.

Happy Camp - Easter 1985

Quickly tiring of the photographs, she wanders around the house, studying pictures hanging from walls, picking random books from a shelf, taking in the décor and furniture. Although the rooms are tidy and clean, they harbour an oppressive feel. The abode is a time capsule from a different era. The cottage's threadbare and sparse appearance reflects the life of a man who embraced cloistered solitude. She returns to the room where Dinkel is examining the diaries.

'Anything else?' she quizzes. 'No explosive letters revealing a darker side to his life? No scraps of paper with an elusive name or telephone number scribbled on it?'

'Not so far.'

She huffs. 'Okay. I'll leave you to it. Skim read all the diaries, then head back to the station.'

Dinkel gazes disdainfully at the mountainous pile. 'All of them?'

'Yes, all of them.'

'But there's over sixty!'

'I'm sorry; have you something better to do? This is your job, Dinkel. You're a detective and detectives investigate.'

'Ma'am,' he replies, dispirited.

'And go through all the photos and see if you can find any that show Selwyn with a woman who is *not* his sister.'

As she heads to the door, a paperweight on the desk catches her attention. She lifts the weighty glass orb from its pedestal and spins it around in her fingers. Encased inside the crystalline glass is an acorn. Inscribed on the wooden plinth are two Latin phrases, Glandis Societas, and underneath, Lumen Pastorum. Prisha is taken with the smooth, heavy feel of the object and its minimalist beauty. She places it back down on the desk and heads outside.

———◦———

If the cottage at the rectory was timeworn and jaded, then John Wilkes' home in Dalehouse is the opposite. The outside skin is the ubiquitous Yorkshire stone, common to, and in keeping with the area. But the interior is a modern, tastefully decorated bungalow, with long, high windows, and sliding glass doors that allow magnificent views of the undulating hills to encroach inside. Lush, chocolate brown carpets adorn the floors, and the furniture is stylish but not overstated.

John Wilkes enters from the kitchen carrying a tray and places it down on the coffee table in front of Prisha. He hands her the cup and saucer.

'One black tea with a drop of cold. And please help yourself to a slice of Battenberg cake.'

'The tea is fine, thank you.' As she sips from the bone china, she wonders why tea always tastes better when it's served in an elegant cup. She watches attentively as Wilkes pours a splash of milk from a tiny jug into his tea. He drops two teaspoonfuls of sugar into the liquid, stirs, then takes a seat opposite Prisha in a comfortable leather couch. He's measured, unhurried, a man who appears at ease in his own skin. Although in his early eighties, he has the countenance of a much younger man. With no obvious frailties he appears to be in rude health.

'It came as a bit of a shock,' he states. 'I've been away at a spiritual retreat and workshop in North Wales for a week. I received a call from Selwyn's sister, Myfanwy, late on Monday evening. When she said Selwyn had passed away, I initially thought it was from natural causes. But she then informed me the police were treating the death as suspicious. Although, I suppose most deaths are suspicious until proven otherwise, unless, of course, it's patently obvious.' He pauses, hoping for clarification from Prisha. None is forthcoming.

She places her cup and saucer back on the table and pulls out her notebook. 'This spiritual retreat in North Wales, where was it and when did you arrive and depart?'

A flicker of surprise crosses his face. 'It was held at Henllys Hall in Beaumaris, Anglesey. I arrived last Wednesday and returned home last night.'

'You were there for the full seven nights?'

'That's correct.'

'Could you give me a brief history of your relationship with Selwyn Morgan, Mr Wilkes?'

'Certainly, although my memory is a little hazy these days on specifics. I think I first met Selwyn around the mid-sixties a year or so after I'd graduated from university with my theology degree. After I was ordained as a priest, I became the vicar at St. Hilda's in Hinderwell. Selwyn had a dual role as sexton and verger. He performed all the odd jobs around the place and helped with the church services. I was there for five years before I moved to a larger parish in Giggleswick. We lost touch for a while, but when I became Bishop of Knaresborough in 1981...'

Prisha's eyebrows arch alarmingly. 'Sorry, did you say bishop?'

'Yes.'

'Oh, I didn't realise. How old were you when you became bishop?'

'Forty-one.'

'Isn't that young to be a bishop?'

Wilkes chortles in a self-deprecating manner, which irritates Prisha. 'There's no age stipulation, and I certainly was not the youngest bishop ever, but yes, in general terms, most people are ordained in their early to mid-fifties.'

'Apologies, I interrupted.'

'In 1981, our paths crossed again. Due to financial pressures the church was undergoing, Selwyn had become somewhat of a peripatetic. That means...'

'I know what peripatetic means, Mr Wilkes. He moved around tending to more than one church.'

His face hardens. 'I didn't mean to insult you, inspector.'

'You didn't. You were saying?'

With a mixture of embarrassment and displeasure at the chastisement, he continues.

'Ahem, yes, I was Bishop of Knaresborough until 1985, after which I was handed an overseas posting.' He stalls as he takes a sip of tea and bites into a Bourbon.

'Overseas?'

'Yes. Firstly, the Falkland Islands, then Gibraltar. I returned to the parish of Pickering in 2006 and remained there until my retirement in 2010.'

'And you were still a bishop?'

'An honorary bishop.'

'And you kept up your friendship with Selwyn after retirement?'

'Yes. We shared many interests apart from the obvious. We are, sorry, we were keen gardeners, and both had a love of British history. I felt Selwyn retreated from life somewhat after his retirement, which I thought was a bad move. Inevitably, we all age. But I believe that if you keep active - physically, mentally, and spiritually then it slows the ageing process. Energy out equals energy in.'

'It's a wise philosophy. Apart from Selwyn's sister, and you, did he have any other friendships or acquaintances?'

He shakes his head. 'Not to my knowledge. He'd visit Myfanwy for a fortnight each year, and he still attended Sunday service at Pickering each week, but apart from that he lived a rather reclusive life.'

'When was the last time you saw him?'

He takes a sharp intake of breath. 'Without consulting my diary...'

'Roughly.'

'I'd say last September or October. I made a point of visiting him a couple of times a year and would occasionally stay the night. And the last time I spoke to him by phone was on Christmas Day to offer him the season's greetings.'

Prisha reflects that the portrayal of Selwyn Morgan never wavers. 'I take it he wasn't married, but did he have a past marriage or a partner?'

'No. A confirmed bachelor rather like myself. Although, I was married once, a long time ago. My wife was killed in a car crash in 1983 and I vowed I'd remain faithful to her for the rest of my life.'

'I'm sorry to hear that.'

'Don't be. As I said, it was a very long time ago.' He glances at his watch, appearing impatient.

'I won't be much longer, Mr Wilkes. Did Selwyn ever mention anyone he'd fallen out with, or if he'd been threatened or blackmailed recently or in the past?'

A slow shake of the head. 'No. Never... oh, wait. Yes, I remember an incident some years ago when he was assaulted in Whitby. I cannot recall the exact details, but he'd been roughed up, and the matter was handled by the police.'

'Yes, we know of the incident. But apart from that?'

'Nothing I'm aware of.'

She offers him a warm smile, masking her qualms. The bishop exudes an elusive air of unease, something she can't quite put her finger on, yet it persistently troubles her. She stands and brushes her trousers down.

'Thanks for your time, Mr Wilkes. You've been very helpful.'

'Not at all,' he replies, escorting her to the front door. 'Always happy to help the police. You have a tough job. And please call on me at any time if you have any further questions.'

As Prisha hovers on the threshold, she does have one last question. 'I noticed a paperweight in Selwyn's study. It was a glass orb with an acorn inside. It had the words Glandis Societas and Lumen Pastorum inscribed on the plinth. Any idea what it represented?'

He pulls a blank expression. 'No. And without consulting a Latin dictionary, I've no idea what the words translate to.'

'Selwyn never mentioned it?'

'No. I cannot recall seeing the object myself, but then again, I am not the most observant of creatures. Probably a gift for services rendered from a local parish. They're fond of handing out trinkets.'

'Yes. That's probably it. Goodbye, Mr Wilkes, and thanks for the tea.'

Prisha steps into the car and fastens her seatbelt, staring back at the bungalow.

'With a degree in theology, and a bishop for over forty years, I'd have thought he'd have had a rudimentary knowledge of Latin. But... apparently not.'

As she drives back to her flat in Whitby to grab a spot of lunch, she reflects on the morning. It's ultimately been frustrating and fruitless. She's no nearer a breakthrough now than when she was first alerted to the murder of Selwyn Morgan. All she has is a curiosity about a keepsake paperweight and something not quite right about Bishop Wilkes.

# 12

Dora enters the office and holds her right hand in the air and mouths the words, 'Five minutes.'

Sebastian Thorne places his hand over the receiver and nods his acknowledgement before continuing his telephone conversation.

'I fully understand the implications, Evan, but opinion polls wax and wane like the moon. You mustn't become fixated. It won't be long before the government is accused of another enormous blunder, then your ratings as preferred prime minister will undoubtedly rise again. It's a mere blip. One must look at the overall trajectory over the last eighteen months. Yes, yes, I get it. I'm sorry, but I really must go. I have a media event to attend. What? The construction team has arrived at the demolition site for our new build and it's too good a photo-opportunity to miss. Yes, speak soon. Bye.'

He hangs up the phone, rolls down the sleeves on his Turnbull and Asser sky blue pinstripe shirt, then fastens the cuffs with antique platinum cufflinks depicting a compass and set square.

'Apologies, sir, but we must leave immediately,' Dora implores. 'James is waiting in the Range Rover.'

'Yes, of course.' He frowns. 'I'm beginning to have reservations about Evan Tudor, Dora. I'm not sure he has the ticker to be PM.' He stands and pulls his Tom Ford blazer from the back of the chair and slips into it. 'He can be such an old crone at times. The slightest setback, and he's running around like a headless chicken. Right, how do I look?'

'Impeccable, sir.'

He winces. 'Not too flashy for a demolition site, I hope?'

'No. Anyway, I have hard hats, Wellington boots, and hi-viz vests in the boot of the car. You'll look the part.'

'Excellent. As usual, you're one step ahead of me.'

<hr />

The car twists its way through the back streets of Whitby on the short drive to North Promenade.

Dora hands Sebastian a sheet of paper. 'Some ideas for your speech, sir. I've bullet-pointed them and, of course, you're adept at paraphrasing.'

'Thank you, Dora.' He studies them for a moment before a sly smile eventuates. 'I like the second one, about transformation, and not just constructing buildings but rebuilding lives. Yes, that hits the right tone. But I need a witty or pithy closing statement. It's become something of a trademark of mine. Any ideas?'

Dora taps a pen on her lips. 'Whitby is well known for its spectres and ghostly atmosphere. What about something like this: the town is famed for its historical spectres. Today we lay the ghosts of the past to rest, paving the way for new spirits to rise.'

'Genius. Spirits of hope, progress, and community.'

'Perfect.'

As the vehicle turns onto North Promenade, it pulls to the side as two police cars with flashing blue lights, but no sirens, speed past.

'I hope it's nothing serious.' Seb leans forward. 'James, park about fifty yards away from the site. I don't wish to be seen arriving in a Range Rover.'

'Sir.'

Dora collects the holdall from the boot of the car containing the safety-clothing as Seb exits the car and performs a last-minute check of his appearance in the wing mirror.

'James, we'll be at least forty minutes, so why don't you grab a coffee and a bite to eat?'

'Thank you, sir.'

Dora and Sebastian set off down the road at a brisk click, the cool sea air refreshingly invigorating. As they round the corner, they slow as they witness the flashing lights of the two police cars outside the construction site.

'Christ, what's happened?' Seb mutters. 'Get on the phone to the foreman and see what the issue is. Surely there can't have been an accident already. We haven't even begun the demolition. Pass me the hard hat and vest from the bag. I'll put them on. That way, I won't be initially recognised. Let's take a closer look at what's happening.'

As Dora juggles with her phone and the safety apparel, Seb stares down at her impatiently.

'Never mind, never mind!' He barks. 'I'll ring the foreman,' he declares, stabbing at his mobile. 'Hi Bob, Seb Thorne here. Why are the police outside the construction site? What? Damn and blast. No, I won't be making an appearance,' he yells, ending the call.

'What is it?' Dora asks.

'Some bloody idiots have chained themselves to the perimeter fencing. Come along, I want to see who it is, but I could hazard a guess.'

As they near the site, they hang back on the opposite side of the road and take in proceedings. Five protesters are chained to the fencing. The obvious leader, in the middle, holds a megaphone chanting slogans.

'The rich get rich, the poor get poorer! Sebastian Thorne's so-called Homeless Projects are nothing more than a Trojan Horse. They're not eco-friendly, they're not people-friendly, they are *profit* friendly.'

The media pack is already having a field day as a burly construction worker makes his way forward with a formidable pair of bolt cutters.

Seb Thorne shakes his head in dismay. 'That damned woman again—Amanda Chan,' he hisses, seething inside. 'We can't let her continue like this. We need to do something about her, and quickly, before she attracts even more crackpots to her delusional cause. We need to take her out, Dora.'

Shock ripples across her features. 'You mean kill her?'

He stares back at her for a good five seconds, impassive, poker faced, as if trying to read her mind. Eventually, his lips curl into a smile.

'Good lord, no. There are far more efficient ways of dealing with people than bumping them off. I'm not a Mafia overlord, Dora. No, we'll stick to tried and trusted methods. Everyone has their price. However, we need to tread stealthily with this one as she has a large following. I suggest you make the initial contact. I imagine she could be silenced for less than a hundred K. But we must make it explicit that by paying her off, in no way is that an admission of guilt. All my projects are completely legitimate and above board. Can I leave that with you, Dora?'

'Of course, sir.'

# 13

As Prisha enters the reception at the station, there is what can only be described as a kerfuffle ensuing. Several officers are corralling five handcuffed suspects in front of the desk sergeant who, for once, appears to be losing his patience. One short, slender woman is vociferously strident in her accusations of police brutality, and how Britain is a totalitarian state dressed up in a veneer of democracy.

The desk sergeant is apparently used to her antics. 'Amanda, pipe down. You're giving me a migraine. If you don't button it, this time I'll press charges instead of letting you off with a caution. Understood?'

The woman is obviously a serial nuisance offender and well versed in the protocols of the police station.

Prisha spots PC Kylie Pembroke and waves her over. 'What's going on?' she asks, mildly amused at the commotion.

'Protesters chained themselves to the fencing at a construction site up on North Promenade. The developer plans to knock down two old hotels and replace them with housing for the homeless.'

'Isn't that a good thing?'

'You'd think so. But the ringleader is the social activist, Amanda Chan. She has it in for the developer. She's waging this little vendetta against him. Well, actually it's not little. She has her own YouTube channel with over two hundred thousand followers. Posts videos a couple of times a week about scandals, rip-offs, and corruption in private industry and government.'

'She has a posh accent for a social warrior.'

'Yeah. Spoilt little rich girl. When you don't have to worry about earning a living to pay the bills, you can play at saving the planet.'

'Who's the developer she's raging against?'

'Local hero, Sebastian Thorne.'

Prisha raises her eyebrows. 'Up until a few days ago, I'd never heard of him. Now his name has cropped up twice.'

Kylie grins. 'He's quite handsome for an older man, if you're into that sort of thing. Very suave. Gift of the gab, but also comes across as a decent bloke. Wasn't born with a silver spoon in his mouth, unlike Amanda Chan. Pulled himself up by his own bootstraps. He's the one who's always appearing on BBC's Question Time and is chummy with the Labour Party. He donates a lot of money to various charities... or so he claims. Anyway, how's the murder investigation at Pickering progressing?'

Prisha rolls her eyes. 'Slow, very slow.'

'It's a weird one, from what I've heard.'

'As bizarre as they come.'

Kylie nudges Prisha in the ribs with her elbow, and winks. 'How's your love life? Still going strong with Adam?'

'Yes, thanks for asking.'

'How many months is it now?'

'Not sure. I don't keep track.'

'You must be doing something right to hold on to a catch like Adam.'

'I think I've found the secret to a successful relationship.'

'Really? Go on then, I could do with a few tips myself.'

'Don't see too much of each other. With his work on the farm and my shift patterns, our time together is limited. That's the key. Keeps it fresh.'

'So, it's not really a relationship. He's more of a friend with benefits. Care to elaborate on the benefits?'

Prisha chuckles. 'He's good in the kitchen.'

'Kinky. On the kitchen table or over the sink?'

'I meant he's a good cook. Hey, we must catch up for a drink after work this week.'

Kylie doesn't get a chance to answer as all the protesters sit down en masse and start to sing We Shall Not Be Moved.

Prisha spots Frank weaving his way through the chaos, appearing decidedly grumpy. She scurries to the entrance and grabs him by the arm.

'Heading out?' she quizzes.

'Aye. I've spent the morning trying to catch up on paperwork. It's like the Sorcerer's Apprentice scene from the Disney film, Fantasia, where the broom can't be stopped from fetching more and more water. The paperwork is the same. Get through one batch and another pile materialises.'

Prisha hasn't a clue what he's talking about. 'Ah, I see. I've just finished questioning John Wilkes from Dalehouse.'

His face brightens as he pushes open the door and steps outside. 'Good. Let's walk and talk. Fancy some fresh seafood? Cockles, oysters, mussels?'

Prisha licks her lips. 'I could go a tub of cockles.'

'I'm in the mood for half-a-dozen oysters. Come on, look lively.'

The seaside town is alive with the chatter and bustle of tourists and the constant cries of seagulls creating a vibrant, living soundscape. Walking in unison, their footsteps create a rhythmic pattern against the pavement. The melodic cadence blends seamlessly with the tranquil flow of the nearby river.

'What did Wilkes have to say for himself?'

'At face value, nothing of consequence.'

'But?'

'Not sure, except there's something off about him.'

'I like that. Instinct. Let's hear it, then.'

'John Wilkes first met Selwyn Morgan in the mid-sixties when Wilkes was the vicar at St Hilda's in Hinderwell. He moved around a bit before being ordained as Bishop of Knaresborough in 1981.'

'That's why his name rang a bell. Wasn't there some brouhaha Wilkes was involved in?'

Prisha's lips arch downwards. 'If there was, he didn't mention it. But then again, why would he?'

Frank rubs the back of his neck. 'I'd have been on the beat only a few months at the time he was ordained, but I seem to recall something dodgy. I'll have a word with Meera. She has a memory like a supercomputer.'

The scent of the sea strengthens as they approach the promenade.

'Anyway, Wilkes got an overseas posting in 1985 to the Falkland Islands, then later to Gibraltar.'

Frank halts and touches Prisha on the arm, as the sun casts soft shadows on the ground.

'Do you understand what that means?'

'No.'

'He must have committed, or at least been accused of, a wrongdoing. If he was shipped out to the Falklands, that's the church's way of giving him an almighty rap over the knuckles. Moving to Gibraltar is a signal the ice is thawing, and he'll be let back into the fold at some point. How long before he was back in the UK?' he says as they continue walking.

She checks her notes, the paper rustling in the breeze. 'He returned to Pickering in 2006 and retired in 2010.'

'Was he still a bishop?'

'Yes. Well, an honorary bishop. I'm not sure what the difference is.'

'It's bishop by title only. It means he still enjoys the trappings of the office but has no authority. Yep, whatever misdemeanour he committed he was punished for.'

'Interesting, but I'm not sure it has any relevance to the investigation. All that was nearly forty years ago.'

Reaching the seafood kiosk, they are engulfed in the tang of vinegar and briny shellfish.

'Don't be too dismissive, Prisha. Some wounds can fester a very long time.' He orders the seafood and slaps his money on the counter.

'Perhaps. Anyway, last week he was away on some spiritual retreat in Anglesey. I checked with the place he stayed at, and they confirmed he was there all week, so we can definitely rule him out as a suspect in Selwyn Morgan's death. He said Selwyn was a confirmed bachelor and in his later years barely mixed with anyone. Besides that, he didn't provide much new information about Selwyn beyond what we already know.'

Frank is handed his change, as they grab the oysters and cockles and tuck in.

'Not much progress, then.'

'No. When the victim appears to be a mild-mannered man, living a humble, some may say—monotonous, unvaried existence, it offers up very little in the way of clues. There appears to be nothing inflammatory, or even remarkable about Selwyn or his past.'

'Did Dinkel come up with anything of note?'

'Not so far. I left him with sixty years of diaries to trawl through, much to his disdain.'

Frank chuckles, his laughter melding with the distant sound of crashing waves. 'Poor bugger. You said there was something off about Wilkes.'

'Yes. Would a bishop be expected to have a rudimentary knowledge of Latin?'

'They certainly would. Latin plays a big part in Christian liturgy and theology, and they'd no doubt be trained up on biblical languages and church history before they were ordained. Why?'

'Wilkes played dumb when I mentioned something to him in Latin.'

'And?'

'Oh, nothing really. Just something I might chase up.'

The taste of the cockles lingers on Prisha's tongue, sea, and salt vividly present, as Frank savours his oysters.

'How are the cockles?' he asks.

'Delish. Your oysters?'

'Heavenly. Like swallowing the ocean. Right, come on, lass, we better head back to the station.'

As they make their return journey, Frank broaches a prickly subject.

'These potential health issues I have, has made me think about my future.'

Prisha's frown deepens. 'Please don't tell me you're going to retire.'

'Keep your wig on. No, well, not for another year or two. But I feel it's time for me to take my foot off the accelerator, melt into the background a little. I also intend to take more holidays, and make sure I have most weekends off. Which means you'll need to pick up the slack. I know you already put in way more hours than you're paid for, so you need to find ways to work smarter, not harder. You've a good ally in Zac, and Dinkel will improve. Trust me. I'll still be around to offer my advice and guidance, but the day-to-day ops and logistics I'm leaving to you. You run the team as you see fit. They're yours now. You give the orders. Of course, I still want to be in the loop and up to speed with developments. And one last thing; this is all unofficial, between me and thee. Can you handle it? Because I think you're more than ready.'

Prisha nods thoughtfully. 'Yes. I'm ready.'

There is no elation in her response.

# 14

# Thursday 27th April

Jeanie Beckinsale sings along to the Sound of Music emanating from the car speakers at a suitably moderate volume. It's her favourite, Do-Re-Mi. She's not the greatest singer in the world, or even in Dalehouse, which is only a tiny village, but when alone in the car she occasionally gives it her all and sings like no one's listening, which is probably a good thing.

She reached pension age three years ago and tried retirement, but the truth was, she was bored. She informed a dozen or so of her favourite customers she was coming out of retirement, and they willingly employed her services again. After all, good cleaners are hard to come by. In truth, it's only part-time. Four mornings a week, eight till midday. Not only does it put a little extra cash in her pocket, but if the customer's at home, then it means a good old natter over a cup of tea and cake or biscuits. Being a widow can be a lonely affair and you take your company where you can.

The return to part-time work also means she appreciates her free time more. Now she savours the afternoons when she can do as she pleases. When you have all day, all week, all month to do whatever you want, it can become exhausting filling the hours. Her new routine has provided her with a sense of purpose and put a bounce in her step.

Parking outside the bungalow, she exits the car and retrieves the small basket of cleaning materials from the back seat. Today is one of her favourite customers. A lovely old man, well-travelled, educated, refined, kindly.

She smiles as she walks past his car parked in the driveway. That usually means he's home, unless he's gone for a walk, and he always has a slab of Battenberg cake on the go. She knocks on the door and tries the handle, but it's locked. Pulling the set of customer keys from her pocket, she finds the right one, coloured purple, and slides it into the lock.

'Yoo hoo! Mr Wilkes, it's only me, Jeanie!' Bustling into the front room, she glances around the tidy living area, but there's no sign of him, or any sign of recent activity. Placing her basket on the table, she follows a corridor that leads to the guest, and master bedroom, and bathroom.

She tries again. 'Yoo hoo! Anyone home? It's me, Mr Wilkes, Jeanie.' She pauses and reflects. Usually, if he goes for a walk, he leaves a note for her on the dining room table along with her cash payment, always a little more than she charges.

'Maybe he's forgotten,' she murmurs to herself. She notices his bedroom door is ajar and for reasons she cannot explain, experiences a rush of panic. 'My God, what if he's had a heart attack or stroke during the night? He's no spring chicken.' She tiptoes closer and gently pushes at the bedroom door. 'Mr Wilkes, it's me, Jeanie. Are you decent?'

The door creaks open and she pops her head inside.

Bedsheets are slightly rumpled, but there's no sign of Mr Wilkes.

Bemused but not overly concerned, she sets about her chores; vacuuming, dusting, emptying the bins and dishwasher, wiping down surfaces.

After an hour's easy toil, she decides it's time for a cuppa and a slice of cake. All her customers tell her to help herself if they're not around and she feels no sense of imposition in doing so.

Entering the kitchen, she refills the kettle and flicks the switch. She pulls out the bread board and places the Battenberg cake onto it, then cuts herself a generous slice as she hums the tune to Edelweiss. With a teabag at the ready in a mug, she pours the steaming water into it and repeatedly dunks the bag up and down. As she does so, her eyes wander to the kitchen window and the beautifully manicured lawns and flowerbeds in the back garden.

She blinks, pauses, then blinks again.

In the centre of the lush grass is an anomaly, something white, uneven, with a jarring splash of red.

She hasn't noticed it before.

*Maybe the gardener has planted a new flowerbed? But it's an odd place to put it, right in the centre of the lawn.*

Fumbling for her spectacles that hang on a chain around her neck, she places them on the bridge of her nose.

The world sharpens into focus.

She blinks once more, fearing her eyesight is playing tricks. Disbelief makes way for terror.

The scream lodges in her throat, but when it does belatedly escape, it's so loud it could curdle blood.

There will be no Battenberg cake today.

## 15

Zac parks up behind Doctor Whipple's E-Type Jag in Dalehouse just as the good doctor attempts to navigate his hulking frame into his car.

He turns to Prisha and grins. 'This should be fun.'

'You're cruel. But I agree. It is amusing.'

'It's like watching a giant, arthritic grizzly bear attempting to climb into the cockpit of a Spitfire.'

'Come on, let's quiz him before he buggers off.'

They exit the car together. 'I don't see the rush. There'll be another ten minutes of labour-intensive effort before he drives away.'

They sidle up to the car. 'Good morning, Doctor Whipple,' Prisha declares.

Whipple, who is struggling to manoeuvre his ginormous foot past the threshold of the door, is taken by surprise and bangs his head on the roof. He glares malevolently at Prisha.

'Considering you have yet another gruesome and macabre killing on your hands, I see nothing good about the morning, inspector.'

Prisha suppresses a smile. 'It was merely...'

He cuts her off. 'Yes, yes,' he grumbles impatiently. 'It was merely a superfluous platitude without meaning and lacking in verisimilitude. A trait which the British have in abundance. Words are precious, inspector. They should be employed in a discretionary and judicious manner. Say what you mean and mean what you say. Everything else is bunkum.'

'Fine. I'll get to the point.'

'No need,' he huffs, still tugging at his trouser leg, attempting to lift the errant foot into the car. 'You want to know the deceased's name; the nature of his untimely demise, and dare I say, estimated time of death.'

'I think I know his name already.'

Whipple ceases his exertions and eyeballs her with incredulity. 'How could you possibly know that?'

'Mr John Wilkes.'

His eyes narrow to slits for a moment before he resumes pulling at his leg. 'The manner of this unfortunate soul's demise is a veritable facsimile of the previous decedent we meticulously examined, but days past. Pertaining to the chronology of this lamentable event's occurrence, one might postulate a parallel timeframe; that is to say, betwixt the hours of ten post-meridiem on the yesternight and the fourth hour ante-meridiem on this day. It is my considered opinion, inspector, that you are contending with an individual of a serially lethal disposition. '

'You mean between ten last night and four this morning?' Zac queries, wishing to clarify the time of death in his own mind.

'That is what I said, sergeant!' he bellows as a bead of sweat sprouts on his forehead despite the cool morning.

'Okay. No need to shout. Here, let me help you get your leg inside,' he offers helpfully as he places his hand under the doctor's calf.

Whipple knocks the hand away with contempt. 'Rest assured, sergeant, my need for external assistance is non-existent. I possess a degree of agility and suppleness that would be the envy of a gymnast gracing the Olympic pantheon.'

'Suit yourself.'

With one last gargantuan effort, the miscreant appendage squeezes into the footwell as Whipple huffs and puffs, the bead of sweat breaking free and rolling down his nose.

'Now, where are my keys?' he mutters as he contorts to the left, attempting to generate enough room to search his coat pocket with his giant hand.

'You ever thought about cutting a hatch in the roof, doctor? That way, you could climb in and out with ease. Maybe install a slide.'

Whipple returns a withering glare whilst laboriously extricating his keys from the confines of his jacket. 'I am inclined to surmise your remark is an endeavour at jocularity, is it not? If otherwise, then permit me to elucidate that such a proposition is not merely ludicrous in its essence but would incontrovertibly wreak havoc upon the fiscal appraisal of a vehicular artefact of such classic provenance. Now, unless you have any further enquiries?'

Prisha nods her head in deference. 'If we have, we'll save them for the post-mortem. Thank you, doctor.'

They watch on in amusement as the great doctor drives off.

'Like I've said before, that guy has undergone a triple humour bypass.'

Prisha turns and stares at the SOCO vans and police barrier tape. 'If Whipple was the warm-up act, then it's now time for the main show. I'm not looking forward to this. Come on, Zac, let's get the protective gear on and see what Charlene has to say.'

The back garden is a vibrant tapestry of red and white roses, lavender, hydrangeas, climbing wisteria, and foxgloves. A grand holly tree stands proudly, its dark green, prickly leaves interspersed with bright red berries, while an ancient oak looms at the garden's edge, casting a protective shade. This botanical haven, with its lush, jade-green lawn, is a testament to nature's splendour and human toil. Birds chirp and sing, content with their lot, as bees zigzag from blossom to blossom like a drunken man searching for the next pub. A confusion of heavenly aromas glides in on eddies wafting from nearby fields.

Nestled within this quintessential English garden, which, in mid-Spring, teems with life, the crime scene presents a stark contrast to its bucolic setting. The tent and the figures bedecked in white overalls, painstakingly scouring the area, tell a different story. In this oasis of life, death is a gatecrasher. For inside the small marquee lies Honorary Bishop John Wilkes, naked and spreadeagled in a crucifix fashion. Through each upturned palm, a tent peg impales him to the earth. Another peg pierces the very centre of his forehead. His dismembered genitalia lie at the side of his head, and once again, the cryptic, indecipherable motif seared into his brow.

Prisha's mouth puckers in consternation as she turns to Charlene Marsden. 'Similar, but not exactly the same. His ankles haven't been broken and there's no candle up his rectum.'

'Correct,' she says, handing Zac a small torch. She drops to her haunches and beckons Prisha to do the same. 'However...' she trails off as she very gently uses two wooden paddles to prise open the jaws. 'Zac, shine the light into the mouth. See it?'

Prisha squints. 'I can see an obstruction, but what is it?'

'I can't be one hundred per cent certain yet, but I'd say it's a rather large bratwurst sausage. It's been forced down his throat. I've bagged a tiny sample for analysis.'

'Christ,' Prisha whispers, rising slowly as the implication becomes transparent. 'It's sexually motivated,' she says, thinking out aloud.

Zac winces. 'You think the perpetrator did this to two old men for sexual kicks?' he asks, clearly not convinced.

Prisha's mind is racing. 'What? No. Not the perpetrator. This is retribution. The candle and the sausage are symbols for the penis. The killer may have been sexually abused by Selwyn Morgan and John Wilkes. I'm sure I don't need to spell it out for you.'

'Oh,' he replies as the penny drops.

Prisha's eyes flick onto Charlene. 'Anything else of note?'

'Not yet. My team is scouring the house and the bins. Oh, there was one odd thing from the swabs we took from Selwyn Morgan's body. You remember his head and chest were wet, and we thought it may have been dew?'

'Yes?'

'Well, it wasn't. It was urine. We sent the swabs for analysis, and they arrived back early this morning.'

Zac shakes his head. 'We are dealing with one seriously fucked up fruit-loop here.'

'Could you tell whether the urine came from a male or female?' Prisha asks.

Charlene shakes her head. 'No. There's little to no cellular matter in urine unless someone has a urinary tract infection, then some cells may dislodge.'

'What about oestrogen or testosterone levels?'

'Urine is mostly made up of waste matter and water, and without getting too technical, it doesn't generally contain the hormones themselves but rather the metabolites—the metabolism of the hormones in the body. Hormone analysis is typically unreliable in determining gender with any conclusive reliability. If you and Zac were to each give me a fresh sample sealed in a bottle, then the results would be superior, but still not conclusive. However, the urine on Selwyn had been there for some hours at the mercy of the elements, therefore degrading the sample further.'

'Okay, thanks Charlene. Me and Zac will have a wander around. We'll try to keep out of your team's way.'

She pulls at the flap of the tent and breathes in the heady scent of gorse blossom, the sweet bouquet mingling with the crisp morning air.

Zac follows her as his eyes scan the back garden. 'You don't think a woman is capable of that, do you?'

'I don't rule out fifty per cent of the population based on some outdated stereotype of women as solely caring and nurturing mother-figures. The only thing I'm certain of now is the link between Selwyn Morgan and John Wilkes, and that they were killed by the same person. And we possibly have a motive—retribution. Right, you take the inside and I'll take the outside. Then we better question the cleaning lady, Mrs Beckinsale, if she's calmed down yet.'

They wander off in separate directions, deep in thought. Prisha stalks down the side of the house and spots a SOCO carefully rifling through a wheelie bin that has been laid on its side. The bin must have been emptied recently because there are only a few items bagged up to take back to the lab. One clear plastic evidence bag catches her attention.

'Excuse me, can you pass me that?' she says to the SOCO, pointing at the object.

'Sure,' he replies, handing her the sealed bag.

Prisha holds it aloft and gazes in amazement, then asks the SOCO to hold it as she takes a quick photo on her phone.

'A clue, ma'am?'

'Quite possibly. Can you analyse this for fingerprints and DNA as a priority?'

'Of course.'

'Thanks.'

She disrobes from her protective gear at the side of the car and places a call to Dinkel.

'Ma'am?'

'Dinkel, where are you?'

'I'm back at Selwyn's cottage.'

'Hell, you're still there. I hope you're not swinging the lead?'

Dinkel isn't even sure what the expression means, but he's quite certain he hasn't been swinging anything, lead or otherwise. 'Excuse me, ma'am, but there are sixty diaries to go through, times by three hundred and sixty-five days. You do the maths. That's a lot of reading,' he replies in a justifiably aggrieved manner.

'I hope that's not truculence I detect in your voice, Dinkel?'

'Sorry, ma'am, but it's these damned diaries. I've had more enjoyment reading my electricity bill. I'm sorry the poor man died, especially in the manner he did, but it's safe to say Selwyn Morgan was possibly the most boring man on the planet.'

Prisha can imagine what Zac's reply would be to that statement, but she refrains from articulating it. 'I take it you've not come across any possible leads, then?'

'No. But I'm now an expert in how to deadhead rose bushes, train wisteria, and graft cherry cultivar on a Gisela rootstock to promote rapid growth.'

Prisha smiles at Dinkel's pain. She regrets her inference he may have been tossing it off. The junior officer has many faults, but he's not scared of hard work and dogged diligence. Good traits for an officer.

'Okay, take a deep breath. How long before you're finished?'

'Another two to three hours on the diaries. Then there are the photos. I found another box. Hundreds of the buggers. What do you want me to do with them?'

'Finish reading the diaries, then bring the photos back to the station.'

'Very good.'

'Anyway, that's not the reason I'm ringing you. Where are you sitting?'

'At the desk.'

'The other day, as I was leaving, I noticed a glass paperweight on the desk. It had an acorn encased inside. Can you see it?'

'Yes. I'm staring at it now.'

'Good. When you're finished, bag it and bring it back as well. Make sure you're wearing gloves before touching it. Oh, and good work, Dinkel.'

She ends the call as Zac approaches. 'Nothing so far inside the house. And the cleaning lady has nothing illuminating to offer,' he states. 'How'd you go?'

'We have another common thread between John Wilkes and Selwyn Morgan—a glass paperweight containing an acorn. It was in his wheelie bin, but yesterday when I asked Wilkes about an identical one I'd seen at Selwyn's cottage, he denied all knowledge of it.'

'Do you think the killer put it in the bin?'

'No, I don't. I think Wilkes did.'

'Why?'

A tingle shoots up her spine. 'By getting rid of it, he was trying to distance himself from something. But what, and why?'

# 16

Prisha momentarily closes her eyes as the old professor enters the living room carrying a tray. She likes a good cup of tea and the occasional biscuit as much as anyone, but in Yorkshire, quite frankly, it borders on the ridiculous. Visitor—tea; tragedy—tea; gossip—tea; boredom—tea; joyous occasion—if not alcohol, then tea; It's tea, tea and more tea. Then they'll put the kettle on to make a fresh brew. Some clever clogs even capitalised on this addiction by creating Yorkshire Tea. As far as Prisha is aware, the rolling hills of North Yorkshire contain not a single tea plantation.

'Here's your tea, inspector. Black with a drop of cold. And please, help yourself to a Garibaldi biscuit if you so desire.'

She desires not, but humours the old man, anyway.

Taking the wafer-thin biscuit, studded with squashed raisins, also known as squashed fly biscuits, she replies, 'Yummy. My favourite.'

'I take it you occasionally work with my old friend Charlene Marsden?' he says, taking a seat at a desk opposite Prisha in his old-fashioned study.

'Yes, quite often.'

He reflects fondly. 'She's a wonderful woman. We've been chums for... well, as long as I can remember. She's a veritable minefield of interesting facts and funny anecdotes.'

'Yes, she is a lovely lady. Someone who I could happily spend more time with.'

He becomes serious as he sips from the cup. 'Now, what's all this about? Charlene's text message was engagingly cryptic.'

'I believe you were a professor of semiotics—the study of symbols?'

'That's correct. It's still my passion, despite my retirement some years ago.'

'And semiotics is to do with symbols from the ancient world and different religions?'

He chuckles, but not in a condescending manner. 'Semiotics deals with symbols stretching from time immemorial to the present day. We are surrounded by symbols all our waking lives. Consider it a subliminal language.' He picks up a pen and hands it to her.

'For example, consider this everyday object. The humble ballpoint pen. Tell me what you see?'

She studies the pen. 'It has BIC printed on it with a cartoon picture of a person with a large round head, presumably referring to the ballpoint, and they're holding a pen behind their back.'

'Exactly. Now look out of the window at your car, the Skoda Octavia. The badge at the front. Have you ever considered it in any detail?'

*Of course I bloody haven't.* 'No.'

'It's a winged arrow enclosed in a circle. The sleek, and rightward pointing arrow, adorned with streamlined wings, conveys a sense of swift movement and progress. The design encapsulates a feeling of liberation and forward momentum, aptly symbolising the ethos of a car manufacturer. Traffic lights are similar the world over, another symbol. Every sporting team, club, association, political and religious organisation in the world has an emblem or logo. All symbols.'

Prisha puts her tea down on the desk and pulls a photo from an envelope. 'Well, I hope you'll be able to help me with this, then. But before I show it to you, I must warn you it's in relation to two recent murders we are investigating, and it must be viewed in absolute confidentiality.'

The professor jiggles his spectacles on. 'You have my word, inspector.'

She has no reason to doubt him. 'A burn mark, or branding, was left on the forehead of both victims by the killer.' She hands him the enlarged photo.

He picks up a magnifying glass and studies the image intently, his brow creased in bewilderment. A good thirty seconds elapse before he pulls a sheet of paper from his drawer and picks up a pencil. Painstakingly, he recreates the rather indistinct markings onto the paper, but makes the sketch fill the whole page.

'And what are your thoughts on it, inspector?'

Prisha tilts her head to the side. 'I think it's the oval shape of a head with an eye in the middle. It either has a short crop of fuzzy hair high on the brow or it could be a hat. As for the arched line pointing out from above that, I'm not sure.'

'Hmm... that's not an eye. It's an Ichthus or Ichthys.' He strokes his chin. 'Then again, maybe it is an eye as well, serving a dual purpose in the symbolism.'

'Ichthus?'

'Ichthus is one of the many symbols of Christianity. The word is Greek, meaning fish. You may have seen the stickers on the rear windscreens of believers. I'm no theologian, but I believe Jesus urged his disciples to become fishers of men and bring them into the folds of the faith. It was also used as a secret sign in times of persecution.'

'Ah, that makes sense,' Prisha notes, her mind quickly scrambling over random thoughts. 'And what about the head?'

The professor takes his glasses off and stares at her. 'I've not come across such a symbol before, but bear with me while I check my reference books.' He stands and turns towards the colossal bookshelf on the back wall, then halts, his hand gripping the upright of his chair. He cackles like a madman and spins around. 'Eureka!' he shouts, making Prisha jump.

'What? What is it?'

'The symbol represents growth and maturity under the watchful eye of a religious mentor.'

'I don't understand?'

Picking up his sketch, he turns it one-hundred-and-eighty degrees. 'We've been looking at it from the wrong angle. That's not hair, nor a cap. It's a cup. The strand at the bottom is a peduncle, or a stem. And the oval face or head is a blasted acorn!'

# 17

Prisha is busily populating the whiteboard with the latest updates for Operation Gorse Bush.

'Zac, I'm just about ready. Can you tell Frank?'

His eyes trail along the carpet to Frank's office door, then return to Prisha.

'Why don't you tell him? Have you lost the use of your legs?'

'Because I outrank you, sergeant,' she replies with a cheeky grin.

He puts his coffee cup down. 'Okay. Where's Dinkel when you need him?' The sound of breaking glass resonates from the tiny kitchenette at the end of the office. 'Silly question. That's the third breakage he's had this week.'

'Fiddlesticks!' Dinkel's anguished cry carries through into the incident room.

Zac scrunches up his face in disdain. 'Was Dinkel recruited from the set of Downton Abbey? The man's a throwback to the 1920s.' He marches over to Frank's office and taps on the window and gives the thumbs up signal.

Prisha continues aligning her findings on the board as the sound of tinkling glass is dropped into a bin.

'I can tell by the look on your face that you're onto something,' Frank's voice booms out. 'Like a rat up a drainpipe,' he adds as Dinkel makes an appearance, red in the face.

Prisha claps her hands together. 'Okay, gather round everyone. A quick debrief on the two murders.'

Frank takes a seat whilst Zac and Dinkel lean back on nearby tables, arms folded. There's the merest hint of anticipation in the air.

She points at two grainy black and white photos of the victims.

'Selwyn Morgan murdered sometime between 10 pm Sunday evening, and 4 am Monday morning. Likewise, John Wilkes, killed between 10 pm last night and 4 am this morning. Nearly identical crime scenes. Pinned out, crucifix fashion with tent pegs through their upturned palms, and a tent peg driven through the forehead. Both with a burn mark to the brow, both with their genitalia removed and placed at the side of the head. Differences: Selwyn had a candle inserted inside him, and Wilkes had an obstruction stuffed down his throat. Zac, did you catch up with forensics regarding the analysis of the fragment they took from the crime scene?'

'Yes. It's definitely pork meat. Until the post-mortem is carried out and the object is removed completely, we won't know for sure, but at this stage it appears to be a bratwurst sausage that was inserted into the throat.'

Frank rubs the back of his neck. 'I think it's safe to assume it's the same perpetrator. None of the details of Morgan's death have been released to the media, so we can rule out a copycat killer. What about forensics?'

Prisha shakes her head. 'Little to nothing. Which means the killer is forensically aware, making sure they don't leave DNA, fingerprints, or fibres behind.'

Zac nods in agreement and says, 'Indicating the murders are pre-planned and carefully coordinated. We're not dealing with a random nutjob, but a clever, calculating nutjob.'

'I agree,' Prisha concurs. 'There is one footprint from the Pickering murder. A size eleven. It may be a red herring, but let's keep it in mind.'

Frank cracks his knuckles. 'If it is connected, then it suggests a male. Not many women wear size eleven. I know both victims were in their early eighties, but what was their constitution like? Were they still fit enough to defend themselves?'

Prisha considers the question and says, 'Both men were still active and didn't have any noticeable ailments. But I'd say Morgan was frailer than Wilkes, who made a point of keeping himself fit. Morgan may not have been capable of offering much resistance, but Wilkes was, if only minor.'

'And nothing under Morgan's fingernails? Skin? Blood? Hair?'

'No. Maybe we'll be luckier with Wilkes.'

Zac crosses his legs. 'If it comes back blank, then it would indicate they were either taken by surprise or knew their attacker.'

Prisha nods in agreement. 'Exactly. Turning to the branding on the forehead; Charlene Marsden believes this could have been made by a signet ring or medallion with a raised embossed image on the object. It would have been heated to quite a high degree to create the burn mark. This could have been achieved by a small handheld blowtorch with the object held by a pair of pliers or suchlike.' Prisha takes a sip of water, taps at the whiteboard, and continues. 'We know how they were killed, but *why* were they killed? Connections: Wilkes and Morgan were old friends going way back and had kept in touch, with Wilkes visiting Morgan a couple of times a year. Both were servants of the church. Morgan a verger and sexton all his working life. But here's the interesting thing: John Wilkes was ordained

Bishop of Knaresborough in the early eighties, a quite lofty standing in the C of E hierarchy. He remained in the position up until 1985. For reasons yet unknown, in 1985, he was relocated to the Falkland Islands. Ten years later, he moved to Gibraltar. As you know, these British territories have significant military presences. Although Wilkes still held the title of Honorary Bishop, he primarily served as a chaplain to the troops stationed there. Frank, can you explain the significance of this?'

'Certainly. Dispatching a bishop of such esteem to a remote outpost like the Falklands is, in itself, a profound reprimand. Particularly for a role as humble as a chaplain. Not that I'm disparaging chaplains. Nevertheless, from bishop to chaplain is a significant step down in ecclesiastical authority and responsibility. This suggests he was either involved in a serious misdemeanour, or closely linked to one. However, revoking his bishopric would have certainly attracted intense media scrutiny, something hallowed institutions are loath to do. Conversely, discreetly relocating him for two decades could serve to deflect unwanted attention. It's important to note, these are my speculations rather than confirmed facts. I'll offer further insights after Prisha's briefing.'

'Thanks, Frank. I questioned John Wilkes yesterday afternoon at his home in Dalehouse, the site of his murder. It was merely to ascertain his relationship with Selwyn Morgan, and if he had any insights into who would want to harm him. I drew a blank. Now, here's another interesting point. In Morgan's cottage, I noticed a glass paperweight containing an acorn. On a plinth, beneath, two Latin phrases.' She points at the photo taken of the paperweight. 'Yesterday, as I was leaving, I mentioned the paperweight to John Wilkes. He said he'd never noticed it at Selwyn's cottage, adding that he was not particularly attentive. I also asked him if he knew what the Latin phrases translated to. Again, he said he didn't know. I'd already looked up the phrases, thanks to Google translate,' she says tapping her fingernail on the board beneath the words. 'Glandis Societas translates as Acorn Society or Acorn Fellowship, and Lumen Pastorum as Light of the Shepherds. Frank, would you care to elaborate?'

'Sure. Alright, let's take a step back in time for a brief history lesson. For centuries, Latin was the cornerstone of the church, particularly in Western Christianity. It wasn't just the language of choice for theological discussions and church governance; it was woven into the very fabric of their services and rituals. When the Church of England emerged during the Reformation, it embraced this legacy, infusing its liturgies and ceremonies with a rich tapestry of Latin. Fast forward to the 1980s – being a clergy member in the Church of England wasn't just about wearing the collar. It meant you'd likely spent years at university, immersing yourself in theology or related disciplines. And it wasn't all Greek and Hebrew for biblical studies. Latin played a crucial role too, offering a gateway to understanding the deep-rooted doctrines and historical nuances of the church.' His voice rises in cadence. 'A bishop ordained in the eighties would undoubtedly have a fair grasp of Latin. It was part of their intellectual toolkit back then.'

Zac rubs his face. 'John Wilkes lied?'

Prisha holds one palm out. 'I believe so. An identical glass paperweight was found in the wheelie bin at Wilkes' address. Zac, did forensics lift fingerprints from the paperweight?'

'Yes. The results came in thirty minutes ago. They contain prints of Wilkes and Jeannie Beckinsale. I contacted Jeannie, and she denied putting the paperweight in the bin.'

'The only people who knew the significance of the object would be Wilkes, and possibly the killer.'

Dinkel appears confused. 'You think Wilkes put it in the bin?'

'Yes.'

'Why?'

'If I came back to question him and noticed it, or returned with a search warrant, I'd have known he'd lied. By getting rid of it, he was distancing himself from Selwyn Morgan, or his past.'

Dinkel is not entirely convinced. 'You said the paperweight is significant, but as yet, I don't see how, apart from the fact that Wilkes lied about it.'

Prisha grins. 'Patience, Dinkel, patience. All will be explained.' She taps at the image on the board of the burn mark imprinted onto the foreheads of both victims. 'This afternoon I visited an old friend of Charlene Marsden, professor of semiotics, Marcus Eldridge. It didn't take him long to figure out what this little motif represents.'

Eyes widen as she fumbles in her jacket pocket and extracts a folded sheet of paper.

'Come on then,' Frank says. 'Don't keep us in suspenders.'

Prisha tacks the professor's pencil sketch to the board.

Frank rises and takes a step closer. 'Well, I'll go to the foot of our stairs!'

Dinkel shoots Zac, the self-appointed Yorkshire dialect interpreter, a quick glance. 'Your DCI is suitably surprised.'

'Ah,' Dinkel replies.

'In fact, one could say he was flabbergasted.'

'What?'

'Never mind.'

'It's a bloody acorn with the Christian fish symbol, the Ichthus,' Frank states. 'This is getting interesting.'

Prisha nods thoughtfully. 'The professor said it may symbolise a watchful, religious eye with the acorn representing growth, maturity, wisdom.'

'From little acorns, mighty oaks grow,' Frank murmurs. 'Over breakfast this morning, I had a chat with Meera. I asked her about John Wilkes. She has a razor-sharp memory. My wife can remember perceived slights I made from fifteen years ago and still manage to dredge them up to clobber me over the head with. Anyway, she does recall an event from the eighties which took place up on the moors where a young lad died, drowning or something, and Wilkes was part of an organisation that ran a camp for underprivileged kids. If the lad's death took place in 1985, then it may explain Bishop Wilkes' sudden fall from grace. I meant to chase it up today, but I've been waylaid with bloody medical consultations.'

Dinkel nearly explodes with excitement. 'Ma'am,' he says, raising his hand in the air like a schoolboy desperate for the toilet.

'Yes, Dinkel?'

'The diaries.'

'What about them?'

'1985!' he declares, clearly agitated.

'Get on with it, man,' Zac grumbles.

'There were pages missing from Selwyn's diaries from 1985. April and August, if I remember rightly. They'd been ripped out. And another thing,' Dinkel states as he rushes to his desk, and excitedly flicks through the box of old photographs. The others follow him, intrigued, and watch on in silence at his frenetic searching. 'Where is it?' he mutters to himself. 'It's here somewhere. I know I saw it. Aha! Here we go,' he says as he lays the photo out for all to see.

Mouths fall open as all eyes gaze upon the battered, fading, black and white photograph.

A dilapidated stone barn stands as a backdrop to a countryside scene. At its forefront, a row of eight boys, pre-teen. Behind them are three adults. The men exude a sense of pride and joy, their arms folded as they smile broadly. Kneeling in the foreground is a striking younger man, his handsome features accentuated by a pair of sunglasses. Two of the men are instantly recognisable; Selwyn Morgan and Bishop John Wilkes, albeit a lot younger. It appears there was an unveiling ceremony moments before the picture was taken as a white sheet lies on the ground below a sign mounted on wooden posts. It reads:

HAPPY CAMP

Discipline, Godliness, Fun.

1985

# 18

Outside, dusk embraces the sky, as a melancholic twilight descends upon the evening. The promenade, partner to the meandering river, comes alive under the soft glow of twinkling streetlights. Amidst this tranquil setting, a lone trawler embarks on its nocturnal voyage, chugging resolutely towards the harbour entrance, ready to brave the restless waters of the North Sea in search of the night's harvest.

Inside, the atmosphere in the incident room is oppressively stuffy, with the overhead ceiling fans doing little more than lazily re-circulating stagnant air. Despite this, there is a manifest tension shared between the officers. They are oblivious to the delights outside, unaware of the fusty ambience inside.

'Is everyone singing from the same hymn book?' Frank asks in his deep baritone as everyone clusters around Prisha, gazing intently at the photograph in her hand.

'I think so,' Prisha replies, studying the children. 'Is this camp a key to the murders?'

Zac sucks air in through his teeth, creating a soft whistling sound. 'You think someone is intent on settling old scores?'

'Possibly. At first sight, it seems innocuous enough. Wilkes and Morgan were part of the church and were involved in taking children on camp. That's no big deal. But the fact Wilkes lied about, and then disposed of the paperweight, puts a new slant on things. He had something to hide.'

With heart in mouth, she turns the photograph over, only to be disappointed. It merely reads: Happy Camp 1985. She was hoping for a list of names identifying everyone in the snapshot.

'You can't have it all on a plate, Prisha,' Frank says, sporting a knowing grin.

She places the photo back on the table as a welcome surge of adrenaline courses through her bloodstream.

Tapping at the photo, she whispers, 'One of these children could be our killer.'

'Or one of the adults,' Frank adds.

She notices Zac as he takes a sly shufti at his wristwatch, which involuntarily makes her do the same.

*Nearly six.*

Adam will already be at her flat preparing dinner. What she really wants to do is to spend another three hours working on the investigation, but she must rein in her enthusiasm. Zac has a young family waiting for him at home. Frank already looks washed out. And Dinkel... well, God only knows what Dinkel gets up to on a night.

'I think it's about time we all knocked off for the day,' she declares, hiding her disappointment. 'But before we do, a couple of minutes preparing for tomorrow. We know Morgan and Wilkes are on the photo. Let's see if we can identify the others. Dinkel, first thing in the morning, I want you to head over to Morgan's cottage and retrieve the 1985 diary. Bag it and take it to forensics. Point out where the pages were removed. Ask them to check for any pen or pencil indentations on the adjoining pages. It's crucial they use non-destructive techniques. We can't afford any damage to it. Those impressions, if any, could be key evidence in a future historical investigation. Tell them it's a top priority and to fast-track it if they can.'

'Ma'am.'

'Zac, I want you to chase up the facts about the boy who died on the moors. I want the how, whys, and wherefores and, most importantly, the date when he died. There must be a police record of the event archived away. Then dig out a copy of the coroner's report and the post-mortem findings on the dead boy. When you have the boy's name, track down his family and old friends and obtain their version of events. We'll need to scan this photo and reproduce good quality prints. Take a copy with you when questioning people.'

'Got it, Prisha.'

'Dinkel, after you've returned from forensics, I want you to trawl through the archives of the local newspapers from early April until the end of 1985. They're bound to have reported on the death, but let's see if any reporter was sniffing into something more sinister than an accident.' Pausing, she peers at Frank. 'Are we okay for overtime?'

'Yes. Already authorised. You can work late if you must, and on Saturdays, but don't work Sundays unless absolutely necessary.'

'The day of the Lord?' Zac quips.

'Daft bugger. It's the day for family and friends. A chance to unwind.'

Prisha nods her agreement. 'Right, let's call it a day. As Frank would say, rest, recuperate and reinvigorate. I'll see you all tomorrow.'

Prisha and Frank watch on as the other two briskly exit the room.

'Well done, Prisha. That was textbook.'

She winces apologetically as Frank loosens his tie. 'I felt a little awkward barking orders while you were standing there.'

'Nonsense. Remember our little chat from earlier?' He saunters casually towards the door. 'You have the respect of your team and in return, you show them respect. That's an important trait, Prisha. Look after them and they'll look after you. A refreshed officer can produce more work in an hour than an exhausted officer can do in a day.'

'Thanks, Frank. Night.'

He pulls at the door and turns to her. 'How much longer are you going to be here?'

'A few minutes. I just want to scan the professor's sketch and upload it into the system.'

He offers her a fatherly smile. 'Aye. I believe you. Night, love.'

As he disappears, she allows herself a moment to savour the pride of another minor breakthrough.

# 19

# Friday 28th April

For Zac, his morning has gone from bad to worse. In fact, if truth be told, he's what is colloquially known as pissed off. Not turning red with rage and imagining he has a backpack full of hand grenades to throw at fellow road users, but neither is he whistling Zip-A-Dee-Doo-Dah.

A wonderful day—it is not.

The harbinger of doom materialised innocuously enough. It began with a hastily bought bacon and egg butty to fill the yawning gap in his stomach as he made the journey from Whitby to the Police Archival Evidence Site. While navigating a badly signposted sharp bend, he momentarily lost full control of his bacon and egg roll, and vehicle. This resulted in the egg falling onto his lap, then the seat cover. The resulting calamity left a large suspicious stain on his trousers, somewhere between his inner thigh where his left testicle normally resides.

. Despite pulling over to clean up the mess, the egg disaster left a slightly dry, white, crusty mark that could not be removed.

To the casual, innocent observer, the stain may appear as nothing more than slovenly habits and poor personal housekeeping. To those with a suspicious disposition, the evidence is damning. Even Zac thinks it looks like a semen stain on his new black chinos.

But how did his day begin?

Despite triple checking the online archives of historical investigations at the station, he could not locate anything related to an accidental death of a young boy on the moors, in 1985. There were a handful of accidental deaths that year, and deaths by misadventure. These included two drownings at sea, and three deaths involving stolen cars. But the boys involved were in their mid-teens, not pre-teen.

He was left with no alternative than to take the one-hour drive to the archival storage facility in the hope the original documentation, if it existed, was still intact.

Without the name of the dead boy, or a specific location where the death occurred, he wasn't looking forward to the search. And now, to make matters worse, especially after the egg saga, standing in front of him is a jobsworth of the highest order wearing an official lanyard around his neck.

He's an older man with a bald head, beady eyes, and seemingly devoid of a personality. Completely humourless, of course, he guards his archives with a bulldog tenacity which borders on the fanatical and would have granted him a seat one row down from Hitler and Himmler at the Nuremberg Rallies, maybe sandwiched between Joseph Goebbels and Hermann Göring.

Zac finishes filling out the three-page form and pushes it back across the counter along with his warrant card, and driver's licence, his eyes falling onto the lanyard of the archival officer; Stephen Keepwell.

*Figures.*

The officer tut, tuts and shakes his head as he adjusts two pens, one black, one red, on the counter into a neat row.

'Is there a problem?' Zac asks.

'Yes, there is. Your rank is sergeant.'

'So?'

'Under the Police Act 1997, and the Freedom of Information Act 2000, it specifically states that access to the physical inventory of the archival management system is only permitted for officers with a rank of inspector or above. An officer below this rank can be granted access if form AARP-1057 is completed and signed by a superior, with rank of inspector or above.'

'The last time I came here I didn't have to go through this rigmarole, and I certainly didn't require authorisation from a superior.'

The officer's ears twitch in excitement. He detects a breach of protocol. 'Really, sir? I can assure you I was not on duty that day. Can you recall the officer who you interacted with?'

'Can I hell. It was years ago.'

He nods thoughtfully, disappointed. 'Hmm... probably before I transferred here. Things were lax, sloppy, before I arrived.'

Zac knows he's onto a loser. 'Fine. You have my email address on the paperwork. Can you send me a link to the form AP whatever...'

'AARP-1057 - Archival Authorisation Request Proforma-1057.'

'... yeah, yeah, and I'll forward it to my boss so he can download it, then sign and return.'

'I'm afraid that's not possible, sir.'

'You do surprise me. Why not?'

'Because AARP-1057 can only be accessed by archival officers, level 2 and above, who have been granted clearance.'

'What's the point of a form that grants access if nobody can bloody access it?'

'Access to confidential records must be managed with probity and due diligence. We can't have any old Tom, Dick or Harry walking in here to have a good rummage around.'

'I'm a police officer; CID, working on a serious murder investigation and the information I'm looking for is not on the digital archives.'

'Highly unlikely,' the archive officer sniffs, a hint of arrogance in his voice. 'Our transition to digital records, starting in 2000, adhered to the most rigorous standards of meticulousness. Every page, every report, every photograph was scanned with an exacting eye for detail. It's exceedingly rare for anything to have evaded our comprehensive digitisation process. Perhaps it doesn't exist online because it never did exist?'

'Give me strength. Are you and me on the same side or what?'

'What side may that be, sir?'

'The side of justice!'

'I'm merely following the well-established rules, protocols, and...'

'Yeah, yeah. Do I need to fill in a proforma to breathe the air in this glorified wastepaper basket?'

'Just doing my job, sergeant.'

Zac rubs at his face, trying to keep a lid on his rising anger. 'Look, please explain how I can receive permission to enter the archive facility.'

'Form AARP-10...'

Zac slams his hand on the counter as he finally loses it. 'If you quote that number one more time, I'm going to shove those two pens up your fucking nostrils until they pierce that pea-sized brain of yours. Now, tell me how I obtain access to the archives? Otherwise, I'll call my DCI, explain your intransigence, and ask him to come to the facility to sign the form. And trust me, my DCI has a short fuse and a long, fucking temper. If he has to come down here, I can guarantee you, your day will turn into a tsunami of liquid shit. You'll need a roadsweeper truck to come in here and suck up your entrails. Cleaners will spend days trying to retrieve you pulverised eyeballs from the fucking ceiling. Okay... so, what's it to be?'

The officer puckers his lips and looks down his nose at Zac as he weighs up the flouting of archival management system protocols against a verbal tongue lashing from a grouchy Yorkshire DCI, and the possible evisceration of his internal organs. He adjusts his pens slightly and clears his throat nervously.

'On this occasion... I'll see what I can do.'

Zac sighs with relief, having won his battle against the human filing cabinet.

'Thank you.'

The jobsworth's gaze falls onto the disconcerting stain on Zac's trousers. He twitches twice, then disappears out the back, clutching his pens.

# 20

Dinkel is a simple creature, unencumbered by artifice or the inclination to engage in mind games. He embodies the principle of WYSIWYG - what you see is what you get. His authenticity and honesty are refreshing traits which may be beneficial in some professions, although it's hard to think of one. Yet Dinkel isn't in any old profession; he's a police officer, where his straightforwardness might not always work in his favour. The criminal elements he encounters will perceive his transparency as a vulnerability to be exploited, rather than a merit. Even his own colleagues might exploit his naivety to advance their careers over his.

For now, though, he remains shielded within the safety of the incident room, embraced by those willing to protect and mentor him. Initially, he was merely endured, stepping into the shoes of a fallen comrade. But gradually, like clearing skies after a storm, tolerance gave way to acceptance. With each passing month and added experience, the perception of his peers has subtly changed. To claim he's revered would be an overstatement; even 'respect' might seem too generous. But 'regard'? Yes, his fellow officers now look upon him with a certain regard. Nevertheless, his lack of guile is a worry. One day, it may be his undoing.

'Ma'am, ma'am, ma'am!'

Prisha pulls her eyes away from the computer screen as Dinkel rushes across the office. In his exuberance he accidentally barges into a chair, sending it careering into a table, scattering a pile of papers onto the floor.

'Ma'am, ma'am, ma'am!' He brandishes a sheet of paper in his hand, performing a good impersonation of Neville Chamberlain—peace for our time?

'Calm down, Dinkel. You're in danger of popping a vein. What have you got?'

'It's from forensics. The electrostatic detection worked. They've managed to lift something from the blank pages of Selwyn Morgan's diary.' As he passes her the sheet, she studies the list of handwritten names between the faint ruled lines of the diary page.

Boys vetted and approved for Happy Camp

Mike Ross - Aged 12

Ted Fairchild - Aged 12

Tom Maplin - Aged 10

Brian Lovejoy - Aged 10

Paul Kirk - Aged 11

Derek Farrell - Aged 12

Ian Longhorn - Aged 10

Malcolm Pearce - Aged 11

'Excellent work, Dinkel.'

'Thanks, ma'am, but I didn't have much to do with it. Forensics should take the credit.'

She barely hears him as she focuses on the top line. 'Nevertheless...' Her eyebrows knot downwards. 'Vetted and approved,' she murmurs slowly. 'Odd choice of words for boys selected to go on an outdoor education camp.'

Dinkel peers over her shoulder. 'Maybe it means they received permission from their parents, or possibly they needed to make sure the boys were fit and healthy to participate.'

And therein lies the difference between innocence and experience, eagerness and scepticism. Where Dinkel sees a rudimentary ticking of the boxes, Prisha sees something deeper. To her, the word 'vetted' is wrapped in a shroud of foreboding. And 'approved' - approved by whom?

'There are eight names, altogether ma'am, which tallies with the number of boys on the Happy Camp photo.'

'Take a step back, Dinkel. We can't jump to conclusions. What we must do, and when I say we, I mean you, is identify the boys on the photograph and see if they align with this list.'

His face creases in confusion. 'And how should I do that?'

She does well to hide her consternation. 'Investigative research,' she replies coldly.

He offers her a nervous smile in return. 'Righto, I'll get onto it straight away,' he says, wondering how in hell's name he's going to tackle the task.

'Before you do, make copies of the diary entry, then scan it and load it onto the system.'

The door slams, making both officers spin around.

'What a bloody morning!' Zac yells as he strides to his desk. 'I've just had to deal with a jobsworth from hell. If you took every traffic warden that's ever existed and mixed them with every car park attendant and ticket inspector on the planet, then the accumulative effect would be my jobsworth, a sort of Frankenstein's Nitpicker. Anal-retentive, pedantic, little knob-jockey! You'd think he was guarding the codes to the nuclear button. And to make matters worse, he's a bloody civvy! He was obviously bullied at school and probably a bedwetter until his early teens.'

Prisha grins. 'But did you get what you went for?'

Zac throws a file onto the table. 'Aye. I've obtained a copy of the police report. Young lad called Tom Maplin. Died August 1985. Poor little bugger drowned.'

———◦———

There's something melancholy about historical documents. They are silken threads that weave and wind back through the years to a time that lives on in nostalgia. A fading photograph, a police report, a snapshot of an era that seemed simpler, better, not as fucked up as the present. But it's merely a mirage, a delicate trick the mind plays on itself. Nothing was simpler, or better. There were still murders, paedophiles, rapes, random and planned acts of extreme violence, and senseless cruelty. Technology marches forward, ever evolving, but the essence of humanity remains a constant, unchanging sculpture forged from our DNA. Our capacity for both great kindness and profound malevolence remains steadfast. The seeds of good and evil are planted into our beings before birth. Whether they flourish or remain dormant is down to nature and nurture... and our own free will.

The air is filled with the occasional soft clatter of a keyboard and the stale smell of coffee, the rocket fuel of the incident room. Like peas in a pod, the officers stare at the whiteboard and the police report from 1985, as Zac reads it out.

'Incident Report: Suspected Accidental DrowningDate/Time of Report: 12 August 1985, 09:30 amStation of Record: Fulford Road, YorkReporting Officer: DCI Jack HargreavesAssisting Officer: DI Dai DaviesIncident Location: Vicinity of Kettlewell Farm, adjacent to the River Rye, near Nunnington, Ryedale.

Summary of Incident:Received a call from Dr Blenheim regarding a suspected drowning incident involving a male juvenile on the moors. The call was made from Kettlewell Farm, Nunnington. Landowner - Mr Seth Baldwin. DI Davies and I proceeded to the location for scene assessment and preliminary inquiries.

Scene Assessment:Arrived on-site at approximately 10:05 am. Found ambulance services present; the victim had already been declared deceased by medical personnel. The victim, identified as Tom Maplin, aged ten, was observed on a stretcher, awaiting my arrival and inspection of the body.

Witness Accounts:Per Dr Blenheim and corroborations from adults present, the camping group retired around 9 pm the previous evening. By 8 am the next day, Tom Maplin was discovered missing. Following an extended search, his body was located in the River Rye by Dr

Blenheim and a minor, Mike Ross, approximately one mile from their accommodation.

Observations:The deceased exhibited a pronounced contusion on the upper right forehead, consistent with a fall. The nearby makeshift stepping stones across the river were examined and noted to be slippery underfoot. Rigor mortis suggests the victim may have fallen in the preceding night or early hours of the morning. Additionally, minor bruising observed on the arms and neck has been attributed to a rugby game played the day before the incident.

Next of Kin:The deceased's next of kin was notified by a uniformed police woman.

Preliminary Assessment:Initial findings lean towards an accidental death scenario. Awaiting comprehensive reports from pathology and coroner's inquest to conclude the investigation.

DCI Jack Hargreaves'

Silence ensues for a moment as the officers digest the information.

Zac sports a smirk. 'Frank, if I presented you with a report like that today, how would you react?'

'I'd kick your arse from this office to the end of the east pier, then throw you in the bloody sea.'

'Thought as much. The big question is, and as you were around in those days, would this be typical of reporting back in 1985?'

Frank sighs. 'Unfortunately, it probably was, although not by all. I vaguely remember DCI Jack Hargreaves, although I never worked with him. From memory he was very old school, heavy drinker. Passed away years ago.'

Zac taps at the report on the board. 'The odd thing is, Kettlewell Farm near Nunnington falls under Ryedale and Whitby police jurisdiction. Why were the York boys called in?'

'Could be any manner of reasons; short-staffed, lack of qualified officers on duty. And York is about twenty minutes nearer to Nunnington than coming from Whitby. What's more peculiar is that a DCI should initially attend what appears to be an accidental drowning.'

Prisha flits between astonishment and scepticism. 'The report is sloppy at best and downright suspicious at worst,' she says, moving nearer to the whiteboard. 'He hasn't even bothered to list the names of those who were in attendance at the camp, nor has he conducted interviews with the other adults or boys. There's no description of the weather conditions; no portrayal of the camp itself. And what about this Doctor Blenheim? Was he part of the camping group, or was he a local doctor called to the scene? The report doesn't make it clear.' Glancing at Zac, she asks, 'Is that all there was? No pathology report, no coroner's findings?'

'Nope. Just the solitary police report.'

'That's also suspicious.'

Frank takes a seat. 'Hang on, Prisha, before you get your Miss Marple knickers in a twist, you need to understand that it wouldn't be the first time case notes and evidence have gone missing. Things get filed away and put in boxes. Departments merge and move buildings. Boundaries change. And once everything was digitised back in the late nineties, all the old investigations, evidence, and paperwork were transported to the archival facility where they were unpacked and filed away. There's plenty of opportunity for things to go astray without it specifically having nefarious implications.'

'Yes, I suppose.' Studying the report again, she smiles and shakes her head. 'Unreal. I see the next of kin was informed of Tom's death by a police woman in uniform. It's good to see they had some use for women in those days apart from making the tea and being a piece of skirt to ogle.'

'Aye, we've come a long way,' Frank concurs, noting her hefty sarcasm.

'Not far enough,' she murmurs. 'Right, as sketchy as the report is, it at least gives us something to build on. Zac, find out who this Doctor Blenheim is and if he's still alive. Then liaise with the coroner's office to obtain a copy of the inquest findings into Tom Maplin's death. The coroner's report should also note the pathology findings and who performed the post-mortem. Tom Maplin was somebody's son, grandson, friend. Yet, that report diminishes him to a mere statistic documented with the same detachment as a minor traffic incident. Dinkel, find out all you can on Tom Maplin.' She grabs her phone and backpack from the desk. 'Frank, can you ring around your old boys' network and see if DI Davies is still alive?'

'He's not. I attended his funeral about five years ago. Where are you going, as if I need to ask?'

'Kettlewell Farm... to see if the Happy Camp barn still exists.'

———◦———

Frank removes his fingers from the Venetian blinds for the fourth time and huffs.

'That lad doesn't know whether he's Arthur or Martha.'

He sidles from his office and confronts Dinkel, who has been pacing back and forth, sitting then standing, fidgeting, wringing his hands, and occasionally rubbing at his face.

Frank presents himself in a friendly, old-uncle-style manner. 'Ah, Detective Constable Clementine Dinkel. How are you going, lad?'

Dinkel is caught off guard. 'Yeah, erm fine, Mr Finnegan...sir.'

'Hmm... you look like a man who has lost a shilling and found sixpence. You're fair mithered.'

Dinkel, aged twenty-six, blinks incoherently. Frank may as well be speaking double-Dutch.

'Sir?'

Expelling air like a frustrated bull, he tries again. 'Let me rephrase it; your face is a quagmire of confusion gazing out of a cracked window.' It doesn't help, as more befuddlement spreads across Dinkel's face. Frank places an arm around the young officer's shoulder. 'What I'm trying to say is—you appear troubled. A trouble shared is a pain in the Aristotle, but try me.'

'Oh, I see.' He hesitates. 'The thing is, Prisha, ahem, DI Kumar, has asked me to find out about the boys listed in Selwyn Morgan's diary.'

'And?'

His face reddens. 'There are eight names from 1985 and no date of birth.' Averting his eyes, staring at the grubby carpet, he states, 'I'm not sure where to begin, sir.'

Frank chuckles. 'I understand. Let's work through this together. Take a seat. Now, tell me where you think you should begin,' he adds as Dinkel flops into a chair.

'Well... the General Registry Office; births, deaths and marriages?' he states expectantly.

Frank nods in agreement. 'Not a bad place to start. But most of the boys' first and last names are not unusual around these parts. And as you stated, with no exact date of birth, you could be trawling through fifty or more hits for each name. Very time consuming. Try a bit of lateral thinking first. What do we think those boys had in common?'

Dinkel grimaces as if the thought process is physically painful. 'I suppose... yes, I think... they may have all come from a disadvantaged background; dysfunctional family; care or foster homes.'

Frank beams. 'Well done, son. Now you're thinking. And remember, we're talking about 1985, so some places may still have been referred to as orphanages. Nevertheless, I'd say the majority of care facilities would have been run, or at least overseen, by the local council. So, where's your starting point?'

Dinkel leaps to his feet. 'The local council archives?'

'Good lad. Now ring ahead and speak to someone in the know, then get yourself down there—yes?'

'Yes, sir!'

As Frank walks back to his office, he mutters under his breath, 'Some winkles are harder to prise out of their shells than others. Doesn't mean they're not worth the effort, though.'

# 21

As Prisha drives through North Yorkshire's vibrant greenery, the tight coils of tension that silently took up residence in her neck and shoulders start to unwind. Fields brim with optimism; the air, fresh and hinting at summer, carries the scent of wildflowers and cut grass, elevating her mood.

Past quaint villages, the car's hum mingles with life's distant sounds, anchoring her in the present. Newborn bleating lambs pierce the quiet. Budding trees flash by her open window, casting patterns of light and shadow across her face, as leaves swoon in the sunlight.

As the River Rye comes into view, its waters a tranquil companion to the road, she finds herself drawn into the peaceful rhythm of the landscape. The drive becomes a brief respite, a chance to breathe and be momentarily lost in the serene embrace of spring's amazing wonder.

Turning off the main road, she gazes upon the long meandering track that leads to a farmhouse on top of the hill. The car slows as it navigates the typical bumpy gravel track, hemmed in by drystone walls on either side. As she reaches the top of a blind crest, she panics and immediately veers violently to the left as a tractor bears down upon her. The tractor swerves and comes to an ungainly stop, kicking up dust and debris as the engine idles.

A middle-aged man, with a weathered appearance, opens the cab door and grins at her.

'Christ, love. That was a close shave. A few seconds earlier for either of us, and you'd have been pushing up daisies.'

Prisha takes a deep breath and kills the engine. 'The dangers of living on a farm, eh?' she replies with a laugh. She exits the car and flashes her warrant card. 'Inspector Kumar. Are you from Kettlewell Farm, by any chance?'

'Aye. Blake Baldwin's the name, pleased to meet you,' he replies, stepping down from the cab and shaking her hand.

'Likewise. You any relation to Seth Baldwin, who owned the farm back in the eighties?'

'Yeah, he's my old man.'

Prisha feels a stab of excitement. 'Really? Is Seth around?'

'Oh aye, he's around all right. About five miles that way,' he states, pointing towards the village of Nunnington.

'Six feet under in the cemetery.' He allows himself a wry chuckle which cloaks his obvious sadness.

'Oh, I'm sorry. When did Seth die?'

'Twenty years back. Heart attack sitting in the back garden on a warm summer's day, drinking a bottle of Newcastle Brown. We found him there on his favourite bench with a contented look on his face, still holding his glass of beer. Didn't spill a drop. He was always careful with his ale. There're worse ways to go,' he reflects. 'Anyway, what can I do for you, Inspector Kumar?'

'I am heading-up the investigation into two recent fatalities. Information has come to light that suggests a possible connection between the victims and an outdoor-ed camp that was held here back in the mid-eighties; 1985, to be precise. I was wondering...'

He nods and smiles. 'You'd be talking about Happy Camp.'

Her eyebrows arch. 'Yes. That's it.'

'I'm heading to that field right now. I have my ewes and lambs in there at the moment. It's better pasture.' He gesticulates indiscriminately into the distance.

Prisha follows the point of his finger, but to her, it's just another blaze of greenery divided by seemingly haphazard walls.

'Right, I see.'

Blake nods towards the long, low trailer attached to the back of the tractor stacked with a dozen square hay bales.

'I'm about to drop some meadow hay off for the ewes. It's full of wildflower and clover. Lot of nutrients. It helps with milk production and really gives the lambs a boost. I can take you there now, to Happy Camp, and show you around?'

'Thank you, Blake. That would be very helpful.'

His reassuring smile dissolves as his gaze falls upon the Ford Fiesta Prisha is driving.

'Now then, lass, I'm not sure your car is built for some of the tracks we have to access, so you have two choices; you can either climb on the back with the hay bales, or you can sit on my lap in the cabin. I know what I'd prefer.' He immediately blushes at his unintended faux pas. 'Erm, what I meant to say was, I know which you'd prefer... not me.'

Prisha chuckles and quickly grabs her backpack from the car as she replies, 'I know what you meant. I'll jump on the back.'

'Righto. Do you need a leg-up?'

'No thanks.' She places one palm on the trailer and effortlessly leapfrogs aboard.

'Blood and dust. I wish I could still do that.' He steps onto the footplate of the cab and calls out, 'Hang on to the side bars, as it can get very bumpy. Shout out if you want me to stop.'

'Will do.'

—◈—

There's a sorrowful, lonely feeling to the stone barn. It exudes an aura of neglect, abandonment. Sad and reticent, as if ashamed of a guilty secret, head bowed. As Blake attempts to push open the door, Prisha stares at the wooden sign outside the entrance. The exquisite relief carving of the letters, as seen in the photograph, has suffered the ravages of time. Once a proud and inviting marker, it has succumbed to the unyielding forces of nature. It leans at a forlorn angle, as though yearning to relinquish its hold on history and surrender to the earth below. In the damp climate, the wood has become a feast for decay, slowly being reclaimed by moss, rot, and the ceaseless appetite of woodlice, and earthworms beneath. Each day edging closer to becoming one with the soil it once stood guardian over; the very soil it was born from. She traces a finger over the weathered letters.

HAPPY CAMP

The rest of the wording has long been obliterated, but Prisha remembers them exactly:

'Discipline. Godliness. Fun. How much fun went on here?' she whispers.

Blake places his shoulder against the door and imparts a hefty shove. Jarringly, it relents as a flurry of dust descends.

'Here we go,' he says in his naturally jovial manner. Prisha follows him inside as he explains the layout. 'As you can see, this was the kitchen area. Basic by today's standards, but back in 1985, it was more than adequate for a cabin-type retreat. Sink, and tap fed by rainwater, collected from the roof into a concrete tank out the back. No running hot water, of course. Here's the classic Aga cooker, with six hotplates and two ovens. Wood fired. From here, they'd cook their food and boil water. Then we have a larder, cupboards, table and chairs.' He pushes at another door. 'This was the bunkhouse for the boys. Slept eight in total. Four bunks, if I remember rightly. The beds are long gone, of course.'

Prisha stares at the cramped confines of the room, her eyes lingering on the solitary, diminutive window high up near the eaves.

*In the heat of summer, it would have been stifling.*

Blake wanders back through the kitchen and to another door at the far end of the downstairs room. This one swings open effortlessly. It's much larger, at least twice the size of the bunkhouse.

'And this is where the adults slept.'

She notes the three large windows, and the rags of curtains, disintegrated over the years.

Noticing another door, halfway along the room, she points and asks, 'What's behind there?'

'Take a look.'

Walking gingerly, as if stepping over gravestones, she pushes at the door. A side room, of sorts, with no windows. It emits a smell which is instantly unpleasant. Musty, with a tinge of something else she can't quite place. For reasons she can't explain, she shivers despite the warmth of the day. She quickly retreats back to the kitchen. Spinning around, taking in her surroundings, she nods towards a narrow staircase that leads upstairs.

'And what's up there?'

Blake flinches, shrugs, fidgets. 'It's a tiny room. Not sure why they built it or what it was used for. Too small for a bedroom. This barn was built by my great grandfather back in the Victorian era. It was used to store hay on small lofts to protect them from the elements and wet ground. Hence the height. The ground floor was mainly used to store farm machinery.'

Prisha climbs the creaking wooden steps until she's confronted with the final entrance. A sturdy, wooden door, with a small gap between the bottom sill and floorboards.

With no great relish, she twists the ring-knocker handle, languishing above an ancient keyhole.

She enters the dark chamber. A few shafts of light pierce the rugged stone blocks where the mortar has crumbled to dust. Pulling out her keys, she turns on the micro torch attached to them. She can stand upright in the centre of the room, but if she ventures left or right, she has to stoop as the sloping rafters impede her movement.

Blake was right. It wouldn't even fit a single bed. Maybe storage, she thinks.

The weak beam from the torch picks out something scratched onto the back wall. Nearing, she notices graffiti etched into the rough timber frame. The words start off innocently enough;

*Mike Ross woz ere 85*

*Misery Camp*

As she moves along the wall, the words darken.

*Help?*

*No More!!!*

*I wish I was dead*

Then... a crude picture of two stickmen. One bent over, the other behind with what she presumes is a large erection, and a happy smile on his face.

A sense of dread washes over her. 'My God,' she murmurs, 'this wasn't a storage room, it was a cell.' Taking a step back, she bangs her head on a rafter and drops the torch. 'Ouch! Damn it,' she curses.

Absorbed by ghastly visions and the fusty smell, she is oblivious to the creak of leather boots on the stairs behind her as she crouches, searching for the torch.

# 22

The Lily Pool at Pannett Park is an oasis of tranquillity in the heart of Whitby. The small geyser from the water fountain complements the serene atmosphere. Dora is waiting on a bench as she scans her mobile messages, separating the wheat from the chaff, the consequential from the trifling, the critical from the trivial.

As Sebastian Thorne's personal assistant, there's never a dull moment. Somewhere in the recesses of her mind, she must have heard the footsteps approaching, but they were drowned out by the white noise of her employer's hectic business and private life. Meetings, interviews, TV appearances, cutting the ribbon at a new high-tech shopping precinct in Leeds built by Thorne Developments. Apart from the business side of things, she also advises him on what clothes to wear for each event; collects laundered suits from the dry cleaners; purchases new ties, underwear, vests, shirts, sunglasses, even shoes. Organises restaurant reservations, books airline tickets, and hotel suites. She even scans all the latest media each day to compile a list of what's happening from around the planet, from the deadliest deeds on the world stage, to what artist is trending most on TikTok. She presents Seb with a one page, A4, bullet-pointed sheet every morning, where he'll quickly digest the information, occasionally quizzing her for more detail on a certain subject. He likes to present an aura of the modern renaissance man with his finger on the pulse of world events, even if it is a sham. Basically, Dora is his second brain and body. He's in the unique position of living two lives at once, even if one of those lives technically belongs to someone else.

'Dora?'

The voice startles her. She looks up. 'Amanda Chan. Glad you could make it,' she says, offering Sebastian Thorne's nemesis a warm smile.

The smile is not reciprocated. Amanda's rather stern face is partially masked by large, round sunglasses. 'I'm not in the habit of partaking in clandestine meetings with the lackeys of corrupt businessmen. Whatever you have to say, then say it now, and I can be on my way.'

Dora sighs. 'At least give *me* a chance. You may detest Mr Thorne, but you don't even know me.'

'Okay. Answer this one question; why do you work for him?'

Dora tilts her head to one side and considers the question. 'I need a job. Mr Thorne pays exceedingly well. He's charming and considerate most of the time, and it keeps me on my toes. I like to keep extremely busy. It makes my down-time so much more enjoyable.'

'I need a job,' she sneers derisively. 'I bet's that what the guards at Auschwitz said.'

Dora bristles. 'Don't be ridiculous. You can hardly compare Sebastian Thorne to murdering Nazi scum who committed mass genocide on a race of people.'

'Do you wipe his bottom for him?' she asks mockingly.

'I would if he asked.'

'You disgust me.'

'In a previous life, I was a carer at a nursing home. I got used to cleaning bottoms. Once you've done a few, it's just another job.'

'How the hell did you become Seb Thorne's PA?'

'It's a long story for another day. We're not here to talk about me. Now, are you going to sit down so we can have a meaningful adult chat or are you going to persist with your adolescent rants, like a spoilt, privileged brat?'

Amanda softens somewhat and takes a seat on the bench. She pulls out a cigarette from a packet and sparks up, holding the smoke for a while before blowing it out in a long satisfying stream.

'You have until I finish this cigarette.' She proffers the packet to Dora.

'No, thank you. I don't. It will kill you.'

'Something or someone has to kill you.'

Dora almost laughs at the irony. 'Yes, you're right. You're quite willing to line the pockets of the executives of the tobacco giants who have caused tens of millions of deaths over the years, and who now flood third world countries with cheap cigarettes to get people hooked, like cheap drug dealers and pimps. And yet you save your rancorous, vindictive spite for a local, hardworking businessman who came from nothing and has made a success of his life.'

'Save me the press release bullshit. There are many battles to fight, Dora. One must choose carefully which hill you are prepared to die on.'

'You seem to have a preoccupation with death. Be careful what you wish for.'

'So, why has Sebastian sent you?'

Dora chuckles. 'He hasn't. He knows nothing of this meeting. I'm not sure he'd approve. I've done some background checks on you, Amanda. I hired a private investigator. It was your last name that intrigued me—Chan. I assumed it was of oriental origin, Chinese, perhaps. But looking at you, there's not an ounce of mixed blood in your veins. Pure, white Anglo-Saxon. But your last name isn't really Chan, is it? You changed it by deed poll from Chandler—Amanda Elizabeth Chandler, only daughter of Sir Brendan Chandler, CEO of GMAX Corporation, a major arms manufacturer. The latest Forbes rich list had your father placed at a rather lowly number twenty-two. Still worth a few billion, though.'

Amanda draws on her cigarette and puffs out three smoke rings. 'So?' she replies, not in the least bit concerned.

'I never did find out what the family rift was about. Although, I guess it's obvious. You don't approve of daddy making weapons to kill people.'

'I've disowned my family. I haven't spoken to any of them in over three years. And if you were trying to dig up some dirt on me, to use as a bargaining chip in my campaign against Thorne, then you must have realised by now that you've wasted your time and money.'

'You're sharp, but I knew you would be. Yes, you're whiter than white. Apart from a number of arrests for public nuisance, disturbing the peace and trespass, there's nothing of any note.'

'Are you going to get to the point?'

Dora glances at her watch. 'Yes. I'm running late. The thing is, you're not only a public nuisance, but you've become a nuisance to Mr Thorne. He's at a critical juncture in his career. It's not a very well-kept secret that Sebastian has political ambitions. Of course, if he becomes a public official, he will step away from all his business interests in an act of probity.'

'How noble of him.'

'But you are the fly in the ointment. And don't flatter yourself. When I say a fly, I mean a rather minor irritating fly, nothing more. So, I want you to drop your irrational, unfounded campaign against him. In return, I can offer you fifty thousand pounds in cash. With that sort of money, you could put down a hefty deposit on purchasing your own place. I've seen where you live in that squalid basement flat.'

Amanda rises, drops the cigarette onto the ground and grinds it in with her heel. 'I doubt *you* are offering me the money. You mean *he's* offering me the money? A moment ago, you said he knew nothing of this meeting.'

'He doesn't. And yes, it will be Mr Thorne's money. I can be very persuasive.'

She scoffs with contempt. 'You must think I'm cheap. Fifty thousand. Do me a favour.'

'Okay. Name your price.'

'I don't have a price,' she turns on her heels and walks away.

'How does one hundred thousand sound?'

She stops and turns around. 'One hundred?'

---

Dora stabs at her phone as she hurries back to the car.

'How did it go?' Seb asks.

'Let's say it was contentious.'

'What's her price?'

'The bidding stopped at one hundred.'

'Good. So, it's sorted?'

'Not quite. She said she'd think about it and get back in touch.'

'Damn and blast her! When?'

'She didn't say. But don't worry. It's just her way of having a little power trip. I think she'll ask for one hundred and fifty. If we make her a final offer of one-twenty-five, she'll bite our hand off.'

'Hmm... well, I hope you're right.'

'I think I am, sir.'

'But remember this, Dora, in every endeavour you undertake in life, one must always have a Plan B.'

'I have already anticipated that, sir.'

A chuckle echoes down the line. 'Of course you have. I wouldn't expect anything less. Pray tell.'

'If we can't silence her with money, then we play her at her own game. We employ the services of a well known social media influencer to wage a campaign against her. We already have a small dossier on her *and* her father's business interests. When people find out who the real Amanda Chan is, she'll be completely discredited. If push comes to shove, we can also release her home address, bank details, and mobile number to turn up the heat. Considering her privileged upbringing, I doubt she has the stomach for a dirty fight. It will be all done through an intermediary, so there can be no link to you, Sebastian.'

'I like it, Dora. You make a formidable opponent. However, it does raise the question; why don't we utilise Plan B now?'

'Time, sir. If you want this problem solved quickly, then hard cash is by far the quickest route. Plan B could take many months to implement before we see any return.'

Thorne roars with laughter. 'You missed your vocation, Dora. You should have gone into business.'

Ending the call, she allows herself a satisfied smile. 'I already have, Sebastian. I already have.'

# 23

The tractor door slams shut, as farmer Blake Baldwin returns with his backpack. He places it on the table outside the entrance to the barn, stops, then stares at his bloodstained hands and tuts. Spinning around, he spots the outside tap close to the decrepit Happy Camp sign. Turning the handle, the pipe coughs, splutters and gurgles, as a thick slurry of muddy gunk spews forth. He lets it run until the water turns clear, then methodically washes his hands removing all traces of the blood. Satisfied, he returns to the table, brushes down a rickety old chair and pulls out his lunchbox from his backpack.

He smiles apologetically as Prisha returns. 'How was it?' he asks. 'Do they still flush?'

'Yes. The toilets were surprisingly clean apart from a few leaves.'

'Good. Must have been built well. They run off rainwater and a septic system. Take a seat.' He pulls the lid off the plastic tub and offers it to Prisha. 'Wife's homemade mini quiches.'

'No, I couldn't. It's your lunch.'

'Afternoon snack, actually.' He lifts one out and places it on the table in front of her. 'Excuse hands, but I've just washed them. Had blood on them from lambing earlier. One ewe had a breached birth.'

Prisha picks up the quiche. 'Thank you. It came out back legs first?'

'Aye. Bit of blood and guts, but they're doing fine. Sorry about earlier, scaring you half to death, creeping up on you like that.'

'Don't apologise. I haven't been sleeping well and I'm a little on edge. I jump at my own shadow at the moment. So, how much do you remember about Happy Camp?'

'Quite a bit. What do you want to know?'

'Everything.'

He laughs as he devours the quiche in one mouthful and takes another one from the box. 'Okay, best I start from the beginning. Dad wasn't into organised religion or God. That's not to say he wasn't a spiritual man, he was, in his own way. He believed in a natural order, you know, the seasons, the earth, the elements. He was also a good man; kind, compassionate, nurturing, loving.' He chuckles. 'That's not to say me and my brother wouldn't occasionally get a clip around the lug 'ole now and then if we played up. My mam was a little different. She went to church most Sundays, was big on Christmas and Easter. Wasn't a zealot or anything, but she had a quiet faith. Anyway, to cut a long story short, a guy came to her local church one Sunday, and she got talking to him. He was setting up a charitable organisation, can't remember the name of it now, but he was looking for a small piece of land or a field and an old barn to renovate into basic accommodation. The plan was to take disadvantaged kids away for weekends and during school holidays. Instil in them a love of nature, walks and outdoor activities, that sort of thing. Eventually, after a lot of pestering, she persuaded dad to let them use this field whenever they wanted. The organisation would be responsible for doing up the barn and outbuildings and making it habitable, out of their own pocket. Of course, dad was a true Yorkshire man and, as you know, you don't get owt for nowt round these parts. In return for free use of the field, the kids and adults would help on the farm occasionally during busy times: harvesting and lambing, fixing broken walls and such like.' He pulls a cup and a bottle from his backpack, unscrews the lid and pours out the yellow, cloudy liquid into the cup. 'Wife's homemade lemonade. Last year's batch, of course. Here, take it, I'll sup from the bottle.'

'Thank you.' She takes a gulp. 'My goodness, that is delicious. You're a lucky man.'

'Aye, and I know it. Now, where was I?'

'Helping out on the farm?' she prompts.

'That's right. Both parties agreed to the arrangement, and that's when it started. They first arrived for the Easter school break.'

'1985?'

'I can't quite recall the exact year, but if you say it was 85, then I'll believe you. They really set to work on the old barn and after two weeks or so, they'd knocked it into shape. Nothing flash, mind. Pretty much as it is today. Put a concrete floor in and windows. It was watertight and windproof. Offered protection from the elements.'

'Did you visit?'

'Yes.' He hesitates. 'Initially.'

'How old are you if you don't mind me asking?'

'Forty-eight.'

Prisha does a quick mental calculation. 'You'd have been about ten or eleven in 85?'

'Aye, sounds about right. I came down with my dad on the first day they arrived, and we introduced ourselves. All the kids came from troubled backgrounds, broken homes, and orphanages, that sort of thing. But they weren't bad lads... just been dealt a rough hand, that's all.'

'No girls?'

He raises one eyebrow. 'No. No girls. No women. Only men and boys. Didn't think much of it at the time.' The inference lingers in the air. 'Over the next week, I'd pay a visit in the afternoons after I'd completed all my chores on the farm. We'd have a kick around with a football or a game of cricket, or rugby, but to be honest, they were hard at work most of the time fixing up the barn. I remember visiting once or twice during the second Easter week and something had changed.'

'In what way?'

'Couldn't put my finger on it. It was just the vibe. The first few days they were here, it was all laughter and frolics.'

'Did you ask any of the boys why the mood had changed?'

He frowns at the distant memory. 'I may have. I think they said they were knackered through all the hard work. Anyway, Easter came and went and over the next few months sometimes a couple of adults would turn up with two or three lads to continue the renovations at weekends: painting and building an outdoor barbecue area, plumbing for the toilets and showers, smaller jobs. I didn't take much notice. Then they returned en masse for the school summer holidays. Me and my brother were flat out on the farm. Dad would pay us three pounds each a day. Might not sound like a lot these days, but it was a bloody small fortune for a young kid back then. Six weeks hard graft and I bought myself my own Chopper.'

'Chopper? You mean an axe?'

Blake guffaws. 'No lass! A Raleigh Chopper bike. You know, big handlebars, a long padded seat with a back rest. Three-speed gears mounted on the crossbar in front of the seat. That bloody gear stick caused me some pain over the years,' he adds with a knowing smile. 'I'm surprised I managed to have kids.'

She's intrigued. 'Why?'

'Why do you think? Hit an immovable object, and you'd slip forward straight into the gear stick. Not as bad for girls, if you get my meaning.'

'Oh, I see.'

'I've wandered off topic.'

'Summer holidays?'

'Aye, that's right. I can't recall the exact day, but it would have been sometime in August. A blisteringly hot day. Dad let us finish our chores early. I set off from the farm and took a shortcut through the fields. As I neared that wall over there,' he nods towards a timeworn stone wall about fifty yards away, opposite the barn, 'I heard voices. Climbed up the wall and poked my head over. The boys were all lined up, receiving a reprimand of some sort. Then one lad was picked out, Mike Ross was his name, and he was made to take his shorts and underpants down and touch his toes. Then the bastard gave him a right bloody belting.'

'Belting?'

'Aye. With a cane. It was brutal. I mean, he was really going for it, no half measures. It wasn't six of the best, it was more like eighteen of the best with everyone else watching on in silence. And the thing was, he was enjoying it.'

'The adult?'

'Aye. He was almost slavering. I think he was getting off on it, you know, sexually.'

Prisha shakes her head. 'Sweet mercy,' she murmurs.

'There was no mercy from that sadistic bastard. I'll hand it to the lad, Mike. He took his punishment. No crying or screaming, he just bit his lip and accepted his lot.'

'Do you know what he'd done?'

'No idea. Some minor infraction, no doubt.'

'What did you do?'

'I was horrified and scared. I slunk away and ran back home. I was going to keep shut about it, as kids often did in those days.'

'And these days.'

'True. But later that night I told my mam and dad what I'd seen.'

'How did they react?'

'Dad fell out of his bloody tree. Went ape-shit. Never seen him so angry in all my life. He intended to go, right there and then, and have it out with the bastard, but mam calmed him down, told him to sleep on it and have words the next morning with a clear head.' He reflects wistfully. 'I suppose she was worried it may escalate into violence. He was wound up like a bloody grandfather clock, he was, which was unlike dad. He wasn't prone to anger, much less violence.'

'And the next day?'

He leans back in his seat, puts the lid back on his lunchbox, and drops it into his bag. 'It was mid-morning. Sorry, I'm using farming time; what I meant, it was about 9—9:30. There's a loud rap on the front door and that bastard's on the front step, wanting to use the telephone. In a wild panic, he was. Said one of the lads had drowned in the river. He called an ambulance. Obviously, well before the days of mobiles. Then later, a couple of coppers showed up. Plain-clothed, like you, possibly CID, I can't recall. The older copper was very intimidating. Anyway, that was that.'

'Did the officers question you or take a statement?'

'Not really. I told them what I'd seen the previous day, but they weren't interested. They said it was a different lad who died, so what I'd seen was irrelevant to their investigation. I did overhear my dad having sharp words with them afterwards, outside, but it fell on deaf ears.'

'Did your father react in any way?'

Blake chuckles, then grins. 'Oh, aye. Later that day, he drove down here to Happy Camp in the tractor. Me and my brother were on the trailer, the one you rode on, actually. When we arrived, he told us to stay where we were. He marched right up to that bastard, spun him around, and clocked him one right on the chin. Went down like a sack of spuds. Out cold. He then shouted at the other adults and told them to pack their things and get off his land and to never darken his doorstep again, otherwise he'd be getting his shotgun out. Later that day they were gone, never to return.'

'Jeez. What a tale. I didn't want to interrupt your flow, but you kept referring to—that bastard. Can you remember his name?'

'I can remember his name all right. It was the doctor—Doctor Blenheim.'

# 24

Prisha finishes taking photographs of the inside and outside of the barn on her phone. She takes a seat opposite Blake, unzips her backpack, pulls out an envelope and places it on the table. 'I hate to keep you and take up your time. I know how busy farmers are.'

'Don't worry, love. The days are getting longer at this time of year. I can catch up.'

She slides out a photograph of Happy Camp, the one acquired from Selwyn Morgan's cottage, and hands it to him. 'Take your time and see if you can recollect any names.'

'Well, look at that,' he says in amazement. A pleasant smile is rapidly overtaken by a deep frown. 'I'm afraid names are not my strong suit, inspector.'

'That's fine. Anything will help.' She's made a conscious decision not to show him the list of names from Selwyn Morgan's diary. It could elicit confirmation bias and muddy the waters. She wants him to recall the names from memory, not from suggestion.

He taps at the photo. 'That's Doctor Blenheim, the sadist, front and centre. And that lad there is Mike Ross, the lad who had six bells of shit whacked out of him. Nice kid. Acted tough. Always brown as a berry.' He pauses for a moment as a reflective gaze crosses his face, then taps at another figure. 'And this skinny little lad was the poor bugger who drowned. Won't ever forget his name—Tom Maplin. Suffered with a terrible stammer. And now I'm struggling. Hang on, I think the boy next to him was called Ted... Ted Fairchild. That's right. Quiet, shy type. I think Mike Ross sort of took him under his wing, looked out for him.'

'What about the adults?'

He massages his stubble. 'Oh, now you're asking. This fellow here...Melvin, perhaps? No, no... Selwyn. Aye, that's right.'

'And what about this man?' she asks, pointing at John Wilkes.

'That was the reverend. That's how everyone addressed him. Not sure what his last name was.'

Prisha indicates at the young, handsome man in the photo. 'This one intrigues me. He must be a good twenty years younger than the other men and at least ten years older than the boys.'

Blake chuckles. 'That's Cyclone, as he was known then. And he *was* a bloody cyclone. Could turn his hand to anything, building wise, and was fast. A real craftsman. I doubt the renovation would have happened so quickly if it hadn't been for his skills. He was all right, or at least I thought he was, at first.' He pauses as he peruses the photo again. 'Selwyn was pretty quiet. The reverend was strict, but the doctor was a nasty piece of work, and arrogant.'

'You said Cyclone seemed all right at first. What did you mean?'

'As part of the survival skills, one evening Cyclone and the doctor showed the lads how to set snares to catch rabbits. When I was growing up, rabbit pie or stew was on the menu at least once a fortnight. Anyway, the next day, Cyclone, me and a couple of the other lads checked on the snares. We'd snagged one rabbit, a big fat doe. I told Cyclone it was pregnant, and he should let it go. What he did next was why I changed my view about him.'

'I'm not sure I want to hear this. What did he do?'

'Held it up by the back legs, pulled out a hunting knife and split it down the middle. Didn't even knock it out, first. I'll spare you the gory details. Life and death is a normal cycle on a farm, but you don't treat animals that way. They deserve respect and to be treated humanely.'

'Christ, he sounds like another psycho. Why would he do something like that? Was he trying to impress you and the boys?'

'No, I don't think he was. He had a ruthless streak to him. That's probably why he got to the top.'

Prisha closes her eyes for a second and shakes her head. 'Sorry, you've lost me.'

'Cyclone is that big shot property developer, Sebastian Thorne.'

Prisha's eyes widen. 'Are you absolutely certain Cyclone and Sebastian Thorne are one and the same?'

'One hundred per cent. I mentioned it once to the missus when he came on TV a few years back.'

'Well, well,' Prisha mutters, gazing intently at the photograph. 'The plot thickens. What about the other boys? Can you recall their names?'

He winces. 'No, I'd be guessing. Wouldn't want to lead you up the garden path.'

Prisha jots the names he did remember in her notebook. 'One last favour; can you take me to the spot where Tom Maplin drowned?'

'Aye, course I can. Hop on the trailer and we'll go there now.'

The River Rye is not much more than a wide stream and would barely cover Prisha's knees at its deepest point, but what it lacks in majestic power it makes up for in beauty. She takes her shoes and socks off, rolls her trousers up and wades into the water, squealing with delight at the icy coolness.

'It's sandy,' she says, turning to Blake.

'This spot is, yes,' he replies, humoured by her behaviour.

She gazes at the stepping stones that straddle the river, fifteen in all, some protruding a good six inches out of the water.

'Were the stones always here?'

'No. The Happy Camp folk placed them there. There's a grand walking track on the other side. I suppose they didn't want to get their shoes and socks wet as they set off on a walk.'

She walks tentatively across the stones. 'Some of them are a bit slippery underfoot.' Making her way back to the bank, she dries her feet on the grass and rubs them with her sock. 'Do you believe Tom's death was an accident?'

Blake lays out on the grass, rests his head into the cradle of his outstretched fingers and palms, and closes his eyes.

'I'm not sure what I believe. All I know is those lads were physically and emotionally abused at that camp. As for sexual abuse, well, I can't say. I never witnessed anything and none of the boys ever confided in me.'

'They wouldn't if they were scared to death. The stickman in the tiny room, you must have seen it. What do you make of that?'

'It could have been a crude record of actual events, or it could be childish graffiti. How many graffiti drawings of male genitalia do you observe on walls and bus shelters?'

'True. There are a lot of other pointers. The two small rooms. The fact there wasn't a female in the group. It was almost like a cult, with the doctor as the leader, or maybe not the leader, but the second in command. The disciplinarian.'

Blake sits up, puzzled. 'When I nearly ran you off the road, you were extremely coy about your investigation, which I understand. But is this a cold-case you're reopening into historical child abuse? It would be nice to know if I'm going to be overrun with police officers and forensic people visiting the farm?'

Prisha slips her socks and shoes on and rises. 'No, it isn't about that, not yet, anyway. There were two rather brutal murders last week. One was Selwyn Morgan, the other was the man everyone referred to as reverend. He was Bishop John Wilkes.'

Blake stands, concerned. 'Really? You think someone has come out of the woodwork to bump them off?'

'It's one possibility we're working on.'

He stares at the ground. 'If that's true, then it probably does point to sexual abuse.'

'Maybe. Then again, the deaths may not be related to Happy Camp at all. By the way, we haven't released the dead men's names to the press yet. So, if you could...'

'Be discreet? Your secret's safe with me, lass. I'll say nowt to no one.'

'Thanks. Right, I best make tracks. I could stay here all day. It's such an idyllic spot, despite its history, but I've taken up enough of your time. If you could drop me back at my car, it would be appreciated.'

A grin creeps across his face. 'Not so fast, young lady. I helped you out, now it's your turn. I have hay bales to load into the outbuilding, a couple of bales to spread out in the field for the ewes, and two lambs to bottle feed. You up for it?'

She beams. 'Why not. One good deed deserves another.'

# 25

Frank emerges from his office with his jacket slung over his shoulder and gazes upon his officers all beavering away at keyboards. Files, reports, and photographs are strewn across various tables.

'Haven't you lot got homes to go to?' he barks, glancing at the clock on the wall. He receives little response, bar a cursory apologetic smile from Dinkel. 'Well!' he bellows, finally getting everyone's attention. 'Are you going to give me the end of day debrief or not?'

Prisha and Zac rise and move towards the crime board.

Prisha performs a neck stretch. 'It's been a highly productive day, Frank.'

'I'm glad to hear it,' he says, sliding into a chair and extending his legs.

She nods at Dinkel. 'Clem, would you care to elaborate on your eventful day?'

'Certainly ma'am. As you know, Selwyn Morgan's 1985 diary had some pages ripped out. The document examiner from forensics used electrostatic detection to identify pen indentations on an adjoining page. That gave us a list of eight boys' first and last names.' He drags an image across the whiteboard and double taps it to enlarge the diary page, listing the names. 'As you will note from the Happy Camp photo, there were eight boys on that snap. Bearing in mind that we think Happy Camp was set up for disadvantaged children, I started my research with the council archives, searching care homes from the 1980s.' Smiling broadly, with obvious pride, he adjusts his tie. 'After no more than an hour, I hit the jackpot,' he adds, touching the whiteboard. A photo of a building flashes up.

'That's the old rectory in Pickering,' Zac states.

'It certainly is. In 1973, it was turned into an orphanage. The building was still owned by the church, but the day-to-day running of the operation was undertaken by council and social services. It finally closed its doors in 1990 and the rectory fell into a state of disrepair until it was sold off for redevelopment a decade ago, whereupon it became Peasholm Manor, retirement apartments. From the social services records, I came across these.' He taps the board again and eight ID type photos of pre-teen boys appear on screen, almost like mugshots, with their full names, age, and parents' names displayed beneath. 'All spent varying amounts of time at the rectory orphanage. Most importantly, all were residents in 1985.'

'Good work, Dinkel,' Frank says. 'Carry on.'

'Last Monday I attended a training day which focused on the latest artificial intelligence being used in crime detection. The training was conducted by a civilian specialist from York. I emailed him the images of the eight boys and the Happy Camp photo, and asked if he could use AI to definitively match the boys' mugshots to the camp photo.' Pausing for dramatic effect, he scans the faces of his colleagues.

'Stop milking it, Dinkel,' Zac states, yawning after a long, tiring day.

'Ahem. Yes. The AI can never be *completely* accurate. But it came back with a certainty of ninety-six per cent.'

Frank pulls at his earlobe. 'Hang on, so you're saying the mugshots from the council archives match with the photos of the boys on the Happy Camp photo, or near as damn it?'

'Yes, sir.'

'Excellent. Good old-fashioned police work, well, apart from the AI part. Thorough, very thorough,' Frank says.

'With a positive ID on the boys, my next task was to search the birth and death records. I contacted the General Register Office and put in my request. They were extremely helpful. Within a couple of hours, I ascertained the following information: five of the boys from Happy Camp are deceased.'

'Five out of eight?' Frank exclaims. 'That's disproportionately high. If they were aged between ten or twelve in 1985, then they'd only be in their late forties today.'

'Correct. The death certificates make for unsettling reading, sir.'

Prisha moves forward. 'Well done, Dinkel. I'll take it from here.'

'Ma'am.'

She takes a deep breath. 'A few days ago, we had very little solid evidence to go on. Now we have an abundance of information. Feast or famine. Remember the acorn motif and the Latin inscriptions? Well, thanks to some good work by Zac, searching the archives of the Charity Commission, we have another small breakthrough. I have collated what we know so far into a summary.' Placing a finger on the whiteboard, she drags a document from the left to the centre and enlarges it.

### Operation Gorse Bush

Happy Camp Links

Charity: The Acorn Fellowship.Registered with the Charity Commission January 1984. De-registered

September 1985.Trustees: John Wilkes (Bishop) | Henry Blenheim (Doctor) | Selwyn Morgan (Verger/Sexton)

Happy Camp Photo (Easter 1985)

Adults from left to right

John Wilkes (Bishop) unveiling Happy Camp sign. Aged 45. Murdered, aged 83 - second victim.

Selwyn Morgan. Aged 43. Murdered, aged 81 - first victim.

Dr Henry Blenheim. Aged 45. Alive aged 83. Former Home Office pathologist, and surgeon.

Cyclone, AKA Sebastian Thorne (kneeling, front) Aged 19. Businessman. Alive aged 57.

Boys from left to right

Brain Lovejoy – Aged 10: Died in 1995 from a drug overdose. Aged 20.

Paul Kirk – Aged 11: Died in 2005 from alcohol poisoning at an all-night party. Aged 31.

Derek Farrell – Aged 12: Died in 1998 from organ failure due to long-term substance abuse. Aged 25.

Tom Maplin – Aged 10: Died from drowning in 1985 at Kettlewell Farm / Happy Camp - Nunnington.

Ian Longhorn – Aged 10: Died in 1993. Took his own life. Hanging. Aged 18.

Mike Ross – Aged 12: Whereabouts unknown. No police record. Now aged 50 – if alive.

Ted Fairchild – Aged 12: Whereabouts unknown. No police record. Now aged 50 – if alive.

Malcolm Pearce - Aged 11: Whereabouts unknown. Police record. Now aged 49 if alive.

**Summary**

Of the eight children identified in the Happy Camp photo, we know for certain five are deceased. Three, whereabouts unknown.

Of the four adults in the photo, we know two are recently deceased, and two are alive.

Prisha frowns as she points at a name on the board. 'Malcolm Pearce has a police record as long as my arm. His first run in with the law was when he was sixteen. Caught with a small amount of cannabis on him. He attended a drug awareness course. From then on, he migrated to theft, burglary, dealing and growing cannabis and served varying amounts of time. Each time he's released from prison, his criminal activities ratchet up a notch. He was released six months ago after serving a five stretch for possession and intent to supply a class A drug—methamphetamine.'

Zac shuffles forward. 'I nicked him about ten years ago or longer when I was in uniform. A tall skinny guy with wiry ginger hair and not the sharpest tool in the shed, but harmless.'

'Has he any convictions for violence?' Frank asks.

Prisha shakes her head. 'No. Just theft and drug offences.'

Frank's barrel chest heaves. 'Correct me if I'm wrong, but are you inferring the killer is one of the five surviving people from the camp photo?'

'I'm not inferring it, Frank. I'm almost certain of it.'

'Blood and sand. Okay, okay, let me play devil's advocate for a moment. You have two prominent and distinguished men on your summary, Doctor Blenheim and Sebastian Thorne. Now why would they bump off Wilkes and Morgan after all this time?'

'I'm not certain, yet, but it could be to do with the death of Tom Maplin.'

'Prisha, it was a drowning, an accidental death. As tragic as it was that a young lad lost his life, no one has ever accused Thorne or Blenheim of anything untoward. To suggest either of them would bump off two octogenarians on the slim chance that an incident from nearly forty years ago should surface is stretching the envelope. Plus, Blenheim is eighty-five years old. Bit long in the tooth for creeping around in the dead of night, I'd have thought. As for Sebastian Thorne, it's fanciful to suggest he would murder the victims in such an outrageous fashion. Why not pay someone to do his dirty work? And a bullet would be a damn sight quicker and easier than buggering about with tent pegs, burning motifs into their heads, and slicing their meat and two veg off?'

Prisha takes a sip of water. 'A smokescreen, possibly? Make it look like the work of a ritualistic maniac, and the last person we are going to suspect is an articulate, suave, entrepreneur like Thorne, or a former Home Office pathologist. Anyway, this might not be about Tom Maplin's death. I have no proof of sexual abuse at the camp, but we do have the farmer, Blake Baldwin's witness account of physical abuse. Plus, the fact five of the eight boys died prematurely, and appeared to have led dysfunctional lives. We know people who suffered childhood sexual abuse often struggle with it for the rest of their lives. Let's for a moment say there was sexual abuse of the boys. Even a whiff of a rumour like that has ruined many successful careers in the past. You know what it's like these days on social media, when the armchair warriors whip themselves into a frenzy.'

Frank is not convinced. 'Nah, I don't buy it. Your logic is all wrong. If there was abuse, then the most likely candidates to seek retribution would be the abused, not the abusers. If it is Thorne or Blenheim, then why haven't they taken out the three remaining boys from the photo?'

'Firstly, we don't even know if they're still alive. And secondly, you're assuming this murder spree is over; it's not. It's a work in progress as far as I'm concerned. Anyway, you're missing my point. I'm not saying it is Thorne or Blenheim. But I *am* saying, out of the five people possibly still alive, I'm certain one of them is our killer.'

'A word of warning, Prisha; I'm not questioning your theories, but you need to leave the door ajar for other possibilities. I've seen this too many times over the years, when an investigating team becomes fixated on one theory to the detriment of everything else. The Yorkshire Ripper investigation is one such case that springs to mind. Their top brass became obsessed with the Weirside Jack tapes, which ultimately turned out to be a hoax. You've put all your eggs in one basket with this Happy Camp theory of yours.'

'And not without good reason, Frank. The acorn motif burnt into the foreheads of the victims; the charity was called the Acorn Fellowship. The trustees? Three of the adults in the photograph. I'd say that was pretty strong corroborative evidence.'

'It's not evidence. It's conjecture. What about the three remaining lads? They're more likely candidates.'

'I agree. But I'm covering all bases. Anyway, let's move on.' She turns to Zac. 'What have you got?'

'I have a little stick of dynamite.'

'Really?'

'Yes, really.' He grins, as he taps at the whiteboard and pulls up a series of scanned documents. 'I managed to obtain a copy of the coroner's report from the inquest into Tom Maplin's death.' He zooms in on one image and quickly scrolls through all the legalese. 'Pretty standard fare. Nothing earth shattering. No smoking gun. There were mild rebukes for the adults in charge of the children at Happy Camp. Duty of care, responsibility, blah, blah. Each adult was questioned: John Wilkes, Henry Blenheim, Selwyn Morgan.'

'Seb Thorne wasn't put on the stand?' Frank quizzes.

'No. Apparently he wasn't there the morning they found the boy's body.'

'That corresponds with Blake Baldwin's account too,' Prisha adds.

Zac continues. 'Each of their statements was similar. They were shocked and saddened by young Tom's death, but they all believed he woke in the middle of the night, or very early morning, and went off exploring. As they were all asleep at the time, they were unaware of his actions. The coroner gave them a slap on the wrist, then returned with his findings of accidental death.'

'Where's the dynamite?' Prisha asks, mildly disappointed.

'Patience. The pathology report was attached as an appendix to the coroner's report. Again, nothing out of the ordinary.' He zooms in on the next document. 'This is a summary of the report. I'll read it out. *Whilst attempting to cross the river, the boy, Tom Maplin, apparently slipped, resulting in a fall where he sustained a significant head injury, likely causing unconsciousness. Subsequently, he fell into the water, where, unable to respond due to his injuries, he succumbed to drowning.'*

'Bit basic by today's standards, but it matches the accounts of the adults,' Frank states.

'Couldn't agree more,' Zac replies as he flips to the very end of the report.

All eyes rest on the pathologist's name and signature.

Frank grimaces, puzzled at the anti-climax. 'Stuart Hartley, Junior Pathologist. Am I missing something?'

'It's not just you who's missing a connection,' Prisha adds.

Zac's eyes twinkle as he scrolls the document down a little further. 'Here's your dynamite, Prisha. Feast your eyes on the senior supervising pathologist, acting in a purely educational capacity.'

'Sweet merciful crap,' Frank gasps.

'I don't believe it,' Prisha says, moving closer to the board. 'The senior supervising pathologist was Doctor Henry Blenheim.'

'I've also tracked him down. He's alive and living in Robin Hood's Bay,' Zac declares, mightily pleased with himself.

'This is beginning to smell worse than a trawlerman's jockstrap who's been at sea for a week,' Frank says, slowly scratching at his neck. 'Maybe your Happy Camp theory has got legs.'

Prisha's mind is buzzing. 'It's not only got legs, but arms, torso and a head, a very ugly head. How can the person who was at the camp, found the body, and was responsible for the boy's welfare have been allowed to participate in the post-mortem? It's a conflict of interest.'

'I think the term supervisory capacity is a nice get-out clause,' Zac says. 'It indicates he was overseeing a junior doctor but had no direct involvement in the post-mortem.'

'That's bullshit!'

'It happens,' Frank states. 'It's not normal practice. Who knows the whys and wherefores? Short-staffed, a sudden glut of deaths, could be any manner of reasons.'

'No. There was only one reason he was there; to make damn sure the boy wasn't checked for signs of sexual abuse. Zac, I want you to find the junior doctor and question him. It wouldn't surprise me if all he did was sign the autopsy report.'

'Okay, but he could be anywhere, and the chances of him remembering one specific post-mortem from thirty-eight years ago is a big ask.'

'Nevertheless, find him.'

Frank rises wearily. 'What's your plan of attack, Prisha?'

'Tomorrow morning, I intend to pay a visit to Sebastian Thorne, and Doctor Blenheim, and I also intend to have a little chat with Amanda Chan.'

Frank scowls. 'Amanda Chan, the social justice activist and royal pain in the freckle?'

'Yes.'

'What the hell has she got to do with any of this?'

'Just a gut feeling. Amanda Chan is waging a very public campaign against Thorne, and I'd like to know why. Maybe she knows something we don't.'

# 26

# Saturday 29th April

An aromatherapy diffuser bubbles away on the countertop. Billows of steam, infused with frankincense, waft through the reception area, creating a calming ambience. A tropical fish tank at the far end of the room emits a bluish light as fish languidly glide by, their vibrant colours a stark contrast to the tastefully decorated walls. Gregorian chants softly echo from unseen speakers as Prisha closes her eyes for a moment and relaxes into the comforting leather chair.

She takes a deep breath and whispers to Zac, 'It's like being at the massage therapy centre.'

'Not like any massage parlour I've ever visited. Let's hope for a happy ending.'

She slaps him on the leg. 'Don't be smutty.'

'Inspector, Mr Thorne will be with you shortly. He's presently on an international business call.'

Prisha opens her eyes and smiles at Sebastian Thorne's personal assistant, Dora. 'Thank you. There's no rush. I was just saying to my colleague how relaxing and calming the atmosphere is.'

Dora nods gratefully. 'Yes. We employed a Feng Shui consultant to design the layout. Now, can I offer you a drink while you wait?'

'Not for me, thanks.'

Zac is more forthcoming. 'Aye. A coffee would go down a treat, thanks, Dora.'

'Americano, espresso, cappuccino, latte? One shot, two shots? Milk, soy milk, almond milk?'

Zac is taken aback. He was expecting coffee granules from a jar. 'Oh, erm, an espresso double shot, with a drop of cold water, would be just the ticket. Get the heart pumping.'

'Coming right up.'

They watch on as Seb Thorne's super-efficient PA disappears through an automatic, sliding glass door.

'This reception is more comfortable than my bloody living room,' Zac murmurs as he shoots a glance at a young, female receptionist behind the counter.

'A bit different to the incident room, eh?'

'Aye. Eh, you haven't forgotten I need dropping off at the dentist by half-past, have you?'

'You've reminded me three times, so no, I haven't forgotten. It's only a check-up.'

'That's not the point. Six week waiting list to get in. Ridiculous.'

'Calm the farm. We'll be only here twenty minutes—max.'

Within a few minutes, Dora returns with the coffee. 'Mr Thorne will see you now. If you'd like to follow me.' Zac hurriedly swallows the mouthful of coffee and follows Prisha and Dora into a small lift. It glides silently heavenward and comes to a graceful halt. A slow hiss and the doors slide open. They all step out into another magnificent office, two storeys up. It offers three-sixty-degree views via floor-to-ceiling smoked glass windows. A handsome man sitting behind a long walnut desk rises and strides briskly towards them.

Dora performs the introductions. 'Mr Thorne, this is Inspector Kumar and Sergeant Stoker from North Yorkshire Police.'

'Excellent! Pleased to meet you both. I admire the extraordinary job you do. I've always thought it takes a special kind of person to devote oneself to the noble calling of police work.' His smile is warm and effusive as he shakes their hands then ushers them towards two chairs in front of his desk.

'Will that be all, Mr Thorne?'

'Yes. Thank you, Dora. I'll let you know if I need anything.' Dora disappears into the lift as he stifles a chuckle. 'I'd be lost without her,' he says, nodding at the lift door as it closes. 'An absolute godsend when I found her. She does the work of three. When she applied for the position of PA, I knew within thirty seconds of the interview that she was the one. I don't always act upon intuition, but on this occasion, I did. And thank God.'

Prisha studies his twinkling blue eyes and slicked back hair, a mixture of luxurious black dappled with streaks of grey. 'Yes. It must be nice to have your own personal assistant.'

His eyes narrow. 'I note your inference, inspector. And believe me, I realise I'm in a privileged position and I'm extremely grateful for it. But it wasn't always the case. Now, what can I do for you?'

Prisha pulls the photograph from the envelope and slides it across the leather-bound desk.

'We're investigating a double murder.'

Thorne lifts the photograph, mouth agape. 'Good lord! Now this is a blast from the past. I'd forgotten all about Happy Camp. Where did you get this from?'

'Two of the men in the photograph are the murder victims. Selwyn Morgan and Bishop John Wilkes. The photo was found at Mr Morgan's cottage in Pickering.'

'I'd heard the local news about the murders, but had no idea who the victims were.'

'No. We haven't released their names to the media for operational reasons.'

'Who would want to kill them?'

'That's what we want to ask you. When was the last time you had contact with either man?'

He places the photo back on the desk, obviously mesmerised by the image. 'Contact? I think the last time I had contact would have been at Happy Camp not long after this photograph was taken. And that would have been...' closing his eyes, he pinches the bridge of his nose between thumb and forefinger.

Zac helps him out. '1985, perhaps?'

He sits bolt upright. 'Yes, I think you're right. If I remember correctly, we began work on the old barn during the Easter of that year and my involvement ended at some point during the summer. It must have been the school holidays as all the boys were there, so probably in August of the same year.'

He lifts a small, ornate dagger from a wooden cradle, leans back in his chair, and spins it around and around in his left hand.

Zac leans forward, apparently mesmerised by the object. 'Is that a sgian dubh by chance?'

Seb grins. 'Yes, it is.'

'May I?'

'Certainly,' Seb replies, handing him the tiny dagger, hilt first.

Zac studies it intently, much to the annoyance of Prisha. 'This is a thing of rare beauty,' he gushes.

Seb chuckles. 'My wife bought it at auction for my fiftieth birthday. It has provenance back to Bonnie Prince Charlie. Apparently, he gifted it to Flora MacDonald for helping him escape to the Isle of Skye, as he evaded capture from the Duke of Cumberland.'

'Get out of here!' Zac explodes, missing Prisha's angry glare. 'You mean the Bonnie Prince *and* Flora MacDonald handled this very dagger?'

'It's been assessed by at least a dozen experts where all but one agreed it is the real deal. The hilt is made from rare bog-oak with a motif of a Scottish thistle. And the jewels are sapphires.'

Zac turns to Prisha. 'Do you know what this is?'

'A small letter-opener?'

He sneers. 'Heathen. This is living history.'

'I'm not sure it's living.'

'It's a ceremonial dagger worn as part of the Scottish Highlands dress. It slips down the inside of the sock. It must be worth a small fortune,' Zac states, mesmerised.

'Let's just say there wasn't much change from two hundred and fifty thousand pounds.'

Prisha coughs. 'Ahem, if we could all refocus,' she says, this time catching Zac's attention.

'What? Oh, aye. Sorry.' He hands the dagger across to Thorne, who carefully places it back in its plinth.

'Apologies, inspector. Now, where were we?'

Prisha leans forward. 'Can you tell me of your involvement at Happy Camp, Mr Thorne?'

Leaning back in his high leather chair, he folds both hands over each other. 'I was in the adventure scouts when I was in my teens. In those days, there was a strong bond between the scouting movement and the church. Less so these days, of course. One Sunday I was approached by Bishop Wilkes to help out on a new project initiated by the church.'

'Why you?'

'My father had his own building firm. Small and not very successful. My father was a good man, and a fine tradesman, but he was no businessman. I was an apprentice joiner and being a small business, I was a sort of Jack-of-all-trades; bricklaying, plumbing, plastering, concreting, tiling. The only thing I stayed away from was the electrics. If you make a mistake in any of the other trades, it can be costly and embarrassing. Make a mistake with electrics and you can kill someone.'

'I see. But you haven't explained how Bishop Wilkes knew you in the first place. I conducted a little research and, according to what I read, you grew up in Leeds, where your father's building firm was located. John Wilkes was Bishop of Knaresborough, which is a long way from Leeds. How did you cross paths with him?'

'I'll try to cut a long story short. My family and I were parishioners of our local church, Saint Mary's in Beeston, a suburb of Leeds. In those days, it was not uncommon for thieves to strip church roofs of all the lead flashing and sell it for scrap. I always kept abreast of the latest developments in building materials, even from an early age. Aluminium flashing with a bitumen undercoat for adhesion and water repellence was in its infancy in the 80s, but it was available. After a Sunday service, I suggested to our local vicar he should employ us, i.e. my father's business, to replace the lead on the roof with aluminium before thieves stole it. The amount of money raised from selling the lead would offset the cost of the project. If he waited until the thieves stole it, he'd end up with nothing but a huge repair bill. It just so happened that Bishop Wilkes was the visiting clergy that day, performing the service. We got chatting, and he told me about this enterprise he was trying to get off the ground to help disadvantaged children spend more time in nature. He asked if I'd be willing to help as a charitable act. I agreed. I saw it as a free holiday. If you've ever visited Beeston, then you'd appreciate the lure of the North Yorkshire countryside.'

'What was it like, Happy Camp?'

He tilts his head and sighs reflectively. 'Initially, the atmosphere was joyous, one of fun. There was a lot of hard work, but there was also down-time when we'd play games with the boys; cricket, football, touch-rugby, treasure hunts, that sort of thing. But by the time I came back for my second stint in the summer, the mood had changed.'

Zac crosses his legs. 'In what way?'

'The atmosphere was more sombre... no, not sombre.' He pauses, searching for the correct words. 'The feeling was tense amongst the children.'

'Tense?' Prisha prompts.

'Yes. An undercurrent of... fear is too strong a word, but maybe trepidation could describe it better. The joy had disappeared.'

'I see. Did you ever witness any abuse, sexual or physical?'

He shuffles slightly in his chair. 'Sexual? No. Physical and emotional... yes.'

'Can you elaborate?'

'All the boys came from broken homes. They hadn't had the best start to life, and one or two of them could be mischievous, errant in their ways, a bit of a handful. The elders, as they were known, were strict disciplinarians, especially Doctor Blenheim. At first, if a boy misbehaved, they might receive a verbal tirade, an occasional clip around the ear. But as time went on, the reprimands became more severe.'

'In what way?'

'Canings. Manhandling the boys, throwing them around. There was a small room at the top of the barn. Its original intent was to be a storeroom. However, it soon became known as the Retribution Room. Boys were locked in there for hours on end as a punishment.'

'And what do you remember about the death of one of the boys; Tom Maplin?'

He nods, his expression sorrowful. 'Yes. Young Tom. A timid lad. I'm afraid I can't enlighten you.'

'Were you at Happy Camp on the morning his body was discovered in the river?'

'No. I'd departed the previous evening.'

'Why?'

'My work was done.'

'But why not wait until the next morning to leave?'

His right index finger taps on the desk. 'To be honest, inspector, I'd had enough and couldn't wait to leave. The afternoon before Tom's death, I'd been working at the back of the barn on the ablution block, finishing off the plumbing. The Elders had two bells. One was a handheld bell they rang to round the children up at mealtimes or morning prayers. Then there was this bloody great big bell they'd hit with a leather mallet. Its toll was deep, booming. You could hear it from miles away. It was struck in three-second intervals.'

'Its purpose?'

'It was called the Retribution Bell, and for good reason. Anyway, that afternoon the Retribution Bell was sounded. I remember thinking to myself—here we go again. Everything went quiet, then I heard Doctor Blenheim shouting and screaming. I stopped work and crept around the side of the barn. The boys were all lined up in a row. It was a stinking hot day. The doctor pulled one boy out, made him drop his shorts, then caned him. It was barbaric, disturbing. I'd witnessed enough. I returned to my work, skipped the evening meal, and worked through until I'd finished the job. I packed away my tools and left that evening.'

'And since that evening, you never saw anyone from Happy Camp ever again?'

'No. I obviously heard about Tom's death, although it didn't get much news coverage. About three months later, my father died of a heart attack. I took over the business and threw myself into that.'

Zac gazes around the room. 'And from that small family run building firm, you built this empire.'

Thorne smiles benevolently. 'I had a lot of good luck along the way, sergeant. Right time, right place.'

Zac may be in awe of Sebastian Thorne, but Prisha is less impressed. 'How old were you at the time?'

'In August 1985, I'd have been twenty, nearly twenty-one.'

'An adult?'

'Well... yes. I'm not sure what you're implying, inspector.'

'On the afternoon of the caning, can you remember the other adults who witnessed it?'

Seb jabs at the photograph. 'Yes. Obviously, Doctor Blenheim but also Selwyn Morgan, and Bishop John Wilkes.'

'And it was only Doctor Blenheim who administered the punishment?'

'Yes. But the other two were complicit in the brutality.'

'You were an adult. Weren't you also complicit?'

———— ◆ ————

Prisha slides into the car, fastens her seatbelt, then turns to Zac. 'What do you think?'

'He's definitely not a killer.'

'What makes you say that?'

'The guy's all right. I like him.'

'Oh, and because you have a man-crush on him, he's ruled out as a suspect in a double murder investigation?'

Zac is indignant. 'I do not have a man-crush.'

'Then why did you take a selfie with him as we were leaving? It was bloody embarrassing.'

'I wanted to show my lads. Sebastian Thorne is a prime example of how, with a lot of hard work and a bit of nous, you can get on in life. He's just a regular guy who's made good.'

'Regular guys don't have antique daggers worth a quarter of a million pounds sitting on their desk.'

'Okay, smarty-pants; what's his motive? Why, after all this time, would he decide to bump off two guys he knew from thirty-odd years ago?'

Prisha turns the ignition. 'I don't know,' she muses. 'It was very convenient he departed Happy Camp the night before Tom Maplin's death though, wasn't it? And why did he not report the abuse of the boys to the authorities?'

'He was young. Probably intimidated. He was hanging out with a bishop and a high-flying doctor, pillars of society. When you were twenty, would you have had the balls to stand up to people like that? And, Prisha, you have to remember it was 1985. Things were a lot different in those days. We're looking back on an era through the prism of modern day values.'

'Hmm... maybe. But there's something off about him.'

'And another thing; we're investigating the murder of two octogenarians, not what may, or may not have happened at Happy Camp a lifetime ago.'

'You're wrong. The murders of Selwyn Morgan and John Wilkes have a direct link to the events at Happy Camp. Right, I'll drop you off at the dentist, then I'll make my impromptu visit to Amanda Chan.'

Zac scoffs. 'Christ, Prisha, I think you're losing the plot on this one. Amanda Chan is a conspiracy theorist fruit-loop. She has nothing to do with the case.'

'No, she hasn't. But I don't like the smell of Seb Thorne, and maybe she can fill in some blanks.'

# 27

Prisha raps on the door of the basement flat as the music of Bob Marley drifts through an open window, accompanied by the distinct smell of weed. She waits a few seconds, and peers around the tiny, paved garden strewn with litter; chocolate wrappers, empty coke bottles, cigarette packets. Not known for her patience, she thumps on the door, harder.

'Ms Chan!' she bellows.

The music abruptly stops as the door cracks open to the sound of a latch chain being throttled. Stoned eyes peer out via the gap.

'What?'

The voice is posh, and Prisha instantly recognises it from the YouTube videos she watched the previous evening. She holds up her warrant card.

'Ms Chan, I'm Inspector Kumar from North Yorkshire Police. Can I come in, please?'

'If this is a drugs bust, you're wasting your time. It's medicinal, prescribed by my doctor. I have a bulging disc.'

'I'm not interested in the cannabis. I'd like to talk to you about Sebastian Thorne.'

Eyes flicker with surprise. 'Don't tell me the spineless toad has sent you to do his dirty work for him? Come to arrest me for harassment, have you? Well, I can tell you on good authority, he cannot shut-me down by using the para-military lackeys of the despot state to keep me quiet.'

Prisha puffs out her cheeks and sighs. 'Amanda, as much as you may hate to hear it, I am not Attila the Hun. I'm a thirty-one-year-old female who loves running, outdoor activities and a cool breeze on my face. I enjoy spicy food, white wine, in moderation, and I have a boyfriend who is a sheep farmer. I like listening to Amy Winehouse, and my favourite book is Wuthering Heights. Oh, and I love my grandmother very much. Now, are you going to let me in or not?'

The door closes, followed by the slide of a chain, then reopens fully. Amanda stoops to grasp a pile of mail from the carpet, then leads the way down a short hallway and through a side door. Prisha inadvertently scrunches her nose up at the overpowering smell of stale tobacco and weed, then studies the flat. It could not be described as dirty, but it is unkempt, disorderly. The small living room houses a television, a modern sofa strewn with a crumpled blanket and numerous pillows, one accompanying chair, and a small round table. Papers, folders and an assortment of books litter the floor and table. Amanda flops down on the sofa and picks up a packet of cigarettes, sparks up, and places an overflowing ashtray on the arm of the couch.

'Go on then, what's this about?' she queries with a sliver of discontent.

Prisha gazes at her. She's an attractive woman who doesn't much care for her outward appearance. Her dress is long, hippy fashion, she's barefoot, and her hair resembles a bird's nest.

'I've watched some of your videos about Sebastian Thorne.'

'And?' she replies, drawing heavily on the ciggy.

'There's a lot of smoke, but not much fire. It's all hearsay, innuendo, always prefaced with the word—allegedly. Your wording is very precise, almost as if your videos are vetted by a litigation lawyer.'

'If you want to take on the rich and powerful, then you need to be as sharp as them. If you leave the door open, just a whisper, they'll be all over you.'

'I also watched some of your other videos on oil conglomerates, intensive battery farming, pollution by water companies. You make some interesting points. But your crusade against Sebastian Thorne seems... personal, and I wondered why? Do you two have history?'

She snorts with laughter. 'You think I'd have sex with him? Do me a favour.' She spits the words out.

'He's an attractive older man. Restrained testosterone instead of reckless testosterone has its benefits. Some younger women go for that.'

'Not this younger woman. Anyway, he's the wrong sex, so you're way off the mark, inspector.'

'Ah, I see. So, what is it then?'

'Why do you care?'

Prisha shrugs. 'Just curious. Do you know much about his past?'

She taps the cigarette on the ashtray. 'Oh yes, and it doesn't tally with the official version put out by his PR Department or his Wikipedia page.'

Prisha's interest is piqued. 'Really?'

'The official line is that Sebastian Thorne came from a dirt-poor family, dragged up in the backstreets of Leeds. His father had a small building firm that Sebastian worked for and then took over when he died, and that was the seed of his empire.'

'And that's not true?'

She cackles and tokes on the cigarette. 'Being a detective, you'd be aware the best liars are the ones who sail close to the truth. Sebastian never worked for his father. His father was an unemployable alcoholic. He did, however, work for his uncle's building firm. When the uncle died of a heart attack, Sebastian went into partnership with his aunt. He ran the business, and she was a silent partner. After a couple of years, he bought her out for a measly sum. Exactly two weeks after the buy-out, he received a twenty-million-pound contract to refurbish a block of flats.'

'And you assume he knew of the contract in advance?'

'Of course he did. Contracts involving large sums of money aren't negotiated over a fortnight. That was just the start of his duplicitous dealings and shady practices. Another example is of an electronics company he bought into. It was run by an old school friend of his, Alistair Darby, a computer and electronics boffin. The company started doing well, supplying surveillance equipment and data protection to businesses. Then, a smear campaign aimed at his old friend began.'

'What sort of smears?'

'Embezzlement, unlawful practices, intellectual property theft. Seb dog-whistled Alistair to the other directors of the company, defending him while highlighting further irregularities. In the end, the board voted Alistair Darby out of the company. He was handed a golden parachute payment with a non-compete clause and a gag order. After his dismissal, the company was renamed Thorne Surveillance. Six weeks later, Alistair's body was pulled from the sea.'

'Suicide?'

Amanda shrugs. 'Misadventure, apparently. Either way, Thorne was the architect of his demise. Oh, and the sweet irony; Sebastian performed the eulogy at his funeral. Do you see the sort of man he is, inspector?'

'Do you have any hard evidence or sworn statements relating to any of this?'

She snorts her derision. 'No. But I've spoken to people. Frightened people who have been at the receiving end of his tactics. And people who are scared for their welfare don't go on the record.' She stubs the cigarette into the ashtray and rises. 'Follow me.'

She leads the way into a dimly lit office. A laptop computer resides on top of a desk, attached to a larger secondary monitor, pushed up against a back wall. Unwashed coffee cups adorn a side table. The faint smell of patchouli oil intertwines with the aroma of dope. Prisha gazes at the side wall, which contains a huge corkboard covered in photographs and articles about just one man.

Her eyebrows arch alarmingly. 'That looks like a crime-scene board,' she states.

'That's because it is,' Chan replies with a chuckle.

'If a psychiatrist saw that, they'd say you have a paranoid obsessive personality disorder.'

'Don't deride me!' she shouts.

'Okay, calm down. What did you want me to see?'

Amanda picks up a large dossier from the desk and hands it over. 'Read this,' she states as she re-lights a half-smoked stub lifted from a burgeoning ashtray.

Prisha stares at the title - The Homelessness Scam, then passes it back. 'I'm sorry, but I don't have time to study it. If you'd care to give me a synopsis, then I'm all ears.'

Amanda takes a seat, the ember of her cigarette casting a small glow in the darkened room. 'As you'd be aware, Thorne is constructing housing for the homeless in affluent neighbourhoods funded by his company. That's the front. In reality, Seb Thorne's ventures have caused a surge in drug-related activities and anti-social behaviour in those areas.'

Prisha, her interest sharpened, quizzes, 'And the fallout?'

'Local homeowners feel besieged. They start offloading their properties to escape the decline, plummeting the property values as the neighbourhood's reputation nosedives.' Amanda's tone is even, each word laden with gravity. 'Then, another one of Thorne's companies swoops in to buy the properties at a steal. After they've got what they want, they clear out the homeless from the flats, transform them into luxury apartments, and auction them off to the highest bidder. They also refurbish all the other properties they've picked up for a song, wait for the market to bounce back, and then sell those at a substantial profit.' Amanda takes a drag, allowing the smoke to waft into the air.

'It's ingenious,' Prisha states, trying to wrap her head around the enormity of it. 'What sort of profits are we talking?'

'Astronomical.' Amanda breathes out as if the word were smoke. 'Even a modest house in these once-desirable suburbs can go for close to a million. For the grander, more opulent homes? Eight to ten million. Imagine snapping up fifteen to twenty of those properties, sprucing them up, and just biding your time. And the apartment blocks for the homeless? Each sells for one to two million, with around thirty units in each block. You do the sums.'

Prisha emits a low whistle. 'Christ. It's like reverse gentrification.'

'Precisely. And because he's allegedly building housing for the homeless, his journey through the labyrinth of planning and environmental paperwork is fast-tracked. And he's got four of these projects on the go right now, raking in a fortune while masquerading as a crusader for the disadvantaged. A win-win for him.'

Prisha shuffles back, mulling over the revelations. 'But as clever as it is, if true, it skirts more on the edge of moral and ethical bankruptcy than outright illegality. He's too clever for that. If you have any hard evidence, then I suggest your first port of call would be to arrange a meeting with an officer from the Serious Fraud Squad. If there's anything in it, they can bring in the National Crime Agency, and the Tax Office.'

'Unfortunately, as yet, I don't yet have anything which could withstand a barrage of legal eagles ripping it to shreds.'

Prisha isn't sure whether Amanda Chan is a smart amateur sleuth, or a deranged obsessive who smokes too much weed and has an axe to grind.

'Why haven't the mainstream media picked up on these so-called scams?'

Crushing the cigarette butt into the overcrowded ashtray, she paints a vivid picture of influence. 'Sebastian Thorne breakfasts with the elite alumni, lunches with royalty, and by evening, breaks bread with Whitehall mandarins, who orchestrate the levers of British power. And for a nightcap? He sips whisky-on-ice with the globe's media moguls, and dare I say, even chief constables. It's in nobody's interest to see him fall from grace.'

'Except yours?'

She shoots Prisha a withering glance. 'Thorne needs to be stopped. He has an unquenchable thirst for control. I suspect at some point in the future he intends to enter politics. You only have to look back in history to realise men like him wreak chaos and calamity on humanity. To paraphrase a jaded cliche; bad things happen when good women don't stand up. Are you a good woman, inspector?'

'That's not for me to answer. It's for others. I've interviewed depraved murderers who saw themselves as good.' Her eyes fall onto a small digital alarm clock perched on top of the larger monitor, held in place by a large blob of Blu Tack. She finds it odd but also realises the time... and it's not on her side. 'I really need to get moving,' she explains as she turns to leave. 'I wish you all the best with your endeavours, Amanda, and if you do ever find any damning evidence, then heed my advice and contact the Fraud Squad.'

She follows Prisha out of the office. 'Don't you worry. I have a plan to capture Sebastian Thorne in the act. And when I do, the whole world will know about it. Even his closest allies will swiftly abandon him when the story goes viral.' Amanda pulls open the front door. 'Excuse me, inspector, but you never explained your visit?'

Prisha exits the flat, smiles benevolently, and turns around. 'Oh, no reason. I saw you in the station the other day after you'd been arrested. I just wanted to get abreast of the facts.'

Amanda narrows her eyes. 'I see,' she replies curtly. 'So, you *were* put up to this by someone higher up the ladder. A fishing trip requested by Sebastian Thorne. Call on Amanda Chan and see if she has anything concrete on Thorne. Was that it?'

'Not at all. I can assure you it was merely...'

'Save your breath, inspector! If you're not part of the solution, then you're part of the problem. A female in your position should know better. You should be an example, not a disgrace.'

The door slams shut in her face swiftly accompanied by the sound of a chain. She wonders once again if Amanda Chan is delusional. Climbing the three steps back to the main street level, she taps at her phone.

'Dinkel, where are you?'

'In the incident room, ma'am.'

'Good. I want you to dig into Amanda Chan. Find out everything you can about her and write it up in a report. I want her background, her friends, her family, where she gets her money from. I want to know the last time she took a pee. Understood?'

There's stilted silence for a moment. 'Right... I'm not sure how I'm going to know...'

'For God's sake, Dinkel! It's an expression!'

---

The tobacco crackles and blazes as the yellow flame tickles the tip of the cigarette. Amanda Chan breathes in deeply, gazes out of the window, then sips from her coffee cup. Her brow creases.

'Why would a random detective turn up here to ask about Sebastian Thorne? They must have better things to do.' She lazily mulls over the question without finding an adequate answer. Her eyes drift onto the unopened mail. Flicking through the letters, she discards the top three, knowing they contain utility bills, *overdue* utility bills. The last envelope is larger. Her name and address are neatly typed. Intrigued, she peels back the adhesive fold and slips her fingers inside. Now she is puzzled. It's an old photograph of a bunch of kids and a few men. They are lined up in front of a stone barn. To the left is a wooden sign which reads;

Happy Camp

Discipline. Godliness. Fun.

She peers into the envelope, but it contains nothing else. She flips the picture over and stares at the typed label affixed on the back.

Tom Maplin. Died August 1985.

Her eyes scrunch in bewilderment as she studies the image once more and draws on her cigarette, drinks from her cup.

'What am I supposed to do with this? Who sent it, and why?'

Carefully, she studies each of the individuals, but the faces mean nothing to her. She walks to her office and retrieves a magnifying glass from the desk drawer, and returns to the table. The magnification does nothing to enlighten her. She wanders around the room puffing on her smoke.

A buzz of adrenaline releases into her bloodstream.

She moves the magnifying glass back and forth until it's focused on the figure kneeling at the front. Early twenties, wearing shades, handsome.

'Sebastian bloody Thorne,' she murmurs in disbelief. 'Now, what is all *this* about?'

# 28

Hidden by high, rustic brick walls festooned with ivy, the house remains out of sight. Prisha navigates the car off the leafy country lane, gliding through an open gateway, its cast-iron gates welcoming her in. The long gravel driveway leads to a Georgian-era country house, that exudes wealth and status with its magnitude and architectural balance. Guarded by Palladian arches, the imposing panelled door sits beneath a transom window, designed to sprinkle light into the entrance hall. Three storeys of stone facade are punctuated by tall sash windows, while the roof boasts a dozen chimney pots, hinting at the warmth within.

Precise hedges, cut into straight, boxy lines, section off the garden, a home for early flowering plants. Bluebells swish lazily in the breeze, their sweet delicate scent sneaking through the car window, whisking Prisha away to a longed-for past. Gravel crunches under tyres, as an air of tranquillity soothes her troubled mind.

'Holy shit,' she whispers, eyes wide. 'Henry Blenheim was definitely private practice. The NHS doesn't shell out this well, not even for the top doctors.' Her words are a mix of wonder and a nudge towards the considerable wealth required to own such grandeur, far removed from the grind of public healthcare.

Climbing the weathered stone steps, she presses at an ancient bell, the tinkling sound from inside somehow managing to escape through the giant door. The sharp clack of heels on tiles grows louder until the door swings silently open. A woman in her late fifties greets her with a warm smile. Greying hair, tied in a tight bun, sits above wrinkled, kindly features. Her attire is smart, if a little old-fashioned. A crisp white blouse is partially covered by a fawn cardigan, which embraces her slender frame perfectly.

'Inspector Kumar?'

'Yes. Mrs Allardyce? We spoke this morning,' she explains, flashing her warrant card.

'Indeed. Come in. We've been expecting you. Would you care for refreshments? Tea, coffee, iced-water?'

'No. I'm fine, thanks.'

Closing the door, she turns on her heels and leads the way. 'I'll show you through to Doctor Blenheim, although I must warn you, he's not in the best of health.' Prisha follows obediently behind. 'It's a beautiful warm Spring we're having, isn't it?'

'Ahem, yes... yes, it is. A pleasant change from the miserable winter we endured. Do you live on the premises, Mrs Allardyce?'

'No. Mondays to Fridays, I work from nine until four. The weekends, from nine until eleven thirty. I pre-make meals for the weekend and put them in the fridge for Doctor Blenheim to heat up in the microwave.'

Prisha follows her down a long hallway. 'How long have you been housekeeper for Doctor Blenheim?'

'Oh, at least thirty years. In his heyday, he employed several staff. Cook, cleaner, two gardeners, secretary, maintenance man. Now sadly, there's only myself and the gardener left. We have a cleaner who comes in twice a week, but to be honest, most of the rooms are never used. The doctor can't manage the stairs anymore, so we turned one of the drawing rooms into a bedroom. That's where he spends most of his time, lost in his books and his memories.' She taps on a door and enters the room. 'Doctor Blenheim, I have DI Kumar from CID to see you.'

Prisha follows her in and quickly sizes up the situation. The drawing room has lost none of its old charm. The only incongruous objects are a bed, an oxygen bottle, and a wheelchair. A plush high-backed armchair engulfs the old man, an oxygen mask resting on his lap. He pulls his eyes away from a book and places it down on a small antique round table adorned with an array of medicines, neatly arranged in a row. Looking up at Prisha, he offers her a welcoming, if weary smile.

'Come, come. Take a seat,' he implores. His voice is brittle around the edges, but it still carries an air of authority.

Mrs Allardyce spins on her heels. 'I'll leave you to it,' she says, quietly closing the door as she exits the room.

Prisha takes a seat opposite the doctor and pulls out her notebook. She's already ruled Doctor Blenheim out as the killer due to his physical demeanour.

'Thank you for seeing me on such short notice, doctor.'

'Not at all. Actually, it's a rather pleasant distraction. I don't receive many visitors these days. Mrs Allardyce told me you are investigating two suspicious deaths?'

'Yes. I believe they were old friends, or acquaintances, of yours. We haven't released their names to the media yet.'

'Oh dear.'

'Selwyn Morgan was found murdered at his cottage in Pickering last Monday, and the body of Bishop John Wilkes was found at his home in Dalehouse on Thursday morning. We believe they were both killed by the same person.'

Shock and surprise splash across his face. 'Good grief!'

'Doctor Blenheim, can you tell me the last time you saw or had contact with either man?'

His glazed eyes drift to the window and the magnificent greenery beyond. 'Oh... it would have been a long, long time ago.'

'Could you be a little more specific?'

'Yes, sorry. Erm... I haven't seen either Selwyn or John for many years, maybe thirty or so.'

'In the 1980s, the three of you were trustees of a charitable organisation—The Acorn Fellowship—designed to help disadvantaged children.'

His eyes dart from the view outside back to Prisha. 'Yes, yes. That seems like a lifetime ago. But what has that got to do with your current investigation?'

'I think there may be a link between the charity and the deaths.'

His arms fold across each other on his lap. 'How so?'

Prisha has no intention of relaying the details. 'What can you remember about Happy Camp?'

A flicker of surprise as his mouth falls open slightly. 'Happy Camp?'

'Yes.' She removes the photograph from her bag and hands it over. 'The charity was given the use of a barn on land belonging to Kettlewell Farm, owned by the Baldwin family. That barn was known as Happy Camp.'

He takes the photo, reluctantly, and lifts a pair of spectacles, on a chain around his neck, onto his nose. 'Yes, I remember, now.' His gaze drops. 'Dreadful accident. A young boy drowned. I always blamed myself and carried the guilt, even though there was nothing I could have done to prevent it.'

'Tom Maplin, aged ten. Drowned in the river after a blow to the head.' She points at the photo. 'That's Tom, third from the left.' Her sentence is devoid of emotion.

He nods, weakly. 'Yes, that's right. Young Tom.' He clamps the oxygen mask over his nose and mouth and takes four deep rasping breaths, then removes it. 'Inspector, I'm not sure how I can help you. As I said, I have had no contact with Selwyn Morgan, nor Bishop John Wilkes for over thirty years. As for The Acorn Fellowship, well, it was de-registered not long after young Tom's death. Up until that point in my life, I had been involved with the church and various philanthropic organisations. After the incident, I focused on my career and expanding my private practice.'

Prisha considers raising the allegations Blake Baldwin made to her, but resists, despite her temptation. Henry Blenheim was incapable of carrying out the murders, but it doesn't necessarily mean he isn't involved in some other way.

'The autopsy on Tom was carried out by a junior doctor, Stuart Hartley. You were also in attendance. Considering Tom was under your care at the camp, and you were the one to find his body, wouldn't you consider your attendance at the autopsy a conflict of interest?'

His jowls harden as his top teeth clamp down on his bottom lip. 'I'm not sure I care for your inference, inspector. Are you questioning my integrity as a physician, or are you hinting at something more sinister?'

His outward appearance may paint a picture of a frail old man in terminal decline, but his mind is still sharp, answering a question with a question.

Prisha knows the game. 'I'm asking you why you were in attendance at the autopsy.'

The oxygen mask returns to his face for a moment as his bony chest heaves and falls. 'I was purely there in an advisory capacity to ensure the junior doctor carried out the procedure correctly. I had no contact with the cadaver and no input into the autopsy report.'

'Why you though? Why not another pathologist?'

Frustrated, he shakes his head. 'It's half a lifetime ago. I cannot recall the exact details of why I was called upon, but I assume it was because of staffing levels and availability.

Sometimes... needs must. I must say, I find your line of questioning bizarre. You're investigating the recent murder of two men who I haven't seen since 1985, and yet all you've talked about is the unfortunate death of a young boy.'

'Tom Maplin, aged ten.'

'Yes! I'm well aware of the boy's name.'

Prisha offers him a perfunctory smile. 'Moving on; the young man kneeling in front of the boys in the photograph is Sebastian Thorne, also known as Cyclone in those days. When was the last time you had any contact with him?'

He peers intently at the image, his lips imperceptibly curling into a slight smile. 'Ah, yes. Cyclone. There was nothing that young man couldn't put his hand to. A natural born craftsman. I'm not in the least bit surprised he made a success of himself. A pleasant disposition.' He hands the photograph back.

'The last time you saw him?' Prisha prompts.

'I haven't seen Sebastian since the camp.'

'1985?'

'Yes.'

Rising, she drops the photo into her bag. 'Thank you for your time, Doctor Blenheim,' she states, placing her card on the table. 'If you think of anything which might be pertinent to my investigation, no matter how trivial, then please contact me.'

———◦———

Doctor Blenheim was evasive, leaving Prisha uncertain whether his reticence stemmed from declining health and a fading memory or a deliberate attempt to obscure a chapter of his past he believed was long ago buried.

Housekeepers, on the other hand, are a different matter. That's why she's sitting in the large kitchen whilst Mrs Allardyce brews tea.

'As far as you can recall, Doctor Blenheim never mentioned the names Selwyn Morgan or Bishop John Wilkes in all the time you've been here?'

Mrs Allardyce pours steaming water from the kettle into the teapot and gives it a gentle stir with a teaspoon before replacing the lid. She places the teapot in front of Prisha on the kitchen table and readies two cups and saucers.

'No, the names don't a ring a bell. That's not to say he didn't mention them, it's just that if he did, then I can't remember. Milk, sugar?'

'No, thanks. Black's fine.' She pulls two photographs of Selwyn Morgan, and Bishop Wilkes from an envelope and slides them across to the housekeeper.

She studies them briefly and shakes her head. 'Can't say I've ever seen either man before. And these are the men who were murdered?'

'Yes. They were associates of Doctor Blenheim back in the eighties.'

She frowns, concerned. 'Oh dear, you don't suspect the doctor is in danger, do you?'

'I'm not sure. But when I return to the station, I'll discuss the situation with my chief inspector. It may be prudent to have an officer on the grounds for the next few nights between sunset and sunrise.'

Alarm erupts across the housekeeper's face. 'Really?'

Prisha smiles. 'Just precautionary, Mrs Allardyce. They can park up discreetly and keep an eye on the place. If surveillance does go ahead, I'd downplay it to Doctor Blenheim. No point causing him undue stress.'

'Yes, of course.'

'Have you noticed anyone suspicious hanging around or anything untoward happen recently?'

Pouring the tea, she purses her lips and sighs. 'No. Life just plods on around here. Days blend into weeks, months into years. It wasn't always like that, though. The doctor was quite gregarious when younger. He had a large circle of friends, some very influential. He threw some spectacular parties back in the day. But that's many years ago, before he retired, and prior to when his ailments were diagnosed.'

'What exactly is wrong with him?'

'He has chronic obstructive pulmonary disease, hence the oxygen. He was a chain smoker in his younger days. The irony, eh?'

'I noticed he has the shakes?'

Mrs Allardyce takes a seat and cradles her tea. 'Parkinson's. Early stages.'

'Do you administer his medication?'

'No. A nurse calls in each evening about seven. She ensures he's taken his medication and checks the oxygen levels and flow rate. Makes him a cup of tea, then locks up and leaves.'

'I take it he's a bachelor?'

'Yes. He was never that interested in the fairer sex.' Her words hang in the air.

'You mean he's gay?'

Recoiling like a cut snake, she pouts, and turns her nose up as though a bad smell has entered the room. 'I wouldn't know, inspector. What consenting adults wish to get up to behind closed doors is none of my business.'

Prisha internally chides herself for being so leaden-footed. Blowing at her tea, she takes a delicate taste.

'That's so clean and refreshing. I noticed you use tea leaves, not teabags?'

'Call me old-fashioned, but the bags really don't do tea justice. It must be loose leaf or nothing, as far as I'm concerned.'

'I think I'm a convert.' Mrs Allardyce relaxes a fraction. 'Has Doctor Blenheim any living relatives?'

A slight nod of the head. 'One older sister, Joan. She lives in Grassington. I wouldn't say they were particularly close, though.'

Prisha makes a few notes. 'And is Joan married?'

'She's a widow. Her husband died, oh, twenty-odd years ago, maybe longer. A bit too fond of the drink, by all accounts. I never met him, although Joan does visit occasionally.'

'And what's Joan's surname?'

'Hargreaves.'

Prisha jots the name down without much thought, then stares at it for some reason she cannot fathom.

*It's a common enough last name, especially in the north of England.*

A niggle, akin to the light touch of a Nightingale's feather, teases her memory.

'Hargreaves,' she drawls slowly. 'Can you remember what Joan's husband did for a living?' She isn't even sure why she asked the question.

'He was one of yours.'

'One of mine?'

'Yes. A police officer. A detective. DCI Jack Hargreaves. I believe he was stationed at York.'

# 29

Superintendent Anne Banks guards the police budget as if it were her own money. It is one of her many responsibilities. If she allowed all requests for overtime, additional resources, and the hiring of outside experts, her fiscal budget would be in tatters before the end of the first quarter. And that's why she is offering Prisha her most severe scowl.

'I'm not convinced,' she replies curtly. 'Selwyn Morgan and John Wilkes were friends. Their deaths appear to be related. But Doctor Blenheim has had no contact with the deceased since the 1980s. Your only connection between the three men is an old photograph and some misgivings about the pathology report on a boy whose death was recorded as accidental, and a tenuous link between Blenheim and his brother-in-law, DCI Jack Hargreaves. I think you're barking up the wrong tree, inspector.'

Prisha throws a glance at Frank, her eyes imploring him for support.

He places his pen on the desk and rises from his seat. 'Anne, this is a dynamic situation and even though we haven't joined all the dots yet, it doesn't mean our line of inquiry is invalid. I'm with Prisha on this one. I believe the recent deaths are connected to Happy Camp in some way. If we do nothing and Blenheim is the next victim, then it's going to be a bad look. I don't know how much longer we can keep this out of the media. At the moment, all they know is that two elderly men have died, and their deaths are being treated as suspicious. We know the killer only operates in the dead of night, so a single officer on guard between say six in the evening and eight in the morning should suffice. It doesn't have to be around the clock.'

Anne taps her foot on the carpet, clearly agitated. 'And how long for? A couple of days, a week, a month? That's the problem, you see; once you implement a strategy, it's very difficult to terminate it until a result is achieved.'

Prisha clenches her fists, noting the first sign of weakness in the superintendent's words.

'I don't think it would be for long, ma'am. The killer struck late Sunday night, and late Wednesday night. It appears they are in a hurry.'

'And by placing an officer on the ground, won't we scare the killer off? Then they could play a very long waiting game.'

'Ma'am, we are making headway each day. This will buy us more time. I think a week from now we'll know a lot more.'

Anne pouts and takes a deep breath. 'A week?'

Prisha doesn't want to put a timeframe on it, but she realises the superintendent has bowed ever so slightly in the wind. Best not push it.

'Yes, ma'am.'

'I'll authorise four days. From 6 pm until 6 am. And for the first shift, you'll have to use one of your own team. I'll speak with the sergeant and organise for a uniform to take the second shift.' She rises from her seat, smooths her jacket down and heads to the door. 'After four days, we'll review the situation. And inspector, a word of caution; your investigation is supposed to be focused on the recent deaths of two elderly men, not on what may, or may not have happened at an outdoor retreat almost forty years ago. I suggest you review the case so far and re-calibrate.' As she pulls at the door handle, she half turns her head. 'Frank, keep me updated.'

'Yes, Anne.'

They watch on as the superintendent marches briskly across the incident room and disappears.

'It's like fighting a battle on two fronts,' Prisha laments.

Frank nods sagely. 'Aye. The longer you do the job, you'll come to realise that politics plays a big part. But you got what you wanted, so take it as a win. Who are you going to use for surveillance?'

'Dinkel is my only option. I can't afford to lose Zac to nightshift, and he's a young family to attend to.'

'I agree. Dinkel can't get into too much mischief, and it will be good experience for the lad. But walk him through what's required. He's one of those types who needs to be led by the hand, initially. But he's a quick learner. You'll need Doctor Blenheim's permission to be on the grounds and give a heads up to the housekeeper, gardener, and nurse as to what's happening, but play it down.'

---

Sitting in the comfort of a Skoda Octavia, Dinkel is feeling rather pleased with himself. It's his second covert operation since joining CID. First there was the dogging operation, which quite frankly, he'd rather draw a dark veil over, and now, on guard to intercept a serial psychopathic killer. As the full enormity of his responsibilities materialises, his tinge of excitement is slowly eaten up by a niggling dread. He takes his mind off gruesome encounters by flicking through his notebook and reading aloud the instructions Prisha gave him.

'Nurse from VitaCare arriving about seven to administer medication to Doctor Blenheim. She has her own key for entry. Once the nurse has left, take a walk around the outside of the house, and check all doors and windows are secure, then close the main gates. Every forty minutes conduct a perimeter walk around the house and gardens. Anything untoward, then call for back-up immediately. Hand over to next shift at midnight. Do NOT fall asleep.'

Reassured, he scans the radio until he homes in on a local talkback show. He pulls a flask from his backpack and pours himself a cup of milky coffee, adjusts the car seat into a more comfortable position, then relaxes and stares out at the clear blue sky and the magnificent gardens.

Dark clouds gather as the unmistakable rumble of thunder rolls in from the North Sea. Then the rain arrives, introducing itself with a few heavy drops that splatter on the car roof and windscreen. As if sidetracked, it stops instantly... for about thirty seconds, before it returns with a ferocious intensity that drowns out the inane prattling of the radio host, nasally emanating from the car speakers.

Dinkel experiences a shard of unease as he stares morosely at the puddles swiftly forming on the gravel drive. He checks the time; 6:40 pm.

'Hmm... typical. Just as I was about to do a walk around. I'll give it ten minutes to see if it stops,' he mumbles to himself.

He doesn't notice the car until it pulls up alongside the house a good twenty yards away from his vehicle. He turns the engine on and flicks at the windscreen wipers to gain a better view, but the rain is so intense it's like peering through the bottom of a glass bottle. Eventually, he heaves a sigh of relief as a figure emerges from the car. A woman, wearing a face mask and carrying a small doctor's bag, waves at him as she drapes a long coat over her head and scurries down the garden path towards the kitchen door.

'The nurse,' he mumbles, eyeballing the time again. 'She's a little early. I'd have waited in the car if I were her.'

Relaxing, he pulls a cheese and tomato sandwich from his backpack and turns the radio up.

This time Dinkel receives no wave from the nurse as she rushes back to her car and hastily departs. As she does so, the rain eases as the menacing, heavy clouds move northward. A splinter of blue sky and a shard of sunlight create a mini rainbow overhead. Lowering the car window, he sticks his arm outside to gauge the rainfall—nothing but light drizzle.

'May as well do a circuit of the house and make sure all's tickety boo,' he mutters as he turns the engine off and steps outside. The air is clean and fresh, and despite the recent inclement weather, it's surprisingly mild. As he checks the handles on all the doors, and critically assesses every closed and locked window of the large country house, he revels in the delightful scents the rain has kicked up. Floral bouquets mingle with a warm, earthy scent, which imbues him with a sense of peace. Having completed a perimeter walk, he heads down the long driveway towards the huge, ornate, cast-iron gates to close them for the night. As he nears, he's more than a little surprised to see a car enter from the roadway and trundle towards him.

'Odd?' he muses. Standing directly in the path of the vehicle, he raises one palm in the air to indicate the car to halt. He strolls to the driver's side as the car window slides down and an identity card is thrust his way. As he spots the green nurse's uniform, the arse drops out of his pants.

'I'm Nurse Spencer, here to administer Doctor Blenheim's nightly medication.'

———◆———

The scene is similar, but not identical, to the previous murders. The most noticeable difference is that Doctor Blenheim is not outside, impaled on the lawn. The drawing room-cum-bedroom was his place of execution. But in keeping with the previous deaths, he is strewn, crucifix fashion, tent pegs driven through both palms, one through the forehead above the branded motif, genitalia resting in a bloody clump above and to the side of him on the blood-soaked carpet.

Frank stares at Prisha before they both discreetly focus their eyes onto Dinkel, who is standing at the back of the room as white as a sheet, shaking slightly.

'What a bloody mess,' Frank whispers. 'This is going to go down about as well as a case of dysentery in a Jacuzzi with the superintendent. What did you say to him?'

'What could I say? Now's not the time to berate him and put him through the ringer. He's in mild shock.'

'What about an ID on the first nurse, and vehicle?'

'He's vague. It was teeming it down. Didn't get a numberplate and his description of the nurse is generic, to say the least.'

'Female?'

'He thinks so.'

Frank's head nearly explodes. 'He bloody thinks so!'

'As I said, visibility was very poor. He said the nurse wore a skirt and a face mask and threw a coat over her head to protect her from the torrential rain.'

'Therefore, it could have been a man in disguise?'

'Possibly.'

'Height, weight, any distinguishing features?'

Prisha shakes her head, weary and thoroughly pissed off. 'Average height, average weight. That's all he could give me. As for the car, he thinks it may have been a Ford Focus or Ford Fiesta, or similar. Possibly black, dark blue, grey, or dark green.'

'Bugger me backwards. Not exactly textbook CID, is it?'

'No, it's not. Another case of confirmation bias. He was expecting a nurse to arrive, and she did. It played into his expectations, and therefore why would he show much interest in the event?'

'Because he's a bloody copper, that's why.'

'You're preaching to the converted, Frank. But as I said, now is not the time for reprimands. The killer is brazen and must have had knowledge of Blenheim's routine. At least that gives us some more lines of enquiry.'

'How did she... he... bloody hell! How did the nurse get into the house?'

'Not sure. There's no sign of a forced entry, and Dinkel checked all the doors and windows were locked when he first arrived.'

'You said Blenheim lived a pretty solitary life. Who else frequents the house?'

'A housekeeper, a gardener, a part-time cleaner, and an elderly sister who lives in Grassington. All would have been aware of his nightly visits from a nurse, and of course, the nurse herself, who is a contractor to a private medical company.'

Frank is distracted as he gazes through the window at the caravan of SOCO vans rolling along the driveway, followed by Superintendent Bank's car.

He's not in the best of moods. 'Sweet Mary, Joseph, Jesus, and Judas bloody Priest. I need her like a hole in the head. Right, leave the Super to me. You've got enough on your plate. Get Dinkel out of here, the back way. Tell him to write up his report, then make sure he sods off home and gets a good night's rest. Maybe he'll remember something in the morning more illuminating than a car of many colours and a person who may have been a woman... or a man. Strike a light and give me strength!'

# 30

# Sunday 30th April

Zac is surprised to see Dinkel at his desk so early on a Sunday morning. As he strolls across the room, he unzips his bomber jacket and pulls his woolly hat off.

'Morning, Dinkel. Have you shat the bed?'

Dinkel glances at him, jaded, worry lines etched into his brow. 'Couldn't sleep. I suppose you've heard?'

Zac pulls up a chair and sits alongside him. 'Aye, I've heard.'

'Go on then, get it over with.'

'What?'

'You know what. Your quips and piss-taking. Let's get it out of the way.'

Zac rubs at his recently manicured beard, thoughtfully. 'No, not today. You fucked up big style. Last thing you need is me reminding you of the fact that you dropped a right clanger.'

'You just did.'

Zac drapes an arm around his colleague's shoulder. 'Believe me, in the grand scheme of things, this is a blip. A rather large, Zeppelin sized fucking blip, but a blip nonetheless.'

'You're not helping.'

'I can assure you I've made bigger fuck-ups... well, maybe not quite as big as letting a serial killer walk right past me and claim another victim right under my nose, but you get my point.'

'Thanks for your honesty.' He lifts his head from his computer screen and stares forlornly out of the window. 'What will happen to me? Is my detective career over? Will I go back to uniform? Is it the end of my life in the police?'

Zac chuckles. 'Nah. The worst that will happen is you'll cop a roasting from Prisha, maybe Frank, and then you'll be on the carpet in front of Superintendent Banks. There may be an informal review into protocols and procedures to see where we can improve. Risk assessments, What If scenarios, all the usual bureaucratic nonsense, then the findings will be filed away, never to be seen again. That's how the modern world works. It's not about amending for past events or mitigating for future scenarios. We must be *seen* to be proactive in confronting our failures, even if it's just a pen-pushing exercise in futility.'

Dinkel offers a wistful smile. 'I want to make amends, but I don't know how.'

Zac rises and pats him on the shoulder. 'We have a triple murder investigation to solve. Do what you do best and drill down into the boring shit that everyone else tries to avoid. Right, time for a brew and then you're coming with me.'

'Where are we going?'

'To the homeless shelter run by the church on the edge of town. I've had a tip off from my snout. Apparently, one of our remaining boys from Happy Camp is a frequent visitor.'

'Which one?'

'Malcolm Pearce, the guy who got out of prison a few months back.'

---

The Beacon of Hope, nestled within a repurposed Victorian schoolhouse, with a red brick facade and large arched windows, is an impressive and inviting building. It serves as a sanctuary for the homeless. Open seven days a week, it offers nightly accommodation for thirty individuals and serves an evening meal and breakfast. Beyond these basic amenities that most take for granted, it offers a supportive environment with counselling and support groups focusing on mental health and addiction. Legal aid services are available twice a month, assisting people with legal concerns. Additionally, a local nurse conducts weekly visits, ensuring ongoing medical care. The shelter also benefits from strong partnerships with local businesses, offering comprehensive job training and placement programs, helping individuals to rebuild and move on with their lives.

Zac and Dinkel loiter in the hallway and assess the situation. To their left, in a large dining hall, a dozen or so patrons are already tucking into a hearty breakfast. Directly ahead is the kitchen and serving counter. There's an atmosphere of conviviality, as hushed conversations are intermittently interrupted by peals of laughter. Zac spots a man in a dog collar directing proceedings behind the counter in an orderly but genial manner.

'That's Reverend Appleby,' Zac states out of the corner of his mouth. 'We need to be discreet.' Having caught the reverend's attention, Zac nods his head to the side, indicating towards a small side office. The reverend makes his excuses to the kitchen staff and heads to the office, ushering Zac and Dinkel inside.

'Sergeant Stoker, it's been a while. Have you come to help out in the shelter? We are always in need of more hands on deck.'

Zac smiles and juts a thumb sideways. 'This is DC Dinkel, and as much as I'd like to help out in the kitchen, we're here on official business.'

The reverend folds his arms. 'I see. What can I do for you?'

Dinkel pulls a mugshot from his inside pocket and hands it over. 'Have you seen this man recently? Malcolm Pearce.'

Reverend Appleby is dutifully concerned as he studies, then returns, the photograph. 'Is he in trouble?'

Zac shrugs. 'Not sure yet. We simply want to ask him a few questions in relation to a spate of recent deaths.'

'Since being released from prison, Malcolm has made great strides forward in rehabilitating himself.'

Zac's patience is wavering. 'I'm pleased to hear that, reverend, but is he here?'

'Sergeant, as you're aware, this is a place of sanctuary for the less fortunate in society. If I let the police use the facilities to hound and harass my patrons, I will lose their trust.'

'No one's here to harass anyone. As I said, it's a couple of routine questions. I have no intention of throwing my weight around, but the alternative is a search warrant and a bevy of leaden-footed boys and girls in blue stomping all over the place. So, what's it to be?'

Outmanoeuvred, and already running out of time before he takes the Sunday morning church service in an hour's time, the reverend backs down.

'Wait here. I'll make some enquiries.'

Dinkel busies himself studying the pamphlets and notices stuck to a corkboard. 'It warms the heart, doesn't it?' he declares.

'The electric chair? Aye, so I've heard,' Zac replies, distracted as he gazes through a crack in the doorway, keeping an eye on the reverend.

'No, I meant the way humanity can rally around to help the less fortunate in society. I think it's wonderful.'

'If you say so.'

'It's a higher purpose, a calling.'

'Aye.' Zac spots the reverend melt into an alcove with a tall, gangly individual.

'I'd like to help out at some point, you know, to make society a better place.'

'You're supposed to be doing that already by putting low-life scum behind bars. It's your job,' Zac murmurs.

'No, what I meant was...'

'You wheedling bastard,' Zac mumbles.

'I'm not sure that's warranted. I was merely saying...'

'Not you. The reverend.'

'Can you say that about a man of the cloth?'

'I just did. Now shut the fuck up and go and wait at the front gate. I think the reverend has tipped off our suspect.'

Zac slinks from the office and hugs the shadowed walls and makes his way to the alcove.

The reverend materialises from the dark. 'Ah, sergeant, I was just talking with one of my volunteers and we haven't seen Malcolm, for, oh, at least a week. However, if and when he should materialise...'

'Save it for the big man upstairs, reverend,' Zac replies as he spots the door behind him. He forcibly pushes the reverend aside and enters the room. Spare tables and chairs, and an assortment of clothing and bedding, are stacked up in the small anteroom. In the far corner, an external door is ajar. He manages to throw a glare at the reverend before rushing across the room. Outside is what would have been the old school playground. It's enclosed by a tall brick wall topped with black coping stones. Wheelie bins are pushed up against the wall, which stand next to an old, wooden garden shed. Zac rushes around to the front of the old school and spots Dinkel manning the front gate.

'You seen him?'

Dinkel shakes his head. 'No.'

'Wait there,' he commands as he sprints to the back of the building again. Slowing, he approaches the wheelie bins. 'Come out, come out, wherever you are, little piggy,' he sings in a lilting Scottish brogue. He lifts the lid on the first, then second wheelie bin and peers inside. 'Recycling and more recycling,' he states. Lifting the lid on the third bin, he adds, 'Ah, general rubbish.' He stares down into wild, terrified eyes. 'Malcom Pearce, funny meeting you here. Not my idea of five-star accommodation. What's the wi-fi connection like?'

'Mr Stoker.'

He slams the lid shut, grips the handle, pulls it back and wheels the bin towards the shed, where he yanks open the door. Tipping the bin forward, he gives it a vicious kick with the bottom of his boot, spilling the contents, including the suspect, out into the tiny hut. He pulls the door shut behind him.

'Rubbish in, rubbish out.'

Malcolm Pearce ungainly struggles to his feet as he wipes discarded slops from his already grim looking clothing.

'Mr Stoker, what's all this about? I promise you I'm going straight. I'm even off the smack.'

Zac grabs his arm and ruffles the cuffs of his jacket up. 'Of course you are. What are the needle marks? Voluntary COVID booster jabs?'

'That's from ages ago.'

'Yeah, and that's why you've still got bruising.' He quickly searches the jacket pockets and pulls out a small plastic coin bag and studies the contents. 'Four rocks. Naughty, naughty, Malcolm. Looks like crack.'

'It's personal use only, Mr Stoker. For when I have a bad day.'

Zac spins him around and digs his hand into the front pocket of his jeans and pulls a wad of rolled up notes out.

'Personal use, eh? There must be over six hundred quid here. I didn't realise being on the dole was so lucrative these days.' Grabbing him by the scruff of the collar, he violently pushes him backwards, where he lands on top of a stack of bagged compost. 'Right, don't fuck me around. The rocks and money are enough for me to charge you with intent to supply. With your record, you'd be straight back inside. So, play a little game with me, and depending on your answers, I may be able to turn a blind eye.'

Malcolm winces and readjusts his jacket. 'What do you want?'

'Three names from the past; Bishop John Wilkes, Selwyn Morgan, and Doctor Henry Blenheim. Tell me about them?'

Pearce is suitably confused. 'What?'

'You fucking heard!'

'I haven't heard those names since I was a kid.'

'You haven't seen any of them recently?'

'No, of course I 'aven't. We don't really mix in the same circles.'

Zac grabs his wrist and bends it down. 'Don't get smart, sunshine. No witnesses in here.'

'Arrgh! Let go! You're gonna break my fucking wrist.'

Zac releases him and pulls the Happy Camp photo from inside his jacket pocket and thrusts it upon Pearce.

'Tell me about Happy Camp?' he snarls.

Pearce studies the photo with a mixture of utter confusion and fear. 'There's nowt to tell. I went there as a kid a few times. Fucking hated the place. Those bastards made it a nightmare.'

'Who?'

'The reverend, doctor, and Morgan.'

'Why?'

'Why do you think? They were all psychos, but the doctor was the worst.'

'Were you abused?'

'Oh, aye. They'd knock the shit out of us for the slightest little thing.'

'Sexual abuse?'

Pearce averts his gaze onto the dusty wooden floor of the hut. 'I'm saying nowt.'

'Fair enough. Have you spoken with anyone recently who mentioned any of them?'

He grimaces. 'No. I swear to God. To be honest, if you hadn't brought their names up, I would never have thought about them ever again, and for good reason.'

Zac points at two boys in the photo. 'Do you remember these two?'

Pearce squints. 'Vaguely. Erm... Mike Ross, also known as Rosco. And this one, the Freak, he was called. Ted...erm, Ted Fairchild, I think.'

Zac is more than intrigued. 'Why was he called the Freak?'

'He was odd.'

'In what way?'

'You know, weak, effeminate. Never got involved in the games. Quiet, shy.'

'Christ, just because a lad's quiet and shy, you gave him the nickname, the Freak.'

Pearce retaliates, angrily. 'I didn't give him that name. It was the adults who started calling him that.'

'Why?'

'I don't fucking know!'

'Have you seen Mike Ross or Ted Fairchild recently?'

'No. I haven't seen any of those kids for years. We weren't close or anything. We were selected to go on that camp by the adults. It just so happened we were all at the same orphanage for a while.'

Zac taps a finger on the adult kneeling down. 'And what about this bloke, Cyclone?'

He shrugs. 'He was all right, I guess.'

'Did he abuse you?'

'No.'

'What about the others?'

'I don't know... I don't think so. He was always busy working on the renovations for the barn.'

'Do you know who he is?'

He shakes his head in confusion. 'Just knew him as Cyclone.'

Zac snatches the photo back, and hands the wad of notes, and bag of drugs over. 'Does the name Sebastian Thorne mean anything to you?'

'No. Should it? Are we done, here?'

'Aye. We're done for the moment. If I find out you've been spinning me a web of lies, I'll be back.' He pulls open the door and glances back. 'You know, it's never too late. Why don't you get yourself into rehab, then spend the money on a set of decent clothes and look for a job. Reverend Appleby set up this refuge to help people get back on track. All you're doing is using it as a free bed and breakfast.'

Pearce stares past Zac, contrite. 'Yeah, I know.'

'If you don't change, your body will either give up on you, or you'll piss the wrong person off. Either way, you'll end up on a slab before your time. Why not take the last twenty, thirty years you have left and live a good life?'

'I'm not in control of my life, Mr Stoker.'

'Then who is?'

'My addiction.'

———◇———

Prisha blinks and repeats the question. 'Are you absolutely certain?'

'One hundred per cent,' Zac replies.

'How can you be so sure?'

'A copper's nose. Malcolm Pearce knows nothing about the deaths of Wilkes, Blenheim, or Morgan. And I don't think he relished remembering those names. He didn't admit as much, but I'm certain he was sexually abused at Happy Camp. He's certainly not a criminal mastermind. He can barely keep body and soul together.'

Prisha turns to the whiteboard, picks up a pen and strikes a line through the name Malcolm Pearce, then stares at the remaining names.

'And then there were three: Sebastian Thorne, Mike Ross, and Ted Fairchild. Which one is our killer?' she muses. 'The question is rhetorical. We need to investigate each one without presumption.'

Dinkel winces nervously as Frank enters the incident room. His appearance is of a man who would rather be on his allotment than cleaning up another mess.

'Okay, Dinkel, the Super is ready to see you.'

The colour drains from Dinkel's face as he rises from his seat like a man who is to be escorted to the gallows. 'Sir.'

Frank stands in front of him and winks. 'Her bark is worse than her bite. Listen solemnly; nod in all the right places; throw in a few well-timed and contrite ma'ams; and at the end, promise you'll not be a naughty boy again. Easy as one, two, three.'

'Sir.'

'Go on then, what are you waiting for? And remember, the fear of pain is often far worse than the pain. Take your earbashing, then put this episode to bed. I can't have my officers navel-gazing and feeling sorry for themselves.'

# 31

Sebastian Thorne studies the short, perfunctory email for a second time, then clicks on the attachment. He moves closer as the image fills the screen. Reaching across the desk, he picks up the sgian dubh, and spins it around and around in his left hand, contemplatively. A highly intelligent man, he often becomes bored with the machinations of big business. He likes to play games, mentally jousting with foes and friends alike. The thrill he derives from outwitting and outmanoeuvring opponents is an elixir. And now he has a new puzzle to tantalise him. Instead of fearing the unknown, his razor-sharp intellect embraces the challenge. He trusts no one, not even his closest allies. Some may call it paranoia, but it's only paranoia if your assumptions are wrong.

He relaxes back in his leather chair and gazes at the photo of Happy Camp on his laptop screen. The email address from the sender is anonymous, a random Gmail address anyone could concoct within a minute or two.

But he already knows who the architect of the game is. The photograph is supposed to be blackmail, that's what the sender wants him to think, and it is; but that is the secondary purpose. What the anonymous blackmailer could never have anticipated is that Thorne has already deduced their main motive—entrapment, followed by an ignominious fall from grace, his political aspirations in tatters. But he's already one step ahead.

The surge of adrenaline fires his mind as a rush of excitement makes him heady.

He grins, still spinning the dagger. 'Okay, you want to play a game, then let's play the ultimate game. I'll wager everything I have against everything you have. The winner takes all.'

He paces back and forth for twenty minutes, imagining every conceivable scenario. Eventually, he stops at the window and stares out onto the car park below. Something niggles at him.

'It's inconceivable they came across that photo by accident. It's private, or at least it was until the recent murders. Now the police have copies. The question is, how would it benefit the police by sending Amanda Chan a copy of Happy Camp?'

The conundrum occupies him for a few minutes until his eyes are distracted as the small, grey-coloured vehicle enters the car park and reverses into a space. He smiles down benevolently on his PA as she exits the car and strides towards the entrance, always on time, always reliable. His thoughts return to the puzzle.

'The police? No, that doesn't add up. There's no earthly benefit they could obtain from such an action. Then who?' His attention drifts again onto his PA as she nears the entrance, juggling a cup of coffee, a laptop, and a briefcase as she searches for her electronic passkey in her pocket.

'Hmm... an interesting theory, Sebastian,' he mutters to himself. 'It would explain how Ms Chan came to know so much about my business dealings. Enemies often stand in plain sight. Yet it's the dagger hidden in a friend's cloak that one must fear the most,' he adds as he presses the pad of his thumb down onto the tip of the dagger. A bead of blood slowly oozes forth. He puts his thumb in his mouth and sucks as a wry smirk creeps across his handsome features.

The lift door swishes open as Dora marches into the office, her usual unruffled demeanour replaced by a furrowed brow and worry lines around the eyes.

'Ah, Dora, you seem troubled?' Thorne enquires, his mind still in a state of high excitement, his body a peaceful oasis.

'I've just had a call from Ms Chan, sir.'

He slides into his chair behind the desk. 'Really? Well, we have been expecting it. You anticipated she'd increase her request to one hundred and fifty thousand pounds. Were you accurate in your assumption?'

Embarrassed, she removes her spectacles and hastily cleans the lenses on her cardigan.

'No, Sebastian. I was way off the mark.'

'You appear flustered, Dora, which is out of character,' he replies, swivelling nonchalantly in his chair to address her. 'What are her demands?'

'A quarter of a million pounds, carried in a Mackenzie Gladstone Bag, and delivered by you to her flat tonight at 7:30.'

Thorne nods thoughtfully as he pieces the puzzle together, now certain of his theory.

'My, my, she's certainly lifted the ante. She also has excellent taste in her choice of holdalls. Did she proffer any explanation for such an exorbitant sum?'

'Not really. All she said was that you can afford it.'

'And how do you feel about this development?'

'I don't like it, not one little bit, sir.'

'Why not? We were the ones who made the first move with our initial offer. We always assumed she'd raise the stakes.'

'But not by so much. I think we should call her bluff and offer one-fifty. Take it or leave it. After all, she really has nothing on you. As you've said on many occasions, she's a nuisance, nothing more, nothing less. If she won't agree to our offer, then I think we should implement Plan B.'

Thorne ponders her response. 'Ah, yes. Pan B. Remind me again?'

'At arm's length, we fund an already established social media influencer to wage a campaign to discredit her.'

'Oh, yes. I remember now.' He rises from his chair and slowly paces back and forth, then halts. 'I think not. We'll stick to the original plan. Quarter of a million is not to be sniffed at, but in the grand scheme of things it's neither here nor there.'

'As you wish, sir. I'll inform her of your decision.' She turns to leave.

'Not so fast, Dora. Take a seat.'

Slightly unnerved at his response and his request, she slips into a chair. 'Sir?'

Still pacing, he begins. 'I have a confession to make. It's not been easy for me to do, but I've kept you in the dark about something.'

'Oh?'

'Over the last two years, I've built an alliance with the Labour Party, and Evan Tudor in particular. However, this has been a ruse. A way to lift my public profile and present my credentials as not only a successful businessman, but as a caring individual with ethics who feels a profound conviction to help the less fortunate in our crumbling society.'

'Yes, I'm well aware of your strategy, Sebastian.'

'Hear me out. Behind the scenes, I've been working with handpicked experts who have been sworn to secrecy.'

'I... I'm not sure I understand, sir.'

He turns and smiles at her. 'I have no intention of entering politics under a Labour banner, nor a Tory one, for that matter. I intend to launch my own party. I believe that within two election cycles, we will win a majority and be in power. With my public persona, I appeal to the left and the right. To the downtrodden and the aspirational. What do you think?'

'I'm not sure what I think, sir. It's a bit of a bombshell. I hold no reservations in knowing you will give it your all, but even though you are well known in some quarters, you are not universally...'

'Recognised?'

'Well, yes.'

'Fear not. The world has changed, Dora. As we've seen in recent years, in the political arena, people can get away with anything by simply calling out their detractors' accusations as *fake* news. Their support doesn't diminish. In fact, it usually increases. There is no truth anymore. Some people will go to their graves believing the earth is flat.' He strolls to the window and gazes out. 'The old adage, no news is good news, is dead. Today, any publicity is good publicity as it puts you in front of people's eyes. Attention span is diminishing. Deep thought and contemplation are dead and buried. The twenty-four-seven news cycle is the new king.' He turns and smiles. 'And everyone should bow to the new king... even me.'

'I see,' she replies, baffled by his cryptic address.

'You can return Ms Chan's call and tell her I agree to her demands, and I'll be at her flat at the designated time. During the hand-over, I will make it clear in no uncertain terms this is the end game. If she breaks the agreement, then I will grind her into the ground.'

---

Dora follows Sebastian Thorne out of the automatic revolving doors. They stop and face each other on the bitumen of the car park, as the overcast conditions usher in an early twilight.

She offers him a reassuring smile. 'Tonight, your tumour will be removed, Mr Thorne. Metaphorically speaking, of course.'

He offers a pre-rehearsed nervous laugh in response. 'Yes. But tumours can grow back.'

'I don't think so. She's gained her pound of flesh, or so she thinks. Just another armchair warrior with a bit more brains than the rest. Quarter of a million pounds is a lot of money. I'm sure she'll find better things to do than spend her time trawling the internet and posting vindictive, half-baked, conspiracy theories about you. Anyway, if she does come back for a second bite of the cherry, we have Plan B.'

'Yes. You're right, as usual.' He falters, deep in thought. 'Do you know what galls me the most about this sordid episode?'

'What?'

'The insistence the cash be placed in a Mackenzie Gladstone Bag. A British classic for decades. That's another thousand pounds.'

Dora stifles a snigger. 'I've told you before, Mr Thorne—don't sweat the small stuff.'

He huffs and sighs deeply. 'I know, I know. It just irks me.'

'You definitely have the money in the car?'

'Yes. In the boot.' He straightens. 'Okay, how do I look?'

'Like a businessman on top of his game. A man in control, as always, Mr Thorne.'

He hesitates and gazes at the ground. 'One must be stoic in situations like this, Dora. We cannot control what life throws our way, but what we can control is how we react. That is the test. I envisage tumultuous times ahead for both of us. When you have a huge wave bearing down on you, don't try to out-swim it, surf the wave onto the shore.'

Dora is used to his platitudes, wrapped in prosaic language. It's become part of his public persona and has created an almost messianic aura around him, and yet... something about his words tonight unnerves her.

'Indeed,' she replies, almost sheepishly.

He reciprocates with a faint smile. 'Right, I shall go and do the deed, and rid myself of this troublesome priestess. One stone... two birds.'

Watching the car disappear, she feels distinctly uneasy. 'What does he mean—two birds?'

# 32

Sebastian parks his Range Rover on the side street, opposite to Amanda Chan's address in one of Whitby's less well-heeled areas. He adjusts the rearview mirror, quickly checking his appearance. Exiting the car, he grabs the Gladstone Bag from the boot, presses the fob to lock the doors and strides towards the row of flats, his John Lobb Oxford shoes, unaccustomed to such insalubrious surroundings, squeak in trepidation.

'Hmm... another area for gentrification,' he muses, scanning the dilapidated Victorian era terrace houses. 'Rich for the picking. You see Seb, a silver lining in every cloud.'

Scampering down three stone steps to the basement flat, he regards the scene with disdain. The overgrown, weed infested miniature garden is in a fight to the death with the debris of modern life; fag ends, plastic bottles, fast food wrappers, and syringes sully what could be a magnificent, peaceful sanctuary.

Shaking his head in annoyance, he mutters, 'I had to fight tooth and nail to climb out of squalor. Yet she was born with a silver spoon in her mouth, to the manor born. Now look at us.'

Tilting his head, he sniffs the unmistakable aroma of weed and the distant strains of classical music. He raps hard on the door and waits, his senses tingling in anticipation.

---

Heartbeat thunders, breath - short and rapid. He stumbles over the threshold of the front door, and wipes bile from his mouth on a handkerchief.

His normally acute critical thinking has momentarily abandoned him.

Hesitates, squints into the rapidly fading light. Eyes see terror in the uneasy quiet of the street.

Legs full of jelly, he unsuccessfully tries to take a deep breath, then climbs the steps.

Looks left, then right.

No one.

He half jogs, half strides to his car.

Climbs inside.

Pulls out his mobile phone, hands shaking violently.

Hits the auto-call button for his PA.

'Dora?' he whispers, his mouth dry, throat constricted. The call is answered instantly.

'Mr Thorne, what's wrong?'

'It's gone belly up. She's dead,' he replies, panic coating his words.

'What?'

'Amanda Chan... she's dead.'

'Dead? How?'

'It doesn't matter how. She's dead. Murdered.'

'Calm down, Sebastian! You're not making any sense. The line's bad. You keep dropping out.'

'She's dead! Bloody well dead.'

'Sebastian, I've never heard you like this before. Take a few deep breaths, then tell me what's happened.'

'She's dead.'

Dora pauses. 'Are you certain?'

'Yes, I'm bloody certain!'

'Did you check her pulse?'

'No, of course I didn't check her pulse! She's dead.'

'Okay. Stop saying she's dead. Where are you now?'

'On the opposite side of the street to her flat.'

'Has anyone seen you?' she asks with concern.

'No... I'm not sure. I don't think so. Christ, what a fuck-up,' he laments with a tidal-wave of regret.

'Where's the money?'

'Damn it! I've left it in the flat. I'll need to go back and get it.'

'No, Sebastian, don't! It's too risky. Right, listen to me. Take a moment to regain your composure, then drive sedately back to HQ and park up in the car park and wait for me there. I'll come out to you. We can work this out, but we need clarity of thought.'

Her calming tone reassures him. 'Should I call the police?'

'Say that again. You dropped out.'

'The police; should I call the police?'

'Not yet. We need to assess the implications. Understood?' Her voice is more forceful, like a mother's.

He glances in his wing mirror and spots car headlights approaching. As it nears, he realises it's a police patrol car. 'Damn and blast,' he hisses, slumping down in his seat.

'Sebastian, did you hear me?'

He relaxes as the patrol car hangs a left at a junction and disappears. 'Yes, yes, I heard you.'

With a hint of suspicion in her voice, she says, 'Mr Thorne, answer me this one question; did you kill Amanda Chan?'

The Range Rover rolls into the car park, only dim sidelights showing. The car creeps to the furthest corner, which is engulfed in shadows. He carefully reverses into a parking spot and kills the engine. Thorne HQ emits a soft, bluish light, a beacon of refined tranquillity, in contrast to the ghouls that claw at Sebastian Thorne.

He pulls at the glove box and scrabbles around inside. The cold metal of the hip flask kisses his fingertips. The top comes off with a pop and he nervously takes a swig of the single malt whisky, then coughs violently. It's a rare occurrence when he drinks. But sometimes, needs must. One more sip and he bangs the corked lid into position and returns the flask to the glove box.

'Shit,' he mutters, staring at the revolving doors, thirty feet away. 'Where is she? Should I call again?'

The distant sirens divert his attention. A long wail rises and descends smoothly, but as it increases in volume, it turns into high-pitched yelps, indicating urgency.

'Police cars or ambulance? Calm down, Sebastian. They can't have possibly discovered her body yet.' His assertion does nothing to assuage his raw, aching fear.

The blue flashing lights bounce off the building, and creep stutteringly across the glass facade. He pushes back into the leather upholstery, hoping it will swallow him.

The sirens are now deafening, even louder than his erratic heartbeat.

A squeal of car tyres and three patrol cars, and one unmarked car, screech into the car park and hurtle headlong towards the corner.

'Oh no, how the hell...'

The vehicles corral the Range Rover, blocking any exit.

He recognises the officer who jumps from the Skoda Octavia.

'Sergeant Stoker,' he whispers as his worst nightmare takes another catastrophic turn.

The door is yanked open. He gazes in shock at the stern face as fear morphs into weary defeat.

'Sebastian Thorne, I am arresting you on suspicion of the murder of Amanda Chan. You do not have...'

The Sergeant's words turn to white noise as Sebastian realises this could be the beginning of the end to his glittering career... or maybe not. It was always a high-stakes game he was playing.

'Surf the wave, Sebastian. Surf the wave,' he silently repeats to himself.

As the patrol cars depart the scene with the suspect inside, Zac saunters over to the entrance of Thorne HQ as Dora emerges from the revolving doors, wringing her hands.

Zac smiles. 'Thanks for the tip off, Dora.'

She shrinks back in revulsion. 'I can't believe this has happened. I was torn, I'll admit as much.'

'Torn?'

'Yes. I'm not sure what happened. He was supposed to drop the money off and then leave. When he called me, he was in a panic. I've never heard him like that before. He told me she was dead, murdered.'

'I see,' Zac says, puzzled by events. 'Maybe we should step inside, make a cup of tea and then I can get a statement. Nothing is making sense at the moment.'

Lost in her own private hell, she doesn't hear the words. 'My loyalty to Mr Thorne is beyond reproach. But when I asked him, and he answered, then I was torn, but only for a few seconds.'

'You keep repeating the word torn. Torn between what?'

'My loyalty to Sebastian, and my own conscience; to do the right thing.' She pauses before gazing into Zac's eyes. 'I asked him, you see.'

'Asked him what?'

'I asked if he'd killed Amanda Chan.'

'And his response?'

'He said... I did kill her.'

# 33

# Monday 1st May

The normally measured, alluring persona has evaporated, replaced by confusion and trepidation. Sebastian Thorne is as flustered as a rabbit that's accidentally wandered into a ferret's pen. And who wouldn't be disconcerted?

Police interview rooms are purposely built to contain three key elements: a bare, sterile environment to reduce distractions; hard walls and surfaces to enhance clarity of speech; and lastly, they are designed to strip away any hint of bias or intimidation... unlike a court of law, where legal professionals strut around grandiose chambers in ancient costumes and wigs, putting the fear of God into everyone.

Despite its simplicity, the windowless environment presses down on the uninitiated, like a leaden weight, not too dissimilar to a prison cell.

Could that be a fourth, more sinister reason for the design?

⸺◆⸺

Sebastian Thorne's barrister, *not any old solicitor*, is a legal luminary. He's represented royalty. Only the best for Mr Thorne, for he can afford the best. Not that money should be a factor in the pursuit of justice. Right or wrong, guilty or innocent—wealth and influence should hold no sway. For we are all born equal, just some more equal than others.

Zac finishes reading the caution, then shuffles the manilla folder into position on the white table.

'How did you sleep, Mr Thorne?'

'I've had better nights, but overall, not too bad. Can't say I'm keen on the outfit, though,' he replies, tugging at the standard police issue tracksuit.

'Sorry about that, but your clothes were required by forensics.'

'Yes, I fully understand.'

'I believe your PA is due in soon with a fresh set of clothes for you.'

'Good, good. My wife is overseas at the moment, visiting her family in New Zealand.' Thorne sits upright and clears his throat. 'Before we begin, Sergeant Stoker, I intend to be brutally honest and frank with you. My barrister has advised me to answer none of your questions, but after careful consideration, I don't believe that is the best course of action... at the moment. I'm sure when you hear the full version, *truthful version,* of events, it will become clear that I had no involvement in Amanda Chan's death. I wish to clear this matter up, or at least clear up my involvement in this affair, as quickly as possible. That way you can focus your efforts and resources on apprehending the real culprit.'

His words are music to Zac's ears. Typically, getting a suspect to talk is like trying to wring sweat from a stone.

'Very good. Let's start at the beginning, then, Mr Thorne. The floor is yours.'

Thorne shoots a sideways glance at his barrister, who appears less than impressed his high-profile client is ignoring his sage, and very expensive advice.

'Are you aware of the campaign Amanda Chan has been waging against me? The YouTube videos? Disrupting my media conferences? Chaining herself to fences at construction sites?'

'Yes. We are aware of that.'

Thorne sighs relief 'Good. Now, despite what anyone may think, Ms Chan was a nuisance, not a threat. Her allegations, or inferences against me and my businesses, are complete falsehoods. However, her continued, and sustained vendetta was becoming problematic for me.'

'How so?'

He shuffles uneasily in his chair and sweeps his locks back. 'I have political aspirations, sergeant. I've reached a point in my life where I feel I have more to offer. A new vision for the country. A fresh start. As you may be aware, there will be a general election within the next twelve months. If things remain the same, there will be a new government and Evan Tudor will be our next PM. Undoubtedly, a slew of older MPs from the Tory Party will not have the stomach for opposition and will stand down, so initiating a by-election in their constituency. I intend to put myself forward as a candidate in one of those constituencies.'

'And Amanda Chan's campaign against you could undermine your political ambitions?'

The barrister fails to disguise an exasperated grunt.

'Yes. Exactly.'

If this guy is trying to build an iron-clad motive for murder, he's doing a good job, Zac thinks.

'Which brings me to the events of last evening. A few days ago, via an intermediary, I made an offer to Ms Chan. A hundred thousand pounds to cease and desist in her unfounded claims. This was not a bribe, for I have nothing to hide, nor was it blackmail on her part. It was supposed to be a consensual business arrangement. Ms Chan did not agree to the offer, but yesterday she came back with a revised amount she'd be willing to take.'

'How much?'

'Quarter of a million pounds in cash.'

Zac's eyebrows are in danger of leaving his forehead. 'And did you agree to her demands?'

'Yes. But let me clarify, it wasn't a demand.'

'That's a lot of money to get your hands on at short notice?'

'I keep a large sum of money in my home safe, so I have access to it at short notice. Sometimes the fastest way to sort out business issues is by cash.'

Zac would love to delve deeper, but his primary objective is the murder. 'I see. You mentioned an intermediary to set up initial contact with Ms Chan. Who?'

His gaze shifts up and to the right. 'I'd rather not say.'

'You said you'd give a truthful account. I need the name of your intermediary to verify your account.'

'Very well. It was my personal assistant, Dora. Dora King. But that is the only part she played in this tragedy, as a go-between.'

'Noted. Carry on.'

'We arranged to meet at her address last night at 7:30. I collected the money into a holdall, a Gladstone Bag to be precise, and turned up at her flat at the agreed time.'

Zac has plenty of questions already, but when a river is in full flow, don't build a dam.

'Okay, you have the money in the bag, and you drive to Ms Chan's flat at 9b Ashdale Terrace, arriving there at 7:30?'

'Yes. Well, I arrived a minute or two early.'

Zac scribbles a note down. 'What next?'

'I went down the steps and knocked on the door. There was the distant sound of classical music coming from within and a strong smell of cannabis. There was no answer, so I knocked again and called out her name. When there was still no reply, I tried the door and let myself in. I walked down a short hallway, turned right into the living room, and called out again. Still no reply. I noticed a door towards the back of the room that was ajar from which subdued lighting shone, along with the music. I pushed open the door and saw Ms Chan sitting in front of her computer screen with her back to me with headphones on. I called her name again but still got no response. I happened to glance at the wall and noticed it was plastered in photos and newspaper clippings of myself. That's when I first had misgivings about my actions.'

'Why?'

The barrister huffs his annoyance but remains mute as Thorne continues.

'Because I perceived it as obsessive behaviour to the point of mania. I pondered her mental condition.'

'Where's the bag containing the money at this point?'

'It was in my right hand, but as I gazed upon the wall, I placed the holdall on the floor. I decided I wanted to finalise the deal and get out of that place as quickly as possible. I'm not easily unnerved, sergeant, but there was something not quite right about the situation. I moved forward and gently tapped her on the shoulder, but received no response. I felt distinctly uneasy. She was seated in an office swivel chair, so I spun it around. And that's when...' He rubs at his tired face. 'Her image shall haunt me for the rest of my days.'

'You assumed she was dead?'

'There was no assumption, sergeant. She had a knife thrust up to the hilt into her left eye. Her left cheek had a streak of blood down it. She was obviously dead, murdered. Nobody would take their own life in such a horrendous manner.'

'What did you do next?'

'I staggered back. I may have fallen to the floor. I can't quite remember. I then bolted from the flat, ran up the steps, across the road and jumped into my car.'

'Your Range Rover?'

'Yes. I sat there for a few minutes, then I rang Dora.'

'Did you pick the bag up containing the money as you left?'

'No. That was the last thing on my mind. I'm ashamed to admit, I was consumed with fear and horror.'

'You called your PA, Dora King?'

'Yes.'

'Roughly what time would this have been?'

He shakes his head, slightly distracted. 'I don't know. I didn't check my watch or phone. If I arrived around 7:30, then I suppose I would have been inside the flat no longer than three to four minutes at the most.'

'Can you remember the conversation you had with Dora?'

'I told her what I'd seen. I was in a fluster, and I can't recall exactly what I said. But she told me to drive calmly back to the car park.'

'The car park at Thorne Development's headquarters?'

'Yes. She said she'd help me work through it and decide on the best course of action. She asked if I'd killed Ms Chan, to which I replied, truthfully, I hadn't.'

'Can you remember the exact words that were exchanged?'

He sighs. 'Erm... she said something like, answer me this one question. Did you kill Amanda Chan, to which I replied, I did not kill her.'

'And then what?'

'That's it. I arrived in the car park and waited.'

'Why did you wait?'

'Dora told me to sit in the car until she came out. Within a minute of parking up, you arrived and arrested me.'

The barrister leans across the desk. 'Sergeant, I'd like to suspend this interview for thirty minutes so I can instruct my client.'

'Certainly. For the record, interview adjourned at 9:16 am.' Zac rises and pushes his chair under the table.

'Sergeant Stoker?' Thorne asks.

'Yes?'

'The media; what statement have you released to them so far?'

'Standard fare. We said we are investigating a suspicious death, and an individual is helping us with our enquiries.'

'My name hasn't been released then?'

'No. But these things have a way of coming out. The mainstream media is bound by legal obligations, but as for social media... well, it's the Wild West.'

Zac enters the incident room and is immediately confronted by Frank and Prisha.

'Did you watch the interview?' he asks.

'Aye,' Frank nods. 'He's not doing himself any favours, is he? He may as well have stuck with the original duty solicitor instead of bringing in a heavyweight barrister who he's totally ignored.'

'I think his brief is in danger of popping a roid. If you wanted a textbook version of what *not* to say in a police interview, then Seb Thorne has just written it.'

'A sign of innocence, perhaps?' Prisha proffers.

'Or arrogance. Anyway, evidence doesn't lie.' Zac rubs at his beard and turns to Prisha. 'You questioned Dora King, yet?'

'No. I've just been going over her witness statement. I'm about to question her now.'

Frank slides into a chair. 'Prisha, show him the photograph.'

'What photograph?' Zac asks.

Prisha pulls her phone out. 'Dinkel is still with forensics at Amanda Chan's flat. He just sent this through.' She hands him the phone.

'You're joking me?'

'I jest ye not.'

'The Happy Camp photo. How did Amanda Chan get her hands on it?'

'Who knows?'

Zac is baffled. 'What the hell is going on here? I can't make head nor tail of it.'

Frank takes a sip of tea and reflects. 'I'm beginning to think your initial theory may be correct, Prisha.'

Prisha scrunches her eyes up. 'Initial theory?'

Frank is a little surprised. 'You thought Thorne could be behind the murders of Morgan and Wilkes. Now, with the death of Doctor Blenheim, and Amanda Chan, it suggests maybe he was cleaning out all the skeletons from his cupboard before his tilt at politics.'

Zac nods in agreement. 'I'm inclined to agree.'

Prisha picks up an envelope off the table. 'I think you two need to take a cold shower,' she advises.

'What does that mean?' Zac asks, bemused.

'The Happy Camp murders were not committed by Sebastian Thorne.'

# 34

Dora King has the appearance of a frightened kitten, sitting behind the bland table in the interview room. As Prisha enters, she immediately detects Dora's nervousness and tries to put her at ease with a warm smile.

'Thank you for coming in, Dora. I understand this must be a distressing time for you.'

She winces and clasps her hands together. 'Yes, it's all foreign to me. I've never been involved with the police before. Am I in trouble? Am I a suspect?'

Prisha offers her a reassuring laugh. 'No, of course not. You're here as a witness, that's all. I'll try to make this as quick and painless as possible.' She pulls out a chair and takes a seat opposite, placing the folder on the table. 'I've read through the witness statement you gave to Sergeant Stoker last night, and I see you've also been given a copy by the duty sergeant. I simply want to go through it step by step and ask a few questions. If you remember anything else during our conversation, then please feel free to let me know, however inconsequential you may think it to be. If at any time you wish to have a break, then just say. Good?'

'Yes. Thank you.' Her fraught expression remains.

'Is anything the matter, Dora?'

'I feel bad. So guilty. Mr Thorne has been wonderful to me. There's nothing I wouldn't do for him.'

'Why are you feeling guilty?'

'Because I rang the police and told them what had happened. I betrayed his trust. I fought with my conscience. I really did. But I had to do the right thing, didn't I?' she implores.

'Yes, you did. It's what every good person would have done. When someone we care for has committed a crime, it's only natural for us to want to protect them, to help them. But when it comes to murder, we can't protect them. I can fully understand your present feelings. But the fact is, Dora, you had no other choice.'

Wringing her hands together, a weak smile narrows her lips. 'Yes. I suppose you're right.'

Prisha pulls the sheaf of papers from the envelope and flicks through them. 'In your statement, you said Ms Chan had been an *irritation* to Mr Thorne for about eighteen months.'

'Yes, that's right. I'm sure you've seen her YouTube channel and her outlandish accusations, all of which are completely false.'

'Yes, I've watched her channel. You said there were two incidents last week involving Ms Chan. One outside Thorne HQ during a media conference announcing a new initiative for homeless housing, and later in the week when you accompanied Mr Thorne to the official opening of the construction site, up on North Promenade. You've explained the sequence of events, but did Mr Thorne say anything to you after either incident?'

Her head droops as her eyes stare at the table. 'Ahem, after the media conference, and once Evan Tudor and his entourage had left the building, Mr Thorne turned to me and said that Ms Chan was like a tumour, and tumours needed removing.'

'He definitely referred to her as a tumour?'

'Yes.' She becomes alarmed. 'But he was speaking metaphorically, not literally, you understand. Mr Thorne has a very poetic vocabulary.'

'And what about at the construction site when Ms Chan and some of her supporters chained themselves to the fencing?'

'He was angry, which is extremely rare for him.'

'And what did he say?'

'Oh dear, this doesn't sound good.' Hesitation.

'Go on.'

'He said... I can't remember the exact words. My mind's a jumble.'

'Take your time, Dora. No rush. An approximation of what he said will be fine.'

'He said something like, it's time for us to take her out.'

'Her?'

'Ms Chan.'

'And how did you react?'

'I was shocked. I asked him the question—you mean kill her? He gazed at me with a severe frown for a moment, which scared me. Then he smiled and said—of course not. He said he was a businessman, not the mafia, and that everyone had a price. Then I understood what he meant.'

'And what did he mean?'

'Well, it's obvious. He intended to pay her off. He asked me to arrange it.'

'And did you?'

'Yes, sort of. I contacted her, and we met in Pannett Park near the water fountain. I offered her fifty thousand pounds in return for her to cease her campaign against Mr Thorne. She cocked her nose at the offer. As she was leaving, I offered her one hundred thousand pounds. She stopped and said she'd consider it.'

'Let's be clear here; you were offering Ms Chan money from Mr Thorne with his full knowledge and blessing?'

'Yes, of course. I don't have that sort of money, nor the authority to obtain it. Sebastian... Mr Thorne is an experienced negotiator. He instructed me to go in with a low offer first. He knew she'd reject it, and I was to up the price. He predicted she'd reject that after a few days and request more.'

'And did she?'

She half-laughs. 'Yes. It was like Mr Thorne had written the script. He said Ms Chan would request one hundred and fifty thousand and we'd counter with our final offer of one hundred and twenty-five. It would be a take it or leave it ultimatum. But that's not exactly what happened.'

Prisha flicks through the statement. 'You told Sergeant Stoker that yesterday, around about midday, you received a call from Ms Chan. She said her price was a quarter of a million pounds and it was to be hand delivered by Mr Thorne to her flat at 9b Ashdale Terrace, at 7:30 pm.'

'That's correct.'

'Was Mr Thorne privy to the conversation?'

'No. I went to his office immediately I'd hung up and told him about the call.'

'How did he react?'

She shrugs nonchalantly. 'He appeared at ease. It was double what we were, sorry, what he was anticipating paying, but it didn't fluster him at all.'

'During these negotiations, did Mr Thorne engage with Ms Chan at any point?'

'No. It was all done through me. That's what I do. He sometimes endearingly refers to me as his paracetamol. I make his headaches go away.'

'You're fond of him, aren't you?'

Her cheeks flush as she averts her gaze. 'He's been good to me and he's very generous.'

'Is there an attraction?'

Shock ripples across her face. 'If you mean sexually, then no. I mean, he wouldn't look twice at me.'

'You're ten years his junior.'

'I know what I am, inspector, and I'm hardly a catch. And you've seen Mr Thorne. Not only is he handsome and charming, but he has an aura about him. When you're in his presence, you feel anything is possible. It's like an electric field.'

'Okay, I get it. You're not sexually attracted, but you are in awe of him?'

She blushes again and murmurs, 'I suppose.'

Prisha turns a page on the statement. 'Back to the payment. Ms Chan requested the money be delivered in a specific holdall?'

'Yes. A Mackenzie Gladstone Bag.'

'That's extremely specific.'

'I assumed it was a little dig at Sebastian.'

'How do you mean?'

'Mr Thorne takes great pride in his appearance. He only wears the finest clothes, from the top British brands. Asking for a Mackenzie Gladstone Bag was Ms Chan's way of acknowledging she was aware of this.'

'You think it was designed to irritate him?'

'Yes. And it worked. He was slightly put out by the request.'

'Can you describe the bag?'

'It was a matt tan colour, eighteen-inch. Mr Thorne has a wardrobe in his office where he keeps a set of clothes in case he needs a last-minute costume change. He also has several travel bags, one being the Gladstone Bag in question.'

Another quick glance at the witness statement. 'You said you followed Mr Thorne out into the car park last night, just before 7:15?'

'That's right.'

'Was he carrying the bag?'

'No. Earlier in the day, he'd returned home to get the cash from his safe. He said the bag was in the boot.'

'Did you see it?'

'No. But I had no reason to doubt him.'

'Quarter of a million pounds is a lot of loose change to have hanging around.'

'He keeps a lot of cash on hand to, as he says, oil the squeaky wheels of industry.'

'Meaning?'

She fidgets in her chair and appears embarrassed. 'Mr Thorne is a big supporter and believer in the union movement. He pays workers on his sites over and above the standard rates, plus bonuses. However, on occasions in the past, he has come up against corrupt union officials who can cause delays in construction by instigating go-slows, walk-outs, protracted negotiations. Hence why he keeps such a large sum of cash on hand.'

'You mean he pays corrupt officials to ensure his construction schedule doesn't fall behind?'

'It paints him in a bad light, but yes. Lost time can cause cost blow outs in the tens of millions of pounds. You must remember, he's the victim here. Not the perpetrator.'

She has a quick glance at her notes. 'Mr Thorne left the car park around 7:15. Then what?'

'I received a call from him at about 7:35. He was clearly distressed and in a state of panic, which greatly disturbed me.'

'Can you remember what he said?'

Dora grimaces. 'I'm exhausted, Inspector Kumar. I can't recall the exact words.'

'I understand. Give me the gist.'

'He said she was dead. I asked him who. He replied, Amanda Chan. I asked him if he was sure, and he said yes.'

'Did you ask whether he'd killed her?'

She squirms in discomfort. 'Yes, I did.'

'And what was his reply?'

She gulps and stares at the back wall. 'He said, yes, I did kill Amanda Chan.'

'Are you absolutely certain?'

'Yes.'

# 35

Zac's dream run has come to an end. Sebastian Thorne's expensive lawyer has had strong words with his client during the recess. Every question posed is now met with a firm, but polite, "No comment."

He decides to play his trump cards. Removing a photograph from a folder, he places it in front of Seb Thorne.

'Exhibit A.'

Thorne's eyes widen in horror. 'No,' he murmurs, barely audible.

'The murder weapon. A small dagger known as a sgian dubh. This particular dagger is quite distinctive, as it has a handle of black bog-wood and is inlaid with sapphires. It's uncannily similar to the one I handled in your office a few days ago. And more importantly, it has your fingerprints on the handle. Can you explain that, Mr Thorne?'

He turns to his lawyer in slow motion. 'This doesn't make any sense.' The lawyer imperceptibly shakes his head and Thorne replies, 'No comment.'

'After you'd left Ms Chan's flat and returned to your car, you called your personal assistant, Dora King. We have taken a witness statement from Miss King and my colleague has recently finished questioning her.'

Thorne's jowls harden. 'Dora has no part to play in this except as an intermediary between me and Ms Chan.'

The lawyer sighs and rubs a hand through his hair.

Zac continues, hoping to provoke a reaction 'It was Dora who alerted the police to the death of Ms Chan, while you were driving back to the car park. That's why we were able to arrest you so quickly.'

Eyes narrow in suspicion. 'No comment.'

'You placed her in an invidious position. Does she do the morally right thing and call the police, or does she remain loyal to her employer?'

'No comment.'

'When you spoke to her by phone in your car, you informed her of Ms Chan's death. According to your earlier answers, during that conversation Dora asked if you had killed Ms Chan. You replied that you hadn't, didn't you?'

'No comment.'

'Because herein lies the crux of the matter. Your recollection of that conversation, and Dora's version, are mostly the same apart from one significant divergence. When she posed the question as to whether you had killed Ms Chan, she says you replied, I did kill Amanda Chan.'

As he leaps to his feet, the plastic chair shoots backwards, upturning and skidding along the floor. 'That's a bloody lie! She'd never say that. That's not the truth. She's confused or misheard me.'

The lawyer closes his eyes and sighs.

—◦—

Frank stares warily at the clock on the wall. Time is another perennial miscreant detectives must deal with.

'Time is ticking. We have ten hours left before we either charge Sebastian Thorne or let him go. I know where my inclinations lie. Before we come to any decision, your thoughts?'

Zac stifles a yawn. 'The only emotional response from Thorne was whenever I mentioned Dora's name. When I told him Dora's version of their telephone conversation, he lost his shit.'

'I'm not sure we can put too much weight on that telephone call. If Thorne was as panicked as he made out, then maybe Dora misheard his reply.'

Prisha taps her teeth with the end of a pen. 'Dora King played the loyal, distraught secretary a bit too well for my liking.'

Frank nods. 'I detect your inference, Prisha. Let's for one moment assume Thorne is telling the truth. Is there any way Dora could be the killer, and she's set him up?'

Zac shakes his head. 'No. Even if she had a motive, there's no way she could have left Thorne HQ after Seb, arrived at Amanda Chan's flat before him, committed the murder and left before he arrived. I've checked the security footage from Thorne HQ and it shows Seb and Dora walking across the car park towards his Range Rover at 7:14 pm, and him returning at 7:52, and parking up. Dora was the only other person in the building, and she didn't leave. There's a security camera inside the front doors and she passes by it on a number of occasions during the timeframe.'

'What about the dagger?'

'We scoured Seb's office, Frank, and the dagger is missing.'

'It appears to be an open and shut case then.'

Prisha rises and performs a cat-stretch. 'All the evidence seems to indicate it was Thorne, but the psychology is all wrong. Sebastian Thorne is a cool customer, shrewd, clever. Let's say he did want Amanda out of the way, permanently. He has no history of violence. He hasn't even received a speeding ticket. It's completely out of character for a smart, intelligent high-achiever to suddenly turn into a killer, take his own distinctive dagger, kill a person, leave his fingerprints on the handle and admit to his PA he committed murder.'

Frank stands and pushes his chair under the desk. 'Are you forgetting Blake Baldwin's account of how Thorne butchered the rabbit at Happy Camp? And Ms Chan's allegations against him about his former business partner? Just because he has no record doesn't mean hasn't killed before. Does anyone know the real Sebastian Thorne and what he's capable of?'

# 36

Even with the benefit of full-length, white protective overalls, there is still a nip in the air. Prisha pulls the zip up to her neck and gazes down the street. Watery daylight creeps through the leafy tree-lined avenue as if stalking the rundown Victorian terraced houses converted into flats.

'Ah, Prisha, I thought you'd like to see this,' Charlene Marsden calls out from the basement flat as she emerges from the front door.

Prisha ambles down the grubby steps with a gnawing sensation in the pit of her stomach. Hunger and tiredness have joined forces to create a fog of mild nausea.

'Morning, Charlene.'

'Morning. We're nearly finished, and the cleaning services are due in thirty minutes.'

'What have you got?' Prisha replies as Charlene holds open the front door into the hallway and leads her through the living room and into the back office, the scene of the crime.

Charlene points at the swivel chair, then at the computer screen.

'Care for some role play?'

'What's my role?'

'The deceased, of course. I'll play the killer.'

'Great. I always get the good parts. Where do you want me?'

'Take a seat facing the computer screen. Of course, this is only my initial hypothesis.'

Prisha sits in the chair and stares at the monitor. 'Be gentle.'

Charlene chuckles. 'There's nothing gentle about murder, but rest assured, you won't feel a thing. I believe Amanda was sitting at her desk, facing the computer screen. The killer stalks up behind her and plunges the knife into her eye.' Charlene's right hand, clenched as if holding a dagger, reaches over Prisha's right shoulder and ever so gently, comes to rest over her left eye.

'And as she was wearing headphones, she wouldn't have heard a thing. Would her death have been instant?'

'If the weapon pierced the brain, then yes, loss of consciousness would have been rapid.'

'Seconds?'

'More than likely.'

'Would she have had time to scream?'

Charlene shrugs, non-committal. 'We all react differently to sudden and unexpected pain. I remember pulling a nail from a piece of wood with a claw hammer once. It suddenly gave, and I hit myself in the forehead with the damn thing. The pain was intense, but I didn't utter a single word. Well, not until later. Of course, you'll need to discuss the mode of death with Doctor Whipple. I'm sure he can elucidate in far more detail and prosaic language than I can.'

Prisha rises from the chair. 'Hell, I forgot about him. Has he been and gone?'

'No. He was indisposed. But we've taken extensive photos and videos of the scene. There are small amounts of blood splatter on the monitor, keyboard, and desk. We've taken swabs and fast-tracked them for analysis.'

'Wouldn't a dagger to the eye have caused a lot more blood loss?'

'You'd think so, but if the dagger was thrust in a straight trajectory, it may have missed the ophthalmic arteries and the internal carotid artery within the cranial cavity. Even if it severed them, the bleeding would have mostly been internal. There's no indication of blood on the chair.'

'What about the tests you ran on Thorne's clothing? Have you got the results back yet?'

'Yes. They're devoid of any DNA belonging to Amanda Chan.'

'You're joking?'

'No, I'm not.'

'Nothing?'

'A big fat zero.'

Prisha spots Dinkel hovering near the entrance. 'You can come in, Dinkel. Forensics are finished. How'd you go?' she asks as he ambles towards her.

'None of the neighbours saw or heard anything.'

'What about the flats above?'

'The first-floor flat is empty, and the flat above that, well, the occupants are fond of their wacky baccy.'

'Stoners?'

He nods and raises his eyebrows. 'Yes, ma'am.'

'The Happy Camp photo; where did you find it?'

Dinkel nods at the corkboard lined with clippings about Sebastian Thorne. 'Pinned to the board.'

Charlene interrupts. 'We've dusted the photograph and lifted two distinct prints.'

'Excellent. Maybe that will tell us how Amanda Chan managed to get her mitts on the photo.' She returns her attention to Dinkel. 'Security footage?'

His face brightens. 'Yes. The house two doors up captured a Range Rover parking up on the opposite side of the road last night at precisely 7:29 pm. A male exits the vehicle, but it's dark and it's impossible to tell definitively whether it's Sebastian Thorne or not.'

'Number plate?'

'Afraid not. But here's the interesting thing; the driver opens the boot and pulls out a bag, a holdall. He then crosses the street towards the victim's flat, then moves out of view of the camera. At 7:34, a similar man is seen walking briskly, in what I'd called an agitated manner, back across the road and enters the vehicle. There's no movement for about a minute, then the car drives off.'

'Was he still carrying the bag?'

'No. But he seems to pull something out from inside his coat as he entered the car.'

'What do you mean by something? A bunch of flowers, a white rabbit, a balloon sausage dog?'

Dinkel shrugs his apology. 'Impossible to say, ma'am. You'll understand when you view the footage.'

Prisha bites her bottom lip. 'Hmm... well, the timeframe tallies with the accounts given by Thorne and Dora King. And there was definitely a bag. So, what the hell happened to it? What time did Dora King call the police?'

Dinkel removes his notebook and flicks through the pages. 'Miss King's call was registered at 7:40, and the first officers on the scene arrived at the flat at 7:47.'

Her face creases in mental thought. 'Thorne arrives back at his car at 7:34. He makes a call to Dora which, according to the telco logs, lasted less than a minute. Let's call it 7:36. Then four minutes later, Dora calls the police. Why a four-minute gap?'

'Maybe she was unsure what to do for the best.'

'Possibly. So somewhere between 7:36 and 7:47, someone must have entered the house and taken the bag. Are you sure the security footage didn't capture anyone else between those times?'

'Certain ma'am. But it has a limited field of view. Whoever entered the flat must have done so from the opposite direction, out of range of the camera. Perhaps an opportunist?'

'No, I don't buy that. It's too much of a coincidence. The chances of such a serendipitous event occurring would be in the billions. Right, thanks Charlene, and well done Dinkel.' She turns to leave. 'I need breakfast and a strong coffee.'

Dinkel trots alongside her like the family poodle. 'Ma'am, I was doing some work on Operation Gorse Bush yesterday.'

'Good.'

'I went through that large box of photos belonging to Selwyn Morgan.'

'And?' she says, stepping outside into fresh air, pulling at the zipper on her protective suit.

'I've made some observations.'

Impatient and frayed at the edges, she snaps. 'Dinkel, at this stage I'm not interested in your observations. I want evidence and facts. We still have two names from Happy Camp unaccounted for: Mike Ross and Ted Fairchild. Your number one priority is to track them down. I've told you that multiple times. Now, once you've finished here and written up your report, I want you to focus on those two names. Understood?'

With his wings clipped, Dinkel acquiesces. 'Yes... sorry, ma'am.'

# 37

Miserly Joe's Cafe is teeming with mid-morning customers: trawlermen, council workers, taxi drivers, tradesmen, and three very hungry detectives.

The waiter places two Full English Breakfasts down on the table, and one small plate of toast. Frank stares enviously at the food in front of Prisha and Zac; rashers of bacon, two fried eggs, baked beans, fried mushroom, black pudding, grilled tomato, and two slices of fried bread. He averts his jealous gaze and stares disparagingly at his lightly buttered toast.

'Christ,' he mutters under his breath as Prisha and Zac attack their food like hungry wolves. 'Okay, let's have a pow-wow, discreetly. I want you both to give me your theories, half-baked ideas, and stabs in the dark regarding Thorne and the murder of Amanda Chan.'

Zac stops chewing and eyeballs Frank, intently. 'You can't use that term these days, Frank.'

'What term?' he replies, clearly befuddled.

Zac takes a surreptitious glance around. 'Pow-wow,' he whispers. 'It's considered cultural misappropriation and potentially offensive. Using the term casually dilutes and misrepresents its significance to the Native Americans and First Nations communities.'

'Sweet merciful shite! Thank you, Greta Thunberg. Looking around this caff, I don't spot many Native Americans tucking into a bacon butty.'

'Nevertheless.'

'Fine, fine. God forbid we should offend anyone. We won't have a pow-wow. We'll have a chinwag. Is that term okay to use?'

'I'm not taking sides, Frank. I'm just saying.'

Prisha can't resist a smirk. 'Okay, I'll go first. I'll explain why I don't think Thorne is involved in the Happy Camp murders. The three murders were meticulously planned and executed. They were particularly brutal and symbolic. The killer was cool, calm, and methodical. If Thorne did kill Chan, and I'm not convinced he did, then why were the murders so completely different?'

Frank huffs indignantly. 'I'll admit that suspecting him of the Happy Camp murders is stretching the bow, but I cannot believe you have doubts about him killing Ms Chan. The murder weapon was Thorne's antique dagger. It had his fingerprints on it. He admitted being at the flat.

His PA has signed a witness statement saying he confessed to the murder. Motive, means, and opportunity. I'm not sure how clear cut you want it to be, Prisha?'

'I suspect a set-up, Frank,' she says, dipping her fried bread into the beans and taking a large bite. 'Charlene said forensics have examined Thorne's clothes for blood and came back with nothing.'

Zac nods enthusiastically. 'No blood on his clothes or his hands.'

Frank smears jam onto his toast and takes a nibble. 'Assuming for one moment it is a set-up, then the only likely suspect who had access to the dagger is Dora King. And yet she was captured on security cams at Thorne HQ. Zac, how far back in time did you check the footage?'

'Right, back to the morning. It shows Thorne arriving at 7:30 am, followed a couple of minutes later by Dora. She leaves the building at midday for thirty minutes before returning. Thorne departs at three in the afternoon and returns at six. I'm assuming he drove back home to collect the money from his safe. At 7:14 CCTV shows Dora and Thorne talking in the car park, before Thorne drives away, and Dora returns to the office.'

'Anyone else in the building that day?'

'No.'

'So, a quiet day?'

'Very quiet. It was a Sunday.'

Frank scratches his head. 'And why were they working on a Sunday?'

'According to Dora, Thorne is a workaholic. It's not unusual for him to ask her to work the weekends. She's generously compensated.'

Prisha slurps on a strong black coffee. 'Amanda Chan's body was still warm to the touch when uniform arrived on the scene at 7:47 last night, indicating she'd not long been dead.'

Frank raises his eyebrows. 'You're being rather cavalier with the timings. The term—warm to the touch—is not a technical expression. You're well aware that a body inside a house, with a comfortable ambient temperature, cools at about one to two degrees per hour. Which means Amanda Chan could have been killed at least a couple of hours before uniform arrived, and the body may still have been warmish.'

Zac chuckles as he wipes baked bean sauce from his beard with a tissue. 'Warmish? Now you're at it.'

Frank takes a gulp of tea, then spreads jam on his last slice of toast. 'What I'm saying is, let's not manipulate the facts to suit our narrative. In all likelihood, Chan probably was murdered not long before the body was found. But let's not discount the possibility that she could have been killed any time between 5:30 and 7:30 when Thorne arrived.'

'Which still means Dora King was not the killer.'

Prisha mops up egg yolk with a slice of anaemic bread. 'Okay, two scenarios. One; Thorne wanted to silence Chan. He follows his true and trusted method—money. He initially assumes he can pay her off for a hundred to a hundred and fifty grand. Somehow, Chan comes into possession of the Happy Camp photo and uses it as a bargaining chip to squeeze more money out of Thorne. Whether he has anything to hide in relation to Happy Camp is a discussion for another day. However, he'd assume that Chan would use the photo in her campaign against him. Guilty or innocent of any wrongdoing, it would all smell a bit iffy and could jeopardise his political aspirations. He agrees to pay the quarter of a million and drop the money off himself. Walking into the unknown, he takes along his antique dagger as protection. He arrives at her flat, lets himself in, then notices she's preoccupied, wearing headphones with her back to him. In a sudden aberration, he sees a permanent way out of his predicament. He kills her, then realises the full enormity of his actions, panics and flees the building and calls his trusted PA and confesses all, assuming she'll keep the secret. She doesn't. In the cell overnight, he has time to think, and realises he doesn't have a leg to stand on. His only defence is to say Chan was already dead when he arrived.' She pushes the plate away and smiles. 'Okay, you two play defence counsel.'

Zac leans back in his seat and pats his stomach. 'Why no DNA on his clothes or body?'

'Pure luck. Charlene said that most of the bleeding would have been internal.'

'But with blood splatter on the computer screen and keyboard, you'd assume there would have been blood on his hand and on his sleeve. Which would mean he must have worn protective, disposable clothing of some sort. But no disposable clothing has been found. We searched the sewers and nearby alleys and gardens. And even if he was canny enough to wear protection, wash his hands, and miraculously dispose of protective clothing, then why leave his dagger and the money behind to incriminate himself?'

Frank nods at Prisha, deep in thought. 'And scenario two?'

'The lead up is the same as scenario one. But this time when Thorne arrives, he lets himself in, wanders to the office and discovers Chan's body. Shocked, he panics and flees the building, completely forgetting about the money.'

Zac grimaces. 'Hang on, that's Thorne's version.'

'Yes.'

'You believe him, despite all the circumstantial evidence?'

She considers the question carefully. 'I'm edging that way.'

'The dagger is crucial in all this.'

'You're right. The only people who had access to the murder weapon are Thorne and Dora King. The only people who knew of the pay-off were Thorne, King, and Chan. Thorne denies he told Dora that he'd killed Chan. Dora says the opposite. You see where I'm heading with all this?'

Frank leans forward. 'Dora was at the office when Thorne arrived at Chan's flat. CCTV confirms she did leave the office during the day, but not within the timeline that matches Chan's death. As Zac said, Dora King could not have murdered Chan.'

Prisha offers a grim smile. 'Not personally, no. But she could be the architect behind it.'

Frank pulls at his earlobe. 'You think Dora King has an accomplice?'

'Maybe.'

Zac nods in agreement. 'That could explain the missing money. The accomplice arrives before Thorne, kills Chan, waits in hiding and when Thorne panics and flees, they simply stroll out with the Gladstone Bag full of a quarter of a million quid.'

Frank taps at the table. 'There is one major flaw to the theory.'

Prisha nods in agreement. 'Yes, I know. How did the killer know Thorne would leave the money behind?'

———◦———

Frank glances out of his office window, then nods at Prisha.

'Brace yourself, lass. Incoming cruise missile.'

Prisha throws a look behind her as Superintendent Banks marches across the incident room like someone in a hurry.

'She's not going to like it, Frank.'

'I think that's the understatement of the year.'

The Super bustles into the office, a ball of barely concealed annoyance and impatience.

'Ah, Frank, Prisha. Sit, sit,' she orders as if talking to her dog. 'I'm up to speed with the Amanda Chan murder. Have you charged Sebastian Thorne yet?'

'Not yet, Anne,' he replies as he and Prisha flop into their chairs.

'What's the hold-up? He admitted to being at Ms Chan's flat around the time of the murder. His fingerprints are on the murder weapon. The murder weapon *is* his antique dagger, and he confessed the crime to his PA. Plus, he had a strong motive. It's an open and shut case. Ms Chan's father, Sir Brendan Chandler, has many influential friends. The Chief Constable has been copping some flak, which, in turn, means I've also been copping it. We need to move quickly. I realise Sebastian Thorne is a well known, and in some quarters, much loved figure, but we cannot be seen to be dilly-dallying because of someone's reputation.'

Frank prepares himself for the onslaught. 'The thing is, Anne...'

Like a masochist searching for their next thrill, Prisha jumps in.

'We're not charging him, ma'am. We're going to release him on bail with conditions, pending further investigation.'

Superintendent Banks sticks a pinky in her ear and waggles it around. 'Sorry, I think I may have misheard you, inspector. For one ghastly moment, I thought you said you were going to release him on bail.'

'That's correct. I did say that, ma'am.'

She glares at Frank. 'Tell me I'm dreaming.'

'I'll cut to the chase, Anne. We believe Thorne may have been set-up by his PA, Dora King, who may have an accomplice that carried out the murder.'

Her foot involuntarily taps a drum beat on the floor. 'May have been set-up? May have an accomplice? The word—may—has never filled me with confidence, especially when put up against evidence and hard facts. You have five minutes to explain yourself and make a damn good case for Thorne's release. Otherwise, I'll pull rank and charge Thorne myself.'

———◇———

Frank and Prisha stride out into the incident room feeling quite chipper with themselves.

'I'll take that as a win,' Frank states.

'Me too. I think she began to waver when you started talking about a miscarriage of justice, and how a high-profile individual such as Sebastian Thorne would generate a tsunami of media attention, and therefore, police scrutiny.'

'Aye. It was a low trick preying on her weakness, but sometimes you have to play dirty. Remember that, Prisha.'

'Don't worry. I will.'

'However, we can't keep her at bay forever. We need to move both investigations along rapidly, otherwise she'll be snapping at our heels.'

With the team gathered around the whiteboard, Prisha claps her hands together.

'Okay, guys, this is the state of play as it stands; Sebastian Thorne is still our prime suspect, on paper at least. But, as counter intuitive as this sounds, he will be released on pre-charge bail with these conditions: he doesn't return to Thorne HQ; has no contact with Dora King; he surrenders his passport; a curfew between 7 pm and 7 am; daily reporting to a police station; and a prohibition on discussing the case publicly. That's not to say he's off the hook yet, but it offers us a chance to explore the theory that he may have been set-up by Dora King, and her possible accomplice.' She turns to Zac. 'Prepare the paperwork for an intercept on Dora's phone. It requires the authority of the Secretary of State and approval of a Judicial Commissioner, so make damn sure it's watertight. They don't grant those warrants willy nilly.'

'Got it.'

Eyeballing Dinkel, she states, 'I need you to uncover everything about Dora's past. Find out her birthplace, her family background, friends, acquaintances, employment history—every single detail, down to what she had for breakfast this morning.'

Dinkel scribbles in his notebook, then squints for a split second, bemused until it dawns on him. 'You're speaking metaphorically, right, about the breakfast?'

'Give me strength,' Zac murmurs.

Prisha masks a smile. 'Yes, Dinkel, it was metaphorical. Frank, can you ask Superintendent Banks to authorise round-the-clock mobile surveillance on Dora King?'

'Leave it with me.'

Zac holds a pen in the air. 'Prisha, what about the media? If Seb Thorne is innocent, even a whiff of this would seriously damage his future political aspirations. You know how certain elements of the press, and public alike, don't let the truth get in the way of a good story.'

'We've already limited disclosure on the murder. Our official line is that we're investigating a suspicious death, and a person of interest is helping us with our inquiry. I've liaised with our media relations team and asked them to be extremely circumspect when replying to questions about the case. They've agreed to follow the well-trodden path of—a complex investigation, presumption of innocence until proven guilty, plus the caveat of the potential legal implications of prejudicial reporting. But in the end, Zac, we can only control what we control. We must act without fear or favour.'

'I'm sure Mr Thorne's PR team can handle any fallout. We already have warrants to search Thorne HQ and Sebastian's home, but considering our suspicions, should we also secure a warrant to search all digital data at Thorne HQ and Thorne's personal electronic devices?'

'Yes, definitely. I'll leave that with you.'

'Thanks a bunch.'

'My pleasure.'

'What about a warrant for Dora King's home address and personal devices?'

'No, not yet, and I'll explain why. If Dora is the architect behind the murder, then she's demonstrated extraordinary cunning, suggesting she'll be ultra-cautious for a while. Our reaction? Total indifference—treat her like she's not even on our radar. No direct contact. Should she reach out to us, keep responses vague, citing confidentiality to avoid jeopardising the investigation. But remember this—suspecting her of involvement in the murder of Amanda Chan and proving it beyond reasonable doubt in a court of law are worlds apart. We require evidence that not only convinces *us* but leaves a jury with no option but to agree.'

'Aye, fair point.'

'I want to allow surveillance time to operate without Dora being on her guard, which may take a few days. If she even has an inkling we suspect her, then she'll no doubt tip off her partner in crime.'

Dinkel half raises his hand. 'Ma'am, do you see a connection between Amanda Chan's death and the Happy Camp murders?'

Prisha's left cheek twitches. 'At this point in time, no, I don't. The common denominator between both cases is Sebastian Thorne, but I don't see any correlation between Amanda Chan and Happy Camp... well, not yet anyway. They are two separate investigations. But as always, never discard the possibility altogether. And Dinkel, once you've completed the tasks I've assigned you for this case, then I want you back on the Happy Camp murders. Remember, we need to find the whereabouts of Mike Ross and Ted Fairchild.'

'Yes, ma'am. It's seared into my brain.'

'Good. Does everyone know what they've got to do?' She's greeted with nods and affirmations. Clapping her hands together, she shouts, 'All right everyone, let's move—action stations!'

# 38

# Eight Days Later – Tuesday 9th May

The chat around the incident room is muted as an air of frustration and defeatism advances with every ticking hour. Prisha and Zac are seated side by side, chastened by their lack of progress. Only Dinkel seems actively engaged as he hammers at his keyboard and whistles a melancholy tune. Although, the word tune, is being generous.

'I wish he'd quit his warbling,' Zac says, throwing daggers to the back of Dinkel's head.

Prisha gazes into Frank's office. Superintendent Banks continually paces back and forth in front of his desk. Words cannot be heard, but her animations are deafening.

'She's got her knickers all bunched up,' Prisha notes.

Zac follows her gaze. 'It's a permanent predicament with her. Although, old Franky boy doesn't look too perturbed.'

The door to the office is thrown open as Frank's bulldog head peers out. 'Prisha, Zac, if you have a moment, please.'

They share concerned glances and meander lethargically into the office and close the door. Superintendent Banks gives Zac the once over, indifferent, then glowers at Prisha.

'Frank has updated me on the Amanda Chan murder. We've had Dora King under surveillance for seven days and absolutely nothing. No secretive phone calls to persons unknown. No clandestine meetings.' She brandishes a couple of stapled sheets of paper in her hand and waves them around dismissively. 'The surveillance log. Dora leaves her house at the same time each morning, stops off to grab a coffee at the same cafe each day, and arrives at work by 7:30. At midday she nips out to a local bakery and buys lunch. She leaves work around 5:30 and returns home. The only deviation from her routine is she's visited the supermarket three times, had an appointment with a chiropractor, and dropped her car off at the mechanics twice. Oh, and on Sunday she walked from Whitby to Robin Hood's Bay, had a spot of lunch and a glass of white wine at the Smugglers Ale House, alone, then returned to Whitby by bus and went home. Hardly the routine of a killer trying to hide something. I was going to say the costly surveillance exercise has been a waste of time and money, but that would be wrong. What it goes to prove is that Dora King has nothing to hide.'

Prisha clears her throat, hands behind her back. 'These things can take time, ma'am.'

'How much time?' she snaps.

'That's impossible to say. It could be weeks or...'

'Or months, or even years.'

'I was going to say... or a matter of days before she makes a move.'

'This operation is costing a small fortune. I'm afraid we cannot justify the expense. I'm calling a stop. Today.'

Prisha throws Frank a worried look. 'I think that would be a mistake, ma'am. We need to sit tight and be more patient than her.'

'No. We need to be proactive. I want you to bring her in and question her.'

'On what grounds? We have absolutely no evidence against her.' Prisha instantly regrets her words, realising she's walked straight into the trap.

Anne Banks sports a whisper of a smile. 'Exactly,' the word is spelt out slowly, laced with meaning. 'Absolutely no evidence against her whatsoever. Nothing but a fanciful theory which has not borne fruit. And yet the man who we should be putting under the screw languishes in his ivory palace with his feet up, probably feeling mightily pleased with himself. The media are having a field day.'

'It's not a fanciful theory. The fact is, the only other person who had access to the dagger and knew of the pay-off was Dora King.'

Anne picks up her handbag and slides it over her shoulder. 'You jumped to that conclusion and believed it as fact. Well, it's not a *fact.* It's a theory you've invested considerable time in and conveniently plays to your narrative. And you're wrong. You say the only other person who had access to the murder weapon was Dora King. Are you forgetting about Sebastian Thorne? His prints were all over it. Thorne is our killer. I should never have let you convince me otherwise. I was hoping to keep this investigation under wraps, but now it's the epicentre of every news programme and newspaper front page. The horse has bolted. My phone has been running red hot. Now, bring Dora King in for questioning, and unless she breaks down and confesses all, then release her and focus your activities on Mr Thorne, and other associates of Amanda Chan.' She turns to leave. 'I've been in discussion with the Deputy Chief Constable, Martin Overland, and we've concluded you need more help.'

Frank raises his eyebrows in an optimistic fashion. 'I couldn't agree more, Anne. We are pushed to the limit with two separate murder investigations. More boots on the ground are always welcome. We can split the team into two, with Prisha leading the Amanda Chan investigation and Zac in charge of the Happy Camp murders.'

The Super puckers her lips. 'That's not what I had in mind, Frank.'

'Oh?'

'Today is Tuesday. Unless there have been major developments in the next forty-eight hours, then I intend to bring in a more experienced team from York to take over the Amanda Chan case. Prisha, you can get them up to speed, then hand everything over and focus on the Happy Camp murders. Do I make myself clear?'

She bites her lip and restrains her anger and frustration. 'Yes, ma'am.'

'Good. That's settled then. And don't take this personally. It's in no way a reflection of your team's ability. And as Frank won't be here next week, I shall be stepping into his shoes until he returns from medical leave.' She departs in silence.

Zac throws Frank a confused look. 'Medical leave?'

'I've only just heard in the last hour. Next Monday I'm booked in to have a pacemaker fitted. It's only a day procedure but my doctor advised me to take a week off, just to monitor things. So, for once, I'm heeding his advice.'

Prisha and Zac troop from the office more dejected than when they went in. They collapse into their chairs and stare out of the window.

Zac twiddles a pen around in his fingers. 'I'm not sure what's worse; her scuppering all our hard work or the fact she's going to be a permanent fixture in the office next week? I might book a week's leave. Maybe go fishing.'

'Ooh, ooh.' Dinkel makes a passable imitation of a chimpanzee.

Zac shifts his attention from the river onto Dinkel. 'The whistling's stopped, but now he's regressing back to being a primate.'

'Ooh, ooh.'

'Oi, Pongo, what's the matter? Is there a banana shortage?'

Dinkel turns around, ashen faced, and stares at Prisha. 'Ma'am?'

'What's the matter, Dinkel?'

'Charlene Marsden tried calling you but couldn't get through.'

Prisha pulls her phone out, un-mutes it and notices the two missed calls. 'And?'

'Do you remember last week when they were examining the clothes of Sebastian Thorne for blood or DNA from Amanda Chan?'

A flood of nausea washes over her. 'Please, no,' she murmurs. 'Don't tell me they've re-examined and found something?'

'Yes, and no.'

'I like a man who's decisive and straight to the point,' Zac quips.

'You best take a look at this, ma'am.'

Prisha rises and walks over to his workstation. 'What?' she says, squinting at a photograph of a brown shoe.

'This is Sebastian Thorne's shoe,' Dinkel explains.

'Does it have Amanda Chan's DNA on it?'

'No.'

Prisha shakes her head and silently curses. 'Just get on with it,' she snaps.

Dinkel pulls up another image showing an imprint from a sole of a shoe. 'Do you remember the crime scene from Selwyn Morgan?'

'Yes, of course I bloody do.'

'You may recall they were able to lift a foreign footprint from the site.'

'Yes, a size eleven.'

'Well, the sole and tread-marks match the shoes Sebastian Thorne was wearing when he was arrested.'

Prisha's stomach flips. 'Oh, someone, please shoot me.'

# 39

The beer garden at the White House offers magnificent views over the water. To the left, the tranquillity of the golf course projects a country feel. Zac and Prisha stare out in silence at the grey water of the North Sea as sunlight skips and jumps over the ceaseless waves.

'I was wrong,' Prisha finally says, subdued, self-reflective.

'Looks like it,' Zac replies with a wistful sigh. 'What now?'

'I suppose we bring Thorne back in for questioning and ask him how his shoe print ended up at the murder site.'

'And what about Dora King? Do we question her as Banks requested?'

'What's the point? We have absolutely nothing on her.'

Their concentration is broken as Adam places the tray of drinks on the wooden bench.

'Here we go,' he says in his naturally easy-going manner. 'Pint of Whitby Whaler for Zac. A gin and tonic for my princess, and a pint of Guinness for me.' He takes a seat and on noticing the glum faces, asks, 'Bad day at the office?'

Prisha takes a large gulp of her drink. 'You could say that. We're about to be taken off one murder case; my theories have gone up in a puff of smoke; the media interest in Sebastian Thorne has gone off the Richter scale, and the final icing on the cake is that Superintendent Banks will be a permanent fixture in the office next week, possibly longer. How was your day?'

'Lost a lamb to a fox last night. They're cunning buggers. You can set your traps and think you've got them, then they'll manage to find a way around it. They always seem to be one step ahead. To catch a fox, you need to think like a fox.'

Prisha is accustomed to Adam's farming analogies, and she usually dismisses them without much thought. But today, his words hang in the air, resonating with an unexpected weight.

<hr />

The rain patters against the windowpane as the edges of the curtain shiver in the light breeze, which always finds a way through the old wooden frame. Adam devours his spinach and ricotta agnolotti like a man who has been working in the fields all day. He rapidly flicks through the TV channels with the remote control. Prisha is sitting opposite him on the couch, legs tucked underneath her as she prods and pokes at her food. Her mind is a labyrinth of dark, narrow alleys that forever lead to a dead end no matter how many times she wanders down them looking for a hidden door, a secret opening. As the evening news flashes across the TV screen, Prisha is yanked back to reality as the leader of the Opposition, Evan Tudor, fronts a press conference.

'Wait. Stop. Leave it on the news and turn it up,' she demands.

'Oh, not this windbag,' Adam gripes.

'Shush!'

Evan Tudor steps up to the podium, the sheaf of papers in his hands shaking slightly. He takes a moment to clear his throat before addressing the assembly of journalists.

'Thank you for coming at such short notice. As you will be aware, earlier this week, we received a formal complaint against one of our members, Sebastian Thorne. It was in relation to a criminal investigation which I am not at liberty to speculate upon. The Labour Party launched its own... ahem, its own investigation immediately.' He stops mid-flow to take a sip of water, the whirr of cameras a constant, the harsh lighting magnifying beads of sweat on his forehead. 'Our findings were due to be delivered to a hearing this weekend, after which a decision on Mr Thorne's status would have been reached. However, earlier today we received formal written notification from Mr Thorne's legal representation stating that Mr Thorne has resigned his membership from the Party, effective immediately. Mr Thorne had this to say:

It is with great sadness that I have come to the decision to resign from the Labour Party. I cannot let the unfounded allegations and inferences around my current state of affairs impact upon a party whose values and commitment to fairness and equality match my own.'

A flood of questions rain forth.

'Mr Tudor, was Sebastian Thorne asked by yourself to step down to save yourself further embarrassment?'

'N... no. Absolutely not. Um. I have had no contact with, uh, Mr Thorne.'

Concerning Thorne's financial contributions to the party, Tudor awkwardly dodges the question.

'I'm, um, sorry, but the specifics of future donations are, you know, beyond me. What I can say is, our finances are, erm, remain... remain robust.'

'Will this affect your friendship with Mr Thorne?'

Evan Tudor winces as if in pain. 'My relationship with Mr Thorne was never personal. It was always on a purely professional level, as we both shared a passion to end homelessness.'

'Isn't it true that Sebastian Thorne is godfather to your eldest son?'

He completely blanks the question and points at another journalist.

'Evan, Mr Thorne has been released by police without charge and is no longer a person of interest in the murder of Ms Chan. Why should he have to resign when he's an innocent man, and why did you accept his resignation?'

'I believe it's in the best interests of everyone.'

'You mean your best interests?'

He shakes his head in contempt and murmurs, 'No. You're wrong.'

'Evan, a poll published this morning showed seventy per cent of Labour voters preferred Sebastian Thorne as leader of the Labour Party *despite* him not being a member of parliament. It seems the criminal investigation has only heightened his popularity. What have you got to say about that?'

He attempts a smile which he can't pull off, making him look like an evil sidekick. He sticks a finger down the collar of his shirt and tugs at it, gasping for air. He receives a surreptitious tap to the elbow from an aide.

'The only poll I'm interested in is, um, the one at the next general election. Thank you for your time.'

He hurriedly rushes from the stage.

As the TV is muted, Prisha snorts. 'That was a fucking train wreck.'

Adam nods in agreement. 'Do you think Thorne was asked to resign?'

'Undoubtedly.'

'It's not a good look for Evan Tudor. Not only does he abandon an old buddy in his time of need but then denies they were ever friends. Politicians—they're a different breed, aren't they?'

'Oh, yes. If their talent was as large as their egos, the world would be a perfect place to live in.'

'Is it true what that journalist said about the police no longer regarding Sebastian Thorne as a person of interest?'

She ruminates for a moment and places her half-eaten bowl of pasta on the coffee table, then picks up a glass of white wine.

'No. The Superintendent fronted the media after the news story broke. She may not be a people person, but she is extremely guarded about her choice of words.' She picks up her phone and scrolls the screen. 'I have the transcript of her press conference here. She said—Mr Thorne has cooperated fully with our investigation, and we have agreed that he will remain available to assist further, should the need arise, as our inquiry progresses. However, our focus now shifts to new leads and potential suspects as we continue our work to bring justice for Ms Chan. We ask for the public's patience and support as we conduct this complex investigation.'

'So he wasn't completely exonerated?'

'No.'

'Then why did the journo state Thorne was no longer a person of interest?'

'Either the journalist was reading between the lines, or he'd been prompted to ask the question.'

'Prompted?'

'Yes. Rich and influential people hire PR companies to mitigate fall out from alleged indiscretions. They usually employ specialists in crisis, or reputation management. You see it all the time. They fight back with either snippets and whispers to the mainstream press, and a social media campaign, or they go dark and completely remove themselves from everything until the noise dies down.'

Adam shakes his head. 'There's something to be said for the simple life. Thank God I'm a farmer. I have my own issues to deal with; broken fences, tractor issues, fluctuating prices, but it's small fry compared to what these high-flyers get up to. I couldn't be doing with all the skulduggery and dog-eat-dog. The lying and deceit must take its toll. At least when I fall into the sack on a night, I know I'll have the sleep of the just.' He glances at the discarded food. 'You going to eat that?'

'No.'

'Waste not want not.'

＊＊＊

By the time Prisha climbs into bed, Adam has been fast asleep for two hours. She glances at his small digital alarm clock on the bedside table. He brings it with him whenever he stays over. It's a back-up alarm in case his phone battery dies during the night. She finds the clock slightly endearing and annoying at the same time. The blue light, although faint, pierces the darkness, keeping sleep at bay.

# 40

# Wednesday 10th May

Due to Adam's portable alarm clock, Prisha is pounding the ground at 5 am. She half curses herself, falling for a farmer, and the ungodly hours they keep. But at the same time she's thankful for the early morning starts, which permits her to hit the streets and tracks alone, apart from a few other occasional die-hard runners.

It's her time to think, or not think. Sometimes her mind is a tombola of thoughts trawling over clues and suspicions. Other times it is a blank canvas, ready to receive the impressions of nature; the sweet song of the blackbird, the cry of a seagull, the crash of the waves, the slap, slap, slap of her running shoes.

This morning, though... her mind is abuzz.

Her run takes her to her usual turning point at the old Hawsker Lighthouse high up on the cliffs alongside the Cleveland Way. She pauses, bends and places her hands on her knees, sucking in the salty sea air rising from below.

For some reason, she cannot get Dinkel out of her mind. It's true that he is irritating, to the point she sometimes has to leave the room when he's in full whistling mode. His innocent demeanour also occasionally grates. And his propensity for breaking objects is annoyingly regular.

She rises to her full height and performs a series of leg stretches, then checks her watch. The distraction doesn't last long as her thoughts return to her junior colleague.

'Christ, Dinkel!' she yells. 'Get out of my head and leave me alone.'

Wiping sweat from her brow, she turns and sprints back the way she came.

She slows to a steady walk as she crosses the swing bridge and saunters along the promenade to her usual coffee shop. Awaiting her order, she focuses on the bustle of the fish market opposite.

Sipping on her cappuccino, she crosses the street and approaches a small market stall that is already open for business.

'Morning, love. What can I get you?'

Prisha smiles back. 'Morning. Is the fish fresh off the boat?'

'Aye, caught last night.'

She studies the various species of fish, then points at a tray. 'Can you give me two generous sized fillets of flounder, please?'

'Certainly, love. But that's not flounder, it's turbot.'

'Oh, what's the difference?'

'Well, they may fool the eye, those two. Appearances can be deceptive, you see. Turbot's pricier. It's a rarer catch and tricky to net compared to flounder. Though they look similar, turbot's got a firmer flesh, richer flavour—quite a delicacy, in my opinion.'

'I don't think I've ever tried it. I'll give it a go.'

'Good choice. You won't regret it.'

The fishmonger selects two fillets and holds them aloft for Prisha's inspection. She nods her approval as Dinkel appears like a mirage in her head again.

With the fish wrapped in butchers' paper, and sipping on her coffee, she tackles the steep incline of the Khyber Pass.

She comes to an abrupt halt as though hitting a brick wall. Her gaze drifts out to sea as a rush of excitement electrifies her senses.

'That's it. Similar but different. That's why we can't find Ted Fairchild. We've been fishing for flounder when we should have been searching for turbot.'

As Prisha hurriedly splays the colourised photographs out on the table, she hears the distinctive voice of Zac and Dinkel approaching along the corridor. They enter the room, bickering.

'What do you mean, you don't like football?' Zac quizzes, patently confused by Dinkel's declaration.

'I just don't.'

'I'll have to take you to a game at St. James Park one day, see Newcastle in all their glory, then you'll appreciate the buzz.'

'I've been to plenty of football games when I was in uniform. It's not my thing. There's too much tension.'

'Of course there's tension. That's what makes it exciting. As Bill Shankly once famously said, football is not life or death. It's much more important than that.'

'Who's Bill Shankly?'

Zac shakes his head in despair. 'I give up.' He focuses on Prisha instead. 'These early morning starts are ruining my beauty sleep. I hope this is good.'

'It is. Gather round. And I have you to thank for this, Dinkel. You're a genius.'

Dinkel is surprised. 'I am?'

Zac is baffled. 'He is?'

'Yes, inadvertently. Cast your eyes over the photos featuring Ted Fairchild again.'

Both men stare at the images with bleary eyes and tired minds.

'Yeah, what?' Zac eventually says.

'Ted Fairchild... arms folded. Arms folded. Arms folded. Arms folded,' she states, tapping each image with a pencil.

'You sound like a broken record. What's the big deal? The lad liked folding his arms. So what?'

She points at the next photograph and hands a magnifying glass to Zac.

'In this one, he's bending over, tying his shoelace. Take a closer look.'

Zac homes in on the image of Ted Fairchild. A few seconds pass.

'I don't know what I'm supposed to be looking at. It's a young twelve-year-old lad, tying his bloody laces. I don't see what... oh, I see it now.'

'What? What?' Dinkel urges excitedly.

Zac turns and hands him the spy glass. 'Breasts.'

'Pardon?'

'Breasts.'

'I thought that's what you said.'

Prisha grins triumphantly. 'That's why he, or should I say she, spends an inordinate amount of time with her arms folded across her chest. Ted Fairchild is not a boy. She's a girl.'

------◆------

As Dinkel beavers away at his keyboard, Prisha is still engrossed in the photographs, carefully picking over them one by one.

'Zac, on the whiteboard, can you pull up the first Happy Camp photo? The one where they're all lined up, Easter 1985. Then pull up a later one where they're playing a game of football, and it looks like Mike Ross has just scored a goal. Use the colourised versions.'

'Aye, give me a moment.'

'How are you going with the Births and Deaths registry, Dinkel?'

'Just logging on now, ma'am.'

Zac taps at the board and the Happy Camp photo fills the full screen. 'Here we go.'

'Zoom in on Mike Ross.'

'Hang on... how do you do that?'

'Two fingers, like you do on a phone.'

'Ah, that's it.'

They gaze intently at the smiling face of Mike Ross.

'Now the next one, and zoom in,' Prisha says.

In black and white, it was indiscernible, but in colour, the contrast is revealing.

'He's turned as brown as a berry,' Zac notes.

'Hmm... that's what Blake Baldwin, the farmer, remembered as well.'

'Some people are born that way. The records indicate it was an unusually warm summer. When I'm in the sun for any length of time, I resemble a blood orange.'

'It's your Scottish blood,' Prisha murmurs. 'You're not used to sunshine.' She walks to the board and stares at the face of the young boy. 'He doesn't look like the other boys, does he?'

Zac squints and rubs at his beard. 'No, you're right. He has a Mediterranean appearance.'

They are interrupted by primal grunts from Dinkel.

'Oh... oh. Ooh, ooh.'

'Eh, up? Sounds like Dinkel is in the last throes of an orgasm.'

'Ma'am, ma'am,' he half whispers.

'What is it, Dinkel?'

'The other day I mentioned the names Stanley and Francesca Fairchild, but their only living child was a girl, so I discounted them.'

Prisha and Zac gather round the back of Dinkel and gaze at the monitor.

'Go on,' Prisha says.

'In 1970, Stanley and Francesca had a baby boy named Theodore, but the child died from cot death, or sudden infant death syndrome, six months later. They then had a baby girl in 1973 called Theodora Fairchild.'

Zac eyeballs Prisha. 'They lost a cherished son. Three years later, they're blessed with another child, but it's not the boy they craved, it's a girl. So, they give her a similar name and pass her off as a boy. It has been known to happen.'

'Christ, the poor mite. What a horrendous lie she had to live, and as the years passed, it would have been harder and harder to disguise.'

'Oh, oh... ooh.'

Zac grimaces. 'I thought his whistling was bad enough, but this new habit of his, impersonating great apes, is really beginning to piss me off.'

'Ma'am, you may want to sit down.'

'I'm perfectly fine standing, thanks. Stop being so melodramatic and get on with it.'

'In 2005 Theodora Fairchild married.'

'Who did she marry?'

'A man.'

'Okay, that's progress, Dinkel, but if you could furnish us with the man's name, it may help somewhat.'

'She married a David King and took his surname. They divorced three years later.' Dinkel pulls his face away from the screen and stares up at Prisha and Zac.

'Fuck me blind,' Zac mutters.

Prisha's mouth falls open for a second. 'I don't believe it,' she whispers. 'Theodora Fairchild became Theodora King. Is she now known as Dora King?'

Zac relinquishes a sly grin. 'And if she's one and the same, is she our Happy Camp killer?'

# 41

Most detective work is mundane, some may even call it tedious. Endless records and documents to study. Telephone logs to analyse. Witness statements to probe. Forensic evidence to interpret. Very rarely is there a Eureka moment. But occasionally, one comes along to blow your wig off.

Tiredness, lethargy, despondency have all been banished to a far-off corner. In their place, excitement, anticipation and a fount of energy now reside.

The trouble is, imaginations can run riot in such a scenario and it's easy to jump to assumptions instead of fact checking. Prisha is not about to let that happen.

'Right, I want us to go over everything related to the Happy Camp murders from day one. Let's see if we've missed anything. Dinkel, I asked you a few days ago to do a background check on Dora King's work history. What did you come up with?'

'Nothing much. She's worked for Sebastian Thorne as his PA for nearly four years. Before that, she worked through an agency as a temp PA for various organisations, and also as a secretary. Going further back she...' He clams up, as his cheeks turn a florid red colour.

'What?' Prisha quizzes suspiciously.

'Ahem... about six years ago, she was working for VitaCare Nursing Solutions.'

'Was it a clerical position?'

'No, ma'am. She was a temping nurse.' His embarrassment is acute.

'Sweet shit on a stick,' Zac gasps. 'How could you have missed that after what happened at Doctor Blenheim's place?'

Prisha holds her hand up. 'Easy, Zac. Dora has never been on our radar for the Happy Camp murders until today. It's an easy oversight.'

Zac sucks air in through his teeth and emits a 'Sheeesh.'

'Next question; anyone know what type of car Dora drives?'

'Aye,' Zac replies, nodding. 'A grey Ford Focus.'

Prisha begins to pace back and forth as her mind works overtime.

'Okay. The circumstantial evidence against her is mounting.'

'It's all falling into place, Prisha. Something obviously happened to her at Happy Camp, and at some point in recent times, there must have been a catalyst. Morgan, Wilkes, and Blenheim are all dead, and Thorne has been set-up for murder. This is payback against the adults from the camp.'

'Possibly. But if she did fit-up Thorne, then she needed an accomplice, and that leaves only one person.'

'Mike Ross, the last of the missing children not accounted for.'

'Exactly. Any ideas on his whereabouts?'

Dinkel raises his hand in the air, much to Prisha's annoyance.

'Ma'am?'

'Yes,' she replies through gritted teeth.

'An oddity.'

Zac chuckles. 'This is not a confessional, Dinkel.'

Dinkel ignores him. 'The surveillance report on Dora King over the last week.'

'What about it?'

'It may be nothing.'

Prisha's fists involuntarily clench together, as do her back molars. 'Yes?'

'Dora took her car to the garage, the mechanic's, on two occasions.'

'And?'

'I found it odd.'

Zac bristles with impatience. 'Get to the point, man!'

'Who takes their car to a garage twice in the same week?'

'Someone who has car trouble, you numpty.'

Dinkel takes umbrage. 'Fine, fine. It was just a thought bubble. I just found it a bit of a coincidence, that's all.'

Prisha discounts his comment, then immediately becomes intrigued.

'Coincidence? You mean the fact that she visited a mechanic twice in the same week?'

'No. The fact that the mechanic was the one who assaulted Selwyn Morgan four or five years ago... Marco Rossellini.'

Prisha grins. 'Marco Rossellini? It's possible his name was anglicised when he was younger to Mike Ross. If he was born overseas, it would explain why there's no record of him or his parents in the registry. Okay, let's get to work. Time to catch our foxes.'

# 42

There are no squealing tyres or blaring sirens as two unmarked cars and four patrol cars quietly park up outside the garage, out of view from the entrance. As the officers alight, Prisha and Zac casually lead the small posse towards the workshop.

'Remember the briefing, Zac. We're here about Amanda Chan's death and the missing money. We don't want to alert him to our suspicions of the Happy Camp murders until we have more evidence against him. He's much more likely to open up if he thinks he can get off with a burglary and theft charge.'

'Agreed. Everyone knows the score.'

'Good. Let's do it.'

As they enter through the open roller door, Marco Rossellini is sitting on a stool reading a newspaper and sipping from a cup, obviously his mid-morning break. He barely acknowledges them as they enter.

'Oh, you again. What now?'

Zac waves the sheet of paper at him. 'We have a warrant to search your premises.'

He grins. 'Really?'

His flippancy aggrieves Prisha. 'Yes, really.'

He puts his drink down and rises. 'If you'd care to tell me what you're looking for, then I could save you some time.'

'We believe you could be in receipt of a large amount of cash in fifty-pound notes.'

Rossellini erupts into laughter. 'Ah, I see. Well, search away, but you don't mind if I carry on working, do you?' He nods at a Ford Mondeo suspended in the air on a hydraulic hoist. 'Only I promised a customer I'd have it ready by mid-afternoon.'

Zac turns to the uniforms around him, already bedecked in protective suits. 'Let's start with the Mondeo,' he says with a knowing smile.

After a good hour's fruitless searching, the team of officers are increasingly despondent. Toolboxes, storage areas, cupboards, the Mondeo, and even the toilet cistern were scoured to no avail.

'When's the bloody dog arriving?' Prisha hisses to Zac.

'Should have been here thirty minutes ago.'

They both eyeball Rossellini, who has been permitted to carry on working on the vehicle suspended on the hoist.

'Any news from Dinkel and the other team searching his home address?'

'Yes. Spoke to him a moment ago.'

'And?'

'Nothing, yet. We must be pragmatic, Prisha. It's been well over a week since the murder of Amanda Chan, and even longer since Doctor Blenheim's death. If Rossellini and Dora King are involved, they've had plenty of time to get rid of evidence.'

'Okay. Time to rattle him.' She wanders over to Rossellini, who is upright beneath the car tinkering with the exhaust pipe.

'I believe you know Dora King,' she states.

Without flinching, and still engrossed in his work, he replies, 'Aye. Nice woman. What about her?'

'She brought her car into your garage last week on two occasions. Why?'

'First time was her annual service, then she brought it back a few days later as the fan belt was squealing. I'd put a new one on, you see, and sometimes they stretch a tad after the car's been driven for a while. A few minutes' work to tighten it.'

'I take it you've seen the news recently?'

He shrugs with his back to her. 'Try not to take any notice of it. It's always depressing.'

'Are you aware of the arrest of Sebastian Thorne in relation to the murder of Amanda Chan?'

He pauses and spins around, spanner in hand. 'Yeah, I'm aware. Impossible to avoid that story. What of it?'

'Mr Thorne dropped off a bag of money at Ms Chan's flat. The money has never been recovered.'

He puffs out his cheeks and sighs. 'Look inspector, I'm not sure how or why you think I'm involved in something, but you've got your wires crossed. Do I look like a man who has suddenly come into two hundred and fifty grand?'

Prisha refrains from smiling despite his first mistake. 'You're a cool customer, Mr Rossellini. Nothing seems to ruffle your feathers.'

Another shrug as he turns his back on her and resumes his work as the sound of a vehicle pulling up outside has Prisha glancing over her shoulder. The handler attaches a lead to the sniffer dog and walks towards the workshop, the canine already wagging his tail excitedly in anticipation of a few treats. It lets out a short, high-pitched whine.

Rossellini turns and surveys the scene. 'What's the dog for? You don't now suspect I'm involved in drugs?'

'No, we don't. That's Monty, part of our K9 unit. A pure-bred cocker spaniel. He's on the top of his game. A real high-achiever. He can sniff out the chemicals used in bank notes and get into small spaces.'

Rossellini forces a wan smile, then shuffles out from underneath the car, presses a button on the hydraulic lift, and watches on as the car rises a few feet.

The dog handler and Monty approach Prisha.

'Any particular place you want me to begin, ma'am, or shall I let Monty lead the way?'

'Yes, let Monty do his thing.'

The handler pats Monty on the head and kneels to detach the lead. 'Okay, boy,' he encourages.

'No, wait!' Prisha bellows. She walks to the hydraulic lift and hits a button. 'Stand back,' she commands as the car descends. As the wheels contact the concrete, Monty is released.

Rossellini's cool persona evaporates. 'Why did you do that? I'm still working on the car.'

'Got to begin somewhere. It won't take long.'

He twitches. 'It better not.'

'Two hundred and fifty grand,' she states, as she watches Monty sniff around the vehicle.

'What?'

'You said two hundred and fifty grand earlier.'

'So?'

'I never specified the amount. I merely said it was a large sum of money. How did you know the exact amount?'

Blinks, non-plussed. 'Must have been on the news when that Amanda Chan was murdered.'

Prisha shakes her head. 'No, it wasn't. That information was never released to the media, so how could you have known the amount of money?'

His left shoulder arches back in a stretch. 'Must have heard it from somewhere. Probably down the pub. People gossip.'

'Hmm... that must have been it,' she replies as Monty suddenly takes an interest in the rear drivers-side wheel. The dog yelps.

'Okay, let's remove the wheel and the tyre. Monty's onto something,' the handler shouts.

Prisha turns to Zac and smiles. 'I think it's time we brought Dora King in. Arrange a warrant and stick her in the cells.'

# 43

Prisha shoots the duty solicitor a glance before repeating the question.

'Mr Rossellini, two hundred and fifty thousand pounds in notes were found in your workshop inside the tyre of a red Mondeo vehicle registered to you. On many of the notes, the fingerprints of Sebastian Thorne were detected. You still haven't explained how the money came to be there.'

'No comment.'

'We know the money was paid by Mr Thorne to Ms Chan to end her campaign against him. So, how did you end up with it?'

'No comment.'

'Very well. I am now about to show you a short video clip captured on security cameras at the Jackdaw fish and chip restaurant in Whitby. It's from Sunday 23rd April, the same night Selwyn Morgan was killed.'

The grainy video footage appears on a screen mounted on the side wall. It shows Rossellini, accompanied by a female, entering and leaving the restaurant. He gives it scant regard.

'We questioned you on the 25th April in regard to the investigation into the death of Selwyn Morgan. At that time, you gave your alibi as visiting the Jackdaw restaurant in Whitby.'

'I did, as the footage proves.'

'Indeed, it does. The restaurant staff also vouched for you. However, you originally told us you went alone. The footage shows that you were accompanied by a woman. We believe the woman in the video is Dora King, a customer of yours, and also Sebastian Thorne's personal assistant. Are you in the habit of taking your customers out for a fish and chip supper, or is your relationship with Dora King more involved?'

'No comment.'

Prisha is used to the game, but it doesn't make it any less tiresome.

'Mr Rossellini, did you murder Amanda Chan?'

'No comment.'

'We know Dora King can't have killed her, as she was seen on security footage at the time of Ms Chan's death. The money found in your workshop is the same money

Sebastian Thorne left at Ms Chan's flat on the night of 30th April. Now either you were at the flat that night, or someone else you know was, and passed the money onto you. They are the only two explanations I can think of unless you can offer me another?'

Rossellini rolls his neck, unlocking tension. 'I didn't kill her,' he finally replies, clasping his gnarly hands together.

Prisha manages to hide her shock at the reply. After two hours of questioning, it's the first time he's offered anything other than "no comment".

'Did Dora King tell you of Thorne's meeting with Ms Chan?'

'No comment.'

One step forward, two steps back. 'Okay, as you refuse to offer me any explanations, I'll give you my theory as to what really happened. This was a carefully orchestrated plan by yourself and Miss King. She arranged the meeting between Ms Chan and Mr Thorne. She knew the amount of money involved, she knew the time and place of the hand-over. However, she couldn't be directly involved as that would be too obvious, therefore she needed an accomplice to carry out the deed, at the same time ensuring she had a watertight alibi. You were the accomplice. You intended to enter Ms Chan's flat after Thorne had departed and steal the money. But it all went wrong, didn't it? Did she recognise you? Was there a struggle in which you killed her? Or perhaps you always intended to kill her. The murder weapon, an antique dagger belonging to Mr Thorne, was supplied to you by Dora King. She had access to it. You killed Ms Chan, then stole the money, knowing the dagger would implicate Thorne in the murder. Is that what happened?'

'I didn't kill her.'

'Then who did?'

'Isn't it obvious?'

'Not to me.'

'Thorne must have done it.'

Prisha relaxes back in her seat. 'Okay, let's for a moment assume you didn't kill Ms Chan, and remove murder from the equation. Even with that out of the way, you're still looking at some very serious charges, Mr Rossellini. Burglary, theft, perverting the course of justice, interfering with evidence at the scene of a crime, obstructing a police investigation, tampering with evidence. Burglary carries a maximum sentence of fourteen years; theft seven. But the big one is perverting the course of justice. That can result in a maximum life sentence. Even if the judge was lenient and the sentences ran concurrently, you'd still be looking at ten to fifteen years behind bars. That's a long time for a man of your age. What would you do when you came out?

You'd have no business to return to. You'd need to start again, or maybe you'd be close to retirement age at that point. And let's not forget, the money puts your firmly at the scene of a murder which we'll continue to investigate while you're on remand. It's a bleak outlook, whatever the scenario. So, why don't you do yourself a favour and tell me how you came to be in possession of the money?'

He rubs at his face, clearly agitated. 'If I tell you the truth and agree to testify in court, how would it help me?'

'It would help you greatly... if you're telling the truth. If you fess up and admit you stole the money and tell us everything you know, a judge will look very favourably upon that. They like people who show remorse and accept responsibility for their actions. It's seen as a signal. You're not a bad man who means harm. You were simply overcome by temptation, and we are all prone to that. And, as you have no previous, then I think you'd be judged leniently.'

'And helping the police?'

'Again, another tick in the box.'

'Hypothetically, if I tell you how I came by the money, how long do you think I would get?'

'Hypothetically? Maximum of five years, more likely two. Out after twelve months on good behaviour, less the time served on remand.'

Silence descends like low hanging mist as Rossellini stares at Prisha, then the table, then throws a glance at his duty solicitor, who merely raises his eyebrows in an—it's up to you—sort of way.

'Okay, I'll tell you what happened.'

Prisha offers him a twitch of a smile and shuffles forward in her seat. 'I think you've made the right choice.'

'I have been in a platonic relationship with Dora King for some time.'

'How long?'

Squinting slightly, he rolls his shoulders. 'Four, five years. We don't live together. It's more of a friendship than, well, you know. Dora told me all about Amanda Chan and the campaign she was waging against Thorne. I wasn't really interested until the other week. She said Thorne had agreed to pay Chan off. When she told me the amount involved, I was staggered. I don't know why, but it began to eat away at me. I know Chan comes from an extremely wealthy family, and that Thorne isn't short of a bob or two himself. Two privileged buggers playing silly little games. I've always had to work damn hard for my money and look where it's got me. I get by, just. Life has always been a struggle. Anyway, over the weekend I thought—what if?' He pauses, and stares at the blank wall behind Prisha.

'What if?' she probes gently after a few seconds.

'What if I entered the house after Thorne left and took the money. He wasn't going to miss it and Chan is the heiress to a fortune.'

'And did you?'

'Yes. I was hiding outside. There's a little alleyway that runs along the side of the flats, but you can see down to the basement. Thorne arrived and knocked a couple of times, then entered. A few minutes passed, and he comes stumbling out. He looked distressed. I didn't know why, but most importantly, he didn't have the bag with him.'

'If he'd departed the flat with the bag, what would you have done?'

'I had a knife on me. If Thorne left with the bag, I intended to confront him at the top of the steps and take the money.' He holds his hands up in defence. 'I swear to God, I didn't take the knife to threaten Chan with. It was simply a back-up plan for Thorne. I would never have used it.'

'Okay, but it didn't play out that way, did it? Thorne left without the bag. So how did you intend to steal the money from Amanda Chan? She wouldn't have willingly handed it over to you.'

'It was a simple plan, inspector. I don't have the brains for anything elaborate.'

'Go on?'

'I'd wait until Thorne's car drove away, then rush into the flat in a balaclava and grab the cash. She's a slight woman, so she wouldn't have been much of a threat or hindrance. As it turns out, I didn't need to do that. The door hadn't been locked, so I let myself in, crept through into the living room, then noticed a light in a back room, which turned out to be the office. I entered. It was gloomy, dark, subdued lighting. She was sitting in her chair staring at me, but said nothing. Didn't scream or anything. I saw the bag on the floor, moved forward, stooped, and picked it up. That's when I realised she'd been killed. The dagger in the eye. I turned, and left, and decided to hide the money for a while until things calmed down.'

'What was Dora King's involvement in the plan?'

He stiffens and sits upright. 'Dora had absolutely nothing to do with it. It was all my own doing,' he replies in a slightly aggressive tone.

'Did you confide in her afterwards?'

'No, of course not. That would have been the end of our friendship.'

'Were you wearing gloves?'

'Yes.'

'As you were waiting in the alley, did you see anyone else arrive before Mr Thorne?'

'No.'

'And how long were you in the alley for?'

'About fifteen minutes.'

'So, about 7:20 ish?'

'Give or take.'

'Did you not once stop to consider your actions and report Ms Chan's death to the police and tell them what you'd seen?'

He smiles resignedly. 'And put myself forward as the main murder suspect?' A deep chuckle. 'No, I didn't.'

---

Prisha gulps down the tepid coffee, then follows it up with a large swig of water from a bottle.

Frank is staring out of his office window overlooking the River Esk, hands on hips, swaying back and forth, as Zac scribbles in his notebook.

'We both watched the interview,' Frank states in his deep baritone.

'And?' Prisha questions.

'Rossellini is lying. But as to which part he's lying about, we're not sure.'

Zac lays his pen on Frank's desk. 'Is he retelling a version of events that helps his cause, knowing the cash we found in his car tyre leaves him without a leg to stand on...'

'Or,' Frank interrupts, 'is he lying to protect Dora King? He said he didn't have the brains for an elaborate plan, and yet that's exactly what it was. It was a classic heist, worked out to the letter. We know Dora has the smarts. You don't become a much-valued PA to Sebastian Thorne unless you're as wick as.'

Prisha grimaces, turns to Zac, and mouths the words, 'Wick as?'

He murmurs his reply. 'Very sharp, lively, on your game, cunning.'

She nods her thanks. 'I believe he's covering for her, Frank. And I'm also convinced the two of them are behind the Happy Camp murders.'

Frank finishes his perusal of the river and takes a seat. 'If that turns out to be true, then it would make sense to ensure it looked like Thorne killed Chan.'

Zac scratches his cheek. 'But why not kill Thorne as well? Finish the job off.'

Prisha raises her eyebrows, quizzically. 'I think Morgan, Wilkes, and Blenheim were abusers. Their punishment was death. Thorne, on the other hand, was not an abuser, but he was aware of the abuse and did nothing about it. His punishment is ruination, the lesser of two evils.'

Frank pops a Polo Mint into his mouth, as he suddenly gets the urge for a cigarette. 'All nice theories, Prisha, but evidence is what we need.'

'It's building, boss.'

'Do you still believe Thorne is an innocent party to all the murders?'

'Yes. His only failure is a lack of judgement. He could have easily put together a team of legal eagles and tied Amanda Chan up in the courts for years. Litigation, gag and suppression orders, going after social media sites to remove politically motivated content based on rumours and hearsay.'

Frank rubs at his chin. 'Hmm... and yet he didn't. He went for a simple pay-off. Odd route to take for such a shrewd man, a man of impeccable judgement.' He turns his attention to Zac. 'When do you intend to interview Dora King?'

'In the next five minutes. The duty sergeant has gone through all the preamble with her, and Dinkel is checking her fingerprints on the database right now.'

'Good. Okay, gang, keep chewing at the bone.'

# 44

Zac is fully aware of Dora King's razor-sharp intellect. She will have anticipated her arrest at some point, and played out possible scenarios in her head, and rehearsed her narrative to the nth degree. But she does have one weak link in her chain—she's unaware of the meticulous evidence the team has been building against her. And she won't be anticipating the angle Zac intends to come from.

Instead of starting the interview by asking all the usual questions and receiving all the usual replies, he intends to yank her from her comfort zone by blindsiding her.

After reading the caution, he settles comfortably into his chair and says, 'Ready to begin, Miss King?'

'Yes.'

He opens his folder and slides a copy of the Happy Camp photo across the desk. Dora gazes at it impassively but says nothing.

'Do you recognise this photograph, Dora?'

A shake of the head. 'No.'

'Have you ever seen it before?'

'No.'

'We found a copy of this in Amanda Chan's flat during our murder investigation.' He flips the photo over, taps at the typed words, then reads them aloud. 'Tom Maplin. Died August 1985.'

Dora shrugs. 'I'm not sure what you want me to say, sergeant.'

'Just to confirm, you've never come across this photograph before, ever?'

'That's correct.'

'Can you explain why your fingerprints are on the copy we found in Ms Chan's flat?'

Swallows hard but remains impassive. 'No, I can't.'

'Take another good look at it. The young man, early twenties, kneeling down; do you recognise him?'

'No.'

'It's Sebastian Thorne.'

She gives the image another cursory glance. 'Oh, yes, I see a resemblance now.'

'The boy third from the left is Mike Ross, the boy next to him is Ted Fairchild. The three adults at the back are Selwyn Morgan, Bishop John Wilkes, and Doctor Henry Blenheim, recently deceased. Brutally murdered.'

Eyes flicker, head tilts slightly. 'Why are you explaining all this? I was arrested on suspicion of conspiracy to murder Amanda Chan?'

Zac has no intention of answering questions. His job is to ask them. He pulls another document from his folder and places it in front of her.

'This is a record from the Births and Deaths Registry. Stanley and Francesca Fairchild were parents to a baby boy born in 1970— Theodore Fairchild. Unfortunately, the child died six months later. In 1973 they had another child, this time a girl named Theodora Fairchild. In 2005 Theodora married David King and took his last name.'

Leaning back in her chair, she calmly clasps her hands together, puckers her lips, but remains mute.

The next document is slipped across the table. 'Six years ago, you worked as a nurse for VitaCare Nursing Solutions, a company that supplies registered nurses and healthcare assistants to care homes, NHS facilities, and private homes. During that time, you administered care to Doctor Henry Blenheim at his home in Robin Hood's Bay. You were provided with a key to the kitchen door for after-hours entry.'

Dora takes a deep breath as Zac retrieves a forensic report from the binder.

'At the murder scene of Selwyn Morgan, we obtained a stray pubic hair sample from the body. DNA analysis indicated it did not belong to the deceased, but it is a match to the hair sample we took from you earlier during your custody admittance. We also...'

Dora holds her hand up in the air. 'Okay. You know. No point wasting everyone's time. I won't play games with you, sergeant. I'll tell you everything, and more importantly, why. If you could give me twenty minutes with my solicitor, it would be appreciated.'

Zac is reticent to agree to the request, as he knows the solicitor will strongly advise his client to offer "no comment." Reluctantly, he acquiesces.

---

Zac walks into the incident room to half-hearted clapping from Frank, Prisha and Dinkel.

'Well, well, well!' Frank declares, beaming as he pats Zac on the back. 'You pulled that one out of your arse, didn't you, lad?'

'Calm down, Frank. It's not in the bag yet. Her bloody solicitor could make her change her mind.'

'I don't think so. To me, Dora King knows her own mind. She realises the game is up.'

Prisha winks at Zac. 'I agree, but will she confess all, or be selective in what she admits to?'

Frank harrumphs his indignation. 'What has she got to gain by lying? If she admits to one murder, she may as well admit to all four. Her sentence wouldn't be much different.'

'I hope you're right. The last thing we need is unanswered questions. This needs to be watertight.'

Zac can't resist a smile. 'I'm going out for a breath of fresh air and to grab a coffee. I need to compose myself.'

# 45

With the interview preamble and formalities over, Zac carefully places his pen next to his file notes and nods appreciatively across the table.

'Okay, we're all set. In your own time, Dora.'

'What I'm about to say, sergeant is the whole truth. I'll give you all the details of the three murders.'

*Shite! Three murders. No, that's not a good start.*

'But first, I'll tell you why. Happy Camp is the beginning of this whole miserable episode. I take it you know about Happy Camp?'

'Yes, we've compiled a small dossier about its foundation, the charity, and the trustees. We also have accounts from Blake Baldwin, the farmer's son, and from Malcolm Pearce, one of the boys in the photo.'

She nods thoughtfully. 'Ah, poor old Malcolm Pearce. Another life ruined by that damnable place. Happy Camp was anything but happy. It was a miserable place of hard work, terrible food, and cramped living conditions, but that's by the by. It was also the site of emotional, physical, and sexual abuse by the three elders: Bishop Wilkes, Doctor Blenheim, and Selwyn Morgan. Every single child underwent abuse to some degree or other.' She laughs, as if in disbelief. 'The irony of it all is that my masquerade was the only thing that saved me from sexual abuse. They weren't into girls, you see. Just young boys. I swore that one day I would exact revenge. I'm sure you're aware that five out of the eight boys from the camp had their lives curtailed prematurely due to drink, drugs, suicide, and one suspicious death.'

'Tom Maplin?'

Her eyes become distant, dreamlike. 'Tom was a lost soul even before he went to the camp, and yet... he always had a spark of innocent hope, like things would get better. Maybe they did, in a ghoulish sense.' Her reverie abruptly ends.

'You said—your masquerade. Is it correct that you are in the photograph, and at that time you were known as Ted Fairchild?'

Eyelids flutter. 'Yes.'

'And the tall boy stood next to you—Mike Ross—now known as Marco Rossellini?'

A nod. 'Yes. He was born in Italy. His mother was British, his father Italian. The family moved to Whitby when Marco was very young. His father worked on the trawlers. He went overboard during a storm. The body was never found. Marco's mother struggled emotionally and financially. That's how Marco ended up in the care home. That's where we met. He was singled out the most by the elders, especially by Blenheim. He treated him as a subhuman because of his Mediterranean blood. It's no coincidence what happened to most of the boys from Happy Camp, sergeant. Childhood trauma doesn't end once you become an adult. It lives on like a slow growing cancer. Never forgotten, always there lurking in the shadows, ready to rear its ugly head just when you think you can finally begin to enjoy life. Well, you can't enjoy life, I mean. You can exist, get by, and hope and pray you don't turn into the monster that created you. I fought that curse for many years, but eventually I did turn into a monster, the fiend who murdered Wilkes, Blenheim, and Morgan. My only regret was that I didn't do it sooner. To see them living behind the veneer of respectability turned my stomach. And Wilkes and Blenheim were even revered. How can that be, sergeant? How can men who inflicted so much pain and torment walk around in society with their heads held high and be lauded?'

Zac swallows hard and murmurs, 'I don't know.'

Dora straightens. 'Right, you've heard the why, now for the how. The planning took years. The surveillance of their homes, their routines - hundreds of hours. Most people go somewhere nice for their holidays, but not me. My down-time was spent plotting their downfall. In fact, upon reflection, that was the most enjoyable part. There is a body of thought that believes the reason serial killers kill again is because the death of their first victim is somewhat of an anti-climax. It never lives up to expectation. The real satisfaction comes from the fantasy. I tend to agree. I thought it would give me some release, but it didn't, not really. The symbolism thing was a little melodramatic, but I thought, what the hell, why not? After all, I was only going to do this once... sorry, three times. I thought I may as well push the boat out and make it special. I apologise if that made your job harder, sergeant. It was never intended to throw you off the scent. I knew you'd catch me, eventually. Anyway, I'm waffling. Let's get down to the murders; Morgan was easy, due to his frailty, as was Blenheim, as he was already in ill health. Wilkes was a little harder, but still, I got there in the end.' She pauses, as if reprimanding herself. 'Apologies, I'm getting ahead of myself. We'll go in chronological order. Are you ready, Sergeant Stoker?'

'Yes, Dora. I'm ready.'

Frank taps at his desk with a pen. 'She's admitted to the murders of Morgan, Wilkes and Blenheim, and her account ties in with what we all know. She's not a crank. We never released anything to the press about the acorn motif burnt into the forehead, nor about the use of tent pegs. But...'

Prisha chews on her bottom lip. 'But why has she not mentioned Rossellini being involved? There's no way she could have committed those murders alone. She's of average height and build. She may have been able to overpower Morgan and Blenheim easily enough without much fuss, but Wilkes was fit and active. He must have shown some resistance. I find it hard to believe she could have subdued him and dragged him into the back garden alone. There were no signs of a struggle in his house and no bruising on him apart from where the tent pegs went in.'

Frank nods in agreement. 'And you still haven't questioned her about Amanda Chan's death, Zac.'

Zac rubs at his neck, agitated and tired. 'Yes, yes, I know, Frank!' he snaps.

'Easy tiger. Take a stroll around the block to reinvigorate yourself, then get back in there for round three. If you're getting nowhere, charge her with the three murders, and we can have a go at her another day.'

Zac rises, wearily. 'Aye, you're right. Sorry, Frank. Didn't mean to bite your head off.'

'That's all right. We'll go to the pub afterwards for a few pints, eh?'

'Yeah, I suppose.'

Prisha and Frank watch on as Zac slouches across the incident room, shoulders hunched.

'I've not seen him like this before,' Prisha notes, concerned.

Frank's barrel chest heaves. 'Aye, well, you must remember, Prisha, his two lads are at the same age as those poor buggers from Happy Camp. A bit too close to home. He's probably thinking Dora King should receive a Victoria Cross, not a life sentence.'

'Of course. I never thought of that.'

———⚬———

Zac smiles at Dora across the table, the harsh lighting emphasising the wrinkles and crow's feet on her face.

'Before we begin, I'd just like to say thank you for your previous statements. It's saved us a huge amount of time and resources, Dora.'

A faint, brief smile of acknowledgement. 'No point dragging it out. My work was done. May as well get on with the fallout.'

Zac shuffles uncomfortably at her brutal honesty. 'Yes, yes. I still have a few more questions to ask you.'

'I'll answer them as truthfully as I can, although it has been a long day and I'm feeling weary.'

'This will be the last interview for today.'

'Very well. What are your questions?'

'There was no sign of a forced entry at Doctor Blenheim's house. How did you get in?'

Her eyebrows arch. 'I think you already know the answer to that.'

'Yes, but for the record.'

'When I worked as a nurse for VitaCare, I was given a key for after-hours access to Blenheim's place. I simply had a duplicate cut. People don't often change their locks, if ever.'

'I see. And moving onto the death of Bishop Wilkes; you said you parked up about a half-mile from his house and cut across a field to his back garden and knocked on the patio doors at the back of his house, then told him your car had broken down and your mobile phone was dead.'

'That's correct.'

'You then pulled a knife out and told him to go into the garden and strip naked.'

'Yes, after I forced a rag into his mouth.'

Zac leans back and rubs a hand through his beard. 'You mentioned earlier that Morgan and Blenheim were frail, weak, and were easy to overpower. Wilkes may have been in his eighties, but he was in good health. I find it hard to believe you could have carried out the killing alone.'

'When you hold a knife to someone's throat, it's amazing how easily they'll cooperate.'

'Still, just purely from a practicality side, it would be hard to pin a person's arm out and drive a tent peg through the palm. It would have been a struggle. Was Marco Rossellini your accomplice in the murders?'

'No, most definitely not. Marco knew nothing about the murders other than what he heard on the news. I admit Wilkes was more difficult, but I did it alone, as I did with the other two.'

'Okay, let's move on. The Happy Camp photo you sent to Amanda Chan had your fingerprint on it. I'm struggling with this a little. You were meticulous in ensuring you left no forensic evidence at the crime scenes. The only thing we found was one pubic hair, which we'll come to in a moment. The fingerprint on the photo seems sloppy, not at all in keeping with the way you operate. Why were you so careless?'

'It never crossed my mind the photo would become embroiled in another murder. It was used as a little tempter to tickle the curiosity of Ms Chan.' She hesitates as she studies Zac's pained expression. 'I can see I've lost you, sergeant. Let me explain; Sebastian Thorne was a young adult at Happy Camp, but he never abused the children. However, he was aware of the abuse, of that, I'm certain. I struggled with that for years. Why didn't he come forward and report what he'd seen and heard at the camp? Then it finally dawned on me. Who would have believed him? At the time, he was a young man working as a builder, from a poor background. Was anyone really going to take his accusations against a bishop, an eminent doctor, and a servant of the church, seriously? No, of course not. As the years passed, I watched his rise to the top, and the thought revisited me. I wrote him a letter about eight years ago, under the name Ted Fairchild, with a PO Box as a return address. I implored him to come forward and report the historical abuse. He was now in a position of power and authority and had the ear of many influential people. The police would be forced to take his allegations seriously. They'd have also carried a lot of gravitas should the case have come to court. He replied in a very brief letter. Do you know what he said?'

Zac shakes his head. 'No.'

'He said he could hardly remember his days at Happy Camp, and to the best of his knowledge, witnessed no abuse of any kind. He wished me his best and ended by saying it's always better to look forward in life rather than backwards. I was incensed. The day I received his letter was the day I vowed to bring forth my own justice. In a way, he was the catalyst.'

'But you never planned to murder him?

'No. That would have tarred him with the same brush as the others. They were evil. Sebastian was... is, political. He was protecting his reputation. But he still had to pay his dues. Not death, but a complete fall from grace and public humiliation. I knew it would take time and the best way to plot his downfall was to be as close to him as I could—hence how I ended up as his personal assistant. It meant a career change, and working for various organisations to build my reputation, first as a highly efficient secretary, then as a PA, but eventually I landed the job with Sebastian.'

'And how did Ms Chan fit into all this?'

'Serendipity, sergeant. I had to bide my time until I saw the ideal opportunity. It was no secret to me that Sebastian was engaged in some dubious development deals. I'm no legal expert, so I was never certain if his business practices were illegal, or simply unethical. By chance, I happened across Amanda Chan's YouTube channel and saw my opportunity. I began secretly sending her snippets of information about him. I baited the hook, and she took it. Later, I'd give her anonymous tip offs about his media announcements, which she'd disrupt. When Sebastian suggested he'd pay her off, I couldn't believe my luck.'

'Why?'

'I'd already done my research on Amanda Chan, or Chandler as her real surname is, the only daughter of Brendan Chandler, and the eventual heiress to his massive fortune. I knew she couldn't be bought, even though she was living just above the breadline. It would only take a phone call to mammy or daddy to bail her out if things got bad. Sebastian asked me to sort it out, the pay-off. I met with Chan and offered her fifty, then a hundred thousand pounds. She wasn't interested, although I told Sebastian that she was. I then sent her a copy of the Happy Camp photo to pique her interest.'

Zac winces. 'Where did you obtain the photo of Happy Camp?'

'From Doctor Blenheim's house. I found it in a drawer, whilst searching for a pair of scissors. I called around to see

Amanda Chan the day after I'd posted her the photo, and we hatched a plan.'

'Which was?'

'She would email Sebastian the photo anonymously. He would instantly know it was from Chan and would anticipate an increase in the pay-off money, which is exactly what he did. I then told him I'd received a call from Chan saying she'd cease her campaign against him, but the asking price was now a quarter of a million pounds. He was to deliver the money, alone, to her flat that night at 7:30. Oh, and another stipulation was that it had to be in a Gladstone Bag. Sebastian kept one in a wardrobe in his office. I'll admit, it was petty. But I knew he was fond of the bag, and I derived some pleasure from the fact he'd be handing it over to Chan.'

'Was Ms Chan privy to all this?'

'Yes. The plan was that Chan would record Thorne paying her off. She'd engage in a back and forth with him about his various shady dealings before he left. Then later, I would collect the money from her.'

Zac is puzzled. 'Hang on... I don't get it. Why would you collect the money?'

'Chan didn't want the money. She had what she wanted already; Thorne recorded red-handed paying-off a person who was raising tricky questions about him.'

'And how did she intend to record him; audio, video or both?'

Dora shrugs. 'She never directly specified. I automatically assumed it would be video with audio, to use on her YouTube channel.'

'I see. So, in this deal you hatched with her, you would end up with the money?'

'Yes. But the money was simply a by-product of the main motive... Sebastian's downfall. I realised that once the video of Sebastian went viral, it would only be a matter of time until his ignominious downfall. Then I would undoubtedly be out of work. A quarter of a million would have tied me over for many a year. I live very frugally, sergeant.'

Zac mentally trawls over his recollections of Prisha's interview with Marco Rossellini. 'But you never collected the money, did you? Mr Rossellini did. He has admitted to that.'

She takes a deep sigh and holds her face in her hands. 'Yes, he did. And I shall forever regret embroiling him in this saga. He doesn't deserve it and is completely innocent in everything apart from helping a friend out.'

'Helping you out?'

'Yes. When I received the call from Sebastian, and he told me Chan had been murdered, I had to think and act quickly. I asked him where the money was, and he said he'd left it behind. I wasn't certain what had gone on in that flat, but I knew if the police found the bag of money, then it would be held as evidence, and probably eventually returned to Sebastian. I admit, my critical thinking wasn't at its best. I rang Marco and informed him of the situation. Then I asked him to wear gloves and to retrieve the money and hide it, then to have no contact with me until I contacted him.'

'And what was in it for him?'

'He asked for nothing. I would have eventually given him a fair share once everything had calmed down.'

'That account does not tally with Marco Rossellini's version of events. He said that in casual conversation, you'd mentioned the pay-off. This revelation preyed on his mind and he, without your knowledge, waited outside Chan's flat on the night of the murder. When Thorne left without the money, he entered and grabbed it for himself.'

'He's lying.'

'Why would he lie?'

'To protect me. During his questioning, you must have hinted at my involvement, and to help me out, he concocted the story. I can assure you; my version of events is the truth. Marco's only involvement was as a courier.'

'Alternatively, it could be you who's protecting him. You insist he knew nothing of the Happy Camp murders, and yet I find it inconceivable you carried them out alone. And now you're downplaying his role in the Amanda Chan murder. Why are you protecting him?'

'I'm not. He wasn't involved in the Happy Camp murders and if you had any evidence to the contrary, I'd have heard about it by now. He's innocent, and we can go over and over this until the cows come home, but my version will never change.'

Zac puffs out air and leans forward. 'Okay, a few more questions, then we'll wrap it up for today.'

'Good.'

'The pubic hair we found on Selwyn Morgan's body contained your DNA. We also found urine residue on his face and chest. Can you enlighten me?'

'Certainly, sergeant. I'm not a pervert, if that's what you're thinking. At Happy Camp, the adults repeatedly used a catchphrase—*payback time*. It was issued whenever we'd committed a minor infringement of their authoritarian rules. Well, Selwyn Morgan got his payback from me. They'd already begun calling me the Freak due to my developing breasts, which I tried to hide by wearing baggy tops. They simply thought I had a weird deformity. They had no idea I was a girl. There was a hut at the back of the barn that was called the Purification Hut. That's where they'd take one of us to be "anointed" as they euphemistically called it.'

'To be sexually abused?'

'Yes, after they'd sprinkled holy water on our heads. I was one of the last to go. It was always just before bedtime, and after they'd been drinking, usually red wine, and only when the bishop was in attendance. They took me to the hut and forced me to undress. That's when they uncovered my secret.'

'Christ,' Zac mutters accidentally.

'At first, they were shocked, then amused. They began laughing and taunting me. They pushed and jostled me around, calling me the Freak until I curled up in a corner and began to sob. It was at this point that Morgan, who was worse for wear, removed his penis and urinated over me.'

'Oh, sweet mercy,' Zac whispers, desperately wanting to end the interview. 'I'm so sorry.'

'Not your fault, sergeant. In a roundabout way, I blame myself for the death of Tom Maplin,' she adds, regretfully.

'How can you possibly blame yourself?'

'After they'd humiliated me in the hut, they threw my clothes at me and ordered me to get cleaned up and go to bed. I went to the ablutions block and had a shower. As I returned to the Happy Camp barn, Sebastian Thorne, or Cyclone, as he was known then, was packing up his tools in his beaten up, old Land Rover. Doctor Blenheim and Morgan emerged from the barn, dragging Tom Maplin by the scruff of the neck. They told him that because of me, he was the next to be "anointed". Poor little lad. He had a terrible stammer and was pleading with them that he didn't want to go. He even wet himself. Cyclone drove off, and I went to bed and pulled the blankets over my head. Early the next morning, a search party was set up to look for Tom, who'd disappeared. We split up into pairs. Doctor Blenheim and Mike... Marco, found Tom in the river. He had a large bruise on his head. I guess the truth is lost forever now. But the official version, that he slipped on the stepping stones, banged his head, then drowned, is balderdash.'

'You suspect foul play?'

'I don't suspect, sergeant, I know. I didn't see what happened, but those three monsters were responsible for his death. They were rowdy and aggressive that night. It's possible they went too far, as if child abuse were not far enough. Anything else you want to know?'

Feeling nauseous, Zac replies, 'What? Oh, just a few more questions.' He takes a sip of water from a glass and tries to remain professional. 'Ahem... we found a foreign footprint at the crime scene of Selwyn Morgan. It matched with the sole imprint from Sebastian Thorne's shoe when he was first arrested.'

'Ah, yes. Simply another red herring. As you know, I had access to Sebastian's wardrobe. Sorry if that threw you.'

'What did you use to burn the acorn motif into the foreheads?'

'It was a signet ring I stole from Bishop Wilkes, from the camp. I entered the ablution block one morning and saw that he'd left the ring on the sink. I pocketed it. I'm ashamed to admit I was a little light-fingered in those days. I used a small blowtorch to heat the ring up, holding it with a pair of needle-nose pliers, then pressed it into the forehead.'

'After, or before, they were dead?'

'Before.'

'What did you use to cut off their genitalia?'

'An extremely sharp hunting knife. And before you ask, prior to their deaths.'

Zac swallows hard and involuntarily squeezes his legs together. 'Why was Selwyn Morgan the only one to have his ankles broken?'

'I intended to do them all, but decided it was too much effort. I had to sit on his legs, facing his feet, then get the block of wood in place as he was writhing around. It took too long.'

'We've searched your premises and vehicle, and Thorne HQ, but we have not located a hunting knife, signet ring, or a blow torch. Where are they?'

'At the bottom of the sea. I threw them off the end of Whitby East Pier after I killed Doctor Blenheim.'

'Okay, I think we're done. I just need to formally charge you.'

<hr>

Zac pushes his chair under the table. 'This interview is now over,' he states, turning off the recording. 'I'll give you five minutes with your solicitor, then the duty sergeant will take over to arrange your remand.'

The solicitor quickly rises from his seat. 'Ahem, excuse me for a moment, but I need the bathroom.' He bustles past Zac and exits.

Zac turns and gazes upon Dora King, who has remained calm and composed throughout.

'I know Marco Rossellini is involved Dora, in what capacity, I'm not sure. Whether we ever gather enough evidence against him is another matter. My question is, why are you protecting him?'

She considers the question thoughtfully before answering. 'Hypothetically, if I were protecting him, I'll give you my hypothetical answer. Payback time.'

'Sorry?'

'Marco was like an older brother to me. I lost count of the number of times he took the blame on my behalf and received brutal beatings, not just at the camp, but also at the care home. He was my defender, my protector, and kept my secret until it could be kept no longer. I love him, sergeant. As one loves a brother. Now it's my turn to take the blame—hypothetically, of course. Have you charged him?'

'Yes. At the moment, he's charged with theft. He's on remand.'

'History repeats. Once again, he's punished for my actions.'

Zac makes to leave.

'Sergeant Stoker?'

Hand on the door, he turns. 'Yes?'

'I'm truly sorry for the death of Amanda Chan. You may think I'm a cold-blooded killer, but I'm not. I like people. Some I even care about. But those who are evil need to be held accountable—don't they?'

Zac briefly recalls his own brush with evil. 'Yes. Yes, they do.'

# 46

Zac welcomes the cool, tranquil sea breeze as it wafts over his face. He closes his eyes and turns to the waning sun; the rays lighting up the inside of his eyelids until all he can see is a reddish hue. Prisha places her hand on his shoulder and gives him a friendly massage.

'It was painful, but you got the job done,' she whispers. 'Good work.'

Frank places the tray down on the bench and hands out the drinks. 'Gin and tonic for Prisha. Pint of Guinness for me, and a pint of Whitby Whaler, *and* a double whisky chaser for Zac—the man of the moment. Is this our new local now—The White House?'

Prisha takes a sip of her drink. 'I think so. It has a serenity out here, overlooking the sea.'

'Aye, true enough. Are we ready to talk or do you want a few minutes peace and quiet?'

Zac's eyes spring open. 'Let me get this down, then we'll talk.' He knocks the double shot down in one, grimaces, then takes a hefty quaff of his beer. 'That's better. Okay, ready.'

Frank faces his junior colleagues. 'Three murders solved is a great result, but the pressing question is, who killed Amanda Chan? There are only two suspects, Sebastian Thorne or Marco Rossellini. Whose story do we believe? Dora King and Rossellini, or Thorne?'

Zac places his pint down. 'Dora came clean about the Happy Camp murders. Why would she lie about Chan?'

'To protect Rossellini?' Prisha offers. 'I think we're all agreed she couldn't have carried out all the murders alone. She needed an accomplice.'

Frank holds a finger in the air. 'That's not quite true. She carried out the Doctor Blenheim murder alone, and in broad daylight, not like the other ones, late at night. If she could pull that off, then why not the others?'

'We're still not certain she did kill Blenheim. It's possible Rossellini was dressed as the nurse. And her explanation about why she broke the ankles of Selwyn Morgan doesn't ring true, either. Do you remember early on, when we questioned Rossellini about his fracas with Morgan four years ago? He said when he was a kid, Morgan gave him a good hiding in a graveyard, and as he ran away, he twisted his ankle. What if the breaking of the ankles was

Rossellini's payback, just as Dora urinating on him was hers?'

Frank rubs at his face. 'Hellfire, we could go around in circles forever with this. Okay, let's focus on what could help us find Amanda Chan's killer. This recording Chan was supposed to make of Thorne handing the money over; does it exist, and if so, where in hell's name is it?'

'Digital forensics have been through everything, and although she had some interesting things on her laptop, there's no audio or video of Thorne being in her flat that night.'

'What about one of those video cameras you put the tape in? Did she have one of them?'

Zac lifts his pint to his lips, then puts it down in indignation. 'For God's sake, Frank, those things were analogue and went out with winkle pickers.'

'Did they? I still have mine in the back of the wardrobe somewhere. Unless Meera has thrown it out, which she tends to do with anything over three years old.'

Prisha reties her ponytail. 'If Dora is telling the truth, then a video must exist. But why haven't we found it? And if she's lying, then the only explanation is that Rossellini is the killer.'

'I can't think straight at the moment,' Zac states dolefully. 'My mind is frazzled.'

Frank nods his agreement. 'Aye, you're right. Enough of police talk. Time to put the brain into neutral for a while. Who are Leeds playing this weekend?' he asks, turning to Zac.

'You know I don't watch amateur football, Frank. But Newcastle are playing Man City this Saturday at St James.'

'Oh, very droll. Look at the silverware, lad. That doesn't lie.'

'We've won more trophies than your lot.'

'Aye, but you have to go back to the 1920s. I'm talking about in living memory. Your trophy cabinet should be on the Antiques Roadshow.'

Prisha wanders off with her drink as the good-natured banter continues. Her mind calms as she watches a distant trawler chug through the waves, heading back to safe harbour.

She whispers to herself, reflectively. 'I always believed Thorne had been set-up. But Frank mentioned it recently; Thorne is shrewd. Why would he fall for such an obvious honey-trap as a hand-over at Chan's flat? Hmm...'

# 47

## Thursday 11th May

She stalks down murky ginnels and snickets, hemmed in on either side by high stone walls. They glisten as water weeps down their rough surfaces and splashes onto the ancient cobbles beneath her feet. Pungent wafts of mould and damp assault her nostrils. Hopelessly lost, her racing heartbeat and laboured breath are the only sounds in the sinister maze. A crack of light erupts at the far end of the alley, like a spotlight on a stage, it beckons her onward. A sharp pain stabs at her chest. Her fingers instinctively feel for the amulet around her neck and the small black claw which rests on her breastbone.

It's a warning.

She should turn back, but the puncture of light fascinates her as she creeps forward. Her eyes widen in puzzlement. Dropping to her haunches, she reaches out for the object in the epicentre of the iridescent beam. She holds it aloft, staring as a realisation dawns; she was forewarned by the fortune-teller. The doll's head in her hand stares past her at something behind. Rigid with fear, she slowly swivels her head. High up, perched on a leaky drainpipe, sits a bird, as black as tar, except for the unnaturally grey piercing eyes. The raven gazes down upon her, an omen made flesh. She drops the head. It rolls like a ball and rests in a gutter of dirty water, face down. The bird calls out in a series of rapid caws, its hooked beak resembling a medieval instrument of torture. As the black shadow swoops, Prisha's scream is swallowed by the walls as they close in on her. Panic and fear collide. She sprints, because that's all she has left.

'Prisha, Prisha, it's all right. It's just a dream.'

Panting hard and dripping in sweat, Adam's face comes into focus. 'Shit,' she gasps.

'Was it the usual one?'

'Yes. Trapped in a dark alley. Doll's head and a bloody raven.'

Adam wraps his arms around her and strokes her head. 'It's my fault. I should never have cajoled you into seeing the fortune-teller.'

She breathes in his comforting musk, feeling safe and reassured. 'Don't be daft. It will pass. I only have the nightmares when I'm overtired.' He releases her and pulls a jumper on and slips into a pair of jeans. 'Do you have to go right now?' she asks, glancing at the clock which blinks the digits, 4:31 am.

He pauses. 'I...'

She curses herself for being needy. 'Sorry. You go. I'm getting up, anyway.'

He leans in and pecks her on the lips. 'I'll see you tonight. Maybe we'll go out for dinner. How does that sound?'

She feigns a smile. 'Great.'

His footsteps reverberate down the stairs, followed by the bang of the front door. A few moments later, the familiar guttural growl of the Land Rover is heard. She listens until it fades to nothing. Her eyes fall back onto the clock. She stares at it in a trance.

Throwing the sheets back, she leaps from the bed. 'The clock! The bloody clock. Where is it?'

———⦿———

Zac enters the incident room, closely followed by Dinkel. They both must have been dragged through a hedge backwards because their usually smart appearance is a forgotten memory.

'This better be good, Prisha,' Zac grizzles as he removes his jacket and flops into a chair at the side of her as she pours over the photos on a table. 'Oi, Dinkel, make yourself useful and put the kettle on. I'll have a strong black coffee. Two teaspoons.'

Dinkel stifles a yawn. 'Milk?'

'For fuck's sake. I said black.'

'Oh, yes. Sorry.'

Zac shakes his head in contempt. 'And you reckon we'll make a copper out of him, yet? Not while he's got a hole in his arse.' He drags a hand through his long black locks, flicking the hair back and across. 'So, why the urgent call at five-bloody-thirty on a Friday morning?'

'I've been watching the video that forensics recorded of the crime scene at Amanda Chan's flat. And I've studied all the photos they took, for the third time, and it's definitely not there.'

'What's not there?'

'The digital clock.'

Zac closes his eyes and shakes his head. 'Clock?'

'When I visited Amanda, her laptop was connected to a larger monitor on her desk. On top of the monitor was a small digital clock. It was stuck to the top with a blob of Blu Tack. At the time, it was nothing more than a fleeting thought, but I found it odd.'

'Why?'

'Every computer has a clock in the bottom corner. Why would she need another one on top of her monitor?'

'Who knows? Amanda Chan had all the signs of an obsessive-compulsive personality. Maybe she was fixated with time, you know... what's the medical jargon... chronophilia?'

Prisha resists a smirk as Dinkel arrives with Zac's coffee. 'I think you mean chronophobia. Chronophilia is the sexual attraction to people of a certain age.'

'I do beg your pardon. Ah, thanks Dinkel,' he says, taking the coffee. He does a double-take and stares in disbelief at the cup. 'This may sound like a stupid question, but why are there two spoons in the cup?'

Dinkel yawns. 'You said a strong black coffee with two teaspoons.'

Zac curses under his breath and wearily eyeballs Dinkel as he wanders back to the kitchen. 'And to think, he was his father's most tenacious sperm.' He removes the spoons and places them on a piece of paper on the table. 'What's your theory about the clock?'

'Spy cameras are everywhere these days. They're so small they can be fitted into baby monitors, USB sticks, pens, even sunglasses.'

'And small digital clocks.'

'Exactly.'

'If Chan wanted to catch Thorne on camera, handing the money over, then why not use the cam on her laptop?'

'Too obvious. Thorne may have noticed it.'

'Okay, that's one theory, but I have another one. What if Dora King was lying about Chan?'

Prisha frowns. 'Yesterday you believed her. What's changed?'

'As I was driving in, I thought about what she said to me after the interview ended and I was heading out of the door.'

'What did she say?'

'I remember her exact words. She said—I'm truly sorry for the death of Amanda Chan. I initially thought it was a simple, heartfelt platitude. The sort of thing someone says when they offer you their sympathies after a loved one's died.'

'But now?'

'It could be interpreted two ways. What if it was an admission?'

'You mean Amanda Chan had to be killed to frame Thorne?'

'Yes.'

'What was her expression as she said it?'

'Remorseful, contrite.'

'So, the scenario would be that Rossellini arrives at the flat five minutes before Thorne. He somehow gains admittance, maybe by saying he has a message from Dora

King. He kills Chan, then waits outside for Thorne to arrive. If Thorne departs with the bag, he confronts him with the knife. If Thorne leaves without the bag, all's good. He simply pops back into the flat and takes the money.'

'We believe Rossellini helped Dora in at least one of the Happy Camp murders, even if we can't prove it. Maybe they'd become immune to the horrors of taking someone's life. What if Chan was an expendable pawn in their quest to complete their work—ruin Thorne. Plausible?'

'Entirely plausible. But is it the truth?' Prisha rises and paces back and forth. 'You're not going to like this, but hear me out.'

'Oh, shit the bed. Here we go,' he groans.

'When I had my brief chat with Amanda, as I was leaving, she said that one day she'd catch Thorne in the act and make the world aware of it. That ties in with Dora King's version of events.'

Zac winces as he sips on the scalding hot coffee. 'We're back to square one. We're still no closer to finding out if Rossellini or Thorne killed Chan.'

'Not quite. The clock.'

'Come on, Prisha, you're clutching at straws. It could be in another part of the house, or may have fallen behind a desk or put in a drawer. Hell, it may have been broken, and she binned it.'

'It wasn't binned.' She picks up a clutch of photographs off the table and hands them to him. 'Forensics emptied her bins, bagged everything, then laid it all out on a tarpaulin before taking pictures. There's no clock.'

Zac studies the prints briefly and passes them back. 'I know what your inference is, Prisha. You think Thorne was already privy to Amanda's plan to record him. He killed her and removed the clock himself.'

'It's possible.'

'And the lack of blood on Thorne when he was arrested?'

Prisha winces as Dinkel returns. 'What if he was wearing gloves and some sort of lightweight covering, like a pac-a-mac or poncho?'

'And what happened to his protective clothing and the clock? We arrested him seconds after he returned to Thorne HQ. His car was examined to within an inch of its life and there was nothing. No DNA, no gloves, no protective jacket, no clock.'

'He could have disposed of them on the way back to the car park.'

'We have CCTV and security cam footage that traces his vehicle all the way back from Amanda's flat to his offices.'

'Yes, but it's patchy at best. It's a fifteen-minute drive and his car is picked up at a dozen locations along the route. He could have stopped at any point and dumped the gloves and jacket into a rubbish bin.'

Zac sighs. 'If he did, that evidence will be long gone.'

'I'm not convincing you, am I?'

'Not really. A lot of presumption based upon a digital clock that we don't really know *is* missing.'

'Then let's rule it in or out. We'll grab a couple of uniforms to help us search Amanda's flat again. Dinkel, get onto media relations and tell them to issue an appeal for dash-cam footage for the night Amanda Chan was murdered, specifically along the route that Thorne travelled between 7:30 and 7:45. Be vague in your wording. Say something about a serious incident that happened but omit any specifics. Then, I want you to go over the footage we already have and analyse it in microscopic detail and see if you can pick out any anomalies.'

'Yes, ma'am.'

Zac rises and picks up his jacket. 'By the way, Dinkel... the coffee was shite.'

'Thanks.'

'Pleasure.'

# 48

Pale sunlight creeps into the basement flat like an intruder, tentative, nervous. Its weak glow no match for the harsh, yellowish glare of the ceiling lights.

Three hours have elapsed, and the four officers have scoured every nook, drawer, and cupboard. Searched behind every piece of furniture, under beds, down the back of chairs and the sofa, but there is no sign of the missing clock.

Prisha thanks the two uniformed officers and dismisses them before turning to Zac. 'No clock.'

'It doesn't help us though, does it? If your theory is right about the spy cam, and if Thorne did take it, he will have destroyed it by now.'

'It does help. We can now focus our attention on Thorne instead of Marco Rossellini,' she explains, casting her eye over the office.

Zac peels off the blue latex gloves and drops them into his jacket pocket.

'Let's go over what we have against Thorne. He admits to being in the flat. His fingerprints were on the murder weapon—his antique dagger. He had a motive. That's four ticks for the prosecution. On the other hand, the money he left behind was found in Rossellini's workshop. We have not a jot of DNA evidence against Thorne. Everything is circumstantial. And to muddy the waters even further, a self-confessed serial killer is intrinsically linked to Amanda Chan. It doesn't bode well for a conviction. The defence barrister will create enough doubt in a jury to return a not-guilty verdict.'

Prisha purses her lips. 'You're preaching to the converted. We'll just have to keep digging until something incriminating surfaces.'

As they exit the office, Prisha flicks the light switch off as her eyes wander to the ceiling. She closes the door, then halts and stares at the carpet in a daze.

'What's the matter? Did you leave the chip pan on?' Zac asks, noticing her trance-like state.

She raises her head and peers at him, then turns, reopens the office door, and flicks the light back on. Nodding towards the ceiling, she says, 'Why would anyone have two in one room?'

Zac follows her gaze. A sly grin spreads across his face. 'You don't think...'

'Yes. I do.'

# 49

The lift doors hiss open as Prisha and Zac step forth into the immaculate office of Sebastian Thorne. He doesn't rise from behind his extravagant oak desk but merely rocks back and forth in his plush, office chair as he spins an ornate fountain pen around and around in his fingers.

Prisha cocks her head to one side. 'Mr Thorne, you do realise you are in breach of your bail conditions by being here?'

Thorne smiles, maintaining his composure under scrutiny.

'Inspector Kumar and Sergeant Stoker, welcome. Would you care for refreshments?' His offer contains no sentiment.

'Did you hear what I said, Mr Thorne?'

He chuckles. 'You obviously don't keep abreast of your paperwork, inspector. My lawyer has successfully negotiated a modification of the bail conditions, citing the essential nature of my presence here for business continuity. I assure you, I am within my legal rights to be here. Now, please, take a seat,' he offers, nodding at two chairs in front of him.

Zac glowers at him. 'That won't be necessary.'

'I see. A flying visit.' He places the pen down carefully on the desk. 'I assume this is a courtesy call to keep me abreast of developments in regard to the murder of Ms Chan?'

Prisha nods her head to the side. 'You could say that.'

A grimace, masked as a smile, etches over his face. 'You're being very guarded, inspector.' Glances at his watch. 'But if you could get to the point. I have an overseas call scheduled in five minutes' time.'

'Of course, time is very precious, isn't it? That's why we're so obsessed with it.'

Zac grins. 'Oh aye, time is a conundrum, all right. Tick, tick, tick. You can buy it, save it, lose it, waste it, keep it. It flies, it drags, it can stand still. It doesn't matter who you are, or how wealthy and powerful you may be, but time is finite and there's never enough of it, is there?'

Thorne's face hardens as he becomes bored. 'Unless you have time on your hands, of course. Which I don't.'

'Sorry. I was just killing time.'

Thorne stops rocking in his chair, his face now like thunder. 'Most amusing, sergeant. Now, are we going to play word games or cut to the chase?'

Prisha edges forward. 'I visited Amanda Chan's flat nearly a fortnight ago, as part of my investigations into another case. In her office, stuck to the top of her computer monitor, was a small digital clock. For some reason, it lodged at the back of my brain, stored away but forgotten about. I mean, they're not that common these days, what with smart phones and laptops. Why have a digital clock when you can quickly glance at your mobile? My boyfriend still uses a digital clock. It's a back-up system used in conjunction with his phone. He's a farmer, you see. Early riser. If his phone battery should go flat during the night, the clock still goes off. If I'm honest, it drives me insane, but in relationships there has to be a bit of give and take.'

'You're waffling, inspector. Four minutes until my overseas call.'

'Sorry, forgive me. It was this morning as that damned clock went off at 4:30 am that I remembered about the clock in Amanda Chan's office. As I was woken at a ridiculous hour and couldn't get back to sleep, I decided I might as well make an early start myself. I went into the station and studied all the photos and videos of the crime scene. Not a single shot captured that digital clock. I found it odd but assumed it may have fallen behind the back of something or been put in a drawer. This morning Sergeant Stoker, myself, and two uniformed officers spent three hours searching Amanda's flat from top to bottom.'

He picks up the fountain pen and lightly taps it on the desk. 'I like to think of myself as a reasonably intelligent man, but I don't understand your obsession with the clock.'

'I think it served a dual purpose; it was not only a clock but a spy cam. I believe Amanda Chan had no intention of being silenced by your pay-off. She wanted to video you handing over the hush money. Then she'd have posted it online to her hundreds of thousands of followers. It would have painted you in a very bad light. I suspect it would have been only a matter of days before the mainstream media ran with the story. The British media love a tall poppy to chop down.'

He nods reflectively. 'Nothing would surprise me about that woman. She certainly didn't inherit her father's business acumen, otherwise she'd have learnt that in business, trust is everything.' Hesitating, his confusion dissipates replaced by clarity. 'Wait... I think I understand. You believe the clock may have unwittingly captured Ms Chan's killer. That's why you were interested in it?'

'You're very perceptive.'

His back stiffens as a toothy beam melts over his face. 'Actually, this is excellent news. Not only can you identify the murderer, but it completely exonerates me.'

'That may have been the case if we'd found the clock.'

'It's missing?'

'Yes.'

He glances away. 'Damn and blast!'

'You have your finger in a lot of pies, Mr Thorne. You're involved in a list of companies longer than my arm.'

'I'm a businessman. It's what I do and I'm damned good at it,' he replies, distracted.

'Thorne Surveillance provides hi-tech surveillance equipment to ports, airports, banks, prisons, even the police. Facial recognition, high-resolution CCTV cameras with night-vision and motion detection; biometric scanners for fingerprint and retina identification; drones with thermal imaging. You have a cyber-security team that implements robust encryption systems for businesses to safeguard against data breaches. It's all very James Bond.'

'I am a major stakeholder in Thorne Surveillance, and a director, but I'm not involved at the molecular level. My role is more strategic.'

'PI Home Surveillance is a subsidiary of Thorne Surveillance. More low-tech, aimed at the consumer market. Surveillance equipment for the home; security cameras, doorbells, and baby monitors embedded with discreet cameras. You also provide what I'd call novelty items like spy-pens, spy-sunglasses, and spy-clocks.'

'I'm not au fait with every single piece of merchandise we produce.' He pushes back in his seat, restless. 'I'm not sure where you're heading with all this, inspector.' Another glance at his watch. 'But if you didn't locate the clock, then I'm not sure the reason for your visit.'

Prisha clears her throat and inches forward. 'It was a risky move you made, Mr Thorne. And it almost worked.'

Irritated, he replies, 'I'm afraid you're becoming tiresome, inspector. What was a risky move?'

'The murder of Amanda Chan.'

# 50

He steeples his hands together, elbows resting on the desk, the epitome of relaxed self-confidence.

'Oh dear, you seem to have gone off-piste again, inspector. First, I was the killer, then I wasn't, and now I am.' He flaps his hand up and down. 'You're floundering around like a washed-up mackerel on the beach. Be honest, you really don't have a clue as to what you're doing, do you? And when I first met you, I assumed you were a highly intelligent officer. I'm usually on the money in my assessments of people, but on this occasion, it appears I was wrong. However, I am intrigued. Before I call my lawyer, please feel free to conclude your fantastical fairy-tale.'

Prisha allows herself a whisper of a smile. 'You were probably already suspicious as to how Amanda Chan was getting information on your business dealings. Dora King, your loyal servant, would have been the furthest person from your mind, until, that is, you received the Happy

Camp photo, which would have set the cogs in your mind whirring. You originally told us you couldn't remember much about the camp. I doubt that was true. You'd have remembered Ted, or Theodore Fairchild, the boy the adults called the Freak, and his best friend, Mike Ross, the child with Italian blood. It wouldn't have taken you long to figure out Theodore Fairchild was in fact Theodora Fairchild, or Dora, and Mike Ross was an anglicisation of Marco Rossellini. You saw a perfect way to get rid of three enemies at the same time.'

Thorne smiles. 'And so I murdered Ms Chan with my own dagger and left it at the scene of the crime. Do you think I'd be that stupid?'

'That's exactly what you wanted us to think. The dagger, the fingerprints, your admission you were at the flat around the time of the murder. You knew the immediate suspicion would fall upon you, but you also wagered the police were too smart to fall for the obvious. I mean, as you said, why use your own distinctive dagger, and with your fingerprints on it? You assumed, correctly, we'd conclude it was a fit-up. And who would be behind such a devious plot? The only other person who had ready access to the dagger was Dora King and she couldn't have been the killer as she was here, at your office, when Ms Chan was murdered. Which led inevitably to our next conclusion; Dora had an accomplice, Marco Rossellini. It was only a matter of time before we found the money at his workshop, and then the connection between Rossellini and Dora King. We would have our killers, and you would be fully exonerated in another blaze of publicity. Like I said, it was a risky move. If we hadn't found the money, then our prime suspect would have always been you. It was a gamble, a game of poker, bluff and counter bluff.'

Thorne chuckles and nods his head up and down. 'This is up there with the finest Agatha Christie mystery, except it's balderdash. As entertaining as it is, I believe in a court of law hard evidence is king.' His cheeks subtly expand then relax, conveying contemplation and a non-verbal, perhaps? 'It's true, you have circumstantial evidence but no *direct* evidence. Are you overlooking forensics? Not a jot of Ms Chan's DNA was found on my person. That's a significant oversight on your part for someone accused of stabbing another directly through the eye.'

'Yes, it is. And it puzzled us for a while. For that to have happened, you would have needed to have worn protection.'

'And yet, no such items were found when you arrested me still sitting in my car.' His confidence grows, the sign of a man who has dotted every I and crossed every T.

Zac nods, a resigned smile on his lips. He turns to Prisha. 'What's that famous Royal Mail slogan they used for years?'

'Nothing gets through like a letter?'

'Aye, that's the one.'

Thorne's smug expression freezes, as if carved in stone.

Prisha takes up the cudgel. 'With the help of the council's CCTV and various security cameras from shops, we were able to trace your vehicle nearly all the way back from Ms Chan's flat to your HQ. At 7:42 on the night of Ms Chan's murder you stopped your car, exited outside a Royal Mail post box and posted what looks like a bulging, padded envelope. What was in the envelope, Mr Thorne?'

He smacks his lips together and swallows. 'It was a hefty business document dispatched to one of my contractors. It had been sitting on the passenger seat and I'd overlooked it in the dark.'

'Ah, of course. Minutes after stumbling upon a grisly murder scene, and in a panic, you rush to your car and head back to your offices, *but* you just happen to stop off to drop a padded envelope into a post box. Quite normal behaviour, wouldn't you say so, Sergeant Stoker?'

'Oh, aye, perfectly normal—if you're a cocksure psychopath who believes he's infallible. Although, some may regard it as hubris. What do *you* think was in the parcel, inspector?'

'I'd say lightweight protective coverings containing Amanda Chan's DNA and a digital spy-clock with video footage of her murder and her killer. I'd also guess the parcel was self-addressed, but that's just a stab in the dark, pardon the pun.'

Thorne claps his hands together as if he's had a light-bulb moment. 'Then the path is clear for you, inspector. All you need to do is recover the envelope containing the damning evidence, and you'll be able to lock me up and throw away the key. Good luck with that.' He rises slowly from his seat. 'In all my business endeavours, I adhere to a singular, golden principle: to know one's adversary more intimately than they know themselves. It is crucial to grasp the nuances of their thoughts, their actions, their motivating forces, and... their vulnerabilities. With this understanding, you possess the master key to shape your own destiny. Knowledge is power.' He rubs his hand through his hair, presses the power-on button on his phone, and throws Zac a dismissive glance. 'As you began this session with a word game, sergeant, I'll end the session with one of my own; time is money. You know your way out.'

Zac fumbles in his jacket pocket, pulls out a plastic evidence bag and tosses it onto the desk. It skids across the leather inlay and teeters on the edge.

Thorne picks it up. 'What's this?' His air of superiority gradually dissolves like a foaming effervescent tablet dropped into a tumbler of water.

'A smoke alarm,' Zac replies.

'I can see it's a damn smoke alarm!' he snaps.

Prisha's eyes narrow, her face hardens. 'Amanda had two smoke alarms on her office ceiling.' She points at the one in his hand. 'That one is the real smoke alarm. The fake one is with forensics from which they've already downloaded the video and audio footage.'

Thorne appears dumbfounded. 'I... what? You're not making sense.'

'You underestimated Ms Chan and overestimated yourself. She had a back-up. A spy cam smoke alarm directly above her desk. It clearly captures you stabbing Amanda, then carefully removing your plastic poncho, gloves, and shoe coverings, along with the digital clock and sealing them in a padded envelope. It's not pretty viewing watching someone die. Zac, do the honours.'

Zac reads the caution as Prisha pulls out her handcuffs.

The lift doors swoosh open. Zac navigates Thorne inside and quips, 'Look's like your time's up, sunshine.'

# 51

# 1985 – Wednesday August 14th – Happy Camp

Rosco pulls his dirty T-shirt over his head, kicks his trainers off and removes socks. He slips from his shorts and underpants, then wades out naked into the bristling beck, shrinking at the iciness of the water but determined to wash the muck and grime from his exhausted body. Ted stands on the bank watching him.

'Come on, get in,' Rosco encourages.

'No. I'll get my clothes wet.'

'Idiot. Take them off.'

'No.'

Rosco takes the plunge and lowers himself into a deep gully where the water rushes over him. He submerges his head, and for a fleeting moment, forgets his troubles. Holding his breath for as long as he can, eventually he resurfaces, panting hard.

'Is it cold?'

'It's fucking freezing,' he splutters, energised by the shock.

'Colder than the showers?'

'Yeah. A lot colder.' He wades back to the bank, climbs out and lies on the sun-kissed grass and stares into the cloudless, turquoise sky. 'I'm not coming here again,' he murmurs.

'You don't have any choice,' Ted replies, pulling his eyes away from Rosco's nakedness.

'Stuff them! They don't own me. They can't force me to come here if I don't want to.'

His friend sits down beside him. 'Yes, they can. They can do whatever they want. Put your clothes back on.'

He sits up and grabs his jocks and shorts. 'I'll run away next time if it comes to it.'

'Don't say things like that. You'll only make things worse for yourself. You hungry?'

Rosco slips into his clothes and jabs his feet into his trainers, straining to get his heel in position. 'Starving.'

The buzzing of hornets and the occasional distant bleating sheep are the only intruder on the silence.

Ted reaches for his backpack and pulls out a packet of chocolate digestives. 'Here, help yourself.'

Rosco is reticent. 'Where did you get them from?'

'I brought them from the orphanage. Aunty gave them to me.'

'Liar. They checked our bags when we arrived. They'd have found them.'

Ted takes a biscuit and hands one to Rosco. 'I hid them in the bottom of my sleeping bag,' he replies with an impish grin.

Rosco rams the biscuit into his mouth, then takes another. 'I heard them talking earlier—the elders.' This time he nibbles around the edges of the digestive, savouring every last crumb.

'What about?'

'I think the reverend is arriving today.'

Ted stops chewing. 'Shit. You know what that means. Have they been for you yet?'

'They wouldn't fucking dare. I'll stab the bastards if they do.'

'No, you won't. You're not as tough as you make out. I think there's only you, me, and Tom who haven't been taken to the Purification Hut,' Ted states, his voiced laced with dread.

'Yeah. I know. I hate them.'

'Even Cyclone?'

'Yeah, even Cyclone.'

'Why? He's not like the others. At least you can talk to him, and he's a lot younger.'

'Don't tell me he doesn't know what's going on.'

'Maybe he doesn't. He works from first light until dusk.'

Rosco pulls a look, making him appear older than his twelve years. 'Oh, he knows all right. If you know it's wrong and do nothing about it, then it makes you as bad as them. Anyway, remember the way he killed that rabbit? Bloody psycho. What's the time?'

Ted glances at his watch. 'Nearly five. Come on, we better head back and help with dinner.'

'Ugh! Bloody dinner. Reheated, gristly stew with stale bread while those bastards have steak cooked on the barbecue.' He glances at his hands and holds them aloft. 'Look at the blisters and splinters,' he states indignantly. 'Happy Camp, my arse. It's more like a bloody prison camp.'

'At least the work has finished now.'

Walking through lush fields embroidered with a rolling vista of the moors, the naturally idyllic scene does nothing to lighten the heavy load on their young shoulders. They deftly climb a drystone wall, drop to the other side and stare at Happy Camp in the distance.

Rosco stops and touches Ted on the arm, lowers his voice. 'I know.'

Ted frowns. 'You know what?'

'About you.'

Lines crease his face. 'Oh. What about the others? Do they know?'

'Nah. They'd have been taking the piss otherwise.'

'You won't tell anyone?'

Rosco offers a rare smile. 'No. Your secret's safe with me. Anyway, none of my business. But you can't keep it a secret forever.' He reflects. 'Then again, those twats do, don't they?' he says, nodding towards the converted barn.

The toll of a sombre bell ricochets across summer fields, the sound hitting them in the head like a lump hammer. Their constant trepidation rises to mild panic.

'Fuck,' Rosco gasps. 'The Retribution Bell. Someone's gonna cop it and I bet I know who.'

---

The eight boys are lined up like a row of little tin soldiers, arms by their sides, chests out, shoulders retracted, as they've been taught.

Doctor Henry Blenheim parades before them, holding a cane in his right hand as he gently taps it on his left palm. Sweat drips from everyone in the breathless humidity of a particularly warm summer's day.

'What's the time?' Doctor Blenheim asks, with a grave undertone. He receives no reply as the other adults, all bar Cyclone, peer at the boys with contempt. He stops marching back and forth as his eyes flit from boy to boy. 'Fairchild, what's the time?'

Ted looks directly ahead but says nothing.

'I see,' the doctor remarks coldly as he moves along the line, as if inspecting new recruits mustered on the parade ground. He stops when he reaches Tom Maplin. He taps him on the shoulder with the cane. 'What's the time, young Tom?'

Tom's eyes blink in rapid succession. 'It, it, it, it's p... p... p...' His mild hesitation before answering, which was barely noticeable four months ago, has now developed into a debilitating stammer.

Doctor Blenheim imitates him, blinking his eyes rapidly. 'It, it, it, it's p... p... p...' he mocks. 'Come on, boy!' he bellows. 'What time is it?'

'It, it, it, it's p... p... p... pay, pay, pay...'

'Spit it out lad, spit it out!' he roars.

With great relief to the other boys, Tom finally manages to say the words. 'Payback time, sir!'

'That's right, Tom. It's payback time!' The words emerge in an almost musical, lilting, humorous tone, rising in pitch and cadence towards the last vowel. The performance deliberately adds a macabre splash of colour to the sentence. He turns to the other adults and nods.

Selwyn Morgan smirks and repeats, 'Payback time.' The reverend remains silent, his grave expression conveying his repressed anger. Cyclone grabs a wrench from the back of his Land Rover and heads back to the ablution block keen to finish the plumbing, the last of his jobs.

The doctor continues his Draconian performance. 'A packet of McVitie's Chocolate Digestives has gone missing from the camp kitchen. Now, unless they have grown legs and gone for a stroll by themselves, it leads me to only one conclusion: we have a thief, or thieves, in our midst. A viper in the nest.' He uses his cane to point at the words on the Happy Camp sign. 'Discipline, Godliness, Fun. Without discipline, we cannot commit to godliness. And without godliness, there can be no fun, as we are already on the path to damnation. Evil is as evil does,' he adds in a long, slow drawl, spittle gathering in the corners of his rubbery lips.

Ted shoots Rosco a worried glance. He reciprocates with a cheeky wink.

The doctor continues marching up and down the line. 'You know how payback time works. The boy, or boys, responsible for this reprehensible deed can step forward and take their punishment like a man. If they hide like cowards, then you shall *all* suffer the same punishment. When you steal from one, you steal from all.' He slaps the cane harder into his palm. 'Now, whoever has committed this sin, then at least have the common decency to own up.'

The boys remain mute to the spot as the tension crackles beneath the unrelenting sun, which watches on, an impassive bystander.

From his peripheral vision, Rosco notices Ted trembling. He swallows hard and takes a step forward. 'It was me, sir. I stole the biscuits.'

Doctor Blenheim nods, not surprised by the confession. 'Ah, Mike Ross, I might have known. You know what follows, boy?'

'Yes, sir. A flogging and a night in the Retribution Cell without food or water.'

'That's right. Not your first time, though, is it?'

'No sir.'

'And I doubt it will be your last. Anyone else involved?'

'No, sir. Only me.'

'You wouldn't be covering for anyone, would you, Rosco?' he adds, eyeballing Ted Fairchild suspiciously. 'Was the Freak involved?'

'No sir. I took the biscuits and ate them all, as I was so hungry. No one else knows about it.'

'Hmm... I hope you're telling the truth. After all, birds of a feather flock together.'

'It's the truth, sir.'

Convinced, he rocks back and forth on his heels like a sergeant major. 'I should be disappointed in you, Rosco, but I'm not. You were born a loser. It's in your blood. Rotten trees bear rotten fruit. But still, after all we've done for you...'

Rosco interrupts, incensed. 'You haven't done anything for us apart from work us like slaves and abuse us.'

The doctor's retribution is swift as he slaps him hard across the cheek. 'You've just earned yourself an extra ten strikes for your insolence,' he screeches, red in the face. 'You know the routine. Drop your shorts and underpants and touch your toes.'

'Sir,' Rosco replies. A solitary tear carves its way down the twelve-year-old's grubby cheek, his only show of emotion.

With the flogging over, the boys disperse, dispirited, forsaken. They were doomed before they were born. It was preordained in the DNA of their father's sperm, of their mother's egg. Of the society that failed them; the family, the next-door neighbours, teachers, social workers, foster parents, care homes, councils, schools, and... the predators waiting in the shadows.

The boys never stood a chance.

## 52

# 1985 – Thursday August 15th – Happy Camp

Mike Ross wipes the sweat from his brow and desperately tries to wet his lips, but his mouth is dry. The urge for water is even more powerful than his hunger. Two misdemeanours in two days means another night in the Retribution Cell without food or drink. Voices and the sound of dishes and cutlery being washed float up to the Retribution Cell. He peels himself off the dusty wooden floorboards and peers out through a crack in the stone where the mortar has disintegrated. Male voices and muted laughter drift in the air as twilight descends.

He sees them. The three of them, as they amble towards the Purification Hut at the back of the barn. The doctor has a bottle of red wine in either hand; the reverend carries the glasses, and Morgan has the picnic rug draped over his shoulder, staggering slightly, already the worse for wear.

Mike tries to gulp, but it becomes trapped in his throat. 'Bastards,' he hisses. A gentle tap on the door has him spinning around.

'Mike, it's me, Ted.' A forced whisper.

'What do you want?'

'I've come to say sorry.'

'For what?'

'For stealing the bishop's ring and not owning up. I was going to own up, honest, but you got in before me.'

'Why did you steal it, idiot?'

'Not sure why. It looked nice, the acorn. He left it on the sink. I thought he might think he'd just lost it. I don't have anything nice.' His voice is laced with regret.

Mike sighs and rubs a hand over his buttocks and winces. 'That's all right. It didn't hurt, anyway.'

'Liar.'

'Where did you hide it?'

Sniggers. 'I split a hole in a tennis ball and put it inside. They'll never find it in there.'

'I hope it was worth it?' Mike grumbles.

'No. Not for the belting you had to take. One day they'll get *their* payback time. We'll do it together... yeah?'

Hesitation. 'Yeah, they will. You and me will do them all.'

'And if we get caught, then I'll take the blame for a change. Hey, I have two slices of buttered bread.'

Mike glances down as the meagre feast is pushed under the door atop a rip of newspaper.

'Thanks,' he replies, eagerly picking up the offering and ramming it into his mouth.

'I have a straw and a bottle of water. I'll push the straw through the keyhole and put the other end in the bottle. It may not work, but give it a try.'

Mike finishes chewing, swallows, then kneels and puts his lips around the straw as it protrudes through the keyhole. He sucks on the liquid and manages a couple of mouthfuls before the paper straw bends and prevents any more fluid from passing through. The bang of the hut door outside has him glancing nervously over his shoulder. He rises and sticks his eye to the peephole.

'Shit. It's Morgan and the doctor heading back,' he hisses. 'Go back downstairs. If they catch you up here, you'll cop it. And thanks for the food and water.'

The shuffle of feet and the creak of boards on the stairs indicate his friend's departure before another noise distracts him. The clank of tools being thrown into the back of a vehicle. He squints sideways and can just make out Cyclone as he loads up his Land Rover with various leftover building supplies. The doctor and Morgan stop and talk to him, but they're too far away for Mike to comprehend what they're saying. A gentle and welcome breeze blows a piece of grit into his eye. As he struggles to remove the irritant, the voices below dissolve. He bends over, blinks rapidly, then blows his nose on his grubby T-shirt.

The voices are back.

He sticks his eye behind the crevice and watches on. His stomach flips.

'They've got Ted,' he barely dares to whisper. 'Leave him alone, you bastards!' he bellows at the top of his lungs. 'Ted, run! Run as fast as you can and get away.'

The doctor momentarily stops and glances up at the sandstone walls of the barn, then continues, along with Morgan, to lead Ted Fairchild to the Purification Hut.

'Bastards. Filthy stinking bastards,' he yells, pummelling his palms against the wall. He drops to the floor and pulls his knees close to his chest, despite the oppressive heat. The gutsy throb of a diesel engine fires up, then slowly recedes as the Land Rover trundles away.

'You cowardly bastard, Cyclone,' he screams.

Rocking back and forth, he repeats the mantra over and over again.

'One day, I swear to God, I'll kill the lot of you. I'll make you all suffer. I'll cut your balls off and hammer a tent peg through your fucking heads.'

The hut door squeals open again.

'That's too soon,' he thinks. Taking up position behind the hole in the wall, he spies Ted running from the hut, sobbing, hair wet, desperately pulling his top on and hitching his trousers up. He loses sight of him as he rounds a corner and heads to the ablution block.

'What happened? They'll know now. They'll know he's a girl. Bastards. I hate them. I'll kill them all. I swear... one day, I'll kill the bloody lot of them.'

He watches on as the doctor, and Morgan, who is now patently drunk, march quickly from the hut, laughing and joking as they head back to the barn. The bishop emerges in the doorway of the hut behind them, calmly sipping on a glass of wine.

'Christ, what if they come for me again?' Although he's done it a dozen times before, he searches the tiny room for a weapon in a futile endeavour.

Gruff voices echo out. The squeal of a child, wailing.

The elders emerge, Tom Maplin pleading with them.

Mike puts his eye to the crack and watches on, experiencing a wave of relief, then a wave of guilt.

'Pl... pl... pl... please, s... s... sir. I, I, don't want to... to b, b, b, be an... an... anointed,' Tom Maplin pleads.

The doctor clips him over the head. 'Stop your snivelling, you pathetic creature. It's a rite of passage. All the other boys underwent it without any fuss.' Morgan says something and the doctor laughs. 'Well, yes, all apart from the Freak.'

The door to the Purification Hut shuts and Mike slides to the floorboards.

'I wish I was dead.'

⸻⊙⸻

Exhausted, frightened, battered and bruised, sleep is a blessing even if it is full of monsters, but at least they're imaginary monsters.

He wakes with a start, a slug of adrenaline zapping his body awake.

Voices again.

Male, adult voices. All is quiet from the rooms below. The children in bed, if not asleep, then pretending to be.

Mike peers out of the hole. The bright moon high in the sky illuminates the stunning countryside, shining a light down on Happy Camp.

The doctor has the picnic blanket rolled up over his shoulder as he hurriedly follows the bishop away from the camp.

But there's something odd about the doctor. His walking is laboured. Morgan appears in the hut doorway, then collapses in a drunken heap on the ground.

'What's going on?' he whispers.

The doctor curses and the bishop spins around.

'Oh, Christ, no,' Mike mutters in fear and disbelief, feeling the rise of sick.

The bishop hurriedly tucks the lifeless arm back inside the folds of the picnic blanket, then both men skulk away into the shadows cast from Happy Camp.

Mike rushes to the edge of the room and vomits.

# 53

# Modern Day - Friday 12th May

Frank ushers Prisha, Zac and Dinkel into his office, his pride in his officers, obvious.

'Take a seat,' he instructs. 'Excellent work. A real team effort. I've just come off the phone from the chief constable. He asked me to pass on his congratulations to you all. It's been a successful resolution. Dora King's confession to the Happy Camp murders and the irrefutable video evidence against Sebastian Thorne in the Amanda Chan killing. Superintendent Banks finished her media conference an hour ago and is due in the office at any moment.' He frowns and glances at his wristwatch. 'Actually, she's running late, which is not like her.'

Prisha stifles a yawn. 'What about Marco Rossellini? Are we still investigating him regarding the Happy Camp murders?'

Frank grimaces. 'Let's say the case file is still open. But to be honest, unless he confesses or Dora King changes her confession and implicates him, then we have not a jot of evidence against him.'

Zac nods in agreement. 'Dora won't implicate him. There's an unbreakable bond between those two.'

Frank is distracted as he peers out of his office window. 'Ah, here's the Super now. I doubt she'll break out the champagne and perform the Can-Can, but I dare say she'll have a few complimentary words to say.'

They all rise as Superintendent Banks enters the room.

'Ah, good morning, ma'am,' Frank declares, beaming. 'I was just saying to the gang what an excellent result it's been. A real team effort.'

Her brow furrows as she gazes at each face individually. 'Yes, yes, it was. Well done everyone.' She mumbles the words as though reading the weather forecast.

Frank rolls his eyes at the lacklustre congratulations. There's stilted silence for a moment.

'Ahem, right then. Okay team, back to it. The drinks are on me after work.'

As the three officers troop from the office, the superintendent grabs Prisha by the arm.

'Prisha, stay behind. I have some troubling news. Take a seat.'

Zac halts, glances at Prisha, then Frank, and finally exits, clearly puzzled.

The Super closes the door and takes a deep breath, her usual grey demeanour drained to white as her eyes fall onto Prisha, in an almost pitiful way.

Frank's concern is evident. 'What is it, Anne?'

'I've been on a call with the Deputy Director of MI5.' She stops as though trying to choose her words carefully, but the elongated silence only heightens the tension.

'Anne?' Frank prompts. 'The Deputy Director of MI5?'

'Ahem, yes. They've assigned an officer to help solve a past case.'

Prisha's heart rate accelerates. 'What past case?'

'Tiffany Butler and the missing Russian, Kira Volkov. An officer may be visiting in the next few days to go over the case details with you, Prisha. He's one of their best. A man named Magnus Crawley.'

Prisha's eyes flick between Frank and the Super. 'I don't follow. I can understand them investigating Kira Volkov. She's a threat to national security. But what has Tiffany Butler got to do with it?'

The Super shrugs. 'Tiffany Butler absconded with twenty million pounds in ransom money. MI5 believe the Russian is after the money.'

'We don't even know if Kira is still alive,' Prisha states, her voice rising in pitch.

'That's right,' Frank says. 'The dinghy she escaped in was found adrift, which suggests she went overboard. The waters offshore are treacherous.'

The Super nods, sheepishly. 'Apparently, MI5 have been trialling some new cutting-edge surveillance technology at Heathrow Airport. It uses biometric recognition. It scans everyone that passes through passport control, then sends the data, in real-time, to a supercomputer. AI then compares the data received to a database of high-risk security threats: terrorists, spies, extremists, and such like. Yesterday it flagged a person who is classified as a category-one threat. A surveillance team was assigned to track the suspect. Unfortunately, they lost contact with the target. She was last seen getting off a train in York, then disappeared into thin air.'

Prisha feels woozy. 'She?' Her voice is nothing more than a hoarse whisper.

Anne averts her gaze and shoots a glance at the carpet before lifting her head and making direct eye contact.

'Yes... she. The Russian, Kira Volkov, is back on British soil. Considering the threat she made against you, Prisha, I fear your life could be in grave and imminent danger.'

# Keep In Touch

Your thoughts and feedback are incredibly important. If you enjoyed the book, please consider leaving a review on Amazon or Goodreads, or a review/recommendation on Facebook. Such reviews are not only deeply appreciated, but they also help fellow crime fiction enthusiasts discover and enjoy the DCI Finnegan series. Or even better, why not tell someone you know about the book? Word of mouth is still the best recommendation.

I thank you for giving me your time, a very precious and finite commodity.

In case you've missed any of the books, take a quick look at the **Also By Ely North** page.

All the best,
**Ely North**

**Ely North Newsletter**

Why not sign up to my entertaining newsletter where I write about all things crime—fact and fiction. It's packed with news, reviews, and my top ten Unsolved Mysteries, as well as new releases, and any discounts or promotions I'm running. I'll also send you a free copy of the prequel novella to Black Nab, **Aquaphobia – The Body In The River**

QR code below.

# Also By Ely North – DCI Finnegan Series

Book 1: **Black Nab**

Book 2: **Jawbone Walk**

Book 3: **Vertigo Alley**

Book 4: **Whitby Toll**

Book 5: **House Arrest**

Book 6: **Gothic Fog**

Book 7: **Happy Camp**

Book 8: **Harbour Secrets**

Book 9: **Murder Mystery** – Pre-order (Dec 2024)

DCI Finnegan Series Boxset #1: **Books 1 – 3**

DCI Finnegan Series Boxset #2: **Books 4 – 6**

Prequel: **Aquaphobia** (Free ebook for newsletter subscribers)

*Note: All books are available from Amazon in ebook, paperback, and in **Kindle Unlimited** (excluding Aquaphobia). Paperbacks can be ordered from all good bookshops. **Boxset print editions are one book compiled from three books. They do not come in a box. *** Pre-orders only apply to ebooks.

# Contact

Contact: ely@elynorthcrimefiction.com

Website: https://elynorthcrimefiction.com

Follow me on Facebook for the latest
https://facebook.com/elynorthcrimefictionUK

Sign up to my newsletter for all the latest news, releases, and discounts.

*Newsletter
Sign Up*

Printed in Great Britain
by Amazon